The Crafternoon

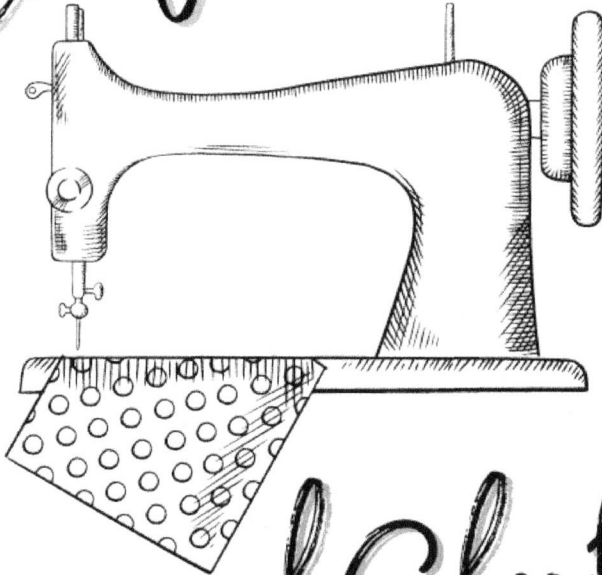

Sewcial Club

SEWING  BEE

J C Williams

You can subscribe to J C Williams' mailing list and view all his other books at:

www.authorjcwilliams.com

Cover design by Paul Nugent

Interior formatting and proofreading & editing by Dave Scott

ISBN: 9798412599052

First printing March 2022

Books by JC Williams

The Flip of a Coin

The Lonely Heart Attack Club
The Lonely Heart Attack Club: Wrinkly Olympics
The Lonely Heart Attack Club: Project VIP

The Seaside Detective Agency
The Seaside Detective Agency: The Case of the Brazen Burglar

Frank 'n' Stan's Bucket List #1: TT Races
Frank 'n' Stan's Bucket List #2: TT Races
Frank 'n' Stan's Bucket List #3: Isle 'Le Mans' TT
Frank 'n' Stan's Bucket List #4: Bride of Frank 'n' Stan
Frank 'n' Stan's Bucket List #5: Isle of Man TT Aces

The Bookshop by the Beach

The Crafternoon Sewcial Club
The Crafternoon Sewcial Club: Sewing Bee

Cabbage Von Dagel

Hamish McScabbard

Deputy Gabe Rashford: Showdown at Buzzards Creek

Luke 'n' Conor's Hundred-to-One Club

Inspired by the wonderful gang at Crafternoon Tea, Isle of Man!

FEEL-GOOD, UPLIFTING AND DELICIOUSLY FUNNY

The Crafternoon Sewcial Club

SEWING BEE

J C Williams

CHAPTER ONE

Charlotte gripped onto her knees, digging her recently-manicured fingernails into the fabric of her borrowed jumpsuit overalls. Overalls that, upon closer inspection, she noticed were littered with the scattered remains of wee winged creatures — various broken corpses of the unlucky insect inhabitants of the sky who'd paid the ultimate price for having the sad misfortune of being in the wrong place at the wrong time. Charlotte swallowed hard, hoping to restore some moisture to the inside of her parched mouth, but it proved fruitless as the surface of her tongue still felt coarse as sandpaper as she ran it over the surface of her teeth.

The noise from the plane engine put Charlotte in mind of an anvil inside a washing machine on its spin cycle. But despite this racket, she could still hear the pulse inside her head throbbing and increasing in tempo with each passing second. "What am I doing?" she asked herself aloud, lowering her head like she was about to offer a little prayer. A course of action she'd already considered several times since the Cessna Grand Caravan had bounced along the runway at Ronaldsway Airport like an excited kangaroo before finally reaching the sky.

Do I need a pee? Charlotte asked herself, moving one of her hands from her knee and pressing down gently on the area of her bladder. She knew she couldn't possibly need one as she'd been to the loo three times in the previous hour back on terra firma, but it didn't stop her from checking once more. Charlotte placed her other hand to her forehead, using her thumb and forefinger to knead the skin on her brow like a baker preparing the dough. "What am I doing?" she said again, followed by a pained moan which was drowned out by the noise of the engine.

She was, however, snapped from her introspection when a firm finger prodded her shoulder blade, followed by a confident, authoritative voice in her left ear, loud enough to be heard over the din. "Everything alright?" the voice kindly enquired.

Charlotte turned her head just enough to see over her shoulder. "Marvellous!" she shouted back, blatantly lying, offering a spirited thumbs-up to demonstrate that all was, indeed, marvellous. "It's lovely up here!" she added for no apparent reason, glancing towards one of the windows with a nervous laugh.

"You'll be fine," Chris, her instructor for the day, submitted with an assured hand on her shoulder. "Just remember to breathe, as I often find that helps, yeah?"

Charlotte took several exaggerated gulps of air in response to this suggestion. "Like that?" she said, forcing a smile, thumb still extended as everything was, after all, marvellous, as she'd just said, and with absolutely nothing at all to worry about. Or at least that's what she kept telling herself, in hopes that she might actually believe it.

"Perfect," Chris said, removing his hand. "Let me know if I can do anything for you," he added.

"Perhaps an extremely large gin and tonic?" Charlotte replied, mimicking the action of drinking such a splendid beverage.

"I'll call over the air hostess," Chris joked. "Would you like a packet of peanuts to go with it?"

"Huh?" Charlotte said, cupping her ear.

"I asked if you'd like peanuts?" Chris said again, only slightly louder.

Unfortunately for Charlotte, however, their transport for the day was distinctly lacking in the creature comforts usually associated with civilised air travel. Indeed, there were no air hostesses dispensing refreshments, no in-flight movies, or, for that matter, any seats to speak of. In fact, Charlotte and her fellow passengers were sat directly on the cold metal floor of the fuselage's spartan interior, crammed in like sardines with their knees tucked into their chests. Also, making things even more intimate was that every plucky jumper was attached (via their tandem harness) to their individual instructors seated inches behind each of them and so close you could feel their breath on your earlobes.

During their induction session back on earth, Charlotte had been fairly blasé ahead of her debut tandem skydive. Indeed, she'd appeared to be relatively unfazed and relaxed, some might say. But Chris, seasoned campaigner that he was — with over nine hundred jumps to his name, according to his earlier tutorial session — could see through the bravado. Of course, he'd seen it all before, and, in his experience, those debutants making light of the situation were often the ones whose resolve collapsed quicker than a cardboard Wendy house in a rainstorm. As was the case with Charlotte. For that reason, Chris was eager to offer words of encouragement at regular intervals on their climb up to a height of thirteen thousand feet.

Thirteen thousand feet high hadn't meant too much to Charlotte, necessarily, when it'd been first mentioned down below. But when it was explained that this equated to roughly two and a half miles above the earth... well, that's when her knees had begun to buckle and the blood had drained away from her face, leaving her a ghostly shade of white. She'd had one eye on the exit sign of their instruction room, and if not for Chris's timely intervention and soothing words, she'd have very likely been in her car and on her way back to Laxey, quick smart.

"We're approaching our desired altitude," Chris noted presently. A statement that did little to calm Charlotte's shattered nerves. "In a moment, you can pop your goggles on, Charlotte," he added. "And then I'll make a further check to ensure we're all connected and that everything is just as it should be."

Charlotte nodded her head, taking a fleeting glance up at the illuminated sign above the door hatch with the words "DON'T JUMP" shown prominently, lit up in red. Knowing this message would be changing momentarily and the light switching over to green — and knowing, further, that she'd subsequently find herself plummeting to the ground at over one hundred and twenty mph shortly after — sent an immediate shiver running down her spine. Including herself, six prospective skydivers sat in two rows, each with their instructors attached to them. Charlotte was unsure how she'd been 'lucky' enough to draw the short straw, exactly, but as a result found herself positioned at the front right of the plane, directly behind the exit and thus shortly the first to be gently coaxed through it. Still, at least by going first she wouldn't be prolonging matters longer than needed, she reckoned, trying her best to look on the positive side.

Charlotte lifted her chin, taking a final recce around the plane, once again wondering what the blue bloody blazes she was doing there and why she'd agreed to it in the first place. She'd taken some comfort in knowing the others on board were also novices like she was, and, as such, would likely be sharing the same levels of angst. Misery loving company, and all that.

However, as she ran her eyes around the interior of the plane, she was greeted with broad grins, some laughter, and one who was even singing! Those seated in the row opposite sported the jolly, relaxed demeanour of folk out for an enjoyable Sunday drive rather than dunderheaded loons who were about to freefall *willingly* towards solid rock.

In return, Charlotte offered an uneasy smile, not wishing to physically convey her panic to a broader audience. "Yay," she said, widening her terrified smile to reveal her dry teeth.

But seeing the friendly faces on the plane looking back at her did raise Charlotte's spirits for a moment. It was comforting, at least, to know that she wasn't to go through this traumatic experience alone. And in fact joining Charlotte for this little adventure, amidst others in the plane's cabin, were the joint architects of this current enterprise — namely, the Crafternoon Sewcial Club's very own resident adrenalin junkies, Joyce and Beryl. Completing the trio in their row was Larry, positioned at the rear, singing away to himself merrily, using a finger to conduct an imagined orchestra without so much as a care in the world as near as Charlotte could tell.

"You're both absolutely bonkers!" Charlotte called over to Joyce and Beryl. "The pair of you!" she added, mouthing the words in exaggerated fashion as she spoke them aloud, in order to make sure she'd be understood over the din.

Joyce and Beryl nodded in unison, happy with the accusation and apparently in full agreement.

It was a couple of weeks earlier when the idea of a tandem skydive had initially been suggested. Joyce had casually mentioned that her ninety-third birthday was approaching at pace and wanted to do something out of the ordinary to mark the occasion. Suggestions of a pottery class, paddle boarding, and even a deep-sea fishing expedition were bandied around, but none of these ideas seemed to particularly tickle Joyce's fancy.

It was then that Beryl had proffered the vertigo-inducing idea of skydiving, recalling how she'd seen a video somebody or other had posted on Facebook, and then remarking to the others that *"It looked like bloody good fun."* Besides the adrenalin rush on offer, and to garner further support of her idea, she further explained to Joyce that you'd likely have a strapping young man attached to your back throughout the course of the jump. *"Not an entirely unpleasant proposition,"* were Beryl's precise words, a statement which had been delivered with a raised eyebrow and a confident bob of the head. There was that, she'd said, and also the added benefit of a temporary facelift to be had by virtue of the wind resistance smashing against your face as you fell to the earth like a stone.

On the strength of such a compelling argument, Joyce had been most agreeable to the notion, and especially taken with the strapping young man portion of the idea.

Larry, for his part, had been preoccupied at the time, busying himself replenishing cups of tea for the thirsty Crafternoon masses (for whom he was kindly volunteering his services), popping in and out of the kitchen area. As such, he'd only caught little snippets of the developing conversation between Joyce, Beryl, and Charlotte. But, liking what bits he *had* heard, and not one to miss out on any form of social adventure, Larry was the first to put his name down to officially sign up for the activity, eager for "a pleasant day out enjoying the Manx countryside," as he'd put it, assuming the ladies would have him. Yes, Larry was definitely up for the idea, he said, further noting that he was actually fairly experienced at tandem cycling, as it should happen, and was more than happy, for that matter, to dig out his dedicated Lycra bicycle shorts to be used on this fortuitous occasion.

It was obvious that Larry had misheard what they'd been discussing, and Beryl and Joyce cackled with delight as Larry bustled back into the kitchen. Joyce and Beryl, mischievous devils that they were, were all for leaving dear Larry to turn up on the day, completely unaware of the misunderstanding and no doubt showing up in his special, tight-fitting bicycling shorts raring to go. Charlotte, meanwhile, hadn't been as keen to leave poor Larry in the dark. Eventually, she had to step in a couple of days later, especially as Larry advised that he'd been planning (at unnecessary personal expense) to head to the shop and purchase a new cycling helmet and accessories for the grand day out.

Still, when Charlotte had revealed to Larry what he'd truly signed himself up for, Larry was still, remarkably, completely up for the new adventure. He didn't even have to give it a moment's thought. *"In for a penny, in for a pound,"* he'd said, agreeing straight away. *"Anything to get the old heart racing!"* he'd quickly added, tapping his chest illustratively. And it was largely Larry's valiant, can-do attitude that had ultimately convinced Charlotte to sign up for the skydive herself. Not particularly a fan of flying (or of falling, for that matter), Charlotte had initially kept her head down on the subject of signing up, skilfully evading the issue each time it was raised. She could have continued dodging the proverbial bullet, but if Larry, Joyce, and Beryl were up for it, well, who was she to chicken out, she bravely reasoned over a nice glass of red with her best friend, Mollie.

And so, back in the present...

"Right. If you'd like to pop your goggles on, Charlotte?" instructor Chris instructed, while checking and double-checking they were attached to each other as they should be. "Do you have any final questions?" he enquired. "Anything you need me to clarify for you?"

Charlotte placed her goggles over her eyes as indicated, shaking her head in the negative in response to Chris's question even though, at that precise moment, she'd likely have struggled to spell her own name let alone recall all of the instructions provided earlier.

Just then, one of the reserve instructors climbed to his feet and edged across to the cabin door, cheerily pointing to the GoPro device attached to his helmet and reminding those watching him that their 'big day' was being recorded for them. He grinned broadly, offering a hearty fist pump in a *you've-totally-got-this* manner before reaching for and then sliding open the door.

While seeing the door remain open was terrifying in itself, the resulting gust of cool air running through the interior of the stuffy plane was at least a welcome relief to Charlotte, who felt confident she could likely have fried an egg on her forehead by this point. With impeccable timing, she glanced up to the light just as it changed from red to green. Ordinarily, if you were at, say, a set of traffic lights, this would be considered a fortunate outcome, but not here. Charlotte wiped the sweat from her brow a moment before she felt a gentle tap on her shoulder. "That's us ready to go," Chris informed her. "So just remember to breathe. And above all, try and enjoy it, yeah?"

Charlotte looked across the plane, first to Joyce, then Beryl, and then to Larry at the back. "You can do this," Joyce said, mouthing the words, followed up with a confident wink.

The next few moments felt like a surreal blur for Charlotte. Chris gave another gentle pat on her shoulder and then, with a further word in her ear, confirmed that it was indeed time to jump.

Charlotte used her heels to pull herself forward, shuffling along like the family pooch relieving an itch on the living room carpet. Every survival instinct was screaming at her inside her head, warning her of impending danger. Yet, here she was, moving closer to the opened door of an aeroplane flying at thirteen thousand feet and doing so of her own volition. Her stomach flipped when her eyes were met by the greenery of the Manx landscape far, far below, and as magnificent as it was, Charlotte couldn't help thinking it wouldn't make for an especially comfortable landing if their chute somehow didn't open.

She gingerly positioned her legs until they were dangling outside the aircraft. "How long do I have to—"

But she didn't get to finish her question because Chris had nudged her forward, and Charlotte Newman was now skydiving.

Cool air smashed into her face, sounding like the static from a microphone battering her ears. She felt an intense wave of exhilaration surging through her body as the wind resistance pushed against her face, initially presenting her with difficulty in catching her breath. What was bizarre and entirely unexpected was that it didn't feel like she was falling like a lead weight, as she had anticipated. Instead, it felt like she was flying like a superhero, and with some degree of composure. It was one of the most incredible and liberating sensations she'd ever experienced.

Through clenched eyelids, Charlotte looked over to the runway they'd taken off from some twenty or so minutes earlier and smiled, knowing that Stanley was down there, somewhere, cheering his mum and their madcap mates on.

Her cheeks jiggled uncontrollably, fighting a pitched battle against the pounding wind, with any lingering thoughts about fear blown clean away. *I'm actually skydiving,* she said to herself, and at that moment she could completely understand why dogs held their head outside the window on car journeys. She felt alive.

But all too soon, just as she was starting to relax, she felt a fierce tug from behind as Chris deployed their parachute which, fortunately for all concerned, opened on the first time of asking. With their rate of descent slowed and the wind-based assault on her ears drastically reduced, Charlotte could now hear Chris talking to her from his rear position.

"How was that?" Chris shouted as they swayed from side to side with the rocking motion of a boat bobbing on the waves.

"Fan... Bloody... Tastic!" Charlotte shouted back, in the absence of anything more articulate to convey her feelings. "I want to go again!"

All was now calm in relative terms following the thirty seconds or so of frantic freefall action. Now returning to earth at a somewhat more leisurely rate, Charlotte found herself able to soak up and absorb the sights, sounds, and smells from her unique vantage point several thousand feet above Castletown dangling from a parachute. "I think I can see Stanley and the others!" she squealed, waving in the general direction of where she thought she could see their cheerleading squad congregated. Whether the gesture was returned, she couldn't tell.

Under Chris's masterly guidance, Charlotte was returned to solid ground safe and sound and without incident. Once released from both her harness and Chris, she eased herself up, placing weight on her still-shaking legs, scarcely able to believe what she'd just done. "Ah! Here come the others!" she said, waving eagerly to the fellow adventurers descending gracefully towards her location like autumn leaves, and relieved to see them waving back.

Charlotte would have been fibbing if she said she hadn't harboured some concerns about Joyce, Beryl, and Larry skydiving at their advanced age. So to witness each one of them landing, one after the other and with prodigious smiles on their faces, was a most welcome sight.

Charlotte skipped over towards Joyce, clapping her hands in glee. "We did it, Joyce!" she shouted ahead of her arrival. "We're now officially skydivers!" she said, punching the air in delight.

Joyce looked up to the newly arrived Charlotte standing before her. "I think I need to readjust my knickers," Joyce announced with a wince. "They're cutting into me like bloody cheese wire."

"Aside from your undergarments being in a shambles, everything else okay?" Charlotte asked, running her eyes over her friend like a trained A&E doctor. "No bumps, bruises, sprains, or pain?"

"I'm fine," Joyce assured her, extending a hand now she'd been released from her harness. "Be a dear and help me up, Lotti?"

The remaining members of the Crafternoon Sewcial Club, Airborne Division, were soon all present and correct, and Charlotte couldn't help but check each of them over for any sign of injury, fussing over them like a mother hen.

"Charlotte, for goodness sake, nothing's broken!" Larry assured her, shooing her attentive hand away like he would a pesky wasp. But he wasn't seriously annoyed, of course, and was obviously grateful for the concern offered. "Now come on, you lot," Larry added, raising his arms like a scarecrow, inviting the others in for a celebratory, team-building cuddle. "How's about that for a birthday experience, Joyce?" he asked, pulling them in close. "I'm not sure how we're going to top that for your next birthday, though?"

"Well, we've got three hundred and sixty-five days to think of something," Joyce offered cheerfully.

"How about hang gliding?" Beryl gamely ventured, a moment or two later, once released from Larry's embrace. "Or, what about that wingsuit flying we watched online in that video, Joyce? Do you remember?" she asked.

"They're both on the shortlist," Joyce advised, tapping the side of her temple to indicate that those options were being safely filed away in the pending tray inside her head.

"Marvellous," Beryl offered, with a particularly gummy grin. And then, "Oh, botheration," she added quickly, placing her hand to her mouth. "I need to go and find our plane," she told the others, glancing skyward, unsure if it'd returned to the airport as yet or was still *up there*, soaring like a bird.

"You're eager to go up a second time?" Larry enquired, following the direction of her eyeline. "I could go again, no problem," he advised, appearing quite taken with the idea and already raring to go.

"No, it's not that," Beryl replied, patting herself down and speaking now through pursed lips. "My teeth must have fallen out. I placed them in my overall pocket before the jump, for safekeeping, but now they're not there. I'm hoping they must be still aboard the plane somewhere, and not, you know..." she said, sweeping her hand over the nearby landscape to indicate the other potential outcome.

"You should've left them in the changing room," Joyce was quick to suggest, and with the benefit of hindsight. "Like me," she added, casting her own gummy smile to happily illustrate the point.

"Oh dear," Charlotte entered in with a smirk. "Just imagine some poor unfortunate soul out for a lovely stroll in the outdoors, only to have Beryl's set of chompers appear from upon high and crack them right on the noggin."

"*Duuuunnnn duun... duuunnnnnnnn dun dun dun dun dun dun dun dun dun dun dunnnnnnnnnnnn dunnnn,*" Larry answered, singing this in response to Charlotte's stated scenario.

"What the...?" Charlotte said, looking Larry up and down once again, wondering if he hadn't perhaps taken a bump to his head after all. "Larry, are you...?" she began, until the meaning of his little ditty registered. "Wait, that's the theme music to Jaws," she said, breaking into a laugh. "It is, isn't it?" she asked, now laughing heartily.

"Come on, Jaws," Joyce said to Beryl, linking her friend's arm and giving her a gentle tug to encourage her along. "I'll help you find that aeroplane, Beryl. But if we could first go for a quick detour to the ladies room? I *really* need to adjust my knickers."

CHAPTER TWO

Charlotte's spoon drew to a halt, coming to rest millimetres above the milk in her breakfast bowl. She peeled her eyes away from her cornflakes, distracted by another pair of eyes she felt certain were staring at her from across the kitchen table.

"Something I can help you with, young man?" Charlotte asked. "Only I couldn't help but notice your eyes boring into me," she remarked, with this being accompanied by a genial smirk.

Charlotte's son, Stanley, sat with his elbows on the table, cradling his chin in his hands, sporting a proud-as-Punch sort of expression and with his own breakfast untouched. "Last week, at school, the teacher invited Gary Eastlake's mum to come in and talk to the class because she'd climbed some mountain in Wales," he said, unloading what was on his mind.

"Oh? You didn't mention that before, Stanley," Charlotte answered. "Was it interesting?"

"I guess," he replied with an indifferent shrug, sounding, in fact, decidedly underwhelmed. "But just wait until I tell my teacher about you jumping from a plane!" he said, perking right up again, extending his arms like a bird taking flight. "My friends will think it's *so* cool that you fell for over five miles at one thousand miles an hour."

Charlotte offered a modest grin in return. "Well, it wasn't quite one thousand miles an hour, Stan," she said, not wishing to entirely dampen his enthusiasm or extinguish the pride written all over his beaming expression. "But it wasn't *too* far away from that, I suppose."

Stanley returned his attention to his breakfast for a moment, stirring the cornflakes around in his bowl, lost in thought. "You know, Mum," he said, after a brief period of further contemplation, "you're just like that secret agent who wears the smart suit, you know, jumping from a plane to escape the bad guys."

"Ooh, I like that idea," Charlotte replied, allowing her own mind to wander, painting a picture in her head. "But instead of a Walther PPK," she went on, "I'd be armed with a crochet hook and knitting needle strapped to either leg. And my mission would be to prevent an evil genius from hijacking a valuable shipment of wool that actually concealed a precious cargo of stolen diamonds, and..."

Stanley stared back at his mum blankly.

"Too much?" Charlotte asked, wondering if she'd stepped beyond the acceptable bounds of fantasy, leaving the safety of its realm and perhaps entering into the outright absurd.

Stanley shook his head in the negative. "No, it's not that," he said. "I just don't know what a Waltherm PDQ is."

"A Walther PPK," Charlotte gently corrected the young fellow. "It was the weapon of choice for James Bond, the secret agent you're thinking about," she explained. "Oh, but instead, I could be *Jane* Bond," she quickly added. "Jane Bond, license to *quilt*," she further suggested, giggling away and pleased with her cleverness.

Stanley narrowed one eye. "James Bond...?" he said, appearing unconvinced. "No, Mum, that's not right. Not him, I don't think. The other one."

"Other one?" Charlotte asked, not aware of any other ones.

"Yeah," Stanley said, removing his spoon from his milk and swirling it around in the air, as if this in some way aided his powers of recollection. "He wears a *suit*, Mum," he reiterated, milk droplets falling from his spoon and onto the surface of the table. "You know him, Mum. You said it was the same actor as Mr Bean."

Charlotte smiled politely, unsure what exactly Stanley was talking about. "Mr Bean?" she repeated back to him, tapping a fingernail on the table. "Oh!" she said in a moment of insight, her son's meaning now becoming clear. "Ah. You're talking about Johnny English and not James Bond," she said, lowering her head, wounded by the blow to her temporarily inflated street cred from this realisation.

"That's him, Mum," Stanley said, pleased to be put out of his misery, so to speak. "You're *just* like Johnny English."

"Hmm, I think we should stick with Jane Bond, licence to quilt, yeah? It's got a nicer ring to it, don't you think?" she offered.

"If you say so, Mum," Stanley answered, giving another shrug. He knew she was wrong, of course, like most adults are most of the time. But he also knew, from vast experience, that it wasn't worth arguing with them about. Usually it was better to just pretend the adults were always right, as that seemed to keep them happy. And he loved his mum, so obviously he wanted her to be happy.

It'd been just three months since the conclusion of the hugely popular Square If You Care initiative. Although, in that relatively short amount of time, both Charlotte's personal and professional lives had enjoyed something of a renaissance, she was pleased to report, to anybody willing to listen (and occasionally to those who weren't).

Her budding relationship with Calum was chugging along nicely, despite several very minor hiccups during their first few dates, a result of Charlotte experiencing an unfortunate run of somewhat less than stellar luck. On only their second date, for instance — an invigorating stomp through the Manx great outdoors — Charlotte had ended up being brought off the hillside by a rescue helicopter after stumbling on a moss-covered rock.

Fortunately, her ankle hadn't been broken, as it turned out, but was just a nasty sprain. But, as the air paramedic was keen to stress (and what Calum had also gently suggested from the outset as well, actually): flip-flops are not ideal footwear in which to go hiking.

Eager to make amends for the fright she'd given Calum, a romantic meal for two — prepared by her own expert hand — sounded like just the solution, she'd felt confident. With Stan dispatched to his dad's for the weekend, it was all about the ambient music, mood lighting, and, of course, Charlotte's mastery in the kitchen. With everything planned to perfection and with military precision, there was absolutely nothing that could ruin what was destined to be a perfect evening. Well, that had been the plan, at least. Regrettably, her delicious starter of steamed mussels with white wine & garlic had other ideas. Sadly, the shellfish hadn't quite understood the brief for the evening. As a result, any ideas Charlotte might have had about concluding a splendid evening upstairs hadn't quite come to fruition, with the only room ending up witnessing any real action being the bathroom as opposed to the boudoir.

Still, if their fledgling relationship could survive the indignity of such an ill-fated experience, then its foundations must be solid, Charlotte consoled herself. And, as a positive spin on the grim situation, the doctor described their bout of food poisoning as only moderate rather than severe. So, every cloud and all that, as Charlotte had cheerily expressed at the time.

But speaking of their fledgling relationship, a niggling concern for Charlotte had been how Stanley would react to her finding another man in her life. At first, he was a little frosty, but this appeared to be more about looking out for his mum rather than any outright hostility directed towards Calum. And soon enough, once they'd got to know each other, the two of them were getting along famously, much to Charlotte's considerable relief. Fortunately for Charlotte, Calum and Stanley shared a common interest, and it was one that had helped them bond. Unfortunately for Charlotte, their shared interest was a fond appreciation for practical jokes, as she soon found herself being the perfect mark for their practical assignments. Still, if it meant being subjected to the occasional water bombing, being unexpectedly covered in baking flour, or perhaps sitting on a craftily concealed whoopee cushion, then that was a price Charlotte was willing to pay for the sake of harmony in her life. Still, not *indefinitely*, though — a fact she'd made abundantly clear to the pair of cheeky pranksters.

On matters away from those of the heart, Charlotte was over the moon that she was now able to describe herself as a full-time crafting teacher, with this added to her already impressive crafting repertoire. As the grateful recipient of a three-year charitable grant provided by Calum's company, Microcoding, Charlotte could now focus her time and energy on expanding her reach island-wide, teaching and promoting crafting skills. Using the methods she'd developed working with Larry and the gang at Make It Sew, she hoped to cater to the needs of both novices to the hobby and those more experienced.

Initially, it had been her intention to focus her efforts primarily on the island's nursing homes. But, on reflection, she was confident she could broaden her scope to include other groups who might benefit from learning new skills, such as schools, for instance. Moreover, only the week earlier, the governor of the island's prison had emailed her, asking if she would consider working with their inmates, a suggestion Charlotte was only too happy to accommodate. The more the merrier, was Charlotte's opinion, as she now had the luxury of available time to commit and, thanks to Amelia's eventual generosity, also had the prize money from Square If You Care burning a hole in her crafting purse.

And so, having dropped young Stanley off to school (after their earlier Johnny English vs James Bond convo, which she felt certain she'd come out on top of), Charlotte eagerly headed to yet another of her newly formed classes — this one at Union Mills Methodist Church, her favourite go-to location — which she'd christened *The Maternity Makers*. Targeted towards mums-to-be and those who'd recently given birth (and with dads also made very welcome as well), Charlotte hoped to provide a friendly environment where new parents could socialise with others in a similar situation. She'd devised an exciting range of knitted and crocheted options for the new members to try their hand at, including cot and pram blankets, baby hats, booties and mittens, and for the slightly more adventurous among them, matinée jackets.

Charlotte arrived to the meeting with plenty of time to spare. She was grateful to see a devoted Larry in attendance, bless his soul, helping out once again, just as he'd promised. And in fact, only a short while after Charlotte had settled in...

"Everybody, please immediately put down your cups and stop drinking your tea!" a flustered Larry called out, having darted from the kitchen and into the main hall. Larry ran his eyes around the room, raising and then slowly lowering his left arm to illustratively reiterate what those in attendance should be doing with their cups. "That's it," Larry encouraged, watching the confused but compliant attendees dutifully follow his instructions, offering them a reassuring smile in the hope it'd hide the panic behind it.

Charlotte was in the middle of a generous quaff during this announcement and, as such, found herself with a mouthful of tea. With cheeks puffed out like a squirrel eating nuts, she wondered if she should try and swallow the tea in one go, or if she was meant to stop drinking it entirely. Based on the urgency present in Larry's voice, she chose the latter, heeding his warning by surreptitiously emptying her mouth with a steady stream into her teacup while hoping nobody was noticing this rather unladylike behaviour. "Larry...?" she said, once her mouth was fully drained and available for speech.

But Larry didn't respond, his attention evidently elsewhere at that moment. "Do we happen to have an Abigail amongst our members today?" Larry asked, looking to each occupied table in turn. "Abigail...?" Larry asked again of the sea of faces staring back at him.

"Hi, yes," a timid voice replied, followed by an ever-so-slightly raised hand. "That's me. I'm Abigail," Abigail replied, cradling a baby in her arms. "Is this about my shoddy parking?" she asked, her cheeks flushed. "Only I was running late, and the car park was heaving," she explained, with a nervous laugh.

Larry shook his head in the negative, heading over to her table. "You're fine," Larry said. "And most of the cars out there look like they've been abandoned anyway, so don't worry," he added, hoping to offer assurance but, in doing so, also calling into question the parking abilities of the other members in attendance.

With the room in hushed silence and folk eager to understand what the nature of the sudden concern was and why they'd been suddenly forced to go tealess, there was little point in Larry attempting discretion at this point. And so, he just came out with what was playing on his mind. "Abigail, my love, there's a plastic beaker in the fridge with your name written on it," Larry said, hooking his thumb over his shoulder towards the kitchen. "Can I please ask if the milk contained in it is the normal sort of milk you'd extract from, say, a cow, or if it is, perhaps, more the sort you would extract from, ehm... *ahem...*?" he asked, twirling his index finger in a circular motion and in the general direction of Abigail's chest.

"Breast milk? Erm, yes...?" she cautiously replied, raising the bonny baby in her arms a bit to indicate who the intended recipient was.

"He's adorable," Larry replied, making cute little cooing noises for the infant's benefit.

"Em... he is a she," Abigail corrected him, although not impolitely. Abigail looked at Larry for a moment, and then, "On the basis you've told us not to drink our tea, and that you're now asking me that question you've just asked me..." she said, turning detective and smartly placing two and two together. "Can I assume you've made everyone's tea using my breast milk?"

Larry's left eye started to twitch as he shifted his weight from one foot to the other. "Yes," Larry offered flatly, in the absence of anything else sensible presenting itself to him. "Yes, I did," he added. "But, it wasn't my fault, you see," he quickly insisted, spinning round and pointing an accusatory finger towards the kitchen. "It was actually all Beryl, my *assistant's*, fault!" he said about the figure standing in the doorway listening on. "*She* was the one that passed me over your milk when I was making the tea."

"I couldn't see the name written on it as I didn't have my bloody glasses on, did I?" Beryl shot back from across the hall. "Besides, *Joyce* told me she'd brought along the milk, so I just assumed she'd put it in that plastic beaker."

"And why on earth would I do that?" Joyce asked, emerging from the kitchen, fearing she was about to be thrown under the proverbial bus by her mate. "That wouldn't make any sense, now would it? The milk I brought along is in the carton as it should be. You just weren't paying attention, were you? Because you were too busy prattling on about that TV series I've already told you loads of times I've never watched."

"Okay, okay," Charlotte said, easing up from her seat with a smirk emerging. She looked across to Beryl and Joyce. "First things first, does young Emma still have enough milk left over for her lunch?"

"Ehm..." said Beryl.

"Erm..." said Larry.

Joyce helped in answering Charlotte's question by fetching the aforementioned plastic beaker and holding it aloft for all to see, revealing less than an inch of milk remaining inside.

"Oh dear, I'm so sorry," Larry said, clearly irritated with himself, offering an apologetic smile to Abigail, and then to baby Emma, whose lunch he'd inadvertently given away. "If I can assist you in getting any more milk, then I'm more than happy to help. Just say the word," Larry graciously offered, though obviously not thinking through the practicalities of such an offer.

"Ehm... it's fine," Abigail answered, pulling in baby Emma close against herself, protecting her chest area from Larry's advances, just in case. "We'll just... erm, I reckon we'll just need to have lunch the traditional way?" she said. "By *ourselves*," she added, just so this was clear.

"Ah, direct from the tap," Larry said, nodding along to her answer. "Excellent choice!" he remarked, sounding like the maître d' at a fine dining establishment. "Right," Larry said, clapping his hands together smartly and turning slowly to address the other members around the hall. "Right. Well. Now we've sorted out that little dairy-related faux pas, how about I go and freshen those teacups for you all?" he asked. "Because I am, after all, the Reverend of Refreshments," he added, reminding everyone of his self-appointed title and one he was particularly proud of.

"Minister of Mayhem, more like," Joyce quipped, along with a cackle. But her joshing was received by Larry with a *you-can-have-that-one* sort of a grin.

Misappropriating a wee one's lunch aside, Larry, Beryl, and Joyce were an absolute godsend for Charlotte and her steadily increasing workload. With their extensive crafting experience and unruffled teaching styles, Joyce and Beryl were *very* willing and able to lighten the load on occasions such as today. One of the predicaments Charlotte encountered when organising any new club or initiative was that she simply didn't know how popular it was going to be, exactly. Similar to when she'd formed the Crafternoon Sewcial Club, she didn't know if she'd have five or fifty people in attendance each week. If it was the latter — which she sincerely hoped it was — then it was a fair assumption that a large proportion of them would be novices to the hobby and thus grateful for some experienced hand-holding and direction. Something Charlotte would, naturally, struggle to do under her own steam no matter how hard she tried. So the offer of assistance was of course invaluable.

Larry, for his part, remained the quintessential host, effortlessly replenishing the cups of the busy crafters, dispensing the occasional well-timed and witty anecdote, and generally willing to muck in with whatever needed doing with gusto and never with any complaint. They didn't *have* to be there, the three of them, generously offering up their time. But they wanted to be. For them, it wasn't a chore, and far from it. They viewed it as an opportunity to socialise with a wonderful group of folks, helping those folks learn a new skill, and generally feeling like they were making a difference in these people's lives — which they often were. And, collectively, they were all part of a team driving forward initiatives strengthening community bonds and having a bloody good time in the process.

With the business of the tea now in the rear-view mirror, Charlotte decided to get up and make the rounds, chatting with her assortment of guests. "Ooh," she said, approaching a table whose occupants were busy knitting baby hats, "I *really* like those colours." Charlotte then took a seat, offering admiring glances around the industrious crafters at varying stages of their projects. She was delighted to know that some of these splendid creations would soon find their way to warming their babies' heads, those babies currently snoozing away in nearby prams. For the other mums — those with presently-expanding tums — they'd have a little while longer to wait before their hard work could be put to proper use.

"Everything okay, Jenny?" Charlotte asked, noting the dogged expression on the lady sitting to her right.

"Hrm," Jenny said, staring intently towards the needles in hand, giving the impression that all was not okay. "Well, I've decided to attempt the pixie hat pattern," she explained. "But I think I may have bitten off more than I can chew..."

"Let's have a look, shall we?" Charlotte said. "May I?" she asked, reaching for Jenny's needles.

"There's supposed to be holes in the design," Jenny began, inspecting the pattern and then comparing it to her own work. "But, I don't know, it looks like one of them is in the wrong place...?" she said, now pointing out what Charlotte had just noticed for herself.

"Ah. What you have here, Jenny," Charlotte said in answer, "is the bane of all knitters. And, unfortunately, something we all experience every now and then."

"Oh?" said Jenny.

"Yep. You have a dropped stitch," Charlotte informed her.

"Oh, fudge," Jenny replied, shoulders sagging. "So I'll need to start again?" she asked wearily.

Charlotte ran her expert eye over the garment, taking a moment to cross-reference it against the pattern she'd taken from Jenny. "Nope. Not at all," she was happy to report a few moments later, putting a dejected Jenny at ease. "You just need to rip it out to the row before the mistake. Fortunately, as you've noticed it now, you'll have that remedied in no time once I show you what to do next."

Jenny wiped the back of her hand across her forehead in exaggerated fashion. *"Phew,"* she said, with a playful rolling of her eyes. "That's a relief. I was worried there for a moment, because just when I'd convinced myself I was getting the hang of this whole knitting business, I had to go and make such a silly mistake. I was certain I'd have to pack it in and call it a day!"

"Considering you'd never picked up any needles until last week, I think you're doing brilliantly," Charlotte offered, along with an encouraging pat on the shoulder.

"I'm just glad I plucked up the courage to come along last week when I did," Jenny commented. "I'm not usually brave enough to get involved on my own, but it did sound like fun," she said. "Plus, I not only get to meet some lovely people and make some new friends, but I also get to create something personal for the new arrival," she added, gently patting her baby bump.

Charlotte offered a warm smile, nodding in response to what she was hearing. "Well, I'm delighted that you did come along, as what you're saying about making new friends is one of the main reasons I formed the class," she remarked. "When I was pregnant with Stanley, I really struggled to meet new people," Charlotte explained. "And if I'm honest, looking back, I found myself a little down in the dumps at times. So, meeting up with mums in the same boat would have been a treat for me back then. Oh, and anything involving crafting is only ever a good thing."

"I *am* starting to understand the crafting appeal," Jenny answered. "Although, I have to say, I wasn't thinking that about five minutes or so ago, I must confess!"

"In crafting circles, we call this frogging," Charlotte advised, as she started to rip out the most recent of stitches Jenny had created.

"Frogging?"

"Yeah," Charlotte replied, ensuring Jenny could see what she was doing, including the technique she was using to pick up the stitches. "I think it's because it sounds like a frog, you know? *Rip it, rip it, rip it...*"

"Ah. Okay," Jenny responded, unsure if she was having her leg pulled. "Although, hopefully, it's something I won't need to do too often?"

Charlotte handed back the work in progress, leaving Jenny to crack on with it. "Just shout if you get stuck," she said, now looking over Jenny's shoulder, a little distracted by the woman presently standing in the opened doorway.

Hoping this to be another new member wishing to join the fold, Charlotte excused herself, scurrying off towards the newcomer who looked as if she was just about to turn around and head back out to the foyer area. "Yes, hello!" Charlotte said, offering up a hearty wave. "We don't bite, I promise!" she joked, approaching the uncertain-looking figure while armed with her broadest of smiles. "Charlotte Newman," Charlotte said, by way of introduction, once stood before the new arrival.

"Ehm, Claudia," Claudia replied, accepting the hand thrust in her direction although appearing slightly intimidated by the tremendously bubbly greeter who'd just bounded over, catching her unawares.

She was young, Charlotte noticed. Late teens, Charlotte estimated, and for a moment wondered if Claudia were perhaps related to one of the other club members rather than a new recruit.

"Are you coming to join us?" Charlotte asked, raising her arm towards the hall. "Or picking someone up, maybe?" she added, attempting to cover all the bases.

"Joining, I guess?" Claudia said, reaching behind her back, gently tugging at something slightly out of view behind her.

"Oh, and who's this handsome young man?" Charlotte asked, as a wee lad appeared. Charlotte crouched down so she was at eye level with the timid-looking young boy now clinging to Claudia's leg.

"This is my son Leo," Claudia offered on her boy's behalf. "And he's currently pretending to be shy, when I can assure you he most certainly is not," she added, dispensing a hair ruffling on him.

"Well, I'm delighted to meet you, Leo. Are you here to knit a dragon, or, perhaps a grizzly bear?" Charlotte asked, offering up a modest growl that sounded more like a cat meowing than the throaty roar of a bear. Still, her shoddy animal impressions at least raised a toothy grin in response. "And, I think we might have some chocolate biscuits, if you're interested?" Charlotte said, returning to full height.

"Yes, please!" Leo shouted, releasing his vice-like grip on his mum and sallying forth bravely into the hall in search of any and all biscuits or biscuit-like items to be found on the premises, chocolate or otherwise.

"Charlotte," Claudia said in a hushed tone, after waiting for a moment until Leo was well out of earshot. "Charlotte, I just wanted to confirm something if I could?"

"Of course."

"My friend told me about The Maternity Makers, but I was just a bit worried we were too old. Well, Leo, I mean, what with him being nearly five. Are we still...?"

"Yes, yes of course. You're most welcome here!" Charlotte assured her, waving Claudia's concerns away. "Honestly, you're fine. When I introduce you to the others, you'll see we have pregnant mums, new mums, grandmothers, and even two dads amongst the group today. Think of us as one big happy family where the common denominators are children and crafting. Oh, and for today, chocolate biscuits as well."

Charlotte turned towards the hall, leading the way. "Is there anything in particular you wanted to learn today?" Charlotte asked brightly, about to reveal the menu of crafting options that awaited her new recruit. "Claudia...?" Charlotte said, when she looked and saw that Claudia had remained anchored to the spot, with no signs of moving.

"Do you think I could..." Claudia began, trailing off and staring down to her feet.

Charlotte stepped back over to the young woman. "Yes?" she asked gently, probing for more information.

"Leo's very worried about the upcoming school year, and..." Claudia said, raising both her head and the plastic bag she was carrying, but before she could finish her sentence, her lower lip started to tremble.

"Hey now, what's all this about?" Charlotte said, quickly offering a tissue retrieved from her pocket. "Are you upset now that he's off to *big* school?" she asked. "If so, it's perfectly natural, Claudia. I know I sobbed for at least an hour when I left my Stanley there for the first time."

Claudia shook her head, wiping away the moisture from around her eyes. "No, no, it's not that," she said, taking in several lungfuls of air to compose herself. "Oh, what on earth must you think of me turning up like this?"

"You're fine," Charlotte assured her again, resisting the urge to cuddle someone she'd just met and settling for administering a comforting arm rub instead.

"It's just that I didn't have any school uniform for my little Leo," Claudia confided eventually, once her lip had stopped trembling. "Fortunately, the charity shop had some nearly-new donated items," she said, indicating the bag in her hand. "But it's all too big, and the trousers drown him. He's terrified the other boys will tease him about it. You know how children can be sometimes. And Leo's been really upset about it, saying he doesn't want to go into school dressed like this. So, I thought I'd come along today, and see if there was anything that could be done...?"

"May I?" Charlotte asked, taking possession of Claudia's bag. "Do you want me to teach you how to adjust them?" Charlotte said, reaching inside and noting trousers, a coat, and a couple of jumpers folded in there. "We can certainly do something with the trousers, at least."

Claudia perked up in response to this. "Would you?" she said. "I mean, is that the sort of thing that you teach people in your class?"

"Not usually, no," Charlotte answered, handing the bag back. "But we jolly well do now, Claudia. We can't have young Leo tripping over his trousers at big-boy school, can we?"

Claudia shook her head, with a smile emerging. "Thank you, Charlotte. I really appreciate it."

"You're very welcome. Now, let's get you inside so we can fashion Leo some trousers that actually fit," Charlotte declared, inviting Claudia into the hall.

"Mum, mum!" an immensely excited Leo suddenly called out, tearing towards them. "Mum, a man in the kitchen called Larry gave me this, and he said I could choose whichever one I wanted inside!" he announced, holding up a sizeable biscuit tin larger than his head. "And they've *also* got lots of *cake* in there," Leo added, taking his mum by the hand, eager to show her where the good stuff lived.

"Who knew a crafting club could be so exciting for a young boy?" Charlotte joked, escorting both of their latest recruits towards the soon-to-be-formed alterations station (after a quick stop in the kitchen for promised refreshments, of course).

CHAPTER THREE

Stanley Newman couldn't wait for the third Sunday of each month, April through to September (weather permitting). Not only did he get to spend quality time with his mum and Auntie Mollie, but he also had the opportunity to nourish his oft-famished piggy bank by putting in a solid shift toiling on Mollie's stall.

The hugely popular and well-attended Douglas Farmers' Market, located on the grounds of the historic Nunnery estate, offered the island's hardworking food producers an ideal venue to showcase their delicious products. And, fortunately, the tremendous Manx public was only too pleased to turn out in their droves to procure what was on offer, supporting local business in the process.

Sure, it was a bit of an upheaval for Mollie & co, shifting crates of produce from the farm shop she managed to her stall for the day. But the effort was usually rewarded by the uptick in takings through her till and magnificent advertising for her shop. Plus, in Charlotte and Stanley, she had two eager assistants, ready and willing to lend a hand and lighten the load, all while having a jolly good laugh.

"That's the last one from the van, Auntie Mollie," Stanley confirmed, handing over the wooden crate he'd been ferrying. "Chard and aubergines," he reported, adjusting his Manx tartan flat cap once his hands were free, as it was a touch lopsided due to his considerable efforts thus far.

After relieving him of this final load, Mollie removed the contents and added them to her already alluring display of fruit and veg carefully arranged on a large wooden table. "I love that a ten-year-old boy even knows what chard and aubergines are," Mollie remarked over her shoulder, extending the young lad an appreciative wink. But he was already gone, wandering off to see what tempting provisions were being sold by the other stall-holders, with his previously stated preference being the sweeter the better. "I think our helper might have spotted the ice cream truck, Lotti," Mollie observed, noting the direction in which he was heading. "Oh, and by the way, I absolutely adore his little hat, Lotti. Did you make it?" she said. "Ah, what am I thinking, but of *course* you made it. After all, it's *you* we're talking about," she then playfully remarked, and in a manner intended as a distinct compliment.

Mollie shifted her attention when there was no response received. "Hello? Earth to Lotti," she said, upon seeing her friend staring vacantly into a box of freshly dug carrots as if she'd been mesmerised by them like a charmed snake. "Hello, Lotti..."

"Oh, sorry," Charlotte said eventually, snapping herself back into the present. "I'd love one if you're going."

"Going?"

"For a cup of coffee or tea," Charlotte said. "I'd love one."

"Okay. But what I was *actually* saying was about how much I admired Stanley's hat," Mollie replied, along with a mild eye-rolling.

"Ah, yes. When we were watching Countryfile last week, he spotted a farmer wearing one, and thought it would be the ideal headgear for today's market. So I went ahead and made one for him," Charlotte proudly related.

"I did actually say you'd probably... ah, in fact, never mind," Mollie said, smirking. "Something on your mind today, Lotti? You don't appear to be your usually attentive self."

"Sorry about that, Moll. When the customers arrive, I'll be bright-eyed and bushy-tailed, I promise."

"Everything okay?" Mollie asked, slipping the loop of her apron over her head and then fumbling with the straps behind her back.

"Yeah, sure, I'm okay," Charlotte said, though without too much conviction, as she removed the elastic band securing a stack of yellow cardboard star-shaped price tags they'd cut out the previous day. "Do you want me to start pricing the stock up?" she asked, reaching for the marker pen resting next to the weighing scales.

Mollie took a step closer, nearer to Charlotte, gently capturing the pen from Charlotte's grip. "Nope, you're fine," she told her, taking one of the stars, and then using her teeth to release the pen lid as both hands were currently occupied. "Seeing as how you're so distracted, I think it's best I do it," she advised, through the temporary obstruction in her gob. "Just in case you put the decimal point in the wrong place and get me fired," she clarified, with as best a smile as she could muster with a pen lid secured between her gnashers.

Charlotte didn't contest this, happy to concede that her friend was most likely spot on in her assessment, given her own presently preoccupied state. "It's just that I can't stop thinking about Claudia," Charlotte explained, dusting away a thin layer of soil that had accumulated on their work surface.

Mollie busied herself writing on the yellow star, in her absolutely neatest writing:

Bugs Bunny's FAVE carrots £2.17 per KG

... after which she proudly set down her handiwork, placing it in front of the carrot pyramid she'd previously constructed.

"Claudia, the girl with the baggy school uniform for her son. Remember the one I was telling you about?" Charlotte said by way of clarification, as Mollie wasn't answering. "It really moved me, Moll, how upset the poor girl was. Honestly, she didn't actually look much older than Bonnie from our Crafternoon club, and my heart just went out to her."

Mollie removed the lid from her mouth. "You were able to adjust the uniform for them?" she asked and, in doing so, confirmed that she'd been listening.

"Oh, yes. And I was able to help her take the sleeves up on the jacket as well," Charlotte said fondly, a twinkle evident in her eye. Charlotte lowered her head, distracted by her own thoughts. "You know, Moll," Charlotte said a moment later, "you can buy a new pair of school trousers from Marksies for less than a tenner, and a coat for, what, maybe thirty quid? But Claudia didn't even have the spare money to buy a pair of trousers, let alone anything else, and she was so anxious about her little boy being teased at school for wearing trousers that didn't properly fit him. Then, when we were able to hem the trousers so they actually *did* fit, she was in seventh heaven when Leo proudly modelled them for us with no longer a care in the world."

"It's wonderful that you're able to use your talent to help," Mollie suggested. "Plus, you've now taught her a new skill."

Charlotte appreciated the words of encouragement but retained a solemn expression. "You know I've never exactly been rolling in cash, myself, Moll. But what I find sad, and struggle to get my head around, is that there are people in Claudia's financial situation who can't afford to buy their precious child something as simple and basic as a decent school uniform." Charlotte placed a hand over her mouth, biting down on her lower lip. "It's not right, Moll," she said, voice breaking. "We're living on an island perceived by many to be fairly affluent, and yet..." Charlotte said, unable to even finish her sentence.

"I know, Lotti," Mollie replied, placing an arm around her friend's shoulders. "And now you mention it, I'm actually feeling pretty guilty about the bottle of red I bought for us to share later on. Thirteen pounds, it cost," she said, shaking her head. "When that same amount of money was all it would've taken to purchase someone like that needy young lad a brand-new pair of trousers," she added, fanning her face with her fingertips. "You're going to get me going in a minute, Lotti."

"Ehm, everything okay?" Stanley asked, returning from his survey mission, a half-eaten toffee apple poised millimetres from his mouth. "What's going on here? Have you two been crying?" he asked, examining their reddened faces and watery eyes.

"What?" Mollie said with a forced smile. "No, no, it's just the onions we've been unpacking, Stanley, that's all," she offered, looking over to Charlotte for corroboration.

"Yes. Yes, the onions. That's it," Charlotte quickly agreed.

"Onions? But I don't see any," Stanley replied, glancing about and noticing the suspicious lack of anything even remotely resembling an onion in the general vicinity. "And wouldn't you need to be chopping them up, before you—?"

"Oh! What's this you have? A toffee apple? You didn't see the ice cream van, then?" Charlotte said, deftly shifting the conversation away from the subject of her emotional state.

"Yeah, I did. But he's only getting himself set up right now, so he wasn't able to sell me anything just yet," Stanley explained with a sigh. "But after all the energy I'd used shifting this lot," he said, indicating to their well-appointed stall, "I was wasting away to nothing!"

"To nothing...?" said Charlotte.

"Right! And luckily, I found somebody selling *these* little beauties before I passed out from hunger," Stanley answered, raising his toffee apple aloft.

"Blimey, Stan, you'd think I don't feed you at home," Charlotte remarked. "Could I remind you that you just had your breakfast of *four* Weetabix a little over, what, one short hour ago?" she said, glancing down to her watch to confirm.

"Yes, I know, Mum," Stan replied, biting off another chunk of toffee-coated treat. "But I'm a growing boy, aren't I, and I need to keep up my strength!" he declared, cheekily tipping his spiffing new hat, which raised a giggle from his two cohorts.

Mercifully, the fleeting threat from a patch of fierce-looking rain clouds overhead trailed away before it came to anything. Fortunately so, because both Mollie and Charlotte were dressed in shorts and a t-shirt, and their stall had no canopy to protect them from inclement weather.

"It's still August," Charlotte remarked, raising an angry fist to the heavens. "I'm not ready to let go of summer, and we need all the fair weather we can get," she said, reprimanding the retreating weather front for even thinking about possibly ruining their day.

"Not long until September, though, Lotti," Mollie was at pains to point out. "And alas, here we are, still cursed with a pair of lily-white legs apiece despite one of the hottest summers in years."

"My legs are *not* that pasty," Charlotte shot back, glancing down at her pins. "Stanley, whose legs do you think are the whitest?" she enquired, once Stanley was finished up serving their latest satisfied customer.

Stanley looked both women up and down in turn, unsure what the correct response was in the circumstance and not wishing to offend either. "Uhm..." he replied, tilting his head as he formulated his answer. "Well, Mum," he said, clicking his tongue against the roof of his mouth, considering it further. "Right. Definitely you, Mum," he decided, assuming this to be the appropriate answer. "Your legs are whiter than the cliffs of Dover, yeah?"

This was definitely *not* the answer his mum had been hoping for. Still, anaemic limbs and the brief, passing threat of a potential soaking aside, the market was proving to be an unbridled success judging by the volume of punters in attendance. Upbeat stallholders merrily dispensed their wares, with their only concerns appearing to be whether their dwindling stock levels would last the day — a most agreeable situation to find themselves in.

And so, during a brief lull in trade after a busy first few hours, Mollie and Charlotte were happy to take the occasion to rest their weary bones in the camping chairs they'd brought along for just such a purpose. "You've got the helm," Mollie said, offering a salute to Captain Stanley as she parked her cheeks down on the rickety green chair. Stan, in response, returned the gesture, pleased as Punch to be the master of this magnificent ship, so to speak. "Some boy you've got there," Mollie remarked, glancing over to Charlotte, sat next to her. "A retail magnate in the making," she observed, watching as Stanley scanned the area, searching for his next punter.

"The absolute best," Charlotte said with a broad smile. "And just look at him in his little hat. Adorable!"

"You know I *can* hear the two of you," Stan pointed out, without shifting his attention away from his duties.

"Love you, Captain!" Mollie said.

"Love you more, Captain!" Charlotte added, at the same time as she was removing the presently vibrating phone from her pocket.

"Hmm? What's tickled you, then?" Mollie asked a moment later, noting the daft grin that had suddenly spread across her friend's face.

Charlotte looked up from her phone with the giddy expression of a lovestruck teenager. "Calum texted me to say he's just arrived."

"Am I in the bad books for dragging you away for the day?"

"Of course not, Moll. Calum knows I'm a girl whose time is very much in demand," Charlotte answered, tapping the buttons on her phone in prompt response to Calum's message. "He's completely relaxed about my hectic schedule. Although I'm impressed he's here today, as I'm fairly certain he doesn't *really* listen when I tell him what I've got on."

"How rude. Although, truth be told, you do tend to jabber on at times, Lotti."

"*How rude,*" Charlotte said, tossing Mollie's own words back at her, although reluctantly nodding in agreement and offering no real defence to the playful slight on her character. "Although, to be fair, I did nearly give the poor chap a heart attack the other week when I was 'jabbering on', as you put it."

"Oh?"

"Yeah, I was filling him in on all my lovely ideas for the new Maternity Makers class, Moll. And, you know me, sparing none of the crucial details."

"I can imagine."

"Anyway, he must have drifted away and misheard me, because he thought I'd actually said I was arranging to join a maternity class."

"Oh! I can see how that might come as something of a shock," Mollie answered. "But that'll teach Calum for not listening."

"Exactly!" Charlotte replied, pushing herself out of her seat, which was no mean feat considering the flimsy camping chair appeared intent on eating her each time she shifted her weight. "Bloody thing," she said once finally upright, casting an uncompromising glare at her assailant. "Anyway, speaking of Calum, he asked if we wanted anything from the refreshments truck," Charlotte said, straightening herself out. "I said we'd have a cup of coffee and a bit of cake?" she advised, looking to Mollie for her blessing.

"Perfect."

"And a Coca-Cola for me, Mum?" Stanley called over, while bagging up a selection of veg for the bearded chap waiting patiently for his order. "After all, this is thirsty work!"

"Already ordered, Stanley," Charlotte answered, and then, "Right, Moll, if it's okay with you, boss, I'll go and lend Calum a hand before we get too busy again?"

"Don't forget to grab me one of those little sugar sachets and a wooden stirrer, if you would?" Mollie said, moving her hand like she was drawing a circle in the air.

Charlotte pushed herself up on her tippy toes, trying to map out the most direct path to the catering trucks through the slew of people wandering about enjoying an afternoon in the Isle of Man sunshine. But whichever way she looked, she was greeted by a sea of heads, so she'd just need to sharpen her elbows and forge herself a path.

"Oh, sorry… excuse me… pardon me… can I squeeze past…?" Charlotte said, as she inched her way through the scrum of folk dawdling along as they inspected the various goods on display. "Ooh, I like your cardigan!" Charlotte called out to one person in particular, spotting what appeared to be a fellow crafter's fine work as the woman shuffled in her direction.

The well-chuffed lady trudged her way towards Charlotte, lowering her candy floss and smiling widely. "Why, thank you," she said, once they were within proper speaking distance. "It's a King Cole pattern," the woman happily informed her, running her free hand over her pomegranate-hued creation.

"The colour is so cheery," Charlotte answered, while taking a mental note to search the pattern out for herself later.

Generally, crafters were like that with each other, appreciative of each other's work and not afraid to engage a stranger so they could bestow praise. Indeed, Charlotte had (on numerous occasions) been the recipient of such unexpected compliments, and each time it did wonders in raising her spirits, leaving her with a spring in her step and an immediate desire to commence knitting again at the earliest available opportunity.

As a result of this mutual crafting appreciation society, even young Stanley could now detect a handcrafted article of clothing from a hundred and fifty paces away. He was like a shark sniffing out a solitary drop of blood in an Olympic-sized swimming pool on such matters. He had to be, because every time he ventured *anywhere* with his mum, there was a real danger she'd chance upon a fellow crafter, with progress to their ultimate destination thus being delayed for an extended, indeterminate amount of time. A nightmare if they were heading, say, towards the toy shop in town, for instance. So, if he could spot the imminent peril well in advance, there remained a chance he could distract his mum or at least take evasive action, altering and avoiding their collision course. It didn't always work, however. Because his mum was, after all, like a crafting Jedi Master. And if Stanley could be compared to a young Luke Skywalker, then his mum was like Yoda, only armed and skilled with a crochet hook instead of a lightsabre.

"Darn it," Charlotte said, having finally navigated her way through the shoppers and then clapping eyes on the collection of catering trucks lined up, though with the magnificent country house as a splendid backdrop. She came to a halt, standing with her hands resting on her hips. The last time she'd seen queues this long, she and Mollie had been waiting for the women's loo at a music festival. The ice cream truck, burger van, BBQ train smoker, and other concessions were, it would appear, doing a roaring trade judging by the number of people waiting to be served. She'd no idea where Calum was, precisely. But considering he was acquiring them coffee and cake, she reckoned the converted VW Campervan with an oversized coffee cup affixed to its roof would be an ideal place to start looking.

At first glance, the queue to the coffee stand appeared modest in comparison to the others. However, as Charlotte drew closer, it was apparent the line was doubled back on itself like you'd find at an airport check-in desk. "Do you lot not have anything better to do?" Charlotte muttered under her breath, despite the fact that she herself was *also* currently hoping for a bit of caffeinated beverage. She scanned the queue for any sign of Calum. "Where are you...?" she said, adjusting her position, looking this way and that, and now wondering if perhaps Calum had decided against waiting.

Confident Calum wasn't in the line for that particular coffee truck, Charlotte had one last nose around just in case there was another one she might have missed, which there didn't appear to be. Just on the verge of giving up on her search, however, she caught a glimpse of a well-dressed, rather dapper-looking chap strolling away from the refreshments area carrying a cardboard tray in each hand. A chap who, in fact, looked remarkably like Calum.

"Calum!" Charlotte called out, though receiving no response. "Calum!" she shouted, breaking into a trot, which proved something of a challenge considering the number of people milling about. "Calum!" she said again, dodging those in her path (offering a friendly smile as she did so), but her voice seemed to be drowned out by the overall ambient noise.

Fortunately, as she wasn't slowed down by carrying several drinks, as Calum presently was, Charlotte soon made up the distance between them, approaching from the rear. "Calum, I was shouting after you like a fishwife," she said, slowing to a walk. "But I'll forgive you because your bum looks so absolutely delicious in those trousers," she graciously offered. This close to him, she should have realised this wasn't Calum at all. But unfortunately, her eyes were currently fixed upon the fellow's pert bottom. Entranced, she extended her hand to give the left cheek a gentle squeeze.

"Whoa!" the man in front said, recoiling as if he'd just been stung by a hornet. He spun around in response, the contents of both of his cardboard trays pitching over and flinging off in every direction in the process.

Even before the first plastic cup had tumbled onto the grass, Charlotte realised, to her horror, that the derrière she'd just had the pleasure of pinching most definitely did *not* belong to her Calum. The only saving grace was that the cups appeared to contain soft drinks rather than coffee. So at least the caramel-coloured liquid soaking into the stranger's baby-blue polo shirt wasn't scalding hot.

"Oh, shoot, I'm so sorry!" Charlotte said desperately, crouching down, but she was far too late to rescue any of the beverages, the last of the liquid now spilling out onto the earth to enjoy its freedom. "I thought you were my... my, ehm..." she started to explain, but then remembering that she and Calum had not officially announced themselves as a couple at this stage in their relationship. "Well, my friend Calum. Calum, who's about your age, and who looks astonishingly like you when viewed from behind," she said, laughing nervously as she scooped some of the fugitive ice cubes back into one of the empty cups. While she was down there, with her fingers raking through the grass, Charlotte couldn't help but notice the shoddy workmanship on the violated man's hems. He was sharply presented (aside from the dark wet patch on his chest), yet the substandard stitching on the end of his trouser legs tarnished his overall appearance, in Charlotte's measured opinion. Of course, not many would have noticed the inadequate alteration, likely something he wasn't even aware of himself. But for Charlotte, these minor (yet important) details stood out like a sore thumb.

"Surely this Calum of yours must be an especially *close* friend, if those wayward hands of yours are any indication...?" the man offered, unamused.

"Hmm, well I suppose you *could* say he's my boyfriend," Charlotte answered, liking the sound of this, actually, and returning to full height. Then, with a polite smile, Charlotte placed the cups that she'd recovered back onto one of the trays still in the man's hand. "You should take it as a compliment that I thought your bum was his, because he's got a *really* nice one," she prattled on, taking a clean tissue from her pocket and dabbing his shirt like she was attending to a glass of spilt wine on a new carpet. "Hopefully, that should come out in the wash," she said with a grimace. "If you like, I could take your shirt with me and have it back to you looking brand-new?" she offered, until the implications of her generous offer dawned on her.

"Thanks, but I'm not sure what my wife would think if I were to return to her with no shirt on as well as no drinks," the glum chap replied, looking down at the damp section of ground soaking up his drinks. "Twenty minutes I was waiting in the queue for them," he remarked, sadly.

"I feel so bad," Charlotte told him. "Would you like me to go and buy you some replacements?" she asked, perfectly sincere, and yet secretly hoping he'd reply in the negative given the time he said it had taken him to successfully procure them initially.

With her generous offer to purchase replacement drinks politely declined, Charlotte offered a further apology before braving the crowds and heading back towards Mollie's stall, the quest for Calum now abandoned. "You're such a bloody klutz," Charlotte said with flushed cheeks and a shake of the head, giving herself a gentle scolding as she progressed.

However, her anguish diminished a few minutes later when she caught sight of Stanley standing front and centre, behind the display, dispensing what appeared to be a bag of spuds and a charming smile to another satisfied customer. Charlotte was also delighted to see the other man in her life sitting in the camping chair next to Mollie, chatting away, with them both letting the young fella do all the work it would appear.

"Here she is!" Calum said, rising up from his seat (with considerably more grace than she'd been able to muster herself, earlier) to greet the recently-arrived Charlotte with a generous peck. "Everything okay?" he asked.

"Oh, yes. Fine," Charlotte replied, taking his hand and looking him up and down with a warm smile. "I went looking for you, and—"

"Utter chaos," Calum cut in with a weary sigh. "The queues were insanely long, so, regrettably, I come to you without refreshments. In fact, it'd probably have been quicker to drive home, fill a flask, nick some cake, and then come all the way back here."

"Were your ears burning, Lotti?" Mollie asked. "Because we were just talking about you, you know."

"About how wonderful I am?" Charlotte asked.

"Of course!" Calum was happy to agree, giving Charlotte's hand an affectionate squeeze. "Mollie was just filling me in on your Maternity Makers class. She said you were a little bit upset, though?"

"Ah. Yes, it was tough to see how distraught that poor mum was about her boy's school uniform," Charlotte answered. "And it really struck a chord, what with me having a young son myself," she said, instinctively glancing over to Stanley for a moment.

"I can imagine," Calum said.

Charlotte went quiet for a bit, staring off vacantly into the distance like the wheels and cogs inside her head were whirring busily away, which, in fact, they were, doing precisely that.

"Charlotte…?" Calum said eventually, uncertain if she was currently deep in thought or if she'd simply finished what she had wanted to say.

"What? Oh, sorry, I was just thinking," Charlotte answered, nibbling her lower lip, which she liked to do when formulating ideas. "When I was looking for you over by the food area," she told him, "I, ehm… accidentally bumped into this one bloke. He looked quite a lot like you from a certain rearward angle, as it should happen."

"Oh?" Calum replied, wondering in which direction this anecdote was going but intrigued nonetheless.

"Anyway, when I was scooping up his ice cubes, I noticed the stitching on his hem."

"That is such a Charlotte Newman thing to say!" Mollie remarked with a laugh.

Charlotte was happy to concede that fact. "More to the point, though, I noticed *the shoddy nature* of the stitching on his hem," Charlotte clarified, an eager expression painted across her face.

"I see," Mollie said, even though she didn't, in fact, see.

"Well, it's a sign, isn't it!" Charlotte declared, although this declaration was met with two polite but somewhat confused expressions.

"It is?" Calum asked, though sounding entirely encouraging and supportive, as he had no wish to dampen the passion evident in Charlotte's eyes.

"Yes, it *has* to be," Charlotte reasoned. "First, Claudia and the oversized school uniform," she said. "And then, just now, I accidentally bump into a stranger, and the first thing I'm drawn to is the sloppy stitching on his hem, yeah?"

At this point, Charlotte gave a confident nod of the head, in a *now-you-both-know-what-I'm-talking-about* sort of way.

"Right," Mollie said, smiling wryly. "When you bumped into this chap, Lotti," she asked, "did you also happen to bang your head at the same time, by any chance?"

"No! Well, at least I don't think so," Charlotte said, giving her bonce a rub for good measure. "Don't you see? So first, Claudia comes along to Maternity Makers, and I then spill that chap's drinks resulting in me clapping eyes on his dodgy hem," she said, offering her own unique form of logic on the situation. "It has to be a sign that there are more trousers out there that need adjusting. A *sign*, Mollie."

At this, Mollie started to laugh, although certainly not in any way unkind. "Are you saying, in some roundabout fashion, that you want to help schoolchildren to get uniforms that fit?" she suggested, figuring this must be where Charlotte was getting to. Eventually.

"Exactly, Moll. And that sort of keen insight is precisely why you're my best friend, as you're always on the same page as me."

"Told you," Mollie said, flicking her eyes between Charlotte and Calum. "Didn't I tell you, Calum?" she added, appearing decidedly satisfied with herself.

Calum nodded his head in response.

"Told you what?" Charlotte enquired. "What's all this?"

"Well, Mollie mentioned to me how the Claudia situation had been playing on your mind," Calum explained. "So she had a sneaking suspicion you were formulating a plan of some kind, although she wasn't sure exactly what you were thinking of. Just as you were returning, I'd been pointing out to her that you had quite a lot on your plate already, though."

"*Pfft*," Charlotte said, dismissing Calum's concerns. "I've only got Crafternoon Sewcial Club, Maternity Makers, and an island-wide rollout of Make It Sew to arrange," she said with a playful wave of the hand. "So, plenty of time to get involved in another worthy cause, I should think. Or at least explore the possibilities."

"Absolutely," Calum said brightly, not sounding entirely persuaded, and yet not wishing to rain on her parade, either.

"Perfect," Charlotte replied. "All I need to do now is recruit some wonderful, kind-hearted souls who'd be lovely enough to lend me a hand," she said. "You wouldn't happen to know anybody that might match that description, would you?" she asked, eyeing up the both of them with a cheeky grin.

"Blimey O'Reilly!" young Stan interrupted, after having just taken care of his latest in a long series of satisfied customers.

"What's wrong, Stanley?" Charlotte asked.

"I'm parched over here!" Stanley announced, removing his hat and using it to fan his face. "I don't suppose there's any sign of that fizzy pop I'd been asking for ages ago...? I'm spitting feathers over here!"

CHAPTER FOUR

Waiting patiently as morning roll call progressed, Charlotte stood, anchored to the spot, smiling for that long that her cheeks ached and her teeth were starting to dry out. She swayed gently from side to side, wondering how the Queen's Guard was able to remain upright and perfectly still outside Buckingham Palace for hours on end, without incident, while she was struggling right now after only minutes.

Ordinarily, Charlotte suspected the taking of the class register wasn't such a protracted affair. But this was Monday morning, and each child appeared intent on regaling Mrs Renshaw with their weekend activities when their name was called out, and with no bit of detail spared, it seemed. Initially, it was cute, Charlotte thought, but twenty-eight anecdotes later, and she was secretly relieved to hear little Robert Zaborowski, the last of the students in class, wrap up his fascinating tale of finding a rare and valuable fossil on the beach only to discover it was actually a discarded BBQ'd chicken wing.

"Well," Mrs Renshaw said, closing over her registration book with a satisfying thud, "it sounds like you've all had a wonderful and eventful weekend. Now, I'm delighted to tell you that, as you can see, we have a very special guest for our arts and crafts lesson this morning. So, class, I'd like you to extend a proper Onchan School welcome to a very talented crafting teacher, Miss Newman."

"GOOD MORNING MISS NEWMAN," the class dutifully called out, in polished unison, extending their very warmest of welcomes.

"Good morning, class," Charlotte politely replied, offering her friendliest of waves in return, and hoping her nerves didn't translate into her voice.

She was surprised to find herself with butterflies in her stomach. Usually, she was confident enough when she stood up at the front, showing a group of people how to thread the right end of a needle. But this was an altogether different proposition than what she was used to. Rather than standing before her usual clientele who eagerly and willingly attended her sessions, this was a class of seven- and eight-year-old schoolchildren looking back at her who really didn't have any choice in the matter. And despite the gracious welcome, some amongst the group didn't seem especially interested. Indeed, one ginger-haired lad sitting on the front row, for instance, seemed decidedly unimpressed to learn more about this first lesson of the day. With a finger shoved up his beak and two heavy eyelids, he appeared just about ready to doze off as Charlotte outlined what she was going to cover in their one-hour masterclass.

As to the subject matter she was presently discussing, Charlotte had agonised all weekend over it, unsure what crafting project to get the children involved with. She didn't want to give them anything overly complex so that they'd get bored and lose interest, but still wanted them to be engaged and hands-on. And, of course, another significant consideration was the issue of health and safety, as Charlotte didn't fancy a lawsuit owing to a child jabbing themselves in the eye with a knitting needle or slicing off the tip of a finger with a crafting knife.

Fortunately, a trip through her hallway the previous evening offered Charlotte the inspiration she'd been searching for, as hung there, presented in an oak frame, was her very own debut crafting project. Inspired by her own work, she decided she'd teach the children the very same project that got her involved in crafting when she was a wee girl: an embroidery sampler. As far as Charlotte knew, it was virtually impossible to injure one-self with a blunt darning needle. (She would still exercise caution, of course, knowing from experience that anything was possible when dealing with young ones.) And considering she had ample supplies in her colossal crafting inventory, it was an ideal task to set them all, she reckoned.

Charlotte explained to the class that their goal was to stitch their own names into the fabric. To illustrate her point, Charlotte held up her own creation featuring the complete letters of the alphabet stitched in several rows in all the colours of the rainbow, which she had completed the night before in preparation for the class. This resulted in three or more audible gasps from her audience, which Charlotte took to be a good sign.

And so, with the grateful assistance of Mrs Renshaw and one particularly enthusiastic volunteer by the name of Chloe, each child was soon in possession of a Binca fabric square (a type of blank embroidery canvas), darning needle, and a variety of different wools to add a splash of colour, as they pleased, to their work. Standing at the front of the class, Charlotte held her darning needle in one hand and a length of red wool in the other. "To get started, we just need to thread the wool through the eye of the darning needle, like *this*," she said, performing the actions as she described them.

Charlotte raised her head, running her eyes around the class, pleasantly surprised to see the class doing as instructed.

"Once we've done that, we just need to ensure that we've tied a knot at the end of the wool," Charlotte went on, pointing to the end of her wool. "Does anybody know why the knot is so important?"

"Ooh... ooh!" Chloe, now back in her chair, called out, fidgeting desperately in her seat and hand nearly touching the ceiling.

"Chloe?" Charlotte said, pointing to the only raised hand in the class.

"It's so that when you complete your first stitch, the wool doesn't simply pull straight through the fabric," Chloe announced, looking to her classmates with a smug grin.

"That's excellent, Chloe," Charlotte answered, nodding her head. "And do we all know how to tie a knot?" she asked of the group.

"Lee Benson doesn't, Miss," Chloe answered, quite enjoying being the centre of attention, it would appear. "That's why he wears those shoes with the Velcro straps," she helpfully added, extending a finger towards where master Benson could be located.

"Yes, I do know how!" Lee shot back, livid at the insinuation. "I only wear these shoes 'cause they're brilliant. Not that you'd know anything about *that*, Chloe."

"Okay, okay," Charlotte said, raising an authoritative hand before matters could escalate. "If anybody here, anybody at all, would like a reminder as to how to tie a knot, then just raise a hand."

With that potential skirmish averted, and no hands raised, Charlotte continued with her demonstration, making every effort to clearly articulate what was required. And to her great relief, the children appeared receptive, with most of them eager to dispatch their needles and get their creative on. Alas, one child remained distinctly disinterested in the proceedings. It was the ginger-haired lad, who looked like he'd just let go of his favourite balloon and watched it float away on the breeze. Still, at least he'd removed the finger from his nostril by this point. So there was that.

"How are we getting on here?" Charlotte asked of the boy with the lost balloon. "Do you need any help?" she enquired, fully aware that the lad's needle was still resting unused on top of his blank, unaltered fabric square. "Would you like me to repeat anything?" she asked, squatting down a little so she could look the lad in the eye.

"Dunno. It's a bit..." he began, pressing out his bottom lip in protest.

"Yes...?" Charlotte asked.

"Girly," the lad declared. "It's the sort of thing my sister does at home," he added, folding his arms across his chest.

"Oh, no," Charlotte said, shaking her head. "Well, I mean, it *is* for girls, yes. But it's also absolutely for boys as well," she told him. "May I ask your name?" she asked.

"That's Liam," Chloe interjected, before Liam could even respond.

"I'm Liam," Liam informed Charlotte, ignoring Chloe and pretending like she hadn't spoken.

Charlotte tapped a finger down on Liam's pencil case. "So you like superheroes?" she enquired, noting the dramatically-posed figures of Spider-Man and Iron Man (amongst several other characters she wasn't quite sure the names of) featured prominently there on the case.

"I suppose," Liam said, raising his left eyebrow a smidge.

"So does my son Stanley," Charlotte was happy to report. "And do you know what?"

Liam shook his head in the negative.

"Well, when he was about your age," Charlotte said, "he used to think crafting was girly as well. Until—"

"Until?" Liam asked, unfolding his arms, leaning forward just a touch.

Charlotte retrieved her phone from her pocket, pressing buttons until her camera roll appeared on the screen. "You see these?" she asked, once she'd located what she'd been looking for, holding the phone out to him.

Liam moved his head a bit closer in order to get a better look at the image displayed onscreen, that image being a head-and-shoulders portrait of an impressively crocheted Iron Man — the very same Iron Man as was illustrated on his pencil case. Charlotte then swiped her finger to reveal an equally impressive crocheted Spider-Man figure, and continued swiping to show off a small assortment of other superhero characters, the names of which she wasn't quite familiar with.

"Cool," Liam offered, right eyebrow now joining the left in its raised position. "You made them?"

"Nope," Charlotte replied cheerfully, popping her phone back inside her pocket now that her student's interest had been sufficiently piqued. "My son Stanley made them. And you know what else?"

"What?"

"Occasionally, he crochets two of the same character and then sells the spare one. As a result, he's made himself close to thirty-five pounds profit last month, and he started by learning what I'm teaching you all today."

"Thirty-five pounds?" Liam asked, incredulous. "With thirty-five pounds, I'd be, like... loaded," Liam marvelled, turning the figure over in his mind and likely charting what he'd do with such potential riches. Then, finally, he reached over to pick up his darning needle. "Your son started with this?"

Charlotte smiled brightly. "Uh-huh. And you can too."

"Cooool," Liam replied, drawing out the 'ooo' and sounding like a ghost impersonator.

Charlotte repeated her earlier instructions to the class for Liam's benefit, suspecting the young fella might not have been giving her his complete attention at the first time of asking. And, with a newly found interest in crafting and his needle threaded, he was soon on his way, hopefully realising that the hobby wasn't as 'girly' as he'd initially believed.

Returning to full height, Charlotte ran her eyes around the class, encouraged that not a word was being uttered, with each of the children engrossed in their work. Indeed, many of them had their tongues hanging out the corner of their mouths, like little puppy dogs — often a sign of intense concentration, Charlotte found from experience.

One pupil, on the other hand, didn't appear to be having too much success judging by his puce-coloured cheeks and fierce expression. But it wasn't Liam this time. Rather, Charlotte observed Lee tentatively pulling his needle through the fabric with a length of red wool following behind. Unfortunately, the knot he'd tied wasn't robust enough, allowing the thread to pass straight through, rendering his efforts fruitless. With his latest attempt proving unsuccessful his frustration was giving way to emotion, and it looked like tears might soon be welling up in his eyes.

Suspecting Chloe's earlier Velcro-based comments to be not entirely without cause, Charlotte very casually made her way over to Lee's desk, not wishing to draw undue attention to his plight. Positioning herself to obscure her actions from the others — and Chloe in particular — Charlotte offered Lee a helping hand, administering a brief-but-discreet refresh on how to tie a knot so he could properly set to work. In doing so, she'd hopefully avert any tears, therefore protecting him from further potential teasing.

"Just jiggle your ruler if you need any additional assistance," Charlotte whispered, so as not to be heard by any neighbouring ears, "and I'll be over, quick as a flash."

With his knot now holding fast, Lee was all set and ready for action. "Thank you," he whispered back, glancing up for a moment before returning to the job at hand, hoping to make up for lost time.

Charlotte continued on with her rounds, weaving her way through the rows of desks, casting an appreciative eye over the progress being made. Some were still working on their first few stitches, while others were racing along, completing two or three letters. But it was evident that they were all getting stuck into their sewing with no complaints offered, which was an immense relief for Charlotte. Eventually, after some time and with all going well, Charlotte returned to the front of the classroom, joining up with Mrs Renshaw once again.

"Wow," Mrs Renshaw said softly, leaning out from behind her desk. "You're a natural, Charlotte," she offered, appreciating the hushed silence and how engrossed everyone appeared.

"Truth be told, I was a little nervous on my way in this morning," Charlotte replied modestly, speaking softly as well so as not to disturb the present quietude.

"Well, you should know that while we're fortunate enough to host several guests each term, this is the first time I've witnessed such an enthusiastic response," Mrs Renshaw assured Charlotte, nodding in the direction of her students. "Ah. I only wish you were here a bit longer with us," she added, glancing at the clock and noticing the time. "Will you be coming back for another visit?"

"Oh, yes," Charlotte answered immediately, not having to think twice about it. "If you'll have me, that is."

"Absolutely," Mrs Renshaw responded, pushing her chair back and rising to her feet. "Shall we see what everyone else thinks about that idea?" she asked, turning her attention to the class. "Okay, class. If you'd like to put your needles down," she advised. "You as well, Liam," she added a moment later, as Liam appeared determined to press on. "Did we all enjoy our embroidery lesson today?" she asked.

"YES, MRS RENSHAW," came the spirited response.

"And would we like Miss Newman to come back and see us again?"

"YES, MRS RENSHAW!" the class shouted back in their loudest ear-splitting pitch, each child sounding intent on trumping the person sitting next to them.

"I think the general consensus is that we'd like you to come back," Mrs Renshaw said with a laugh, while playfully rubbing her ears.

"I'd love to come back and see you all again," Charlotte said, looking over her shoulder and then back again, as if she had a secret to share with them all. "And guess what?" she asked rhetorically, receiving wide eyes in response. "You're all faster learners than most of my adult class," she told them with a wink. "But if you meet any of them, you didn't hear that from me," she added, placing a finger over her lips.

A moment later, the chiming of the school bell sent the children happily scampering towards the door, desperate to maximise every moment of their precious morning break now that their first class had officially ended.

"No running!" Mrs Renshaw shouted as the class spilt out into the corridor, a similar scene likely occurring throughout the school. "Charlotte, before you go, would you like to join us for a cuppa in the teacher's lounge?" she asked, once she could hear herself think.

Charlotte hastily packed away the surplus materials, admiring the results of the children's industrious efforts lying atop each of their desks. "Thanks, that's very kind, but I've got an appointment with your headmistress, as it should happen," she answered. "She's agreed to let me pick her brain on the issue of school uniform, as a matter of fact."

"Maybe next time, then," Mrs Renshaw said. "Would you like me to show you to her office?" she offered.

"Would you?" Charlotte asked, scooping up her bags, which were now a bit lighter than when she'd arrived.

There was something decidedly unnerving about waiting outside the headmistress's office, even at the ripe old age of thirty-three. Sitting there, squeezed into a child-sized plastic chair, Charlotte felt an irrational wave of guilt wash over her. Indeed, the last time she could recall being in such a situation was when she was eight years old and had just been caught red-handed, smuggling her new gerbil into school. Virgil, as she'd named him, had been enjoying a grand day out, happy as you like nibbling on a carrot in her school bag. But the lure of freedom had proved too much, however, resulting in Virgil making a daring bid for freedom, and with Charlotte's teacher mistaking him for a rat and spraining her ankle as she attempted to scramble onto the safety of her desk. The fact that Virgil had appeared lonely at home was not, apparently, considered an acceptable or valid reason for his morning outing, and Charlotte had subsequently been dispatched to the headmaster's office to explain herself.

Fortunately, this had been Charlotte's one and only brush with the school authorities, but the memories were painful, rather like her teacher's ankle that day, no doubt. Interrupting this trip down memory lane just now, Charlotte heard footsteps approaching the door and immediately straightened her back in response.

"Charlotte?" asked the person peering through the opened door.

"Yes, hello," Charlotte said, grateful to be done with her uncomfortable chair. "It's nice to meet you, Mrs Pinkerton," she said, extending a hand as she rose up. She was surprised to find the headmistress was young, perhaps only a couple of years older than she was. She was a lovely woman, wearing a bright, floral-print dress.

"Please, call me Gabby," said Gabby, leading Charlotte into her office.

"This isn't how I remember my headmaster's office," Charlotte remarked, noticing, as she entered, the rather modern-looking glossy white lacquer desk. It reminded Charlotte of a large Tic Tac.

"Oh?" Gabby answered, parking herself down on her lime-green swivel chair.

"I suppose I expected dark wood, harsh lighting, and bookshelves crammed with ancient texts," Charlotte replied, taking a seat.

"Did you go to school with David Copperfield?" Gabby asked with a wry smile. "I could pull my hair back into a tight bun and don my black, full-length dress with a white high-collar blouse underneath if you like?" she asked, continuing with her gentle ribbing.

"I'm sorry," Charlotte conceded, holding her hands up in surrender. "Both you and your office are considerably more stylish and contemporary than what I recall from my more Dickensian schooldays."

"Ah, well, we haven't completely lost the old ways," Gabby replied, conspiratorially. She then reached behind her, producing a sturdy, long-handled wooden object for Charlotte's review, though Charlotte was too busy admiring her surroundings at the moment to immediately notice. "I call this *The Enforcer*," Gabby revealed, with a sinister narrowing of her eyes.

"What's that?" Charlotte asked, only able to see the upper portion of The Enforcer, the remainder of which was still concealed behind the desk.

"We're not supposed to cane the children anymore," Gabby whispered, as if those walking through the corridor might hear their conversation through the closed door. "But I find a well-timed whack with this, or threat thereof, does wonders for maintaining discipline," she said, striking her wooden staff down onto the floor with an imperious thump, like an imposing Gandalf the Grey.

"*What?*" a horrified Charlotte asked. "You're pulling my leg...?" she added with a nervous laugh, hoping that her leg was indeed being pulled.

Gabby held her serious expression for a moment longer, before finally raising the long wooden object for Charlotte's inspection. "Yeah. Just a hockey stick," Gabby said with a mischievous giggle, holding it out so Charlotte could now clearly see it. "I'm helping out with the PE class," Gabby explained, spinning around and placing the stick back from where she'd taken it. "So. Tell me," she went on, continuing her circular motion until she'd rotated a full 360 degrees. "How did the crafting group go this morning? Were the class kind to you?"

"Very much so," Charlotte was pleased to relate. "It's fair to say we had a few late adopters, but once they'd got into the swing of things, they did appear to quite enjoy themselves."

"Well, we're of course very grateful for you spending your time here with us today," Gabby offered. "Right. Now, as to your email..." she said, opening the black leather folder resting on her desktop and fetching a sheet of paper from inside of it. She tapped her finger down, eyes fixed on the printed page.

"I hope you didn't mind me emailing you unannounced?" Charlotte asked. "It's just that I knew I was coming along today, so I thought I'd kill two birds and all that."

Gabby shook her head firmly in the negative. "Oh, no. Not at all, Charlotte," she replied, raising her head. "In fact, the subject of school uniform cost that you outlined is such an emotive one, and one that's often raised by the parents. Of course, as a school, we do what we can to help out. Last year, for instance, we allocated an area of the school library where parents could donate surplus uniforms for other parents to use."

Charlotte's eyes widened in response. "That's amazing," she said brightly.

However, Gabby's downcast expression suggested their new initiative wasn't proving to be the roaring success they'd hoped. "Yeah, it's a work in progress and one we're collectively eager to encourage," Gabby explained. "But the challenge we've encountered is that the parents who'd benefit most from the assistance are often unwilling to come forward."

"Oh, no. Do you know why, exactly?" Charlotte asked. "Are they embarrassed, maybe?"

"I think that's most likely the case, yes. Parents perhaps don't want to be seen by other parents rummaging through a second-hand clothes rail," Gabby answered. "I do genuinely like the ideas you've laid out here about recycling, though," she added, patting Charlotte's printed-out email with the flat of her hand.

Charlotte was heartened by the encouraging response she was hearing from across the Tic Tac desk. Often, bursting with good intentions, Charlotte was guilty of jumping into things feet-first, without factoring in the practicalities or potential pitfalls. Unfortunately, this character trait — endearing as it may have been to some — had, over the years, resulted in some of her endeavours falling at the first hurdle, with her not having considered some of the finer details...

Such as the time, back when Stanley was still in a pram, that Charlotte had identified an opportunity to bolster her paltry bank balance by setting herself up as an importer of luxury fabric from China. Luxurious, yet inexpensive, that is. And with her keen eye for quality and reasonable prices, word amongst the crafting community soon spread, and it wasn't long before she even found herself supplying a local fabric shop who were simply unable to source the products as competitively as Charlotte seemingly could. Unfortunately, however, her entrepreneurial foray came to an abrupt end once her credit card statement landed on her hallway mat. Horrified, she quickly realised she'd not factored international shipping costs into the equation. Additionally, her currency conversion calculations had been somewhat less than accurate as well, she discovered. And to compound the situation even *further*, thanks to her limited grasp of the Chinese language she'd also made a rather large mistake regarding measurement. Specifically, feet vs metres. As a result, Lotti's Fabulous Fabric, as she had named her importing enterprise, had been selling merchandise for half of what she should have been charging. Essentially, Charlotte was selling ten-pound notes for a fiver. No small wonder, then, that her fledgling import business had been so terribly popular... right up until the point she was forced to cease operations.

Still, at least she'd learned from the mistake and often drew on that costly experience caused by what she preferred to describe as a simple, unfortunate "administrative error." And it was for this reason that Charlotte was more careful and more meticulous in her present dealings, going so far as to outline her thoughts in a document akin to a formal business plan ahead of her meeting with Mrs Pinkerton today. And her efforts appeared to be paying dividends if the positive reaction was anything to go by.

"We recycle plastic, we recycle glass bottles, we recycle all sorts of things. Not to mention, just how popular is upcycling old furniture these days?" Charlotte told Gabby. "But, frustratingly, there's still a stigma associated with reusing perfectly acceptable clothes, school uniforms in particular."

"Absolutely. And if we can overcome that, and change people's opinions..." Gabby entered in, nodding in happy approval like a dashboard-mounted bobblehead.

"Exactly!" Charlotte said, fidgeting in her seat due to the creative juices coursing through her. "So, you don't think I'm wasting my time, Gabby? You know, trying to solve a problem that doesn't exist? Because I do that sometimes, more often than you'd imagine."

Gabby took a quick glance at her watch, and then did that disappointed, pained expression you make when you suddenly realise you're meant to be somewhere else. "Charlotte, you're not wasting your time. And I love what you're doing," she said, collecting her leather folder and jumping up from her seat. "I'm at your disposal, and I'd relish the opportunity to work with you on this. And I also meet regularly with the education minister, and the other headteachers, so if you need any introductions..." she added, gathering herself together.

Charlotte stood as well and walked towards the door, a warm sense of anticipation filling her veins. "Are you off to your PE class now?" Charlotte enquired over her shoulder, by way of small talk.

"What? Oh, no," Gabby replied. "As a matter of fact, I've just remembered that I've completely forgotten about last night's detention students," she told Charlotte, letting out an exasperated sigh. "They're still chained to the radiator and must be starving by now," she said, completely deadpan.

"You're pulling my leg again, surely...?" Charlotte offered, perceptive individual that she was.

"Of course. Of course, yes," Gabby confirmed. "Actually, it was rope, rather than chains, now I think on it," she said with a grin.

"I believe I'm going to enjoy working with you, Gabby..."

CHAPTER FIVE

A sharply-dressed woman marched up the street, heels clicking on the pavement, takeaway coffee cup pressed to her rouge-coloured lips. Aside from looking fabulous, the sound produced by her Jimmy Choo shoes also served to alert those in front of her presence, like a train's horn clearing livestock from the tracks up ahead. She offered a curt nod to a pair of suited men who'd obligingly parted ways, allowing her to continue her journey without breaking her stride (and with them stealing a glimpse of her strong, well-toned legs as she passed).

Looking on, sheltering in the doorway of a nearby nail salon, Charlotte couldn't help but be impressed by the stranger's confident swagger. Indeed, the woman reminded Charlotte of the previous weekend, in which she'd enjoyed watching *The Devil Wears Prada* with her fellow movie critic, Mollie, as part of their monthly film club. Of course, Stanley had been cordially invited to watch the film as well (as he always was), but when Mum outlined the synopsis and no aliens, caped crusaders, or cowboys and such were involved, his interest had soon waned.

Charlotte's mind wandered for a moment, imagining what exciting hustle and bustle awaited the lady when she eventually reached her office. But of course Charlotte had never worked in a corporate environment for any length of time, so her experience on such matters was limited mainly to watching certain various American films. And from what she'd seen recently, it all looked a bit too cutthroat for her liking, and she felt confident her elbows weren't nearly sharp enough for a high-flying business career. Also, the prospect of having a boss even remotely like Meryl Streep's formidable character was enough to strike fear into the heart of anybody hoping to climb the corporate ladder.

Fortunately, as it should happen, Charlotte had absolutely no desire to seek out a new career. After all, why would she? She was getting paid to teach crafting, and as far as she was concerned, it was the most incredible job on the planet. And it was because of that incredible job, as a matter of fact, that she presently found herself somewhat chilled in a shop doorway at quarter to nine in the morning.

"Come on," Charlotte said, eyes fixed on the shop opposite, the interior of which, unfortunately, remained blanketed in darkness. She puffed out her cheeks, releasing a steady stream of air, rubbing her hands together in both anticipation and impatience. "Come *on*," she repeated, shifting her weight between each of her feet, swaying gently from side to side. She was like a gambler, desperately waiting for the bookies to open so she could scratch that particular, overriding itch. But rather than a copy of the daily *Racing Post* stuffed under her arm, Charlotte had a book called *101 Crafting Ideas for Beginners* placed there.

Charlotte stirred, edging forward, uncertain if she'd seen a figure through the front window on which her attention was currently fixed. She squinted her eyes, hoping to improve her view, and then...

"Yes!" she declared, pitching herself forward, emerging from the recessed doorway with a spring in her step. Soon across the street, Charlotte squidged her nose up against the shopfront window, feasting her eyes upon the now-illuminated interior.

Debbie, the shop's proprietor, at first remained blissfully unaware of Charlotte's presence, happily preparing her fine establishment for another day's roaring trade. "Good gravy!" she exclaimed, clutching her chest when she suddenly caught sight of Charlotte's snout pressed up against the glass.

Charlotte, in answer, smiled brightly, offering up a friendly wave, and then mouthing the words "Good morning" through the window. "Please let me in," she added, hoping the proprietor was able to read lips. Stepping back, she placed her palms together as if she were offering up a little prayer, which, in essence, she was.

With the door unlocked and cracked open, Debbie raised her eyebrows. Charlotte, a steady customer, was of course not unknown to her. "You're starting early today," Debbie said with a wry smile, offering Charlotte a warm welcome like a pub landlady to her first thirsty punter of the day.

"Lemme in, woman!" Charlotte said, playfully pushing past Debbie to salivate over the goods inside her crafting supplies shop, Bon Fabrics, where Charlotte took in several deep lungfuls of the glorious scent of creation.

Bon Fabrics, located in the main shopping area of Douglas, was just one of the many splendid craft shops that Charlotte found herself frequenting on the regular. Yes, the need to restock her crafting supplies cupboard on a recurring basis was a fortunate side effect of Charlotte's expanding client base, and a duty she was more than happy to perform. So much so, in fact, that Debbie had even joked about having a spare shop key cut for Charlotte and perhaps furnishing her with the code to the alarm system.

With all this shopping to perform on a regular basis, it was a great relief that Charlotte now found herself with a healthy chunk of change in her crafting coffers, thanks in part to the generosity of her one-time nemesis, Amelia. Having secured victory in the Square If You Care initiative by foul play, and feeling decidedly guilty about it, Amelia had very graciously suggested that Charlotte would be best placed to utilise and distribute the winner's cash prize, totalling a little over six thousand pounds. On top of all this, the charity committee at Calum's company, Microcoding, had signed off on Charlotte's bursary, meaning Charlotte was now in paid employment with a guaranteed salary for at least the next three years. As a result of this, it's fair to say Charlotte's financial situation was much less dire than it had been in the past, and she could often be found these days wearing a toothy grin wider than that of a Cheshire cat.

Charlotte placed her well-thumbed copy of *101 Crafting Ideas for Beginners* down onto the shop's countertop, followed by her elbows.

"Right. Kettle's on," Debbie announced, appearing from the shop rear after popping back there for just a moment. "So, not that it isn't a distinct pleasure to see you, Lotti, as always. But I don't often find you lurking just outside, in the street, waiting for me to open up...?"

"Ah! Well!" Charlotte replied, flipping her book to the page marked with a yellow post-it note, and then tapping her finger down rhythmically. "I'm delighted to report I've now got thirteen nursing homes signed up to the Make It Sew crafting community..."

Debbie joined Charlotte, planting her elbows down on the counter. The two of them, side by side, looked like they could have been both waiting to place an order at the local chip shop. "Charlotte, that's amazing!" she said.

"Isn't it?" Charlotte replied dreamily, releasing a contented sigh. "But it's not without its logistical challenges," she added.

"Oh?"

"Yes. At the moment, everyone in each class is working on their own individual projects," Charlotte explained. "I could have some members knitting, for instance, some cross-stitching, some crocheting, some quilting, and so on. Which is fine. However, one person might want to make a bear, someone else might fancy crocheting a hat, and the list goes on. And now, with even more nursing homes joining the family, I'm in danger of having several hundred unique projects on the go at one time, leaving my head spinning round, in a bit of a tizz."

"I can imagine."

"And then it hit me."

"It did?" Debbie asked. "What, exactly?"

"Yes, at two o'clock this morning..." Charlotte said, offering an exaggerated yawn as well as placing her hand up to her mouth, in true sleepy fashion.

"Yes...?" said Debbie.

"I sat bolt upright in bed!" Charlotte happily declared, this sudden, animated change in tack startling poor Debbie in the process.

Charlotte pushed her hand through the air, like a bird in flight, in order to illustrate either sitting up straight in bed or an idea taking form, Debbie wasn't sure which.

"And that's when it hit me," Charlotte went on, continuing with her explanation. "Rather than each of the clubs working on dozens of different projects at once, I was thinking of introducing a simplified menu of options," she said, sliding her book along so it was under Debbie's nose and ready for inspection. "I'm going to suggest a general crafting theme depending on the time of year. And the page you're looking at now is the first one. And all of the designs are perfect for beginners."

"Ooh," Debbie said, lowering her head closer to the page in question. "I *love* crafting *anything* Christmas-related, Lotti. And by getting your members started early, in September, they'll be experts by the time Saint Nicholas arrives. I feel all Christmassy just looking at this."

"Exactly! And with all the groups working on similar projects, my crafting inventory will become considerably simplified," Charlotte said. "And while I won't need to buy so many different supplies, I'll need *quite* a lot more of certain specific types of supplies, if they're all to be working on the same projects..."

Charlotte batted her eyes, looking directly at Debbie across the counter, optimistic of garnering a reaction.

"*So*, by buying in bulk," Charlotte went on, "I'm hopeful of securing a larger discount, perhaps, from my lovely and generous suppliers..."

But Debbie didn't appear to be listening at the moment, still feasting her eyes on the wonderful array of Christmas-themed crafting delights in front of her.

"Ehm, as I was saying..." Charlotte pressed on, clearing her throat.

"Don't worry, I heard you," Debbie said through the corner of her mouth, not looking up, her attention still on the book, but proving she was listening. "And, yes, absolutely. You're my best customer, Lotti. Let's see your shopping list, and we'll see what we can come up with."

Charlotte danced a little happy dance, clapping her finger-tips together in delight. "Aww, yay. Debbie, you're the best!" she said.

"There's just one condition."

"Oh?"

"The kettle's surely boiled by now, Lotti, but I'm too busy deciding which Christmas stocking I'm going to make. And that tea's not going to make itself, if you take my meaning?"

"On it!" Charlotte answered, offering up a friendly salute, and then caressing a set of displayed fabrics on her way to the kitchen like a child stroking an alpaca at the petting zoo.

With the boot of her car stuffed to the gills with fabric and other supplies, Charlotte had set off, merrily heading up the mountain road. Her first appointment was with the Harbour View nursing home, located in the seaside town of Ramsey. She adored the scenery this particular route north provided, with rolling windswept hillside all around and countryside views that never failed to impress. There was a sense of rugged wilderness in this elevated area of the island, although, in truth, you were only ever a few minutes away from civilisation.

Further up the road, the island's only mountain, Snaefell, could be seen ahead, cloaked by a cosy blanket of misty hill fog. It was a challenging climb to the summit on foot, as she, Mollie, and Stanley had experienced during one recent and enjoyable

Sunday morning excursion. However, the reward for one's effort was always worth it. On a clear day, the views afforded to plucky adventurers were always a treat, offering a sweeping vista over the magical little isle in the middle of the Irish Sea. Of course, one could always travel in comfort to the summit if one wished, courtesy of the famous Manx Electric Railway, which Stanley had rightly pointed out at the time. This idea had fallen on deaf ears, however, at least until they'd traipsed several hundred feet higher. It was then that Charlotte, thighs aching — and having just trampled through a particularly large collection of ewe berries (i.e., sheep droppings) — had started to understand the wisdom of her son's suggestion. Still, any aches, pains, or soiled shoes were soon forgotten about once they'd reached the top, courtesy of the sizable mug of hot chocolate they all enjoyed at the lovely Snaefell Summit Restaurant & Café. Perfect refreshment, especially as far as Stanley was concerned, in preparation for the return leg of their journey.

Once Snaefell was in her rear-view mirror, the town of Ramsey slowly emerging into view as she descended further towards sea level, Charlotte's mind wandered to her Christmas-themed crafting menu, a smile appearing at the prospect. She broke into an impromptu chorus of "Jingle Bells," supported by a rhythmic hand-slapping of the steering wheel, thoughts occupied with sparkly tinsel and fairy lights. Of course, Christmas was still a good few weeks away, but she'd already taken a mental note to retrieve her handcrafted festive apparel from the loft for its annual outing, once the time should arrive. *Is Stanley too old for his elf costume?* she pondered for a moment, hoping for at least one more year before he declared himself too mature for such nonsense.

Just then, Charlotte was jarred from her jolly, Crimbo-based reverie by the sound of her phone ringing, connected through to her car speakers courtesy of Bluetooth wizardry she didn't completely understand.

"Charlotte Newman, Crafting Queen, at your service!" she announced cheerily, after having pressed the 'connect' button on her steering wheel. "Hello...?" she added a moment later, when the only sound she heard was muffled voices, like the sort of thing you'd hear when somebody sits down on the phone in their pocket, calling you by accident. *"Is there anybody there?"* Charlotte asked, sounding very much like a two-bit psychic on Blackpool seafront, though not on purpose.

"Oh, it's useless," a frustrated voice could be heard on the other end, increasing in volume, briefly, but then falling away like the caller was moving the phone away from their mouth again. "I thought you were supposed to be able to see them...?" the voice was now saying, suddenly coming into focus once again. The caller sounded female, and elderly.

"Beryl? Beryl, is that you, my love...?" Charlotte asked, recognising the familiar, if intermittent, voice. Charlotte pressed down on the indicator, moving her car to the side of the road. Once safely parked up, she reached for the handset cradled in the cavity below her car radio. "Beryl, it *is* you," she said more confidently, now that she was able to see the caller's identity on the phone's display.

"You're holding the phone the wrong way round, you daft old brush," an equally frustrated-sounding voice could now be heard saying, much to Charlotte's amusement. Charlotte placed a hand to her mouth, stifling a giggle listening to the unfolding conversation on the other side of the call. She knew Beryl was involved, and a logical assumption on Charlotte's part was that the other feminine voice she was hearing belonged to Joyce, what with the two of them being glued at the hip. "Here, Beryl," Joyce insisted. "Chuck it 'ere, and I'll have a look."

"Pfft," Beryl shot back. "Technical advice? From you?" she scoffed. "The same woman who thought my dishwasher was a fridge?"

"One time that happened," came the reply. "And as I told you at the time, Beryl, I didn't have my glasses on!"

"It was only when the milk started to turn that my nose uncovered the mystery of its missing location," Beryl pointed out.

Charlotte cleared her throat, sensing this little exchange could well go on for several more minutes, several additional minutes Charlotte really didn't have to spare. *"Ahem,"* she said. "Not that it isn't a distinct pleasure to hear your voices, ladies, but this is a phone call, not a video call. That's why you can't see me."

"Oh, I heard a voice!" Beryl excitedly announced, followed by what sounded like the handset being wrestled over, and only muffled cries after that.

"Guys?" Charlotte said, waiting for the two ladies on the other end to get themselves together. "Guys...?"

Charlotte decided the quickest resolution to the current situation would be to end the call and then immediately call them back, only this time using WhatsApp video call as Beryl and Joyce had likely intended. Doing just that, Charlotte then leaned back in her seat, supporting her phone at arm's length atop the steering wheel. Mission accomplished, the camera connected and there on Charlotte's screen appeared the familiar faces of Joyce and Beryl, along with Larry as well. The three of them were huddled close together as if stuffed inside a phone box, all peering into the camera.

"I told you I could sort it out, Beryl!" Joyce triumphantly declared.

Charlotte grinned in return, feeling like she'd just woken from surgery to find a collection of relieved faces looking her over in her hospital bed. "Morning, guys," Charlotte said, waving her free hand.

"GOOD MORNING, LOTTI!" the three of them replied in unison, reminding Charlotte of the schoolchildren singing her name in class.

"We're just up in Onchan," Larry explained on behalf of the group. "We've had a delightful coffee, and—"

"Don't forget about the cake," Beryl chipped in, turning to face Larry.

"Oh, yes. And cake," Larry agreed, happy to amend and correct the record.

"Ah, that's nice," Charlotte said, offering a hearty thumbs-up to indicate her approval. "So, did Mabel pick you all up, then…?" she asked.

"I did, and they were a bloody nightmare, bickering the entire way in the back seat like an old married couple, as I knew they probably would," Mabel entered in, followed by an audible tut-tut. "Which is why I insisted Larry ride shotgun, so that I could at least have some peace up in the front."

"Mabel, where are…?" Charlotte began, moving her nose closer to her phone. She'd heard Mabel speaking, sure enough, but there was no obvious sign of her. "In fact, never mind," Charlotte quickly corrected herself, because there at the very bottom of the screen, unnoticed initially, was a stray tuft of hair that Charlotte could only assume was emanating from the top of Mabel's head. "Sorry, Mabel, I didn't see you," Charlotte said gently. "Erm, I still can't, actually."

Mabel was a friend of the others, who still had a car and could drive. More relevant here was that Mabel stood just a bit under four-foot-ten in her stocking feet, which would explain her current submerged, just-out-of-view position on Charlotte's phone screen.

Charlotte glanced at her dashboard clock, knowing she didn't have an awful lot of time to spare right at the moment. "Anyway, it's lovely to hear from you all," she told them. "But can I get an update on the cake later? Only I'm running a little late, and—"

"Ah, roger that," Larry said. "But the reason we're calling is that we've just been into Joan's Wools and Crafts to pick up the package you asked us to collect," he reported.

"Ahh, thanks, Larry," Charlotte replied, smiling at the mere mention of the crafting emporium that brought her so much joy. "I'd have gone myself, but I'm tied up all day," she said. "How about I swing by the nursing home later this evening? You can then tell me all about the cake, as well?"

Larry indulged in a slow, two-fingered caress of his chin, offering up a gentle shake of his head. "Yeah, but here's the thing, Lotti. I'm not sure we're going to get it in the back of the car..."

"I've got only a wee Fiat Cinquecento," a non-visible Mabel explained, from down below, just offscreen. "I'm lucky if I can fit my weekly shop in the boot."

Charlotte narrowed one eye, wondering if the group had perhaps indulged in a tipple or two, as they weren't making too much sense. "Larry, can you not just pop it on your knee?" she asked, eyes flicking to the clock and back. "It's only a few pieces of school uniform."

Larry tilted the camera so that all four were now in the shot, heads floating like the iconic Queen album cover. "Lotti...?" a confused Larry said. "Lotti, there's more than one bag to collect here. In fact, you're probably going to need a van."

"You could open your own clothes shop with that lot, dear," Joyce remarked, looking to the collection of heads around her for confirmation and with that verification being duly dispensed.

Charlotte listened on as each of the group took it in turn to outline how Mabel's small Fiat Cinquecento was woefully ill-equipped to transport the intended package. That package being a surprisingly large collection of virtually-new grey school trousers, gingham dresses, and white collared shirts.

Wishing to kickstart her school recycling initiative, Charlotte had posted a note on Facebook the previous week, hoping to garner feedback on the idea. To her delight it was well-received, with one mum offering to donate a bag full of new primary school uniforms that her son no longer required since moving to secondary school. However, with the initiative very much in its infancy, Charlotte hadn't arranged for formal drop-off points just yet. So, thinking on the spot, Charlotte, as she had with the Square If You Care initiative, suggested Joan's Wools & Crafts as a convenient location. Laura and the team had, after all, so generously supported that previous campaign.

Unfortunately, if what Larry & company were presently relaying was indeed accurate, then it appeared the tentacles of Charlotte's social media presence had a considerably longer reach than she'd imagined. Apparently, several other benevolent souls had read the post and visited Joan's with bags stuffed with surplus uniforms over the weekend as well. Compounding the situation further, Larry now informed Charlotte, two primary schools had just been in, dropping off their entire inventory, eager and willing to support such a splendid initiative.

"You couldn't see the floor for school uniform," Larry advised gravely. "Laura was in the shop on her own, red-faced and frantic, struggling to shift everything into the rear stockroom. We did what we could to help clear the backlog, but it kept right on coming."

Charlotte chewed on the back of her hand, offering a pained sigh. "Was Laura awfully annoyed with me...?" she asked eventually, sinking back into her seat.

"She didn't say as much, no..." Joyce replied, much to Charlotte's temporary relief.

"... But it was likely only because she was out of breath and couldn't really speak," Joyce added, finishing her thought.

"Probably too knackered from shifting all those bags," Beryl contributed helpfully.

"Darn it all!" an exasperated Charlotte moaned, bashing the back of her skull repeatedly against the headrest like her head was on a spring. "Well... okay, thanks," she said after a bit, returning her attention to the Queen tribute band before she developed a headache. "I think I'd better hang up now," she told them, blowing them all a kiss. "Speak soon."

Charlotte took a few deep breaths. She was already several minutes late for her first appointment, but felt there was no alternative but to delay her arrival a bit further. She didn't even need to look up Joan's phone number, consigned to memory as it was.

"Aww, hell," Charlotte said as the phone rang. And rang. And rang. No doubt due to Laura being occupied, at present, with other matters requiring her urgent attention.

"*Joan's,*" a stressed voice replied down the phone, once it was answered eventually. "How can I... assist?" the weary-sounding woman replied.

Charlotte grimaced, unsure as to what to say or how to respond. For a moment, she even considered hanging up in order to give herself more time to try and formulate something, anything, constructive to say. And then...

"Good morning, Laura!" Charlotte offered, as brightly as she possibly could. "It's, em... only me. Lotti. Charlotte, that is. Charlotte Newman? How are things with you...? All good, I hope?"

"Laura...? "Ehm... hello? Laura...?"

CHAPTER SIX

C harlotte drained the contents of her charming, sewing-machine-shaped teapot into two cups, one for herself and one for her ex-husband, giving the teapot a gentle jiggle to aid in the process. A present from Stanley the previous Christmas, Charlotte adored this most recent addition to her already extensive collection. Indeed, there had been occasions where she'd overfilled a teacup or two because she'd been paying too much time admiring the workmanship and design of her treasure, while paying too little attention to the flow of liquid from the device as she should have been. *"It's not only a detailed model of a sewing machine but also a teapot, so it works wonderfully on multiple levels,"* she'd say, or similar words to that effect, regaling any visitors around her kitchen table or, for that matter, anyone else willing to listen.

Many people were an absolute nightmare to buy gifts for, but never Charlotte. With crafting being such a wide-ranging hobby, incorporating multiple strands, as it were, it was usually relatively easy (Stanley and others often found) to procure the ideal Christmas and birthday gifts for her. As such, chez Newman had a passing resemblance to a crafting giftshop.

Charlotte teased open the metal lid on her biscuit tin, in the kitchen at chez Newman, stealing a glance inside and wondering if Stanley's ravenous appetite hadn't already decimated its contents. But, pleasingly, the full packet of chocolate digestives remained entirely undisturbed, her son's favourite foil-wrapped biscuits left intact, along with several other selections.

"It looks like Stanley didn't realise I'd gone shopping yesterday and filled this," Charlotte remarked, offering the well-stocked tin to George for his consideration.

But George had turned away from her for a moment and was now busy at the kitchen counter.

"*Ahem*," Charlotte said, placing the biscuit tin back down, onto the kitchen table. "What, *exactly*, do you think you're doing?" she asked, with the same stern tone you'd use when witnessing someone stepping on your new carpet with a pair of muddy shoes.

"What?" George asked a moment later, feeling Charlotte's eyes burning into the back of his skull. "I'm still sweating," he replied matter-of-factly.

Charlotte shook her head, releasing a not-too-serious sigh, watching him mop up the sweat from his shaven head. "Yes, I can see that. But you're using one of my good tea towels," she explained, passing him over the kitchen roll, although the damage was already done. "A tea towel I'd have likely then used to dry the dishes, mind you, if I'd not just seen you with it wrapped around your baldy bonce."

"That," he said, removing the damp tea towel and holding it aloft, "is the result of hard labour, I'll have you know. Anyway, how is it you're not dripping in sweat as well?"

Charlotte took possession of the desecrated tea towel, throwing it straight into the washing machine drum, wondering if she should have left it to soak in soapy water first, along with perhaps some bleach. "Well, ladies don't sweat, they *perspire*," Charlotte informed George, in response to his question. "And even then, we don't like to do that. It's unseemly."

"And it couldn't have anything to do with me doing the lion's share of the work?" George suggested, offering up an alternative explanation.

Earlier that day, Charlotte had turned up to Joan's Wools & Crafts armed with a nice bottle of red and a potted plant as a peace offering. However, she needn't have worried, as Laura was in good spirits other than sore shoulders from rehousing the overstuffed bags crammed with uniform items, although Laura was grateful for Charlotte's gesture nonetheless.

With Laura appeased (and several unplanned purchases of wool later), the issue still remained as to what to do with all the donations. It was fortunate, then, that Charlotte had only recently repaired several threadbare-in-the-crotch pairs of jeans for Stanley's father, George. Naturally, Charlotte had no intention of charging him for her services, knowing he was just a phone call away if she ever needed any repairs attended to at home, what with him being particularly useful in that department. However, on this particular occasion, she opted to call in a favour for something else instead, requesting his services and use of his van to help clear out Laura's overflowing stockroom. And, as she discovered earlier in the day, Larry & co hadn't been exaggerating in their appraisal of the situation, as George's van had ended up packed to the gunnels. Indeed, there was considerably more than could ever be expected to fit into the boot of Mabel's poor little Fiat Cinquecento!

Unfortunately, Charlotte hadn't had any clear plan on what to do with the items once they'd picked them up. She had no available space in her own modest abode, and George needed his van emptied for work the following day. Luckily, and to her immense relief, her storage saviour had come in the form of Amelia Sugden, her one-time arch-nemesis.

It wasn't that they were bosom buddies now or anything like that, but their relationship could at least be described as thawing. Since they'd settled their differences following the hard-fought Square If You Care competition, Charlotte, to her surprise, found herself very nearly enjoying Amelia's company on the occasions she found herself in it. This was fortunate, as well, considering that Amelia was her boyfriend's sister, and, who knew, maybe even her sister-in-law one day? She could dream, of course (about marrying Calum, that is).

But what their improving relationship also meant was that, given this, when Amelia had learned about Charlotte's predicament earlier — through Calum, after Charlotte had apprised him of the situation — she was straight on the phone to suggest the use of the Laxey church hall, of which she served on the committee. It may not have had the largest storeroom, but there proved to be more than enough space after a reshuffle and general tidy around. After turning up to unlock the hall, Amelia even went so far as to offer the hall as an official uniform recycling drop-in centre once Charlotte's initiative was completely up and running. And rent-free, at that.

There was a time, not so very long ago, when a sceptical-minded Charlotte would have quite rightly questioned Amelia's motives, suspecting them to be for her own selfish gain or furtherment. But following Amelia's successful election campaign (as the political representative for Laxey), she'd delivered on most of the commitments outlined in her manifesto, impressing Charlotte and the good folk of Laxey in the process. Perhaps a leopard could change their spots? Charlotte both thought and hoped so.

"So. Calum...?" George asked cryptically, blowing the steam from his cuppa.

Charlotte placed a hand on her hip, head tilted. "I *told* you, George, he's away on a conference. Otherwise, he'd have been here helping in a shot," she replied, adopting something of a sharpish tone.

George raised an eyebrow in response. "Defensive much, Lotti? I was just wondering how it was all going with the two of you?"

"Oh," Charlotte said, her shoulders relaxing. "Sorry. I just thought... well, I just figured you were..."

"No, nothing like that, Lotti," George answered, rummaging through the biscuit tin. "I like the guy just fine."

"You do?"

"Sure. From what I've seen of him, he seems like a decent enough bloke."

Charlotte parked herself down, opposite George, arms folded on the table like she was about to conduct a job interview. She went to speak but stopped herself, chewing her lip, eyes looking off into the distance.

"Out with it..." George joked.

Charlotte smiled, returning her attention to George. "You know I'd never get involved with anybody who wasn't good for Stanley, don't you?" she said.

George set the biscuit tin down, giving Charlotte his full consideration. So often the joker, he resisted his initial impulse to offer a quip in response, as he could see this was important to her. "You and me both," he offered with a friendly wink. "And it's nice we can still do this," he said, raising his teacup with the words *Sew Thirsty* embossed on the side.

"Drink tea...?" Charlotte teased.

"Well, yes, that. But, more generally, being civil to each other, I mean. Which many in a similar situation aren't. You know, bickering at each other all the time, and such. It's good for us, and even better for Stan-the-man."

Charlotte raised her own teacup, embossed with the words *Knit Happens*, happy to raise a toast. "To not bickering!"

"To not bickering," George repeated, carefully clinking his delicate cup against Charlotte's. "So," he said a moment later, moving the conversation in a slightly different direction, "I was thinking about this school uniform recycling thingy."

Charlotte offered up a panicked expression. "I hope I've not bitten off more than I can chew," she said, reflecting for a moment.

With a KitKat now in hand, having delved back into the biscuit tin and making a quick selection, George waved away her concerns. "You'll be absolutely fine, I'm sure," he said. "Just look at how much you've already achieved this year, setting up I-don't-know-how-many crafting clubs. There's not many people that could do that, Lotti."

Charlotte ran her eyes over his bearded face. "You know, you're actually quite lovely when you want to be, George," she told him. "Well, when you're not defiling my best tea towels, that is."

George broke a row of his KitKat biscuit off, dunking the separated portion into his tea, while nodding in complete agreement. "You're not wrong, Lotti. Just don't tell everybody, as I've got this bearded, surly persona to uphold. Kinda like the Manx lumberjack."

George sucked off the now-melted chocolate, leaving only the exposed wafer on display, like a finger that'd had its skin stripped away. It amused Charlotte, as this was precisely the sort of thing Stanley did when enjoying a biscuit dunked in his own cuppa.

"So," George continued, brushing away a few misbehaving crumbs from the hairy prison that was his beard. "What are you going to call it?"

"Call it...?"

"Yeah, the uniform thingy."

"I'm not sure," Charlotte admitted, after a moment or two's reflection. "Uniform... recycling... something-or-other...?" she said. "I dunno. Why?" she asked, suspecting that her fellow tea slurper may in fact have been giving this very dilemma some prior consideration.

George placed his cup down onto the table, holding his hands out in front, ready to set his stall out. "You told me you wanted to make recycling cool, right? So there's less of a stigma about using perfectly good clothing again?"

"Yes, exactly!"

George's eyes were wide with expectation. He was like a marketing executive making a killer pitch to a new client. "You want to make *recycling cool?*" he asked rhetorically, not wanting or expecting a response. "So, how about..." he went on, moving a hand through the air, helping Charlotte to visualise his idea. "*ReCyCool,*" he revealed, lowering his hand, hoping to gauge the client's response. "It's instead of calling it *recycle*, you see, you call it ReCy—"

"Yes, I get it," Charlotte replied, indeed getting it. "You know, George, when you came up with the *Sewcial* part of the Crafternoon Sewcial Club, well, I thought you'd peaked with that, if

I'm honest," she told him. "But, George, this is brilliant. I *love* it," she said, leaning across the table to deliver a hearty high-five. "In fact, with talent like this, I think you're in the wrong job!"

"Well, my invoice will be in the post."

"Hmm, you can have another KitKat instead?"

"You have yourself a deal," George said, hand already in the biscuit tin.

Later that same day, Charlotte returned to the Laxey church hall just as the life-drawing group were finishing up their weekly class. It was a class Charlotte had been invited to previously by one very animated Beryl, who attended whenever she could manage, along with a small handful of other Crafternooners. The invite had taken Charlotte by surprise at the time, as she never really knew art to be a subject the girls had been especially keen on, despite recalling Beryl perhaps mentioning it once before in passing.

As Charlotte stepped into the classroom area to patiently wait for the class to clear up, she couldn't resist a smile. She also blushed, as she now suspected that an artistic flair wasn't the only thing attracting her Crafternoon ladies like moths to a flame to this particular activity. Presently, pencil, pens, and brushes weren't the only, ehm, *equipment*, so to speak, being packed away. A fairly fit, attractive young fellow, in fact, could be seen only just now covering himself up with a dressing gown, casually chatting away to the group without a care in the world, as if he hadn't just spent a rather extended period of time modelling before them completely starkers.

"Frisky old buggers," Charlotte remarked, chuckling away to herself and quite confident now that scratching an artistic itch wasn't the primary motivation for Beryl and the others attending whenever they were able.

"Was he... was he in the buff?" an incredulous Mollie asked, having just arrived and taken up a position standing next to Charlotte. She likely couldn't help but notice the chap's bare feet, along with the conspicuous lack of trousers on the portion of his legs currently visible. "He looks very, erm... well-proportioned...?" Mollie remarked. Even mostly covered as it now was, the fellow's pleasing figure was still evident.

"You don't know the half of it," Charlotte replied. "If you'd arrived only a few moments earlier, you'd have..."

"Hmm?" Mollie said, not really listening.

"Moll, you know you're staring?"

Mollie tugged on her collar, using her shirt like a pair of bellows to cool herself down. "If I'd known *he* was going to be here, I'd have done something with my hair," she said, still distracted. "And I'd have dusted off my sketch pad."

"You have a sketch pad?" Charlotte asked, but Mollie's attention remained elsewhere. "Hello? Earth to Moll?" Charlotte said, snapping her fingers like a second-rate hypnotist and bringing Mollie back to the room. "Come on, I'll show you what we're up against," she told her.

With Mollie's tongue returned to the confines of her gob, Charlotte escorted her willing volunteer to the rear of the hall, and then through to the storeroom.

Once inside, Mollie cradled her chin between her thumb and forefinger. "Hrm," she mused, as her eyes registered the scale of the job at hand. "And all of those bags are full of school uniforms?" she asked, looking to the pile, then back to Charlotte, and then back again towards the pile.

"Yup!" Charlotte answered.

"Stone the crows, Lotti, there are bloody loads."

"You should try *carrying* them all," Charlotte said wearily, even though, bless his soul, it was George who'd done nearly all of the work.

Mollie took a step closer, poking one of the bags with her index finger. "And you actually think the two of us are going to be able to sort through the entirety of this lot, and all of it this evening?" she asked.

Charlotte laughed at the suggestion. "No, silly. Of course I don't," she said, giving her best mate a playful smack on the arm.

"That's why Bonnie and a few of her friends have also offered to lend a hand as well. They should be here soon."

For Charlotte, there were many highlights throughout her crafting journey that she liked to reflect on, raising a nostalgic smile whenever she did so. Her first cross-stitch monogram, for instance, crafted sitting at her gran's knee. Knitting Stanley's first pair of bumblebee mittens was another thing. And her first sewing machine, a gift from her mother-in-law and the catalyst for turning a wonderful hobby into a rewarding career, was yet another. Then there were the people, amazing and unique characters she'd likely never have met if she'd not taken a chance on herself and dared to fulfil her dreams of becoming a crafting teacher. Also, there was the sense of community she had fostered and enjoyed. Through the crafting clubs, many had found companionship through a common interest. And, for some, it was the reason to leave the house they'd so been hoping for. Charlotte was proud of this.

And while it was nigh on impossible to single out one particular highlight or accomplishment amongst so many (a tremendous problem to have), Charlotte's friendship with Bonnie would always make her shortlist. Initially, Bonnie had only attended the Crafternoon Sewcial Club hoping to complete a cherished quilt (something her mother had started but was never able to finish before sadly passing, taken too soon). With the club's assistance, Bonnie was very pleased to be able to complete what her mother had started, while throwing her own youthful exuberance into the mix throughout the process. Even so, Charlotte had half-expected Bonnie's attendance to dwindle once she'd achieved what she'd hoped to achieve. But to Charlotte's immense delight, this hadn't been the case at all. Bonnie, as it turned out, hadn't missed even a single club meeting, and had since recruited several school friends as new members also. Bonnie was enjoying the sessions so much that she rarely purchased new clothes these days, handcrafting most of her current wardrobe — a talent her chums were now happy to develop as well.

With Bonnie and her friends in their late teens and Joyce and others in their early nineties, it served to prove that crafting, as a hobby, really did span the ages. The diverse age range made the oldies feel young again, and the young 'uns were treated to a master class, benefiting from the wisdom of those who'd been crafting for a lifetime. And when everyone got together, a splendid time was guaranteed for all, with tea consumed by the gallon and an infectious mix of laughter making the rounds, to boot.

Back at the church hall — with nary a naked man to be seen, regrettably — Charlotte, Mollie, and Bonnie, and along with Bonnie's two mates Sarah and Abigail, all stood with hands on hips, buoyed by a warm sense of accomplishment. Empty bags were strewn in the corner of the hall like wrapping paper on Christmas morning, the wooden floorboards very nearly consumed by donated items. It wasn't strictly school uniform items, though, as it turned out, with a variety of things like coats, bags, football boots, and plimsolls amongst the array of objects unpacked.

In a little under two hours, Charlotte and her merry band of helpers had emptied the storeroom, laying out the items into three separate sections that they'd categorised as:

1 – New/nearly new

2 – Somewhat worn, and

3 – Well past their useable shelf life.

Unfortunately, while sections two and three were chock-a-block, the first and most crucial section resembled a clothing shop the day *after* a closing-down sale. And it wasn't that Charlotte wasn't grateful, because absolutely she was. But it was a little disheartening, after all their collective efforts, that most of what they'd received they couldn't use, such as trousers with worn knees, pairs of shoes that didn't match, and school shirts greyer than George Clooney's hair.

Charlotte puffed out her cheeks, releasing a sorry burst of air like a deflating balloon. "On reflection, I think I perhaps should have been clearer as to what *precisely* we were hoping to gather," she said.

"It's not your fault, Lotti," Mollie was quick to point out. "I mean, without trying to sound unkind, who in their right mind would donate something like this to a school uniform recycling campaign?" she said, holding up a black gym shoe with a ten pence-sized gaping hole in the sole, before dropping it back down into section #3. "Maybe you should take down your social media request, if only for the time being?" Mollie offered. "Otherwise, we might end up with loads more items like this."

"Way ahead of you. Already done," Charlotte confirmed, moving her attention to section one. "Well, I see there's still plenty of reusable uniforms," she said brightly, with a smile suggesting all was not entirely lost. "Sure, not as many as I would've liked. But, still."

"And there are at least several winter coats here that look like they've never been worn," Bonnie contributed. "But also..." she added, a thought forming. "In fact, no. It's probably a daft idea," she concluded.

"No, go ahead. What were you thinking, Bonn?" Charlotte pressed, encouraging her to continue.

Bonnie, wearing her latest creation — a wonderful, cream-coloured chunky knit cardigan, Charlotte couldn't help but notice — ran her hand through her flame-red hair. "This section," Bonnie said, using her foot to point to section #2. "It isn't really suitable to be worn, yeah?"

"Agreed," Charlotte reluctantly agreed.

Bonnie dropped down onto one knee, retrieving a red jumper that sat on top of the pile. At first glance, it appeared to be in fairly decent condition, but unfolding the garment, the small splodge of black staining on the chest area indicated its former owner may have owned a leaking pen. "But we could still make something else from them? The good bits, I mean," she said, moving the item over to the group #3 section and placing it there.

"Ooh," an enthused Sarah said, raising her finger skyward, appearing awash with inspiration. "That red jumper, what about making a Christmas stocking out of it, Lotti? You mentioned you were working on festive themes at the crafting clubs, didn't you? So that might fit right in."

With a smile emerging, Charlotte tapped her chin as she took this idea into consideration. "You could definitely be on to something here, ladies," she mused aloud, casting a glance at the jumper. "Last Christmas, Stanley and I made some adorable little Santa hanging tree gnomes," she said. "The material in the jumper would be perfect for Santa's cone-shaped hat, I reckon, and we could use t-shirt fabric to craft his face, with a mini pompom for his nose." Charlotte narrowed one eye, chewing the inside of her cheek, her creative juices in full flow. She walked along the rows of piled-up clothing, deep in thought. "Hmm, so many possibilities..."

"What might we do with the trousers?" Mollie enquired. "Black and grey don't really jump out as being overly festive. Any ideas?"

"Christmas bunting?" Bonnie suggested. "Could be used for either the backing or even the lettering?"

"Perfect!" Charlotte said. "And while some of the clothing items might not be worn again, it's still being recycled, yeah? So, it's ReCyCool!"

"Yep. Sounds good," Mollie agreed.

Charlotte made her way over to a chair, holding the red jumper she'd picked up from on top of one of the piles. "I need to sit down. My mind's working overtime," she said. She draped the red jumper over her knee, caressing it like a cat. Rather than looking out at piles of scruffy, tired-looking clothes, she could now see the vibrant ingredients for what could become one great big Christmas pudding, metaphorically speaking of course. "You know what we can do?" Charlotte said, speaking up again after a minute or two deep in thought. "The nearly new clothing we obviously keep as is, yes? But, anything we make from the rest, we could sell."

"Great idea!" Mollie answered. "And we could have a festive knees-up on the proceeds, yeah?" she offered. "You know, canapés, champagne, oh, and fancy Belgium chocolates...?" she suggested, her mouth beginning to salivate at the very prospect.

"Well, we *could* do that," Charlotte replied. "Or..."

"Or?" Mollie said, suspecting the mention of the word 'or' meant the end of her festive knees-up idea.

"*Or*, we could use any money we make to buy *brand-new* uniforms," Charlotte informed them, running her eyes around the rest of the group. "Then, we can add what we buy to the donated items."

"Yeah, your idea is better, I suppose," Mollie had to admit. "Still, we should buy some Belgium chocolates, though..."

"Ooh, I'm so excited about this!" Charlotte said, rubbing her hands together gleefully. "I wonder what other ideas we can develop. Anyone? Maybe we could do that thing where we throw suggestions around to see what additional ideas we can dream up? What's that word...?"

"Brainstorming?" Bonnie put forth.

"Yes! That's it! Brainstorming!" Charlotte said, getting up to fetch her handbag. She was looking fiercely determined, like she was on a mission.

From her handbag, Charlotte retrieved her notepad and pen, opening her notepad and then holding pen over paper, ready to start writing. She looked up, expectantly, prepared to hear what anybody else might have to offer, but was surprised to see Mollie putting on her coat. "Oh. Where are you off to?" Charlotte asked, disappointed.

Mollie zipped up her jacket. "I know what you're like when you get an idea in your head, Lotti," Mollie told her. "Especially when the notepad gets unleashed. You'll be here all night."

"Oh," Charlotte said, still slightly dejected. "It's just that, well, you're amazing at coming up with—"

"Relax, I'll be coming right back," a smiling Mollie quickly replied. "I'm just off to get us something to replenish the energy levels," she revealed, rubbing her tum, and thus putting a grateful Charlotte at ease. "Everyone good with pizza?"

CHAPTER SEVEN

Charlotte glared at her phone's display, offering it a stern frown, along with several muttered words of a rather choice variety, though fortunately not spoken quite loud enough for the sausage dog sitting on the table before her to hear. She was a lady, after all.

But of course, choice words and stern glances aside, it wasn't her phone's fault that she'd been struggling for the better part of the morning to formulate a new social media post to replace the old one she'd since deleted (as she hadn't wanted Joan's Wools & Crafts to become further inundated with donations to the point where she'd perhaps become barred for life from there, a truly horrific prospect). Trying to think up a new message was proving difficult for her, however. She needed something along the lines of, *"Thank you in advance for your generous donations, but we only require new/nearly new items,"* but without sounding like she was ungrateful, as nothing could be further from the truth. She was acutely aware that failing to get the tone just right could well be misinterpreted as *thanks, but no thanks, we don't need your useless rubbish*. The reason, then, that she was presently agonising over the exact wording to use.

"What's that? You didn't think I'd forgotten you, did you, Frankfurter?" she asked, giving the partially completed dog a two-fingered pat on the head, just to show him he was still a very good boy. And a patient one at that, as he'd been sitting there slightly neglected as Charlotte pondered her vexing messaging problem.

Charlotte took a small handful of fluff, skilfully plumping up the cute little canine's rear legs with stuffing so that his hindquarters wouldn't drag along the kitchen table once he was all sewn up. "Oh, you're so *handsome*," Charlotte remarked, giving the adorable fellow's wee felt nose a gentle squeeze. "Who's a handsome boy, then? Yes, *you're* a handsome boy."

Charlotte adored creating memory items for people, though she'd briefly considered suspending her order book for new commissions simply because her spare time was becoming more and more scarce. But sitting there with Frankfurter for company, Classic FM playing on the radio, and a mug of tea within reaching distance, she knew leaving the book open was the correct decision. Even though she was obviously getting paid for her time, it just didn't feel like work. After all, people didn't smile this much when they were supposed to be working, did they? Moreover, there was an unbridled sense of accomplishment to be had by taking a bag of old clothes, wielding your scissors, and creating a keepsake that would be treasured by somebody for years to come. Plus, Charlotte couldn't deny that the extra cash these projects brought in was helpful at times. For the first time in she didn't know how long, she was delighted to have a few spare pounds in her purse at the end of each month. Along with the welcome income from her new job, this meant she could treat Stanley from time to time, purchase nice things for the house, or even splurge on some personal items for herself, all without worrying about where she'd find the money.

With the precision of a skilled heart surgeon closing up a patient after a triple bypass, Charlotte applied the finishing stitches along Frankfurter's tummy. "There," she said, offering her warmest of smiles, as an impeccable bedside manner was always appropriate at times like this, she felt.

Charlotte admired her handiwork for a few moments, running a critical eye over this latest creation, ensuring the face was properly symmetrical, he was firm in all the right places, and there was no sloppy stitching to be seen. Then, satisfied he was worthy of true pedigree status, she tied a red ribbon bow around his neck, finished off with a decorative gold bell. "Ahh," she said, scooping him up and placing him inside a clear plastic display bag, the sort a florist would use to protect a lovely bunch of roses. "Perfecto!" she declared, placing him on the sideboard to enjoy a nice view out the kitchen window until such time as his new owners came to collect him.

After working throughout the morning since dropping Stanley off at school, Charlotte indulged in a generous, well-earned stretch, reaching her arms high above her and rolling her head around in order to crack her neck. She wondered if there were any official medical conditions directly attributed to spending hours hunched over your latest project. *Crafting curvature of the spine*, perhaps? *Knitting neck*, maybe? She pondered this as she now switched over to easing out the knots in her shoulders, pressing against the flesh there like she was kneading bread dough. However, her self-ministrations would need to wait, distracted as she was, just then, by the familiar metallic thud of her garden gate being closed.

There was no need to look through the kitchen window to confirm the identity of her guest, with Charlotte instead offering a cursory glance towards the kitchen's wall-mounted clock. She walked through the hallway and lifted the latch on her front door, easing the door open to greet her visitor. "You're three minutes late," she announced. "Standards are dropping all around, it would seem," she said, tut-tutting playfully.

"I'll have the crew back at HQ horsewhipped, in order to improve their efficiency, Miss Lotti. That way, I can get out of the starting gate a bit earlier," Postman Harry promised, offering a smart salute in response. "What, too harsh?" he asked, noting the concerned expression on Charlotte's face.

"I think a firm word would suffice, Harry."

Postman Harry nodded his approval. "Very good, Miss Lotti. And may I say it's a rare and unexpected treat to find you in residence."

"I know, right? I seem to be out most days, lately, don't I?" Charlotte answered, taking a step back and with a flourish of the hand encouraging Harry inside. "The consequence of being in gainful employment, as it should happen," she was pleased to convey. "Although not seeing your cheery face every day is a blow," she added solemnly. And she meant it sincerely, because seeing Postman Harry every day was a treat, instantly raising her spirits the moment she clapped eyes on his ruddy cheeks coming up the garden path (along with the rest of him, of course). Like a Berocca tablet, taken daily, a healthy dose of Harry was all you needed to lift you up, giving you a spring in your step for the rest of your day.

Harry stepped gingerly through the hallway, walking with an awkward gait like a gunslinger moseying into a saloon bar after spending far too much time in the saddle. He unburdened himself of his postbag, laying it down on the kitchen floor with a gentle thud, before running his hand over his lumbar region.

"Everything okay there, Harry?" Charlotte enquired, following closely behind. "Only you're walking like you've got a stone in your shoe."

Harry parked himself down on a chair, taking a load off his weary feet. "I'm still struggling after that incident last week," Harry explained with a sigh. "You know the one."

Charlotte placed the already-warm kettle back on, and then gave Harry a blank look. She racked her brains, trying to recall the particular incident he was referring to. But with nothing obvious coming to mind, she was concerned that she perhaps hadn't been listening when he'd told her before. "Ehm... incident...?" she asked tentatively.

"Yes, the—" Harry started to say, but then cutting himself short. "Oh, silly me," he said with a laugh, shaking his head and setting his ruddy cheeks wobbling. "I've not seen you for a few days to tell you, have I?"

"Tell me what?"

"About throwing my back out," he answered. "Bloody sore it was, too. And still is, actually."

"What on earth happened?"

"I really shouldn't say," Harry said, for some reason looking over his shoulder, suspiciously.

"But you're going to anyway…?" Charlotte suggested, filling both of their teacups a few moments later. "I mean, you *have* to, yeah? You can't start a story like that without providing the conclusion. I'm fairly certain it's illegal, and you could even be arrested."

"Well…" Postman Harry began, with Charlotte hanging on his every word. "Well, I was down in the village making a delivery, right? And then—"

"Whose house?" Charlotte interrupted, believing this to be a crucial and vital element of his tale.

"Oh, I can't say," Harry said, looking over his shoulder once more. "That would be against the postman's code. But for the benefit of this, let's call her Mrs X."

"You have a code? In fact, never mind," Charlotte said, placing his cup down in front of him. "Do continue."

Harry took a sugar cube from the china bowl, dropping it into his cup with a satisfying plop. "I was delivering a parcel to *Mrs X*, you see, and it was one of those things where I needed the customer's signature. Well, the door can't have been closed properly, because when I knocked, it creaked open. So, as I've been delivering to *Mrs X* for a few years or more, knowing her well enough, I reckon, I stuck my head inside to announce my arrival. But there was nothing. No response. At this point, I was getting worried, yeah? What if she'd taken a fall or summat? Then with the door opened and only silence inside, that's when I panicked, thinking it might be burglars."

"No!" Charlotte said, jaw hanging low.

"So I shouted even louder," Harry said, picking up the story again. "If there were burglars, I was hoping to scare them off. *GET OUT OF HERE!* I yelled," Harry related, shaking his fist in furious recollection.

"You're *very* brave, Harry."

Harry nodded in agreement, taking a dainty sip of his tea. "That's when I heard something of a commotion. Just then," Harry continued. "And from where I was standing in the hall-way, I had a clear view through to the living room, Lotti. I could see things through the rear window being dropped from up-stairs. And I thought, *NOT ON MY WATCH, MISTER!* So I dropped what I was carrying, marched straight through the living room and unlocked and threw open the patio doors, hoping to inter-cept them. And that's when it hit me."

"What, you realised it *was* burglars?"

"No, that's when the shoe dropped."

"You mean metaphorically...?"

"No. Literally."

"Wait, a *shoe* hit you? That's what you're saying? And that's how you injured your back?"

"Well, it didn't help. But no, that's not the reason. The real damage was done when the bloke dangling from the window ledge lost his grip and landed on me."

Charlotte allowed this little snippet of information to digest for just a moment. "So a burglar landed on you...?" she said, try-ing to understand what Harry was telling her.

"That's what I thought, Lotti, until I realised he was almost naked. Now I'm no Hercule Poirot, that's for certain, but even I know that burglars don't ordinarily go about their business throwing clothes from the upstairs window and wearing only a pair of white underpants. It's not exactly inconspicuous or dis-creet, yeah?"

Charlotte started to snigger, having a very good idea where this story was heading. "You caught your Mrs X in the act, didn't you?" she asked, unable to contain a laugh. "Oh my," she said, placing a hand to her mouth.

"In *flagrante delicto*, yes," Harry answered, taking another sip of his tea. "They obviously didn't close the door properly and mistook my good intentions for her husband coming home," he continued. "That's when the luckless Lothario tried to make good his escape, unfortunately using yours truly as a landing cushion. Fortunately, he didn't fall directly on my head, at least, as that would have been much worse."

"Erm... was he okay?" Charlotte asked, unsure what else she could really say.

"Of course! He had a soft landing!" Harry said with a chuckle, the shock of the incident no longer as raw, it would appear. "The same can't be said for my lower back, though."

"I'll bet Mrs X was mortified. Did she dare show her face?"

"She didn't *want* to, Lotti. But you better believe I made her come down the stairs the instant she was decent!"

"I'll bet. Did you give her a piece of your mind, Harry?"

"No, no, it wasn't that. It's that she still needed to sign for the parcel I was trying to deliver," Harry explained.

"Ah."

"I had a job to do," Harry added. "However, while I was there, I did suggest that she might want to invest in a better lock for the front door."

"Oh, Harry, you poor dear," Charlotte concluded, now the mystery of Harry's impaired gait was explained. She took a large circular tin from the sideboard and removed the lid, presenting the contents for Harry's careful consideration. "Carrot cake?"

After peering inside and taking a generous sniff, Harry leaned back in his chair, all concerns, worries, aches and pains washing away in an instant. "Charlotte, that looks heavenly," he insisted, running his tongue over his lips. "And if you don't mind me saying so, I've missed your cake when you've been out working."

Charlotte feigned a look of disappointment. "Only the cake? What about my scintillating conversation?"

"A close second to your carrot cake," Harry replied, along with a friendly wink.

Charlotte sliced a good-sized portion of cake for them both, topping up their teacups as well while she was at it. And while Harry was making short work of her baking skills, enjoying the fruits thereof, she filled him in on the complications of her

ReCyCool initiative, including the challenge of accepting donations without overwhelming shops like Joan's.

Once his plate was empty, Harry released a contented sigh, right before draining the dregs of his cup. "You know what you need, Lotti?" he said, rising up from his chair, his work not finished for the day and post still to deliver.

"Well, no," Charlotte replied, eager to hear more. "That's why I was telling you, what with you being a wise old owl and all."

"Oi, cheeky. Less of the old, alright?" Harry gently admonished, groaning as he straightened out his spine. "Then again..." he said with a laugh, giving his back another rub. "Anyway, as I see it, Lotti, you can't expect folk up the north of the island to drive for miles and vice versa, everyone dropping off at only a single location. That might discourage people before you even begin, yeah? So what you need, I reckon, is an establishment in the north, south, east, and west, large enough and willing to accept donations for you. That way, you'll minimise the distance people need to travel."

Charlotte smiled politely but was slightly underwhelmed by what was essentially a summary of what she already knew. "Yeah," she said. "That's kinda the problem I'm—"

"Shoprite!" Harry said brightly, as a lightbulb switched on inside his head.

"Shoprite?"

Harry checked his watch, making progress towards the hallway. "Yes, Shoprite, Lotti. They've got supermarkets in all four corners of the island, and their stores are massive. That means people can easily drop things off, yeah? And who knows, maybe Shoprite would even be kind enough to let you put up a few clothes rails in their stores as well. That way, those who need any uniform items can pick a few bits up while they're doing their weekly shop."

"Ooh," Charlotte replied through puckered lips, enjoying what she was hearing. "I like that, Harry. I like that a lot. And it would solve the storage issue of one shop having to carry every uniform design from each school. Instead, we could distribute uniforms for schools in the north of the island to their Ramsey store, schools in the south to their Port Erin store, and so on..."

"There you go, then," Harry said, clapping his hands together in an *I'm-not-nearly-as-daft-as-I-look* fashion. "You should speak with Mike," Harry added, reaching into his delivery bag to hand Charlotte several envelopes secured by an elastic band, lest he forget the reason he'd shown up on Charlotte's doorstep in the first place.

Charlotte accepted them, though paid little attention to the envelopes. She was really only interested in the post if it had wool or something similar inside. "Mike...?" she enquired.

Harry lifted the latch on the front door, turning to face Charlotte. "Mike. As in Mike from three cottages down."

"Thanks! I will!" Charlotte promptly replied, happy to do as instructed, even if she wasn't sure exactly why. "Ehm... why, exactly?"

Harry laughed, although not in an unkind way. "Mike, your almost neighbour," he explained, "is an accountant who happens to work at..." he said, clicking his tongue against the roof of his mouth, introducing a passable impression of the sound of a drumroll. "None other than Shoprite!"

Charlotte narrowed one eye, not appearing overly convinced by this suggestion, and also more than a little confused. "Mike, who drives the red Volkswagen Golf, Mike?"

"That's the one."

"But he's a painter and decorator, isn't he? I mean, I could swear that's what I'd been told. Unless... unless I'm somehow mistaken...?"

Harry shook his head. "No, trust your local postman, Lotti," he told her. "They know and see everything. Just ask *Mrs X*, for example," he said with a wink.

Charlotte placed her flushed cheeks in her hands. "Oh, no. That's really embarrassing, Harry."

"Is it? Why? It's not the first time I've ever—"

"No, no, not that. I mean it's embarrassing for *me*, Harry. Because I was absolutely *convinced* he was a painter, although for the life of me I couldn't say why. But, being convinced he was a painter as I was, and me being the lovely neighbour that I am, I've been giving his mobile number out to anybody looking to have a bit of painting done. And I've also tagged him into dozens of similar requests on Facebook! Bloody hell, he must think I'm as mad as a hatter..."

"That's very kind of you," an amused Harry commented.

"*Darn it*," Charlotte added, remembering something specific she'd just remembered. "Only last week, I stopped him while he was out walking his dog. I was telling him about my flaking fascia boards, and I asked him for a quote to clean them up and give them a proper coat of paint."

"The fact he's usually dressed in a shirt and tie didn't give you a clue he wasn't a painter and decorator?"

"Well, no. I just thought Mike took great pride in his appearance. But now you've pointed it out to me, Harry, well, I do feel a bit daft."

"Anyway," Harry said, walking over the threshold, holding a hand above his head by way of goodbye. "As always, it's been a pleasure, Lotti. And thank you for the cake."

"And scintillating conversation?" Charlotte called after him.

"Always, Lotti," Harry answered, pulling open the garden gate.

"See you soon, Harry. And be sure to give Mrs X my regards!"

CHAPTER EIGHT

ReCyCool Isle of Man

If you have new or nearly new school uniforms, shoes and coats, etc, gathering dust in your cupboard, why not donate them and let them fulfil their potential?

Your generous contributions will go directly to schoolchildren who'll wear them with pride.

Collection points at Shoprite stores island-wide.

It's not just cool to recycle... It's ReCyCool! ☺

Charlotte sat on a trestle table, gently swinging her feet back and forth, adding the final and finishing touch to her social media post, with that finishing touch being the smiling emoji. "It doesn't sound too, you know, too bolshie or ungrateful, does it?" she asked.

Positioned next to Charlotte on the same table, Emma, the nursing home manager, moved her nose closer to Charlotte's mobile phone. "Let me have another read," she suggested, replicating the swinging motion of Charlotte's feet. With a similar blonde bob apiece, the pair shared a passing resemblance, the two of them often confused with each other by some of the more visually-impaired residents.

Once again, Emma read through the post, running her finger over the phone's display, mouthing the words while nodding in approval. "Perfect!" she declared, once she'd finished. "It's friendly, concise, tells you what you need to know, and where to drop the items off."

With a nervous grin, Charlotte pressed the 'publish' button. "There we go," she said, setting the phone down on the tabletop. "I just hope a few people share the post, so the word gets out there."

"Well I'll be certain to, Lotti, you can count on that," Emma answered. "And getting Shoprite's support must be a massive boost for you from an awareness standpoint, I imagine?"

"Oh, Emma, they've been amazing," Charlotte said, pushing herself off the table as the first coterie of crafters made their way through the wooden double doors. "And Shoprite has even offered to place those big metallic recycling bins outside their stores, and they've even allocated a small section inside each location so we can eventually display the clothes."

Charlotte's Make It Sew initiative often took her all over the island, proudly boasting over five hundred attendees each and every month, collectively. There were times, like this evening's class, when Charlotte was flying solo, teaching the group on her own. But on other occasions, Mollie, Bonnie, Joyce, or some of the other Crafternooners would happily pop along to lend a hand. Each visit to every nursing home was like a social occasion for Charlotte. There, she was meeting up with new friends and old, delighted to see familiar faces, eager to see what they'd been working on since her last visit. Of course, some members weren't particularly predisposed to crafting, more interested in attending to have a chinwag over a nice cuppa with their pals. And, for Charlotte, that was perfectly fine as well. After all, this was a community, and one built on the foundation of friendship. If some didn't immediately pick up a crochet hook, they still contributed to the vibrant atmosphere, helping to make attending the clubs a welcoming, enjoyable experience for anyone involved. And whilst some of them might not be crafters just yet, it didn't prevent Charlotte from nudging a knitting pattern under their noses on occasion (along with a piece of delicious cake) just to whet their appetites.

Charlotte relished attending each and every nursing home, of course, all with their own particular charms, but there was something about today's setting in particular that was close to her heart. It was here where she'd first volunteered her teaching skills, turning up on the first week to an audience size best described as modest, and with some even sleeping through her debut class. Yet it was from these humble beginnings that she'd seen her own confidence grow as well as the number of weekly attendees, helping her to realise the potential of what would come to be known (thanks to Larry's brilliant wordplay suggestion) as Make It Sew. Like a proud parent with a magnificent brood, Charlotte adored all of her groups and could never single one out as her very favourite, necessarily. But whenever she was heading along to see Larry & company, as was the case today, the spring in her step became especially springy.

Charlotte smiled warmly when more of the class members arrived. "Welcome, welcome, welcome!" she said, visiting each occupied table in turn, handing out the Christmas crafting menu that she'd created. The festive option wouldn't be for everyone today, as many of the members were still already committed to their present works in progress, but having several available alternatives was always a pleasant problem to be faced with.

"Ooh, I like this," an intrigued Shirley offered, pushing her glasses up her nose. Then, she gently prodded her friend sitting to her left. "You like a nice candy cane, Carol," she said, pointing out that particular crafting option for her mate's consideration. "Or what about this giant advent calendar?" Then, like a hungry diner in a fine restaurant, Shirley ran her finger down the page, stopping briefly on each option to consider the various merits and complexities. "I feel all Christmassy, Carol," she eventually declared with a satisfied sigh. "Oh!" she quickly added, bursting into a fit of laughter, scaring poor Ted sitting opposite in the process. "Christmassy *Carol*," she said, nudging her mate gently in the side, once more. "It's no wonder I feel festive sat next to you, Carol!"

"Good one, Shirley. We must remember to tell Larry that one, as I'm sure he'd appreciate it," Charlotte commented. "In fact..." she said, running a curious eye around the room. "In fact, where is Larry, or, for that matter, the rest of the group?" she asked, noting several lonely tables with seats not being presently warmed by anyone's posteriors. Charlotte walked over to the entrance doors, poking her head out into the corridor, looking this way and that, hoping to find the rest of the members nattering away outside, as they often did. But nothing. "Oh," Charlotte said flatly, after taking a brief glance down at her wrist. "Five past."

Naturally, attendance at Make It Sew was entirely voluntary, but Charlotte couldn't help feeling a touch deflated returning to the dining room. If anything, attendance numbers had grown week by week, so to see a sudden decrease like this came as something of a surprise. "Okay, group," she announced, returning her attention to those seated who were waiting patiently to hear more about this special, seasonal menu they'd so far been teased with, "I know we've not even seen the first festive advert on the telly yet, but let's talk about... Christmas!"

Just then, Emma, who'd previously returned to her duties, appeared in the doorway, casting her eyes around the dining room. "Oh, shoot!" she exclaimed. "Just give me twenty seconds or thereabouts, yeah?" she called out to Charlotte.

And twenty-one seconds later, Charlotte heard something of a commotion emanating from the corridor, sounding like cattle stampeding at feeding time. Before she had time to investigate, her missing crafters appeared, happily chatting away to each other as they merrily filed into the room.

"Did you lot get lost?" a relieved Charlotte joked, extending a welcoming hand and inviting the late arrivals to avail themselves of the empty chairs.

Emma appeared into view again, at the rear of the group, shepherding them with the skill of a border collie rounding up its herd. "Entirely my fault," an apologetic Emma explained. "They were all watching that Sewing Bee programme in the TV room, Lotti. I said I'd give them a knock when you arrived, but it completely slipped my mind."

Charlotte's bright demeanour changed suddenly, her shoulders rapidly sinking like the torpedoed RMS Lusitania. "Wait, what? *The Great British Sewing Bee?*" she said, the panic in her voice clearly evident.

Emma could see the abject horror painted across Charlotte's face. "Don't worry, you haven't missed anything," she advised, in her most soothing tone. "It's not a new series, just re-runs."

Charlotte clutched her chest with one hand, wiping an imaginary bead of sweat from her forehead with the other. "Bloody hell, you gave me a terrible fright just then," Charlotte replied, drawing a long breath, the thought of missing even one episode of her favourite show nearly too horrible to contemplate.

"I'll tell you what. That Patrick Grant can take my inside leg measurement any day of the week!" Ethel, one of the latecomers announced, fanning herself with her hand. She was obviously an admirer of the show's debonair presenter, and the sentiment she'd just expressed was one wholeheartedly shared by several of the other women present judging by the enthusiastic head wobbling.

Emma rolled her eyes and, with a wry smile, manoeuvred Pete's wheelchair so that his knees were comfortably tucked under one of the tables. "Do I need to set the fire extinguisher on you lot?" she asked, casting the table of tittering ladies an amused glance before bringing her attention back round to Charlotte. "Apologies again," said Emma. "How could I forget about *this* group? I mean, *really?*"

Larry, as he entered the room behind the others, offered a brief wave for Charlotte's benefit but appeared flustered, heading straight to the refreshments station — two tables pushed together where the kitchen staff had laid out the hot water urn along with tea and coffee supplies. "Oh, bother," he said, sounding consternated as he removed the cellophane from the cake Charlotte had baked and provided. He proceeded to unstack the teacups, placing each on a saucer with a teaspoon lying on the side.

Sensing Larry's unease, Charlotte followed him over as several of the group retrieved their current projects from the store cupboard. "Everything okay, Larry?" Charlotte asked, placing a hand on his shoulder.

Larry tipped out the contents of the milk carton, filling several miniature china jugs, which he placed out across the table at regular intervals. "I am now, Lotti," he confirmed, testing the temperature of the metallic urn with the back of his hand. "Perfect now," Larry declared, shaking the burn away. "We're ready to forge ahead, and the refreshments station is ready for action, Captain!" he confirmed with an enthusiastic salute.

Charlotte gave his shoulder a gentle squeeze. "Very good, Number One," she replied, returning his nautical-themed form of address.

"And, I'm sorry it wasn't all set up and ready like usual," Larry added, lowering his head like a pooch who'd just snaffled the family's Sunday roast. "Only *that* lot," he said, with an accusing finger, "introduced me to that flipping great show on the telly, didn't they? And now I'm bloody hooked. But I promise normal service will resume next week, Skipper."

Larry then gave Charlotte another smart salute.

"Nonsense, Larry. I understand entirely," Charlotte assured him. "I've been known to record it and watch the same episode at least a dozen times. Just ask my Stanley. The poor lad could probably recite every word of some of them."

"The challenge in the next episode is Hollywood bling," Larry informed Charlotte, tearing open a packet of Bourbon biscuits and placing them so that they formed a perfect circle around a fancy serving plate.

"Come on, my lovely," Charlotte said, aiming Larry towards his seat. "How about we get cracking, and, who knows, you might be able to whip up some Hollywood bling of your own?"

Charlotte couldn't help but admire Larry's commitment and attention to detail. For some, it might have been simply a cup of tea. But for Larry, it was something he took pride in, making sure everything was *just so*, with everything properly arranged and perfectly in place. It was as if he knew that the consequence of his actions, either positive or negative, would directly impact Charlotte. Likely the reason, then, that Larry was as dependable as he was, often willing and ready to go the extra mile. Charlotte didn't know if it was a generational trait, necessarily, but she often observed that her membership 'of a certain age' tended to be blessed with impeccable manners and such. Yes, they were a bit rowdy at times, especially when being egged on by one another, but, on the whole, they were thoroughly decent folk. Consequently, Charlotte was delighted young Stanley relished the time he spent with them all, because as far as role models went you couldn't get much better, in Charlotte's book!

Edith's tongue was extended, pressed flat against her top lip. If it were protruding any further, in fact, she'd be in danger of licking the tip of her nose. With her concentration unwavering, she applied the final few stitches, securing a delicious dollop of cream to her plump-looking Christmas pudding.

"It's incredible what you can do with a piece of brown fabric and a cut-out section of white school shirt," Edith remarked triumphantly, leaning back in her chair to survey the fruits of her diligence.

Distracted by the intoxicating sounds of joyful satisfaction, Charlotte took a walk over to Edith's location, eager for a quick peek. "Oh, yes," Charlotte said, venturing around the table for an admiring look over Edith's shoulder. "Yes, that looks good enough to eat."

Edith, clearly pleased with herself, held up a section of green felt. "Just the holly sprig to add, and then it'll be good to go!" she said, receiving appreciative glances and sounds of encouragement from around her. "Come on, you lot, it'll be Christmas before we know it!" she barked to those sharing her table, though this was accompanied by the flicker of a smile.

Charlotte's Christmas menu was proving to be quite the hit, judging by the number of members keen to enter the yuletide spirit. Several were happily repurposing articles of school uniforms, converting a worn school shirt, for instance into a jolly snowman, diligently following the pattern guide from Charlotte's crafting book. Others opted for the Christmas stocking option, giving some of the red school jumpers a second bite of the cherry and a stay of execution. Of course, these were items of donated uniforms they were using, the pieces not quite ready for the scrap heap, worn or ripped in areas but ideal for turning into Christmas decorations.

It was heartening for those beavering away to know the items they worked on today would likely be brought down from the attic each December to dangle from the tree, or perhaps be draped over the fireplace stuffed with prezzies from the big man in the red suit. Now, rather than being stuffed in the back of the wardrobe, turning fusty, the used garments would be an integral part of the festivities, raising a smile when they made an appearance each year. And if some of their completed products could be sold, raising money to buy new uniforms, well, that was a splendid outcome as far as they were all concerned.

Edith's crew had set themselves the task of creating a Christmas wall-hanging — the centre-page pattern from Charlotte's book — crafted from a mosaic of five-inch green fabric squares that would be five wide and nine in length when stitched together. As such, it was undoubtedly a stern challenge they'd set themselves. Half of them were sewing Christmas puddings onto the fabric backing, ready to form sections of the perimeter, while the others were busy cutting out vibrant red letters from the school jumpers, laying them on the table like a fabric game of Scrabble. Once stitched in place, barring any mistakes, they'd hopefully form the words "Merry Christmas" in the shape of the holy cross, with the *Merry* intersecting *Christmas* like items in a crossword puzzle.

Navigating his refreshments trolley with a wonky wheel and keeping an interested eye on proceedings, Larry weaved his way through the room, anticipating parched mouths with the professional assurance of a sommelier in a Michelin-starred restaurant. By now, he'd long since given up on any pretence of being a crafter, preferring the social side of their engagements, dispensing refreshments along with the occasional anecdote on his rounds.

"Is that you running low, Sally?" Larry enquired, leaning over the table to catch a better view inside her empty teacup before topping her back up, lest the poor dear go without. "You know, Sally," he then said, replenishing the Rich Tea biscuit supply on her side plate, "you want to be careful you don't get any of these Christmas decorations anywhere near your mouth."

Sally broke her attention away from her partially completed snowman. "Oh?" she said, narrowing one eye, suspecting she was likely being set up but intrigued nonetheless. "Why's that, Larry?" she asked, lowering her needle, eager to hear more.

Larry removed the tea towel draped over his shoulder, eyes wide like an excited fisherman who'd just felt a nibble on the end of their line. "Because..." he said, drying off the spout on his teapot, "you'll end up with... *tinselitis*."

Sally giggled like a schoolgirl, swatting him away like a pesky fly, causing the laughter lines to deepen around her eyes. "Did you read that in a Christmas cracker?" she asked.

"You're the only Christmas cracker around here, Sally," Larry suggested with a wink, after which he pushed his rickety trolley on towards the next table where he'd spotted several empty side plates. "Fear not, Larry's here!" he called in advance of his arrival, a packet of Rich Tea biscuits primed and ready.

Charlotte, who was only half listening in from where she was sitting, offered a pained groan and a gentle shake of the head in response to Larry's delightfully dreadful pun. "You'll also need to tell Stanley that one, Larry. He'll love it," she told him.

The willingness of the residents to learn new skills was an inspiration, and seeing those cheery faces around the room motivated her, convincing Charlotte that what she was doing was a good thing. Charlotte adored the jovial atmosphere she encountered at the crafting clubs, comprised of laughter, chatter, cheesy Larry jokes, and often a warm sense of enthusiasm. Tonight, however, felt extra special indeed. Perhaps it was the Christmas crafting menu bringing out a general feeling of goodwill amongst the group, or maybe some of them had been getting stuck into the gin bottle before she'd turned up. But whatever it was, Charlotte looked around the room, soaking it all up. It was as if they all had a twinkle in their eyes like their inner child had just been awoken, daring to dream what Santa might bring down the chimney for them on Christmas morning. Yes, it was still only October, and there wasn't a fairy light to be seen just yet, but she felt like the elves must have sprinkled some of their magic dust in Larry's tea urn. It was a special moment for Charlotte, rather catching her off guard as a small lump formed in her throat. Such was the feeling of overall loveliness that she wouldn't have been at all surprised if Cliff Richard marched through the door right then, singing a rendition of his seasonal classic, "Mistletoe and Wine."

Then, as if somehow able to read Charlotte's music-minded thoughts, Larry tapped his teaspoon on the side of his mug, creating a gentle, steady beat that slowly increased in volume. *"Silent night..."* he said softly, singing the words, grateful to have several pairs of eyes turning in his direction. Larry raised his hand, holding his spoon out like a conductor's baton, smiling broadly. *"Holy night..."* he continued, only this time a mite louder, attracting more of the eyes that'd resisted his initial effort and with those still nattering away falling quiet in response.

Charlotte's jaw dropped. She'd heard Larry whistling often enough and suspected him capable of carrying a tune, but this she'd never expected. His singing voice was remarkable — silky, rich, and deep, like a mug of luxurious hot chocolate on a cold winter's night.

"All is calm, all is bright..." Larry went on, now in his stride and weaving the spoon through the air like a painter with a fresh canvas.

The hushed silence amongst the group broke, as one-by-one others in the room joined in, encouraged by Larry stood in front of his trolley with the wonky wheel. Before too long, everybody was belting out the seasonal classic, some sounding marvellous, others tone-deaf. But that didn't matter. Indeed, such volume was produced that Emma and Ken, the evening receptionist, both appeared in the doorway, watching on and enjoying the impromptu performance.

Eventually, Larry lowered his spoon once the final words of the song escaped his lips. He offered a half-laugh, extending a grateful smile for the benefit of all those gracious enough to provide such excellent choral accompaniment.

Charlotte pushed her chair back, taking to her feet. "Larry, that... was... beautiful!" she said, breaking into applause that was promptly supplemented by others who'd risen to their feet as well.

"Bravo!" Edith hollered, and for someone with limited mobility, she was doing a rather stand-up job in leading the cheerleading committee. "Is this the part where we throw our knickers on stage?" she asked, raising a raucous cheer in from some of the other girls in response.

Larry, for his part, allowed the suggestive comment to wash over him, offering a simple bow in return. "Why thank you," he said, blowing kisses to his adoring fans. "It's a little premature, but I'm feeling all Christmassy watching you crafting. Now, I should think we'll all need to lubricate our vocal cords after that little sing-song, am I right? Right, then! So who's for a top-up?"

Following their unexpected interlude, the members of Make It Sew returned to their crafting projects, teacups once again replenished.

"That really was quite lovely, Larry," Charlotte told him, finding him a minute or so later with his trolley tilted at an angle, attending to the one errant wheel.

"I hope you didn't mind the interruption, Lotti?" he asked, giving the offending wheel a firm slap. "There we go," he said, happy he'd knocked the wonkiness from it. "Now, hopefully, I won't appear like the village drunk when I'm veering around the dining room."

Charlotte extended a hand, helping Larry return to his feet. "You're a man of many talents, Larry," she said fondly. "Singer, trolley mechanic, and the hardest-working crafting assistant a crafter could hope for. You do know how much I appreciate your help, Larry?"

"Pish-posh," Larry answered, waving away her kind words and feigning embarrassment. "It's my pleasure," he said. "It's just a pity that I'm not actually much good at the art of crafting itself."

"That's why we make such a brilliant team, Larry. We're like the guys on The Great British Sewing Bee, yeah?"

"Ab-so-lute-ly," Larry readily agreed, and then, "We are?" he added, happy at the suggestion, just not entirely sure why.

Charlotte linked her arm into his, nodding confidently. "Of course," she insisted. "I'd be the crafty one on the programme. The judge, if you like, and—"

Larry liked the direction where this was heading. "Ooh, ooh!" he cut in, fidgeting like he needed a wee. "And I'd be the one who fills the gaps with humorous remarks, wandering around chatting to the contestants before shouting, *TEN MINUTES TO GO!*"

"Eh, what's that?" a confused Sally called over, after quickly checking her watch. "Here, we've got another half hour, and I've not even touched my brew yet," she said, with an audible tut-tut at the end.

"No, not you, Sally," Larry said, "I was talking about..."

But Sally had already returned her attention to Frosty the Snowman, not particularly interested in what Larry had to say at this juncture as she was determined to carry on with her current project regardless.

"But I'd be funnier," Larry said, speaking to Charlotte again and now back on the subject of what they'd just been talking about.

Charlotte offered a happy shrug, not committing one way or the other but suspecting Larry was most probably right.

"If I were on that television programme..." Larry continued, his mind wandering off at the prospect. "Yeah, if I were on that television programme, the contestants wouldn't get anything done as they'd be too distracted from laughing. Unlike those two muppets on the *actual* programme, I reckon. Well, to be fair, the one with the long hair is reasonably funny, I suppose, but as for the other one..."

Larry went silent for a long moment which, where Larry was concerned, was unusual. "Everything okay?" Charlotte asked, at the same time unlinking herself as she noticed a hand waving from over at Edith's table. "Just coming!" Charlotte advised, to the person in need of assistance.

Larry raised a finger aloft like a flag being run up the flag-pole. "We should do that, Lotti!" he said.

"Do what?" asked Charlotte.

"The Great British Sewing Bee!"

"You want us to go on the show?" Charlotte replied, smiling politely and a little puzzled. "But, by your own admission, Larry, you're not much of a crafter, so I'm not sure I understand," she said over her shoulder, as she headed off towards Edith's table.

"No, Lotti. What I mean is, instead of The Great *British* Sewing Bee, what about The Great *Isle of Man* Sewing Bee?" Larry answered, calling after her. "Just imagine it," he said, rubbing his hands together excitedly. "We'd invite all of the island's crafting clubs to nominate their finest crafters to participate, with the overall winner laying claim to being the island's craftiest crafter! With me providing commentary and witty repartee throughout, of course."

Charlotte stopped in her tracks, quickly spinning round, an intrigued eyebrow raised heavenward. "The Great Isle of Man Sewing Bee...?" she said.

Larry bounced his head up and down. "Yep! Whaddya think?"

"Oh, Larry. I like that idea. I like that idea a *lot*."

CHAPTER NINE

Trees swayed like a collection of punch-drunk boxers, buffeted by the gusts whipping in from the Irish Sea which stripped branches of their golden leaves, creating a crisp carpet of molten-like foliage at the roadside. And while Charlotte may have been sorry to say goodbye to the warm summer months, the island's changing scenery at this time of year never failed to captivate her. Thoughts of blustery walks along Laxey Beach followed by snug, toasty evenings around the log burner always produced a smile, even on the briskest of days.

"Oh, isn't it completely stunning," Charlotte said, pressing her nose closer to the passenger-side window, watching the autumn leaves falling like confetti. "Stanley," she said, now looking over her shoulder, "don't the trees look pretty?"

"Yeah, sure. Just loverly, Mum," Stanley responded, though without bothering to look through the window, as he was more engrossed in admiring the fancy leather seats and posh interior of Calum's car right at present. "Calum, if you dropped me off at school in this," he asked, "would you rev the engine until all of my friends turned round to look...?"

Calum flicked his eyes to the rear-view mirror. "Sure," he answered. "I could also see if I could do a doughnut in the car park if you like? Perhaps create a cloud of burning rubber which we could send wafting across the playground?"

"Could you? Yes, that would be brilliant!" said Stan, in ready agreement, leaning forward in his seat while imagining that very scenario in his mind.

Charlotte cleared her throat in that *I-don't-think-so* sort of way that mums have come to master over the years, her eyes still fixed on the glorious countryside passing by the window. "There'll be absolutely no burning of rubber," she reiterated, just in case she hadn't already made herself perfectly clear.

Burning rubber aside, it's fair to say that Charlotte wasn't particularly clued up when it came to all things car-related. So long as it moved when she pressed the accelerator and stopped when the brake pedal was applied, that was about the extent of her general interest. Stan, however, was most impressed with Calum's new speed machine, as he'd called it, suggesting it might actually be quicker than the Starship Enterprise and the coolest thing he'd ever driven in. It had been for this reason, at Stanley's request, that the three of them had ventured out for a Saturday morning drive around the autumnal Isle of Man.

It was also an ideal opportunity, Charlotte had put forward, to visit the island's Shoprite stores in the process (and then perhaps find somewhere nice for a spot of lunch afterwards). In the wake of her revamped ReCyCool social media post, Charlotte was hopeful her message had been received by the public as intended and that, going forward, the donations of clothing items received would all be reusable by schoolchildren on the island.

First up, then, after a pleasant drive along the famous Isle of Man TT course, was Shoprite's Ramsey location, situated in the north of the island. And even before Calum had pulled off the main road, Charlotte's head was already out of the window, eager to catch a glimpse of the recycling bin.

"Ooh, I can see it!" Charlotte announced, as Calum parked up in the next available space. "Can you see it, Stan? Doesn't it look brilliant?"

Once outside the car, Charlotte skipped across the car park, Stan in one hand and Calum in the other. In a prime position in front of the store, just up ahead, was the green recycling bin. Well, to refer to it as merely a bin would be something of an understatement as this thing was greater than a garden shed, with the word RECYCOOL emblazoned in large letters across the front. "We need a photograph," Charlotte suggested, once they were upon it, reaching into her pocket for her mobile phone. She then looked around for someone who might be able to help.

"Excuse me!" Charlotte said, spotting a passing traffic warden in a high-viz vest, a sausage bap positioned mere centimetres from his gob. "Yes, hello!" Charlotte said, offering him a cheery wave. "Would you mind awfully?" she asked, thrusting her phone in his direction, while taking up a position standing in front of the bin with Calum and Stanley ushered into place on either side of her like bookends.

The traffic warden, who now had tomato ketchup running down the side of his hand from his partially-eaten breakfast, looked to Charlotte's phone, then to his sausage bap, back to Charlotte's phone again, and then up at Charlotte. "You... you want to swop your phone for my sausage sarnie...?" he asked, confused.

"No, no, I want you to take our picture!" Charlotte clarified.

The fellow appeared grateful he wasn't being asked to give up his breakfast, but now seemed even more confused than before. "You want me to take your picture?" he asked. "Right *here*?"

"That would be splendid, thank you."

"Ehm... you do know there's a lovely sandy beach not far from here? And even a scenic boating lake around the corner?" the warden pointed out. "So, you know, if you should want something a touch more pleasant as a backdrop, rather than a bin...?"

Charlotte caressed the green metal behind her because, for her, this was more than just a bin; this was the fruition of her vision. "Thanks, but right here is perfect," she insisted, offering the chap her very smiliest of smiles.

"Alright, suit yourself," the warden said with a shrug, likely figuring simply taking the photo as asked would be the fastest resolution so that he could get back to the business of eating his breakfast as soon as possible and be on his way. He looked around, finding somewhere to set down his sandwich for a moment, and then, sandwich temporarily deposited, licked the ketchup from his fingers clean. That done, he accepted Charlotte's phone and positioned himself accordingly. "Say cheese," he said, snapping the shot. He returned the phone, snatched his sarnie back up, and could then be heard mumbling "Takes all sorts..." to himself as he stepped away, getting out of there while the getting was good.

With the moment captured for posterity and the traffic warden on his way, Calum placed his arm around Charlotte, pulling her in close, a proud grin spread across his face.

"I shouldn't really be this pleased to see an oversized bin, should I?" Charlotte asked, looking first to Calum and then to Stanley. "Is it a bit weird?"

"Mum, you're often a bit weird, but this time you've a good reason to be weird," Stanley offered.

"Oh, in that case... thanks, I think?" Charlotte said, giving the young lad's hair a generous ruffle. "Come on, then. I'll show you where we're going to display the donated clothes."

For many, the drudgery of entering a supermarket to undertake the weekly shop wasn't exactly the highlight of their week. But, for anybody watching on, Charlotte would likely have appeared as the happiest shopper they'd ever seen. Entering the store, she couldn't contain her mad grin, bounding through the aisles like Tigger on a trampoline. Every few steps, she looked over her shoulder, making sure the other two were still keeping pace. Which they were, until Stanley had apparently veered off. "Have we lost somebody...?" Charlotte asked, glancing about.

"Dunno?" Calum offered a moment later. "He was just there a moment ago, and then poof, like magic..."

"Ah. He'll be assessing the store's extensive biscuit selection, I expect," Charlotte replied with assurance, suggesting such detours on Stanley's part were a regular shopping occurrence. "No worries, he'll soon catch up."

Towards the rear of the store, just beyond the shelves of household cleaning products, Charlotte came to an abrupt halt, so abrupt, in fact, that Calum all but collided into the back of her.

"You've certainly got no problem with your brakes," Calum joked, after drawing alongside of her. "Charlotte?" he said, following her eyeline when no response was offered.

Charlotte's attention was currently taken by a wooden shelving unit and two clothes rails, above which the Shoprite staff had kindly displayed the ReCyCool posters that Charlotte had previously emailed through when outlining what the initiative was all about. In addition, the staff had acquired a small handful of student desks and even erected a school blackboard, writing on the blackboard in large chalk lettering Charlotte's own words: *"It's not just cool to recycle, it's ReCyCool."*

The display they'd created looked fabulous, with a fair degree of time and effort obviously being invested into it. It was disappointing, then, that the only visible article of clothing to be had was a cosy-looking duffle coat, hanging there on one of the rails all by its lonesome.

"Hey now," Calum said, noting Charlotte's despondent expression. "That big green bin we've just had our picture taken in front of is probably jam-packed with donations, ready to be unloaded."

Charlotte forced through an optimistic smile. "Yeah, you're probably right," she said, heading over to the duffle coat. "It looks nearly brand-new," she observed, running a hand over the garment, which immediately raised her spirits.

"Oh, wow, Mum. Have they given away all of the uniforms already?" Stanley asked, returning from his thorough inspection of the biscuit aisle. "See?" he continued, before Charlotte had a chance to respond one way or the other. "I told you it was a brilliant idea!"

"Uhm, yeah. Either that, or I think they're probably still unloading the recycling bin," a hopeful Charlotte replied. "Is that a little souvenir?" she asked, clocking the glossy wrapper in his mitt.

Stanley raised up the packet in his hand. "I found those biscuits you really like, Mum," Stanley announced.

"The biscuits *you* just happen to love as well?" Charlotte said, pointing out the obvious.

"Oh. Do I...?" Stanley asked, as if this had never occurred to him, and played no part at all in his selection process. "How interesting. See, they're the ones you're always dunking in your cuppa, so I just wondered, since we were here and all, if you'd like to..."

"Yes, we can buy some biscuits, Stan," Charlotte told him. "And I just love how you're always thinking of me," she added with a chuckle.

"I'm all about the sacrifice, Mum."

Half a packet of Hobnobs later, and the three of them had ticked off the Ramsey, Douglas, and Castletown Shoprite stores and Calum, for his part, was remarkably relaxed, considering there was a ten-year-old snaffling chocolate crumbly biscuits in the rear of his brand-new car.

By this point, Charlotte's initial disappointment at the one duffle coat had been replaced by a feeling of resigned defeat, though it was difficult for Calum to see her so dejected, especially when her intentions had been so selfless and pure.

Back at the Ramsey store, Calum had approached a member of staff, wondering if it would be possible to review the contents of their recycling bin and any potential contents therein. Realising this to be an ideal opportunity to shirk his sweeping duties, at least for a while, the lad had been only too pleased to oblige, acquiring the required keys from the manager's office. But Calum's well-intended idea didn't quite have the Hollywood-style happy film ending he'd hoped for, as rather than finding the belly of the recycling unit stuffed with donated children's uniforms, this particular bin could best be described as malnourished. There had been no clothes to speak of, and the only contents, as they'd soon discovered, were a Breville toaster and a well-thumbed Ordnance Survey Map of Anglesey. Compounding the sorry situation further, the young shop assistant noted that the toaster didn't even have a plug, an observation he'd found most amusing. Sadly, the theme of meagre pickings appeared to be the order of the day, with the other stores they subsequently visited describing donations as similarly underwhelming.

"Take the next left, and I'll treat us all to some lunch?" Charlotte suggested, lunch being something they could at least all look forward to.

"The Café at the Sound...?" Stanley asked, voice filled with hope.

"Yep!"

Calum pressed down the indicator, making the turn as requested. "I could eat, but I thought we were heading to the store in Port Erin?" he asked, flicking his eyes over to the passenger seat.

Charlotte went quiet, chewing on the inside of her cheek. "If I'm honest, I'm not entirely sure there's too much point," she replied a moment or two later. "After all, we've already been to three stores, and there's not enough to even clothe one child," she said, letting out a sigh. "I suppose we could always make them a piece of toast instead...?"

"We'd need to buy a new plug first, Mum, remember?" Stan helpfully reminded her. "There was no plug on the toaster."

Calum stifled a laugh, not sure how it'd be received. "Or, take them on a detailed trip around Anglesey?" he added, once confident of the mood in the enclosed space.

The Sound Café, situated on the island's southern tip, was among Charlotte and Stanley's favourite places. The general location was ideal for sunbathing seals, and offered sublime seaside views, including the Calf of Man, a small island half a mile offshore, and visitors often described the spot as one of the finest coastal vistas you'd be fortunate to come across both locally and in the UK, such was its natural beauty.

Sitting on a wooden bench after they'd all had their lunch, Charlotte watched on as Stanley ran across the wild hillside, hoping to secure an improved view of the rocks below and the possibility of a seal or two. "Stan, please be careful over there!" she called out, even though her words might well be carried away on the firm breeze before they could even reach him. To Calum's amusement, Charlotte squirmed in her seat, half raising her hand like a pupil asking the teacher a question, hoping and failing to attract the young fella's attention.

"Relax, Lotti," Calum said, taking her tensed arm and gently returning it to a resting position. "He knows to be careful, and we both know he's a sensible lad. Besides, when my lunch has settled and I've loosened my belt a little, I'll be running straight after him."

Charlotte nuzzled into Calum's shoulder, wriggling her head until she found the optimum position. "This is just perfect," she declared.

"It is pretty special. Although..."

"Although?"

"I'm just trying to figure out if you're cuddling into me or using me as a windbreak?" Calum wondered aloud.

"A bit of both, I expect," Charlotte happily admitted, sounding completely content, just like a purring cat warming itself in front of an open fire. She issued a nervous laugh, though, watching as Stanley decided a handstand was a great idea.

"Oooh," Calum offered, also watching as Stanley's arms began shaking under strain, his legs flailing above him. "Go on, Stanley!" he called over, clapping his gloved hands together, seconds before the young lad's arms gave up the fight and he collapsed into a crumpled heap.

"Stan, are you—?" Charlotte asked, but the raised thumb and sound of giggles told her all she needed to know, confirming that nothing was broken. "He's always adored coming down here," Charlotte said, turning her attention back to Calum.

"For the stunning views, or for the delectable offerings at the café?"

"Both," Charlotte answered, wiping free a wind-induced tear as she spoke. "Although we'd often just bring a picnic for ourselves. A flask of tea, a packet of sarnies, and a biscuit or two.

Nothing fancy, you know? And we could spend hours down here, exploring the coastline or even looking out to sea for pirates through our binoculars."

"I guess you never found any?" Calum asked. "Because, if you did, I'm sure I'd have read about such a discovery in the newspaper, yes?"

"I think we must have scared them all off," Charlotte replied, giving Calum a friendly nudge. "You know, when his dad and I separated, there really wasn't too much spare cash around for the little things like trips to the café and such. But he never moaned. Not once that I recall. In fact, he'd sit outside, right here on the grass, munching on his sandwiches and feeling sorry for those poor fools stuck inside their nice, safe, warm café, missing out on all the grand adventure."

"You've raised a lovely lad, Lotti. And, because it's not always expected, that's probably why he appreciates it so much when you *do* treat him to something nice."

"Yeah, he's a little cracker, isn't he?" Charlotte said, moving her face away from the shelter that was Calum.

"Where are you going?" Calum asked.

"Me?" Charlotte said, jumping to her feet. "I'm going to show Stanley how to do a proper handstand! You coming?"

"*Pfft,*" Calum scoffed, removing his gloves, stretching out his arms above his head. "You're talking to a primary school gymnastics champion, I'll have you know. In other words, of course I'm coming!"

CHAPTER TEN

And that's two pounds change, Mrs Acaster," Mollie said, taking the coins from her till. "Would you like a hand carrying your veg box?"

Mrs Acaster took a firm hold on her purchase, offering the delightful produce inside an admiring glance. "No thank you, Moll," she said. "I've managed to park just outside the front door, so I think I'll be fine, but I do appreciate the offer."

"At least let me get that door for you," Mollie said, zipping out from behind the counter. "And, I hope your husband's operation goes well, Mrs Acaster," Mollie added, reaching for the door handle. "If there's any reason that you're struggling to get out of the house, you just phone me, and I'll drop off whatever you need on my way home, all right?"

"Thank you, Moll. That's exceptionally kind of you."

Mollie hovered in the farm shop doorway, giving the impression she was inspecting the doorframe or something or other when in truth she was simply making sure Mrs Acaster succeeded in packing away her shopping outside, what with the old girl being a little unsteady on her feet at times. "See you soon, Mrs Acaster!" Mollie offered with a wave, once the car boot was closed over and Mrs Acaster was safe to be on her way. Then, with a contented smile, Mollie went back inside to attend to the massive stack of Halloween turnips that'd been dropped off earlier that morning.

"You're an old softie at heart, Moll," Charlotte remarked, with a cup of tea in each hand that she'd just fetched from the kitchen area.

Mollie balled her hand into a fist, shaking it for Charlotte's benefit. "Don't you be telling anybody about that, because I've got my bad girl reputation to protect!"

Charlotte handed over one of the cups, setting it down in front of her friend. "I'm serious, Moll. I heard what you were saying, and I don't mind admitting I was earwigging into your conversation."

"Nosey so and so."

Charlotte skirted straight around Mollie's response, looking her friend squarely in the eye. "You're very good at what you do, you know? A real asset to this place," she told her.

Mollie, embarrassed by such overt praise, let out a shrug. "I suppose it helps when you enjoy what you do," she offered. "Anyway, are you buttering me up for something?" she said, eyeing Charlotte suspiciously. "First, you tell me you've brought me along a slice of my favourite chocolate cake, which I'm certainly not complaining about, mind you. But *then*, you're telling me about how bloody brilliant I am as well. What is it you're after?"

"How very dare you, Moll," Charlotte replied, placing a hand on her hip, head cocked defiantly. "Do I need an excuse to come along and tell my best friend just how wonderful she is? No, I should think not."

"Fair enough," Mollie said with a laugh, reaching for her cuppa. "Although you know I would do anything for a slice of chocolate cake."

"Ha! You should pop that little statement onto your Tinder profile, Moll," Charlotte advised with a chuckle. "I'm sure you'll be inundated with dating requests from the baking community in no time at all."

"Feh! I've no time for men in my life," Mollie insisted. "Now how about we dish out that chocolate cake you promised me you've brought. Is there any particular reason you're taking so long to serve it...?"

Charlotte removed the plastic food container from her handbag, whipping off the lid and presenting the contents for Mollie's inspection. "I've brought you two bits, Moll. One for now and the other for afternoon tea," she said. "And I reckon it's a good thing I did, as I think you're going to need to build your strength back up after unpacking that lot," she remarked, surveying the boxes of turnips stacked one on top of the other.

Mollie rested her cup back down on its coaster, extracting the slightly smaller of the two pieces of cake, nibbling on it daintily, savouring every morsel. "You know," she said, between nibbles, "I was actually thinking about you this morning, Lotti. And ten minutes later, here you are."

"Oh? We must have that ESP thing going on," Charlotte suggested, wiggling her fingers mysteriously.

"Yeah, I was reflecting on what you were telling me over the phone last night," Mollie told her.

"Which bit, precisely?" Charlotte asked, her psychic abilities apparently failing her already. "Only we were putting the world to rights for over an hour, so..."

Mollie had given up on the ladylike nibbling approach, wolfing down the remaining portion of her cake in one go. "Ermph!" she offered, cheeks full like a squirrel's mouth stuffed with acorns, and holding up her index finger as a placeholder for when she could speak again. Several contented whimpers later, Mollie wiped the excess from around her chops with her tongue. "I was referring to the section of the conversation where you were giving up on this school uniform initiative," she said.

"I didn't exactly say I was giving up on it, Moll," Charlotte protested. "I just said I was reviewing my options, or words to that effect. I don't mind admitting when I'm wrong."

Mollie cleared her throat, a crooked smile across her face. "Rubbish!" she spat out, cleverly disguising the word as a cough.

"Okay, fine. Maybe I *did* say I was giving up on it," an amused Charlotte was forced to concede. "I don't particularly like being wrong, Moll, but the woeful amount of donations are maybe telling me all I need to know, and that the general idea wasn't perhaps one of my better ones, you know?"

Charlotte reached for her tea and took a sip, patiently waiting for her best mate to caress her bruised ego, assuring her she'd done all she could and to just chalk the whole thing up to experience and move on.

"Bollocks," Mollie declared, after due consideration.

"Bollocks...?" Charlotte answered, a little louder than she'd intended. "Bollocks?" she said again, but this time whispering it in consideration of the couple who'd just entered the shop. "That's a bit harsh, isn't it?" she asked Mollie, pushing out her lower lip.

Mollie curled up the corner of her mouth again to show Charlotte she wasn't being overly serious. "Lotti, ReCyCool is an absolutely fabulous initiative. We both know that."

"But I already told you about the one duffle coat and the broken toaster," Charlotte pointed out. "Not exactly what you'd call the hallmarks of a roaring success, now is it?"

With her cake now polished off and hands thus free, Mollie folded her arms across her chest, gently shaking her head. "Remind me how you've advertised it?" she asked, in a tone suggesting she knew the answer already.

Charlotte looked up and to the left, humming to herself as she thought about her response, wondering if this was a trick question she was answering. "Well..." she said, before giving it another few seconds worth of thought, "I've posted about it on Facebook...?"

Mollie raised her eyebrows in a *keep-it-coming* sort of way. "And...?"

"Well, I've been in and spoken to the school. And I've told loads of people."

"And...?"

"And... well, I suppose that's it."

"That's my point, Lotti. One post on Facebook does not equate to a detailed marketing plan," Mollie said, unfolding her arms. "Lotti, I'm not being negative about this. Just the opposite, in fact. But how many people are really going to read one social media post? And as for the recycling bins... brilliant! But, if people don't properly know what they're for, can you really be surprised to find a toaster inside?"

"I suppose," Charlotte said, supposing. "Though it wasn't just a simple toaster, yeah?" she reminded her friend. "Rather, it was a *broken* toaster."

"Okay, let's look at the positives? You've got Shoprite and some of the schools on board with the idea, but in the nicest possible way, are they also spreading the word for you? They might well be, but get on the phone and ask," Mollie said, hoping to rouse her friend. "Lotti, if I thought your idea was silly, I'd tell you in an instant. That's what best mates do. Like the time you dyed your hair pink. Remember?"

"I was going for the cute, punky effect but ended up looking like Frenchy from Grease. And I had to attend a job interview looking like a bag of cotton candy," Charlotte replied, recalling that rather embarrassing affair. "Remind me to listen to you next time."

"I must dig out the photographs of that sorry catastrophe of a hairdo," Mollie said, taking a mental note to do precisely that. "I'm sure Stanley would be delighted to see it," she added with a grin. "Anyway, we digress, Lotti. So, in summary, it's a bloody terrific idea, and what you've done so far is impressive. We just need to knock it up a gear or two, raise the profile and get the word out to the great Manx public."

Charlotte pressed her shoulders back, lifting her chin. She liked what she was hearing. "Yes, we do, Moll!"

"So...?" Mollie asked, swirling her hand in the air, eager to hear what Charlotte's initial ideas were.

"Oh. You're waiting for *me* to speak, then?" Charlotte asked. "I thought perhaps you had some pearls of wisdom to share, and I didn't want to interrupt."

"I didn't really have anything, to be honest. But you need a gimmick of some sort, Lotti, that I know. Something to capture people's attention and make them stand up and take notice."

"I could dye my hair pink again?" Charlotte proposed, but not seriously, really.

"Oh, you should. Imagine the look on young Stan's face when you turn up at school to pick him up looking like a flamingo,"

Mollie replied, playfully rolling her eyes. "Anyway, get your thinking cap on, Lotti, and I'll do the same. For now, though, I need to crack on, as those turnips are sadly not going to unpack themselves."

Charlotte drained the contents of her teacup. "Yes, I need to get going as well, as I've got a Make It Sew class with our friends at the Appledene care home," she explained, glancing down at her watch. "But after that," she promised, tapping the top of her head, "my thinking cap is going straight on."

"You're going to see Surfboard Sam?" Mollie enquired.

"Well, I'm going to see the nursing home residents," Charlotte answered. "But I should think Sam will definitely be in attendance, yeah. What with him being the manager and all."

"Oh," Mollie said with a shrug, playing it cool, as if she hardly cared one way or the other. "Does he ever ask about—"

"*Mollie and Sam, sitting in a tree!*" Charlotte replied with a giggle, singing the words. "*K-I-S-S-I-N-G!*"

Mollie shook her head slowly. "I was only asking."

"You're blushing," Charlotte was happy to point out. "What happened to 'I've no time for men in my life'?"

"Get outta here before I throw a turnip at you."

"So, on the basis that you're like a giggly schoolgirl around him, do you want me to have a word with Sam on your behalf?"

Mollie waved away the offer, appearing absolutely horrified by the suggestion, but then, in contradiction to her facial expression, blurted out, "Yes, Charlotte. Yes, I absolutely do."

Several miles further up the road and Charlotte was still smiling happily away to herself, picturing Mollie blushing over a fella. It brought her back to their school days when, if you were keen on somebody, you'd dispatch your mate to make the initial enquiries on your behalf in order to ask the boy if they fancied a snog.

Sam, or "Surfboard Sam" as Mollie had affectionately christened him, was a blond, floppy-haired chap who wouldn't look out of place smoking funny cigarettes and playing the guitar around a campfire at the beach rather than being the nursing home manager that he was. The girls first met Sam during the recruitment drive for the Square If You Care initiative. With his positive, can-do approach and extensive contacts throughout the island's nursing homes, he'd also proved to be an invaluable contact for Charlotte in her efforts to roll out the Make It Sew classes. Moreover, Sam was somebody whose advice she greatly valued and respected. As such, in a relatively short period of time, he'd become something of a firm friend. And something else that was firm about Sam, at least according to Mollie, was his adorably cute derrière.

Turning off the main road and onto the winding driveway, Charlotte caught a glimpse of the familiar stone turret she so adored through a break in the dense tree cover. And even though she was now a regular visitor to Appledene, her mind still wandered away each time she saw this, full of thoughts of being a fairy princess locked in the tower waiting patiently for Prince Charming to come galloping through the countryside astride a magnificent stallion ready to launch a daring rescue.

Snapping herself out of her joyous daydream, Charlotte then parked up, after which she loaded herself with holiday-themed crafting supplies like a packhorse.

"What on earth are you like?" Sam shouted across the forecourt from where he'd noticed her arrival. Then, once at the foot of the concrete stairs, he quickened his pace. Well, as quick as one could when wearing flip-flops. "Let me help you with those bags," he insisted, rubber soles uneasy on the stone chippings underfoot.

"You do realise it's November?" Charlotte asked, casting her eyes over Sam's sockless feet and denim shorts.

Sam relieved Charlotte of one of the larger bags she was carrying, slinging it over his shoulder. "We've been shifting boxes around all morning, and while it may be freezing outside, it's nice and toasty inside, so perfect conditions for these," he explained, slapping one of his denim-clad hips.

Charlotte chuckled to herself as Sam led the way back inside, picturing Mollie's face looking at where her own eyes were presently drawn to, Sam's pert bum cheeks swinging this way and that with each stride.

"I hope you're not laughing at my shorts?" Sam asked over his shoulder. "Because they're all your fault," he insisted. "I was inspired by your crafting class, so I upcycled these myself from an old denim jacket."

"Of course not, Sam. In fact, I was just admiring the fabulous stitching. So, well done, you," Charlotte told him. "Anyway, what boxes have you been shifting around?" she asked, moving the conversation along.

"It's a surprise," Sam cryptically replied, the rubber soles of his flip-flops scrunching with every step, making it sound like he was walking through a fresh layer of snow. "But suffice to say, some of the staff and residents have been particularly industrious this morning, and I'm sure you'll approve."

An intrigued Charlotte followed close behind, wondering what they'd all been up to, looking around for clues. But she needn't have been so impatient as the answer presented itself the moment they stepped through the oaken front doors. "Oh, Sam!" Charlotte exclaimed, laying down the bags she'd been carrying and then twirling herself around to survey the scene, the reflection of fairy lights sparkling in her eyes. "This is like a winter wonderland," she marvelled.

The staff and residents at the nursing home had evidently been busy. The grand entrance foyer, which served as the reception area, was festooned with tinsel, draped from all four corners, meeting at a twinkling, illuminated star dangling down from the centre of the ceiling. In the corner by the staircase, next to the tastefully decorated Christmas tree, an oversized polar bear wearing a Santa hat gyrated hypnotically in time to the seasonal classics being played over the sound system. And in every direction, the dark oakwood panelling was framed by what appeared to be an endless supply of sparkling lights.

"And just look at the windows!" Charlotte said, while doing precisely that. "It's like something straight out of a scene from A Christmas Carol," she remarked, admiring the snow spray that had been carefully applied to the corners of each window-pane, giving them a certain auld-worlde charm.

"You like?" Sam asked, fully suspecting he already knew the answer.

"Oh yes, Sam, I absolutely adore it. When I was a young girl, I had a yuletide jigsaw, and the image on the box looked exactly like all of *this*," she explained, running her hand through the air, smiling nostalgically. "The decorations continue throughout the building?" she asked.

"Yes, indeed," Sam answered, beaming proudly. "In fact, I'm fairly certain we drained the national grid when we switched the lights on earlier!"

Charlotte cast Sam a quizzical eye. "Not that I'm complaining, you understand..."

"But?"

"But it's like the first week in November, Sam. Aren't we a touch, I don't know... premature?" Charlotte asked.

Sam raised an eyebrow. "You think?" he asked, breaking into a gentle laugh. "Though it's your fault we've all been so eager," he insisted.

"It is?"

"Of course. The guys and gals in your Make It Sew class got wind of your Christmas crafting menu."

"They did?" Charlotte answered with a sigh. "That was supposed to be a surprise for them," she said, though not all that upset by the discovery, really.

"Yeah, a few of them were chatting to their crafting mates at one of the other homes. Apparently, the conversation turned to what projects they were working on, and all was revealed. Then, before you know it, the residents here are digging out their garish Christmas jumpers and old Bing Crosby and Andy Williams albums and so forth. And it was good old Henry and Sid who presented the case for putting the deccies up early, even if it is only November. Of course the tree is artificial, for now, but only because nobody has a real one available just yet."

"And you didn't mind putting them up this early?"

"Me? No, not at all," Sam said, using his foot to adjust the stuffed reindeer that'd fallen against the nativity scene, perhaps as a result of good old Blitzen getting blitzed on one eggnog too many. "The way I look at it is that this is their house, yeah?" Sam explained. "So if the residents want the decorations up at the beginning of November, then who am I to argue?"

"Fair enough," Charlotte answered, nodding. "Oh, Sam. You really *are* a thoughtful chap, you know that?" she told him, giving him the same sort of fond glance you'd offer an adorable little puppy.

Sam escorted Charlotte through the maze of corridors leading to the dining room, where she was delighted to see the Christmas theme continued. However, it wasn't the general decorations, lovely as they were, that initially caught her eye, but rather the fact that more than a few of the Make It Sew members had indeed entered into the spirit of things, dressing up in their finest Christmas costumes. Charlotte placed her bags down, looking around the dining room table where the group members waited patiently for the class to begin. "Oh, yes!" she said, looking over to a grinning Sam, and then back again. "You all look magnificent. Just splendid!"

"They're our Christmas panto costumes from last year," Henry was pleased to report, giving the bell on the end of his green-and-red elf hat a gentle ding, producing a giggle from his neighbours in the process. "Sid and I went dressed as elves," he explained, pointing to his mate sitting next to him, though it was unlikely that Charlotte required any further clarification on this point, what with them both sitting there looking like elves.

Sid pushed his chair back. "Check out my feet," he said, throwing them up onto the tabletop, revealing his green velvet shoes, each sporting an impressive, curly tip.

"They're a thing of beauty," Charlotte suggested, clapping her hands in delight.

And the two elves were clearly in esteemed company, with the main man, Santa himself, sitting across the table from them, gently caressing the white cloud that was his beard. Keeping Mr Claus company, sitting either side, were Rita and Eileen, looking perfectly resplendent dressed in their lovely Christmas pudding costumes.

Charlotte continued with her clapping, unable to contain the smile engulfing her face. "Oh, you lot are just the best," she said, wiping away a happy tear from her cheek. "I was just about to unveil my new mystery crafting programme, but I can plainly see that *that* particular cat is well and truly out of the bag," she told them, giving them a playful wink. "Right, then! Why don't we see what goodies we want to make, yes?"

The Appledene club members flicked through Charlotte's printed patterns, carefully considering the various benefits of each before settling on the designs that tickled their individual fancy. Some of the group were keen to craft items that could be sold to raise money for the ReCyCool project. Others, however, had their hearts set on making something they could gift to loved ones, such as grandchildren, for example. A brilliant idea either way, as far as Charlotte was concerned.

Before too long, knitting needles, crochet hooks, and scissors moved just as quickly as the crafters' lips, who loved nothing more than a good natter in pleasant company.

Charlotte circled the large table, offering an experienced hand, words of advice, or even a second opinion on which colour felt went best with which if required. She was over the moon with the enthusiasm and productivity on display. The only exception to this appeared to be Rita and Eileen, sitting there in their wonderful costumes, but arms planted firmly by their sides and faces tripping them.

"Everything okay, ladies?" Charlotte enquired, kneeling in between the two of them. "If you need any help, you know I'm delighted to assist?"

Rita removed a cream-coloured cap (which represented the fresh cream in her costume) from the top of her head to fan her rosy cheeks. "It's no good, Lotti," she said wearily.

"You don't know what project you want to do?" Charlotte asked, primed and ready to talk through the various options.

"No, it's not that. It's these soddin' costumes," Rita explained, expelling a firm burst of air in frustration. "It's bloody roasting in here."

Eileen nodded, the bead of sweat running down the side of her face confirming that fact. "And more importantly, we can't even reach our knitting needles," she advised, illustrating this very point by attempting to manoeuvre her arms around the rotund belly of her Christmas pudding costume, and failing miserably. "See what I mean?" she said with a sigh. "I can't even reach the bloody table."

"Uhm..." Charlotte replied with a wry smile. "Perhaps it might be an idea to take the costumes off?"

"Oh, we can't do that," Rita shot back. "You see, we're both like proud kilt-wearing Scotsmen under here, if you take my meaning?"

"*Au naturel*," Eileen added by way of further clarification, tapping the side of her nose, which her arm was only just able to accomplish.

"I see," Charlotte replied with a giggle. "Well, perhaps a strategic recess, ladies? Maybe change into something a bit more comfortable?"

Rita replaced the splodge of cream atop her head, looking over to Eileen. "Right. Come on, Eileen," she said, struggling to get to her feet and remain upright in her tipsy, too-large-around-the-middle outfit. "I'm getting all steamed up in this thing."

"You sure you want to change?" Eileen asked. "The loss of fluid might help us squeeze into our Christmas party frocks, wouldn't it?"

"That's a good point," Rita responded, though it looked like the two of them were both intent on a change of outfit anyway.

Charlotte pushed herself up, stepping aside to allow sufficient room for the pair of overly rotund ladies to pass.

"Surely you've not scared them off already, Lotti?" Sam joked as he wandered over, watching the two costumed ladies waddling towards the exit.

"I'm just hoping the pair of them don't try and walk through the doorframe at the same time and get themselves jammed," Charlotte remarked, casting a concerned eye in their direction. "But no, they're just off for a costume change as our two resident Christmas puddings are in danger of being overcooked."

"Well, I can confirm the refreshments are here, and not at *all* overcooked, I don't think," Sam was happy to advise, giving the biscuit tin in his hand a jiggle. "Christmas cookies, baked fresh today, by yours truly," he said, whipping the lid off so Charlotte could have a gander inside. "Oh, and..."

"There's more?"

"Yep. Well, not food-related, no. But as I was cutting out my Christmas-tree cookies earlier, I was thinking about your text message."

"Ah. Which one?"

"The one about your recycling campaign," Sam told her. "You mentioned a 'catchy gimmick to turn around the lacklustre response,' to use your exact words."

"Ooh," Charlotte said, delving her hand inside the biscuit tin.

Sam tilted his head like a curious canine. "Hang on, are you oohing about my biscuits, or about what I was just talking about?"

"Bowf," Charlotte mumbled, half a Christmas-tree cookie now in her gob.

"Well..." Sam answered, pausing dramatically, building up to his big reveal.

"Weww?"

"Well what about a fashion show...?" Sam put forth.

"A fashun schhhow?" Charlotte replied, spilling crumbs from the corner of her mouth.

Sam smiled in response to the unladylike table manners on display. "Yeah, a huge fashion show," he said. "But the kicker is that all the modelled garments are made from recycled clothes, like my impressive shorts. So it fits in with what you're trying to promote, and will hopefully generate some publicity." Sam then raised a finger in another eureka moment. "What about..."

"Uh-huh?"

"Getting some of *this* lot involved," Sam suggested, running his hand in the direction of the seated crafters. "Can you imagine that motley crew strutting their stuff down the catwalk?"

"Oh, Sam," a now empty-mouthed Charlotte said, smiling a crumb-specked smile. "Yes, that idea has potential," she agreed, looking over to her unsuspecting marks, all happily crafting away and unaware they were presently being talked about. "You know, Sam..." Charlotte remarked, looking him up and down.

"Yes?"

"Well, you're athletic, can make your own clothes, bake delicious biscuits, and you're never short of a wonderful idea," Charlotte continued. "It's a mystery to me why you're still single," she said. "You *are* still single, aren't you?" she asked, moving forward a step.

"Uhm... yeah?" a confused Sam said, taking a step back in response, eager to regain some of his personal space.

"You'd be a magnificent catch for any girl," Charlotte told him, coiling several strands of hair around her finger as she spoke. "And throw in your caring nature? Well, I'd say you were the absolute perfect package."

Sam's jaw fell slowly, like an opening drawbridge. "Erm... you haven't been drinking, Charlotte, have you?" he asked, taking a tentative sniff of the air in front of him, trying to detect any trace of alcohol. "Look, you're an absolutely cracking girl, Lotti," he assured her, the remnants of cookie caught between her teeth slightly distracting him. "That is, I mean... you're, you know... very pretty. And someone... surely someone—"

"Not *me*, you silly sausage," Charlotte cut across. "But you can continue telling me how pretty I am if you like...?"

"Perhaps without the biscuit caught in your teeth, Lotti?" a relieved Sam advised. "Then, you'd be a solid seven out of ten, I reckon," he suggested, though receiving a steely glare in return. Just then, a knowing expression washed over him. "Wait. By any chance, are you buttering me up on Mollie's behalf?"

Charlotte was still somewhat unhappy she'd only rated a 7 out of a possible 10, and briefly considered taking Sam to task for such a faulty and grossly mistaken appraisal. But then she relented, deciding to graciously move on. "Yes. Yes, I am," she said. "You've hit the nail on the head."

"A-ha. So is that why she keeps sending me photographs of the night-time sky?" Sam replied.

"The night-time sky? You mean stars and stuff?" Charlotte asked.

"Yeah," Sam confirmed. "Last night, for example, she sent me a picture of a full moon, without any explanation. I mean, don't get me wrong, it was a perfectly lovely photograph and all, but..."

Charlotte smiled an uneasy smile, wondering what on earth had happened to her friend's usually solid chat-up techniques. "Oh!" Charlotte said, placing a hand to her mouth, realisation suddenly dawning. "That might actually be my fault, Sam," she admitted. "You see, I told her about our conversation on astronomy, and how much you liked it and everything."

Sam laughed politely, not really getting the joke. "What are you on about, Lotti? Since when do I like astronomy?"

"Last week in the kitchen," Charlotte insisted, sounding quite confident on the matter. "Remember? You spent a good five minutes or so telling me all about astronomy and the college course you were taking on it."

"I flippin' well knew you weren't listening to me, young lady. I could tell by the way your eyes glazed over," Sam gently chided her. *"Horology,* Lotti. Not astronomy," he explained, tapping the watch on his wrist to indicate what horology was, that being the study of time, and the measuring thereof. "There's quite a difference," he said.

Charlotte started to laugh. "Oh, dear me," she said. "I can just imagine Mollie peering through her curtains, waiting for the ideal opportunity to take a picture of the moon and such."

"I did worry when she sent me a video clip the other day of what she'd described as a shooting star," Sam said, sharing in Charlotte's laugh, but in his case it was more a sense of relief that he now understood the reason for all the strange, random messages he'd been regularly receiving from Charlotte's mate.

"A shooting star's pretty cool, though, even if you're not actually into astronomy?" Charlotte put forward.

"Yeah, but it was an aeroplane, Lotti, not a shooting star," Sam felt obliged to point out. "You could clearly see the lights on the wings flashing. I just didn't have the heart to correct her, as she appeared so passionate about it."

Charlotte pursed her lips, sucking in air through her teeth. "She's going to kill me when she finds out, Sam," she said.

"About it not being a shooting star?"

"No, no, not that. I mean about the whole misunderstanding in general. The whole astronomy thing," Charlotte clarified. "In fact, it would make my life easier if you would—"

"Yes," Sam agreed, before Charlotte was able to finish.

"Yes, as in yes, you like Mollie?" a hopeful Charlotte asked. "And you'd like to go out with her because that would really help me out of that particular pickle?"

"If it means she'll stop sending me pictures of the sky, then yes," Sam was happy to grant. "Lotti...?" he said a moment later, when no response was received. "Lotti, you're doing that eyes-glazed-over thing again, and we know what happened the last time you pretended to be listening to me, right?"

"I'm sorry, Sam. Yes, hopefully no more astronomy-related messages," she answered. "And if it's any *constellation*, I was just thinking about your fashion show idea."

Sam released a pained groan. "Constellation. Yes, very good, Lotti," he said, letting out a chuckle. "So, you like the fashion show idea? I'd be happy to help."

"I do like it," Charlotte said, although sounding as if she wasn't completely set on the idea, actually. "It's just that I might make a tweak or two, if you don't mind, using some inspiration Larry provided me a few weeks back."

"Which was?" Sam asked, only slightly offended that his perfect idea wasn't vigorously jumped upon, precisely as is, without need for modification.

"Well," Charlotte said, eyes sparkling in anticipation. "If I may, I'll borrow your theme of making the final garments from recycled clothes, yes. But rather than a fashion show, I'm thinking of hosting a sewing bee."

"A sewing bee?"

"Yes," Charlotte answered. "I already have a name for it, too. I'm thinking of calling it *The Great Manx Sewing Bee*."

"Hmm," said Sam. "That's not a bad idea at all, Lotti. Not bad at all..."

CHAPTER ELEVEN

The radio alarm clock erupted into life, blaring out the familiar, dulcet tones of Ed Sheeran around the bedroom. But rather than jarring Charlotte from her lovely deep sleep, as it did most mornings, Charlotte's eyes were already wide open.

Ordinarily, she was flat out in the land of nod once her head hit the pillow, and stayed that way, but her mind had been a hive of activity throughout the night, sewing bee thoughts consuming her and making sleep elusive. She was still enthusiastic about the Great Manx Sewing Bee idea, but the physical practicalities of it were presenting some degree of trouble.

On the popular television show bearing a similar name, contestants faced different crafting challenges over several weeks, with somebody eliminated each week. For this local competition to best work, however, Charlotte would need to devise a format whereby the event started and finished on the same day, ideally, with the victor crowned by day's end. Also, it wasn't as if she had an awful lot of time to come up with a proper plan, either. It was now the first week of November, and it was her intention of organising something for the start of December. This would hopefully allow them to promote the event and sell the festive items they'd all collectively been working on, raising additional funds for the recycling initiative in the process.

In addition, with the Christmas period often a financial drain on a large number of families, Charlotte figured a major re-launch of the ReCyCool initiative would be well received in time for the first school term after the Christmas break.

A short while later...

"Morning, Mum," Stanley offered, midway through a stretchy yawn, plonking himself down at the kitchen table where his bowl of Rice Krispies waited patiently for him. "What's with all the bags?"

"*Stanley Newman*," Charlotte scolded him, lifting her head up from her porridge. "I didn't get much sleep, if you must know. And that's not the sort of question you ask a lady first thing in the morning. Or any *other* time, for that matter."

Stanley screwed up his face like he was sniffing the air. "Eh?" he said, reaching for the pint of milk.

"Oh, sorry, Stan," Charlotte quickly added, catching up with his meaning and rubbing her bloodshot eyes. "You're talking about the bags piled up near the front door?"

"Yeah, I nearly tripped over them."

"I couldn't sleep," Charlotte explained. "So rather than toss and turn, I sorted my wardrobe into three piles — wear always, wear sometimes, and haven't worn forever. The last pile is coming with me to Crafternoon today, and I'm going to try and create a new outfit from them, and... I've lost you in this conversation, Stanley, haven't I?

Stanley nodded in agreement. "A little bit, Mum. I was just wondering if that's the sort of thing all crafters do. You know, when they can't sleep? I then wondered why you didn't just count sheep like the rest of us, but I figured the sheep would be too afraid to come near you as you'd probably just grab them and turn them into a cardigan or something."

"Sorry, Stan," Charlotte said with a smirk. "You're losing *me* now."

"I guess it runs in the family," Stanley suggested, returning his attention to his brekkie.

One of the many benefits of being at the helm of her modest crafting empire was that Charlotte didn't need to be sitting behind an office desk at 9 a.m. each day. Weather permitting, this, among other things, afforded her the luxury of walking her son to school each day. Yes, Stanley would occasionally grumble on the mornings he could see his own breath, but without any other distractions of modern life, it was the time of day when they did most of their talking. She'd long since given up on holding his hand as this was now officially uncool, but for Charlotte (and she hoped, Stanley, too), this was a precious time that she relished. It wouldn't be too long before he was off to high school and shaving, and so, for now, Charlotte wanted to keep hold of her little boy for as long as possible. Even if that did involve her listening to a blow-by-blow account of what activity Stanley's favourite YouTuber was presently engaged in, as was the case today.

"Here we are, buster chops. Another day, another dollar," Charlotte announced, a short while later, as they approached the school playground. Charlotte leaned forward, presenting her right cheek for Stanley's consideration. "Before you go…" she said, tapping her index finger on the area of her face where she expected his lips to be placed.

Stanley, for his part, flicked his eyes over to the business end of the playground, where his mates looked too busy kicking a ball to notice him kissing his mum goodbye. "Love you, Mum," Stanley said, giving his mum's cheek a quick smooch that felt, to Charlotte, like a pet fish briefly skimming the surface of the water for fish flakes before plunging straight back down into the depths of the tank. And with that, he was away for a few minutes of footie before the school bell rang.

Charlotte waved to nobody in particular, as her son, by this time, had already scampered off. "Okay… bye, Stanley," she said, what little moisture there was from his perfunctory peck already evaporating on her cheek before the boy had even swung his right foot towards the football. Charlotte released a sigh and a gentle shake of her head, remembering the times that Stanley clung to her like a limpet, demanding she stay by his side until the moment the teacher escorted the class inside. "Ah well," she said to herself, turning to enjoy the brisk walk home.

Then, however, Charlotte caught a glimpse of Amelia in the opposite corner of the playground, holding court with her band of impeccably made-up cronies who appeared to be hanging on her every word, as per usual. Ordinarily, Charlotte would have simply continued walking, making good her escape without giving it another thought. But since they were very nearly related owing to their shared relationship with Calum, and were also now on speaking terms, Charlotte was concerned Amelia would see her sloping off and take it as a personal slight. So, for that reason, Charlotte reluctantly trekked across the playground, grinning in advance of her arrival, preparing herself to suffer whatever witty anecdote it was that Amelia appeared midway through delivering right at present.

Not wanting to interrupt, Charlotte politely hovered on the periphery of the group, smiling like she was privy to the conversation, which, of course, she wasn't.

"... And Tilly was laughing that much that she snorted champagne all over the *maître d'*, if you can just *imagine* it," Amelia concluded, prompting the others to erupt into a jolly fit of the giggles.

Charlotte offered a little laugh, not wanting to feel left out, followed by a contented-sounding sigh as if she were recalling the hilarious memory herself.

"Oh, hello there, Charlotte," Amelia said, catching sight of Charlotte from out of the corner of her eye. "We were just talking about last year's Yummy Mummies Christmas lunch," she explained, setting off another round of laughter at the mere mention of it. "Anyway, enough about us," Amelia said, politely enough, and looking at Charlotte in a *how-exactly-can-I-help-you?* sort of way.

After a long pause, and with several pairs of eyes now trained on her, Charlotte shifted her weight between her feet uneasily, unsure what to say. After all, she'd only popped over in the first place to be polite. "I, uhm, that is..." Charlotte muttered, hoping the school bell would ring at that precise moment.

"Cat got your tongue, Charlotte?" Amelia asked, followed by a snorty sort of laugh. "Don't be shy, Lotti, you're among friends."

"I was, erm..." Charlotte replied, scratching the side of her head, her mind agonisingly blank and nothing of interest to say presenting itself.

"I know what's going on here," Amelia confidently declared to the group as a whole, and then giving Charlotte a wink. "You don't need to be all sheepish around us, Charlotte, and of *course* you can."

"Can?" Charlotte asked with a nervous grin. "Can what?"

"Join us on this year's Yummy Mummies Christmas lunch, of course," Amelia replied. "What are you like, Charlotte? Creeping up on us to secure an invite like that?"

Charlotte literally couldn't think of anything worse than spending an afternoon in the company of the Yummy Mummies, but her brain was seriously letting her down right now in thinking up some kind of excuse to avoid attending. "Ah. I'll look forward to it," she answered, lying her arse off. And then, twenty seconds too late, an actual helpful thought presented itself, though it likely wouldn't be of any use in helping her get out of the lunch date she'd just made. "I did mean to speak to you about something else, Amelia, now I think on it," she said. "But you're busy, so maybe—"

"I was actually just leaving, so you can escort me to my car?" Amelia suggested, while offering the other Yummies a fingertip wave goodbye. "Let's walk and talk," she told Charlotte.

Amelia scooped up Charlotte's arm, linking in like they were the very best of friends. "So..." Amelia began, as they started to walk along, but the ringing school bell cut her off mid-flow. "As I was saying before I was so rudely interrupted," she joked a moment later. "So what's on your mind? You're not going to ask me for my brother's hand in marriage, are you?"

Charlotte looked across to Amelia to gauge how serious she was being. "Ehm, no. No, I wanted to speak to you about a crafting competition I'm planning."

"Oh, silly me. There was me almost buying a new wedding hat as well," Amelia said. And then, "I'm just pulling your leg,

Charlotte. Anyway, a crafting competition? Sounds good. Call me intrigued."

During the short walk to the school car park, Charlotte outlined the rough draft of her plan for the sewing bee crafting competition. Unfortunately, she'd not had time to formulate all of the finer details, but what she was saying to Amelia did appear to be falling on interested ears.

"So it's to raise the profile of your recycling project, then, and hopefully generate funds in the process?" Amelia asked.

"Exactly," Charlotte was happy to confirm. "I reckoned on extending an invite to all the island's various crafting clubs to enter teams into the competition. Originally, I was considering calling it either *The Great Isle of Man Sewing Bee* or *The Great Manx Sewing Bee*. But as it will likely happen in December, perhaps we could call it *The Isle of Man Christmas Sewing Bee*, with fairy lights, tinsel, and costumes? It'll be magical."

"And the winning team takes home the ultimate crafting bragging rights?" Amelia asked, receiving a nod in the affirmative from Charlotte in return. "Charlotte," Amelia said, once they were standing next to her car. "Charlotte, I think it's a perfectly lovely idea."

"I was absolutely going to extend an invite to you and your Laxey Coffee Morning Crew, Amelia. That is, if you think your members would be interested in putting a team forward?"

"Interested?" Amelia scoffed. "If there's the chance of being crowned the supreme island crafters, then yes, I'm more than certain we'll be submitting a team. Maybe even several."

Charlotte was delighted, pleased that her idea appeared to receive such a warm reception. "You'll be a part of the team? I'm thinking maybe three or four people in each."

Amelia shook her head in the negative. "Oh no, Charlotte. I want us to win this competition, so we'll need to get our craftiest of crafters signed up. So, I'll perhaps nominate myself as the team manager instead," she said, reaching inside her handbag for her keys. "Have you sorted a venue?" she asked. "This event could be huge, so you'll need somewhere with ample space."

"No, not so much," Charlotte said with a shrug. "I was thinking about phoning a few of the nicer places to see how much they'd cost."

"Sponsorship, Charlotte," Amelia immediately put forth. "The local corporates will be eager to put their hands in their pockets for a worthwhile endeavour like this, I should think. If you need any help in that regard, just shout."

"I will. Thank you, Amelia."

Amelia went quiet for a moment, mulling over the details of what Charlotte had just relayed to her. "December, you say?" she asked. "That could be a dilly of a pickle, Charlotte."

"It could?"

"Sure, December is Christmas party season, Charlotte. The more desirable venues are booked well in advance. That's why the Yummy Mummies booked their lunch months ago."

Charlotte's shoulders dropped. "Oh, bother. I never thought of that."

"Anyway," Amelia said, opening her car door and climbing into the driver's seat. "Anyway, if it's any consolation, it won't be a problem."

"About the venue?" Charlotte asked, eyes filled with hope.

Amelia waved away the question. "No, silly, not that," she said, though not in an unkind way. "I mean about our Yummy Mummies Christmas lunch. I'm friends with the restaurant manager, so asking him to add an extra chair to our table won't be a problem."

Charlotte forced a smile that must have looked like she had a bout of wind. "Oh," she said. "That's marvellous news, Amelia. I'll look forward to it."

"Splendid," Amelia said, starting up her car. "Right, then. Toodle-pip, Charlotte."

CHAPTER TWELVE

Charlotte knew all too well just how competitive those in the Isle of Man crafting scene were. It was something she'd witnessed firsthand during the Square If You Care initiative earlier in the year. Therefore, it should have come as no surprise, then, that each crafting club/coffee morning group she contacted were desperate to sign on the dotted line, the allure, it would appear, of proving their credentials as the finest crafters on their fair isle impossible to resist. Indeed, many of those she'd spoken to that morning weren't just concerned with the where and when but more with who *else* had also signed up, owing to some previous, unsettled beef or other. Charlotte discovered, for instance, that several members of the group called Stitch 'n' Bitch were embroiled in something of a turf war with another craft club called the Knitty Noras. But she didn't delve too deep into that ongoing skirmish for fear of being somehow implicated.

You couldn't make this stuff up, Charlotte thought. And with the salty language heard on several of these calls, she could easily be forgiven for thinking she was dealing with rival hairy-arsed biker gangs rather than a collection of local crafting clubs. Unfortunately, there was no provision for security guards in Charlotte's event budget, but she was starting to think it might be a prerequisite based on the tenor of some of the conversations she was having. Anyway, with these calls now out of the way, she was now engaged in another matter...

"Yes, that's correct," Charlotte said into her phone. "Either Saturday the second of December or the following week," she confirmed, pacing around the Union Mills church hall as she spoke. Charlotte waited for a few seconds for a response, but what she received was not of the sort she'd hoped for. "Excuse me. Are you *laughing* at me?" she said, placing a firm hand on her hip, even though the person on the other end obviously wouldn't be able to see her defiant posture. "Yes, I *know* it's the run-up to Christmas," she said, raising her voice. "We chose those particular dates so we can sell our *festive goodies,*" she explained. "So that's a no, then, is it?"

Stanley, who'd been earwigging while he placed out chairs for the start of the day's Crafternoon Sewcial Club session, pulled a pained expression once his mum put down her phone. "No dice?" he asked, being the perceptive young chap that he was.

This managed to raise a smile from Charlotte, despite the unproductive nature of this last call she'd made. "No dice?" she replied, repeating her son's words back to him. "Where on earth did you—" she began to say. "Wait, have you been watching those dodgy old American gangster films at your dad's again?"

"I ain't no snitch, lady. You'll never take me alive," Stanley responded, before closing an imaginary zipper over his mouth.

"I'll be having words with Don Corleone the next time I see him," Charlotte told him, removing her angry hand from her hip. "And, yes. Sadly... no dice."

Stanley wandered over to his mum with his cleaning cloth draped over his shoulder. He didn't bother to tell her she was mixing up gangster films with mafia Godfather films, as now wasn't really the best time. "Something will turn up," he said, like a bartender cheering up a down-on-their-luck punter. "Anything I can do to help?" he asked, wiping down a nearby tabletop.

Charlotte appreciated the supportive gesture, moving in and placing her arms around him. "How about you just give your old mum a hug, Stanley?" she suggested, temporarily holding him captive. "Because that always makes everything better in an instant."

"Sure thing, dollface," Stanley said in an exceptionally questionable American accent, and with one eye on his watch.

"Somewhere to be?" Charlotte asked, giving him a squeeze.

"I just didn't want to be late meeting Beryl and Joyce's bus, so I can carry their bags in," Stanley explained, his face pressed into his mum's armpit.

Charlotte planted a kiss on top of his head. "How did I end up with such a wonderful, thoughtful son?"

"Dunno? Luck, I guess?"

With hugs thus administered, Charlotte glanced about. For her, there was something immensely comforting about standing inside the empty church hall a few minutes before the start of the Crafternoon Sewcial Club. Looking around at the vacant congregational seats, bathed in a wash of vibrant colour thanks to the stained-glass windows, it was a welcome moment of tranquillity before the inevitable chaos ensued. But it was this chaos that so warmed Charlotte's heart.

In the relative quiet, she'd be able to hear the sound of the approaching bus and then, distant at first, the giddy chatter, laughter, and occasionally singing, as the gang made their way up the road. Then, finally, the metal gate at the end of the path creaked open, and individual voices were now recognisable. About this time, she would often hear vehicles arriving into the car park at the rear of the building as well, along with, perhaps, the gurgling hot water urn in the kitchen reaching temperature, readying itself for the tea that was soon to please the palates of the arriving mob.

Today was no different, and Stanley, as usual, was first to reappear into view after a purposeful trip outside, loaded up with multiple items, arms fully occupied, like an airport baggage handler. "They're here, Mum!" he announced brightly, though owing to the racket radiating from the foyer directly behind him this was a fact Charlotte was no doubt already acutely aware of.

"Welcome back, guys!" Charlotte called out, walking towards the door with a grin stretched from ear to ear, eager to find out what projects everybody had been working on. "Come on in and get settled," she offered, helping some of the new arrivals out of their coats.

Then, after allowing ample time for everyone to arrive and filter in, Charlotte excitedly called the meeting to order. "It's Thursday. It's four o'clock in the afternoon!" she announced to the merry horde. "Which means it's...?" she prompted, cupping her hand around her ear.

"Crafternoon Sewcial Club!" the gang shouted back, right on cue, raising an enthusiastic cheer.

And so, with the day's club meeting begun, Charlotte was thrilled to see their numbers had swelled once again, with young Stanley having to unload the contents of the store cupboard for additional seating to welcome them all. On each of the tables, Charlotte had laid out a leaflet she'd painstakingly designed to promote the Sewing Bee event, hoping to garner some interest from the members. Although Charlotte remained without a confirmed venue at present, she had at least settled on a format for the event after some considerable deliberation previously. Teams would consist of a maximum of four crafters. Each group would then compete against the other teams in a series of knockout challenges throughout the day, similar to the format of the TV show. Teams would then be whittled down after each round of the competition, leaving four finalists to battle it out, hoping to claim the title of the Isle of Man Sewing Bee champions.

As a twist and to spice things up a little, Charlotte threw in something of a curveball. Each team would only be permitted to submit one finished article to the judging panel in each round of the competition. Therefore, individual teams would need to decide whether they wished to work collectively on one item, or to produce multiple items and pick which one they liked best for submission. Either way, they could submit only one item per round for the judges' review, so the strategy would require some serious consideration.

"So, Lotti..." Joyce said, pushing her reading glasses up the bridge of her nose and examining the information before her. "This sewing bee competition?" she asked without breaking her attention away from the sheet of paper in hand.

"You like what you see?" Charlotte replied, hopeful of a positive response.

Joyce nodded, looking to Beryl beside her to gauge her reaction as well. "Oh, yes," Joyce readily agreed. "So, we're putting a team in?"

"That's the plan," Charlotte said, clipboard in hand to record any potential participants.

"Well, Joyce and I are in," Beryl entered in on behalf of them both.

"And me," Bonnie quickly added from her seat at the end of the table. "I'd love to be in their team, if possible?" she said. "We'd be the dream team, ladies," she said to Beryl and Joyce.

Charlotte scribbled down the three names before they could change their minds. "Marvellous," she said, tapping her clipboard like a drum.

"Our name is already on the trophy," Joyce confidently declared. And then, "You *are* going to join our team, Lotti?"

Bonnie leaned forward in her chair. "Oh, go on, Lotti? It'll be a hoot."

Charlotte continued tapping her pen as she considered her response. "Hmm," she said, weighing up her options. "Well, as the organiser, would it be playing fair for me to join one of the teams?" she asked herself aloud. "Although, then again, I'm not going to be one of the judges, am I? So, it's not like I'm going to have any sort of advantage, I suppose," she continued, talking herself into it.

"Then it's settled!" Bonnie announced, rubbing her hands in delight. "We'll just need to come up with a team name."

Charlotte added her own name to the register. "Well, that's our team confirmed, though I'm not sure about the name just yet," she said. "Hmm, that certainly didn't take long. I'm not sure I expected it to get sorted so quickly," she added, glancing around the busy hall and feeling a bit sorry for the others who might have wanted to join in as well.

"It's not just one team from each club, though, is it?" Beryl asked. "Because you'll likely get at least three or four from the Crafternooners alone, I should think."

"And you might get some takers from your Make It Sew classes?" Joyce reminded her, removing her glasses now she'd read what she needed to.

"Oh, I suppose you're right," Charlotte said, supposing. "Good idea, there needn't be only one team. And if that's to be the case, I'd better let the other groups know it's not limited to just one team per club. I know the Knitty Noras have a fairly large membership, for example, so they'll be wanting to enter more than one team as well, I'm sure."

"*Oooof,*" replied Beryl, shaking her head. "Don't mention that name around me and Joyce, dear," she told Charlotte.

"Oooof indeed," Joyce added, curling her fingers into a fist, cracking her arthritic knuckles in the process.

Charlotte, for her part, smiled away, waiting for a punchline that didn't present itself. "Sorry, I don't follow," she said, not following. "Oh, hang on. I was just hearing this morning about some ill feelings throughout certain factions of the local crafting community. But I didn't know you girls were amongst those involved...?"

"For us, it's all been coming to a particular head this week," Beryl gravely advised. "The Knitty Noras, Stitch 'n' Bitch, and a few of the others who come along to the bingo, you see."

"Bingo?" Charlotte asked, interest piqued. "How come I've not heard about this? I like bingo."

"Monday afternoons at Ramsey Town Hall," Joyce said. "But they're a bunch of thieving cutthroats."

Charlotte looked over to Bonnie, wondering if she had any additional insight into what was still evidently an open wound to both Beryl and Joyce. Receiving a shrug in response, she returned her attention to Joyce. "There seems to be an awful lot of aggression over a simple game of bingo?"

"It's well deserved," Joyce insisted. "Four straight games of bingo, and every time one of the Knitty Noras mob won."

"Then, Kitty Eastlake scooped the progressive jackpot," Beryl added, the vein in the side of her temple now pulsating. "Another member of the Knitty Noras."

"Okay?" Charlotte said, not really understanding what the issue was. "So, is it a case of sour grapes because they walked away with the bingo prize money?"

"Hopped, more like," Joyce answered her. "Kitty's only got one leg, you see. And you know what else she's got?"

Charlotte shook her head.

"A grandson who just so happens to be a bingo caller in his spare time," said Beryl, deftly picking up the reins right where her friend had left off. "Apparently, he was seen outside waiting to give Kitty a lift home at kicking out time, and one of the Stitch 'n' Bitch lot clocked her getting into his car. It turns out she'd been giving him signals for what numbers they needed, and he then did what was required. At least that's what we strongly suspect."

"It's likely been going on for months," Joyce entered back in, cracking her knuckles once more. "Bunch of cheats."

"I see," Charlotte said, taking a step back, eager to move the conversation away from the seedier side of the island's bingo scene before Joyce and Beryl ruptured something. "Right, then! Well, I've got you ladies down on my clipboard!" she said breezily. And then, pointing over her shoulder, added, "Okay, I'd best pop in and see how Larry's getting on with the refreshments."

By the time Charlotte circled the room on her way to check on Larry, she'd managed to sign up an additional four sewing bee campaigners. For a moment, she wondered where the club might display their winner's trophy. "Oh, that reminds me, I still need to buy a trophy," she told herself, jotting down this thought while it was still fresh in her mind.

Stepping inside the kitchen, Charlotte caught sight of Larry as she finished scribbling her note. "Larry, my lovely. I've not even had time to say a proper hello," she said, securing her pen under the spring-loaded clip. "Did you happen to see the fruit loaf I'd left next to the tea urn?"

Larry spun round, extending his arms as he performed an exaggerated bow. "Good afternoon, Lotti. And welcome to my humble kitchen," he told her, using an unfamiliar, deep voice. "It's great to see you today, Lotti," he added, straightening himself up. "But enough about me, tell me about yourself."

Charlotte looked Larry up and down, eyeing him suspiciously, and wondering why he was adopting such a peculiar way of speaking at present. It was the first time she'd spoken to him today and hadn't really noticed his arrival, but she did observe now how well he was currently dressed. "You're looking exceptionally smart today, Larry," she remarked, admiring the tweed blazer he was wearing accompanied by a crisp white shirt and cherry red tie.

Larry waved away the compliment. "So, have you travelled far today?" he asked, continuing on with the curious affectation evident in his manner of speech. "And what about that weather we're having?"

Charlotte narrowed her eyes, wondering if perhaps Larry and Stanley were in cahoots, setting her up for a practical joke of some sort. "What's going on, Larry? Why are you acting so strangely today?" she asked.

"Did I ever tell you about the summer I worked as a Butlins Redcoat?" Larry replied, not answering Charlotte's question directly. "I was quite the commanding presence on stage, according to the critics," he informed her.

"Larry? What's going on?"

Larry hummed and hawed, staring down at his impeccably polished dress shoes, suddenly a bit shy about what he wanted to say. "It's just..."

"Yeah?"

"Well, I was just thinking about what you mentioned on my WhatsApp group, Larry's Lookout," Larry said, referring to their collective communication channel.

"About baking a fruit loaf...?"

"No, not that. Although I had noticed it, yes, and it does smell delicious," Larry answered, breathing in deeply. "But what I was actually referring to," he said, along with a hope-filled expression, "was about you signing people up for your sewing bee competition."

"Larry, my lovely," Charlotte said, as gently as she could, like a schoolteacher about to break the news to a pupil that they weren't going to be in the school play as they'd hoped. "Larry, by your own admission, crafting isn't exactly your forte, so I'm not sure—"

"What? Oh, no, Lotti, goodness no," Larry gently cut in. "I'm hopeless at crafting. You and I both know that," he said with a laugh. "Hence, why I'm in here happily preparing the brews," he added, executing another graceful bow.

"Okay. So?" Charlotte said, waiting for whatever kind of explanation Larry was about to give.

Larry cleared his throat, getting ready to set out his stall. "So," he said, running a hand through his hair. "The way I figure it, Lotti, I'd imagine you're going to be busy on the day of the competition. Organising and crafting and such, yes? And I just wondered if you'd perhaps considered, you know, a host for the event...?"

Charlotte moved closer, placing a hand on Larry's arm. "Is this why you've dressed up, Larry? Because you wanted to be the compère?"

"Pretty much," he said, straightening his tie.

"The job's yours, Larry," Charlotte assured him, agreeing immediately, and happy to do so. "I couldn't think of anybody better suited or qualified, what with your extensive Butlins career and all."

"Splendid! I won't let you down, Lotti," Larry promised, after which he reached inside of his jacket pocket, pulling out a thick wad of index cards on which he'd evidently written himself a batch of notes. "I didn't want to presume, Lotti, but I spent most of last night jotting down ideas for my opening speech, as well as my final address ahead of the prize presentation. Of course, there are also a few witty anecdotes here to sprinkle in throughout the day."

"Larry, you'll smash it out of the park, I'm sure," Charlotte answered. "Just be advised, however, that your duties may also extend to being a bouncer, at least from what I've been hearing regarding tensions between the various crafting factions."

"The bingo lot?" Larry asked, shuddering like someone had just stepped over his grave.

"Yeah. You've heard about this?"

Larry nodded slowly. "I went along once. Made the mistake of talking when they were calling out the numbers."

"Oh. I'm guessing from your demeanour that they weren't too impressed?"

"No, Lotti. Not at all. One of them said that if I didn't shut my gob that instant, she'd come straight over and cut my bingo balls off. So, I've not been back since."

"Oh, poor you, Larry. That doesn't sound very sociable of them. Not very sociable at all."

Chapter Thirteen

Hold up, Mollie!" Charlotte called out, swinging her little arms like pendulums. "My legs don't go that fast!" she said, trailing behind her friend like a duckling chasing after their mum.

Mollie turned to face her running partner, slowing down and now jogging backwards. "Sorry, it's these new trainers," she explained. "They make me feel like I'm Zola Budd."

"Two things," a breathless Charlotte replied, holding up two fingers as she gradually, eventually drew alongside. "Number one, Zola Budd didn't even wear trainers, she mostly raced barefoot," she advised, enjoying a lungful of bracing seaside air. "And number two, I thought we were walking today, not running?" she said. And with that, Charlotte placed a hand on Mollie's arm, preventing any further forward motion whilst she caught her breath and lowered her heart rate.

Mollie gently brushed the hand away, launching into a series of energetic star jumps. "Oi, I've a new pair of jeans to squeeze into tonight and need all the help I can get."

"Sam will think you look fabulous regardless, Moll, like you always do," Charlotte told her. "But please, can we walk for a while?"

Mollie relented, winding down her star jumping session. "Sure, we'll pick up the pace when we reach the next bus shelter, yeah? I still need to burn a few extra calories."

"We're still going for coffee and cake when we're done?" a concerned Charlotte asked. "Because this exercise portion of our afternoon together is secondary, as far as I'm concerned, the cake and coffee part being the most important bit," she suggested, only half-joking (although this meant she was of course half-serious as well).

"Of course. Cake and coffee are still totally on!" Mollie answered, as if this should never have been in doubt. "But by having a gentle jog and burning away a few calories first, it's like we're essentially getting the cake calorie-free," she added, tapping her nose like she had all the answers. Which, to be fair, she often did. And then, upon reaching the next bus stop, Mollie, as threatened, picked up the pace again, leading their exertions along Douglas Promenade with the steady sea breeze offering them a welcome shove along the way.

Despite the huffing and puffing — most all of which being on Charlotte's part — the pair of them enjoyed their Friday afternoon catch-up. With Mollie usually required to work weekends in the busy farm shop, Charlotte made a point of keeping an available slot in her own work schedule, with Friday being designated Mollie and Charlotte time. And even though they spoke most nights, often more than once, the opportunity for a brisk walk — or jog, in this case — followed by a visit to one of their favourite coffee shops was an activity the both of them appreciated and enjoyed. And this particular outing, as it should happen, offered Charlotte the opportunity to dig a little deeper into the details surrounding Sam and Mollie's upcoming first date. Once she'd regained the ability to breathe freely again, that is.

"That bloody promenade doesn't appear that long when you're driving along it," Charlotte remarked, hands resting on her thighs, looking back over the route they'd just covered.

"We're so lucky to have this on our doorstep, though, aren't we?" Mollie replied, watching a plucky dog walker being unceremoniously dragged along on the beach below. "Can you imagine living in a concrete-filled city centre instead of this?" she asked, stretching out her arms and pirouetting like a ballerina. "I love living by the sea."

Charlotte couldn't resist a smirk while stretching out her calf muscles. "Someone's happy, Moll? It's almost as if you've got a date or something."

"Well, who could be dour with a view like that?" Mollie put forth, gazing out over the breaking waves as she performed several deep lunges. "But seriously, it's still a miracle Sam asked me out," she reflected. "Especially after me sending him random photos of the night sky, and, as I've come to learn, lights flashing on an aeroplane's wings."

"Well, you just make sure you're on time for that date of yours!" Charlotte said brightly, purposely breezing right past the subject of astronomy and such in hopes of avoiding discussion on this slightly embarrassing topic. "Anyway, have you decided where you're going?" she asked.

"Yes. Lettuce Entertain You," Mollie revealed, strolling towards the sea terminal at the far end of the promenade, the venue for today's coffee. "It was Sam's recommendation."

"Eh, isn't that a Robbie Williams song?" Charlotte asked, the name sounding strangely familiar.

"Similar, I think, yeah. But this is *Lettuce*, one word," Molly clarified. "Anyway, Lettuce Entertain You is that fancy new vegan restaurant in Peel…" Mollie added, trailing off, almost as if she knew what was coming next.

"Vegan restaurant?" Charlotte answered, following behind now she'd completed her brief warm-down. "But you're the biggest carnivore I know, Moll. So why on earth did you guys decide on a vegan restaurant?"

"Hey, I can appreciate a nice salad," Mollie shot back. "Now and again, at least."

"Is that so?" Charlotte scoffed. "Because remind me how much salad you had with that sixteen-ounce ribeye you demolished when we last went to that American steakhouse, if you would?"

Mollie deliberated on that question for a moment or two. "It was a twelve-ounce, actually," she eventually replied. "And the only reason I didn't have salad was—"

"Because there was no room left on your plate!"

"Hmm, fair point," Mollie was happy to concede, giving a little shrug. "Anyway, it's not all about me, Lotti. I thought it'd be nice to agree to a restaurant that respects Sam's beliefs, you know?"

Charlotte nodded her head in approval at what appeared, on the surface, to be a most generous and selfless gesture on Mollie's part. "Wait, hang on," she said, after a moment's quick consideration. "What do you mean, Sam's beliefs?"

"Well, I didn't want to sit there murdering a prime cut of beef in front of a strict vegetarian, now did I?" Mollie was eager to point out. "It just wouldn't be right."

Charlotte started to laugh, able to read her best mate like the open book she was. "You've told Sam you're a vegetarian, vegan, or both, hoping to impress him, haven't you?" she asked, stepping in front of Mollie and staring her square in the eye. "And this is why he then suggested that new vegan restaurant? Tell me I'm wrong, Moll?"

"I'd love to, but you're not," Mollie said with a sniff. "I just thought it would be a thoughtful thing for me to do to not eat meat in front of him. Besides, I've often toyed with the idea of giving up meat, so now might be the ideal opportunity anyway." And with that, Mollie folded her arms across her chest, ready to accept Charlotte's proper recognition of her selfless act, which was sure to come her way.

"Wait, now I'm even more confused. You think Sam's a vegetarian...?"

Mollie tilted her head, not quite sure what Charlotte was implying. "Uhm, *yeah*," she said, laughing at the absurdity of her friend's question.

This was all too much for Charlotte, who placed the palm of her hand against her sweaty forehead. "I don't know how to break this to you, Moll. But Sam isn't a vegetarian."

"Of course he is," Mollie insisted, although with a little less conviction than before. "Isn't he?"

"Nope. I know this for a fact because he made us both a bacon sarnie last time I was at the nursing home."

"Oh, sugar," Mollie answered, her shoulders drooping. "I don't know why, but I guess I just assumed..."

"You just assumed he didn't eat meat because he's got that whole hippy vibe going on?" Charlotte surmised.

"A little bit, yeah," Mollie replied with a grimace. "Well, you would, wouldn't you?" she reasoned, though not receiving the look of assurance she was hoping for. "Bloody hell, Sam already thinks I'm a bit loopy over the astrology incident, and now I'm a carnivore lying about being a vegetarian."

"You mean astronomy? Anyway, he won't think you're a bit loopy, Mollie, I promise," Charlotte assured her. "He'll think you're *completely* loopy."

"Oh, I'm having a carrot cake baby," Mollie said, caressing her tum as they commenced the return portion of their journey, towards Charlotte's parked car. "It's a good job these Lycra leggings have a bit of give in them," she added, giving the waistband a satisfying snap. "Is there any chance you can stitch some elastic into the waist of my new jeans, Lotti?"

However, Charlotte was deep in thought, staring over at a hotel on the opposite side of the road. And even though they were travelling at a much more leisurely pace owing to their excessive servings of cake, Charlotte still stopped, running her eyes over the handsome Victorian facade. She cradled her chin between her thumb and forefinger, pensive, like an artist plotting their latest watercolour.

"Earth to Lotti!" Mollie said, taking up a position next to her. "What's so interesting?" she asked, looking for what was so captivating.

"I don't think I've tried the Metropole hotel," Charlotte answered, scanning through her memory, and talking more to herself than Mollie. "Or have I?" she asked, turning to Mollie, though again, appearing to be directing the remark more towards herself than her friend.

"For what, exactly?"

Charlotte tapped a finger to her lips, still thinking. "As a venue for the Christmas Sewing Bee," she told Mollie.

"Oh, if you haven't, you should certainly give them a call," Mollie suggested. "I was there for a surprise birthday party, and it's lovely inside. And the function room is massive, Lotti, so plenty of space if you have loads of people showing up. Which you will, of course."

"Perfect," Charlotte said, taking a determined stride towards the Metropole, still not entirely sure if she'd already phoned them previously or not. "No time like the present," Charlotte announced over her shoulder. "Strike while the iron's hot, and all that. You coming?"

"Of course I am, Lotti. After all, you've got the car keys to get us home."

Once inside the Hotel Metropole, Charlotte offered an admiring eye around the reception area, impressed with the polished marble and mirrored walls, somehow without a rogue fingerprint mark in sight. "Oh, this is rather plush," she said to Mollie, picturing this to be the ideal location for her upcoming event.

"Hmm, a bit too plush to be still wearing our sweaty running gear, Lotti. Maybe better to just give them a call?" Mollie proposed, discreetly evacuating a generous portion of Lycra that'd ridden up areas it wasn't invited to be in.

"Well, if we'd walked for the duration like I suggested, you wouldn't be currently having the problem of sweaty running gear," Charlotte politely reminded her, reaching over to the reception desk to ding the brass bell sitting there.

"Good afternoon, madam," a smartly-dressed lad (called Louis, if the name badge pinned to his jacket was any indication) offered, appearing from what was presumably the main office. "I hope I didn't keep you too long?" he asked politely, offering a cordial smile.

"No, not at all," Charlotte replied, impressed by the calibre of the welcome. "I was just admiring your gleaming mirrors, as it should happen. Wondering how you manage to keep them so clean, avoiding greasy fingerprints all over them like I end up with at home from my young one."

"Ah, yes, madam. The secret is that I keep a broom hidden behind the reception desk, and if I see any wandering hands, I promptly administer a good whack to them," the young gentleman named Louis answered, along with the glimmer of a smile. "But seriously, though, our housekeeping team will be delighted to learn of your complimentary feedback," he said. And with that, he moved his hands, fingers hovering above the keyboard in front of him. "Are you two ladies checking in?"

"What?" Charlotte asked. And then, "Oh, no. No, we're not staying here, unfortunately."

"That's our loss, madam," Louis replied, standing down his hands, placing them by his side. "So, how can I help?"

Charlotte sensed that this Louis fellow was an amiable sort of chap. The type who could pull strings, if required, and grease the wheels if the need arose, or so she hoped. She took a step closer, resting her elbows on the reception desk, maintaining eye contact all the while. "What it is, Louis," Charlotte began, flicking her eyes to his name badge, just to make doubly sure she was getting his name right. "My friend here," she said, pointing over her shoulder. "My friend has told me what a wonderful venue this hotel is."

"Always good to hear, madam," said Louis.

"Now, before you start laughing at me, Louis," Charlotte continued, "I was desperately hoping to hire a room next month. Next month as in December." Charlotte scanned his face, but with no laughter lines forming, she pressed on. "I know it's the run-up to Christmas, Louis, and you're likely booked up months in advance. But the truth is, nobody else will have us. I think I've phoned every hotel on the island."

"I see," Louis said, hands raised to his keyboard again. "Can you confirm the date and how many nights you're looking for?"

Encouraged by the fact she hadn't, as yet, received an immediate rebuff, she dialled up her charming smile to at least a nine. "That's the thing, Louis," Charlotte said, offering a quick glance over to Mollie and back. "We don't actually need to book in overnight. We only need the room during the day, and then we'll be out of your hair. So, you could even hire the room out again for the evening."

"You don't want the room for the evening? Just the afternoon?" Louis said, confirming the request to make sure he'd understood.

"That's correct," Charlotte said, flashing her pearly whites.

Louis looked to his left. "Let me just have a quick word with my manager," he offered by way of a placeholder. "Mr Prendergast," he said, making his way towards the office. "Can I borrow you for just a moment?"

Charlotte raised a hopeful fist in Mollie's direction. "I can still turn on the charm when I need to, Moll," she said, drifting away for a moment as she imagined the reception area jam-packed with crafters dressed up in their Christmas finery, enjoying a cheeky glass of sherry and perhaps a mince pie. "I've got a good feeling about this place," she said, unable to contain her excitement, looking into the office where Louis was in deep conversation.

Two or three minutes later, an older chap with a bald head but generous tufts of hair protruding from each nostril presented himself before Charlotte. He extended his neck across the reception desk like a walrus stretching for a bit of sun. "You were asking our establishment's representative, Louis, about room rental?" he said, giving Charlotte and Mollie a long, lingering once-over, and appearing not at all impressed by what he was seeing.

Charlotte nodded her head in the affirmative. "Yes, please," she said, slightly taken aback by the considerably less friendly nature of this new person she was now dealing with. "As I was explaining to your associate, it's just for the daytime, though.

So, if you needed it for the evening, we'd be long gone by then in case that helps our cause?"

The manager shook his head gravely, rolling his eyes and making no effort to contain his contempt. "We're a four-star rated hotel, young lady," he stressed, looking Charlotte slowly up and down. "And for that reason, we're not particularly interested in renting our rooms out by the hour. Given this, you may wish to consider a motel, or perhaps a bedsit, which might be better suited to your particular needs, and, *ahem*, clientele."

"No, no, we'll definitely need it for more than just an hour," Charlotte attempted to explain. "We're expecting it to be very popular, you see, with plenty of visitors."

An amused Mollie, who'd been listening in, stepped forward, taking the opportunity to whisper into Charlotte's ear something about the 'world's oldest profession,' or similar words to that effect. And with her message thus delivered, she quickly stepped back again, waiting for the penny to drop.

Charlotte scrunched up her face, turning towards Mollie. "He thinks we're what...?" she asked, after digesting the packet of knowledge just delivered into her lughole. Mollie simply nodded in response, trying desperately to repel the smirk bubbling away behind the scenes.

"Look here," Charlotte said, turning her attention back to the reception desk. "You think I'm a-a-a—" she stammered, scarcely able to form her words. "A lady of the *night*?" she eventually spat out, stamping her foot down like an angry toddler. Then, she extended her finger in the manager's direction, cheeks puce. "I'll have you know that we're dressed like this because we've just been jogging. And it was your function room I was hoping to hire, not a bedroom for that... thing you're thinking about. I'm a respectable crafting teacher, and my friend manages a hugely successful farm shop, for heaven's sake!"

"The function room?" the confused Mr Prendergast asked, throwing young Louis a look. The manager then expelled a bit of air from his nostrils, causing the protruding tufts of hair to sway briefly as he considered this new bit of information. "I was under the impression you wanted a room by the hour, if you take my meaning?" he said, sounding apologetic now. "Louis, pass me out the function room diary if you would?"

"Well," Charlotte said, her tone conciliatory as well, conscious as she was that she needed this chap on her side. "Well, now that's sorted, I'd like to..."

"Just a moment, please," said Mr Prendergast, opening the diary he'd just been handed. "Right, then," he said, once he'd landed on the proper page, looking back up to Charlotte.

"Yes, well, now we've cleared up that we're actually hoping to book the function room next month, in the afternoon, and not to... well, you know. I'd like to—"

"Wait, the function room? In *December*?" asked an incredulous Mr Prendergast, immediately closing over the diary and letting out an exasperated sigh. "Surely you can't be serious. You *do* know that's our busiest time of the year, booked up months, if not *years*, in advance?"

"So, after all that, you're now telling me you're fully booked?" Charlotte asked.

"Solidly," came the firm response.

"Marvellous," Charlotte said, reaching into the fruit bowl on the edge of the desk. "We're taking these for our trouble," she announced, glaring defiantly as she grabbed one apple and one pear from the selection, giving Mollie and herself something to enjoy on their journey back to the car even though neither of them was especially hungry at this point anyway.

CHAPTER FOURTEEN

Three cups of coffee before sunrise was something of a record for Charlotte. The fourth, however, proved a bit too much of a challenge, and a half-filled mug of tepid liquid was emptied down the kitchen sink before she started twitching due to caffeine overload.

Often so organised, with perfectly respectable diary management skills, Charlotte had been horrified to open an email from an enquiring customer the previous evening. Ordinarily, this would have been a welcome communication, but not so much when they were arranging to pick up the memory bear they'd ordered as a birthday gift. An order Charlotte had completely forgotten about. She was unhappy about it, but it wasn't that she had to drop everything at the last minute to accommodate the order that frustrated Charlotte. Rather, it was more that she'd come so close to disappointing people for their very special day that bothered her. Fortunately, by burning the candle the previous evening and then an exceptionally early start this morning, she'd been able to rectify the situation. Still, that wasn't the point, and Charlotte knew it.

The difficulty was that Charlotte's mind was all over the place. Until now, she'd managed to keep all the collective plates spinning, if only just. Despite all the projects she was juggling, she'd felt fairly confident she could press on with the island-wide rollout of Make It Sew, grow her Crafternoon club, and even continue with the occasional commission or sewing lesson when the opportunity presented itself.

However, her Sewing Bee initiative had been getting her into something of a lather of late, with Charlotte finding herself in the midst of a chicken-and-the-egg sort of scenario. On the one hand, she couldn't widely advertise the event without a confirmed venue. On the other hand, if she did eventually secure a venue but hadn't properly promoted the event in advance, then there was the genuine danger that not enough people would show up for it owing to the fact that they didn't know anything about it.

By her own reckoning, she'd signed up about one-third of the crafting teams needed simply by word of mouth, but it was what to do next that left her uncertain. A little voice in the back of her mind was pushing her to cancel the event entirely or, potentially, reschedule to a time when securing a venue would be less problematic. However, the entire purpose of hosting the event before Christmas, which she kept reminding herself of, was to raise funds and the profile of the school uniform recycling initiative ahead of the new term. In addition to this, many of her crafting friends were busy, already beavering away on festive-themed creations to sell on the day of the event. And those that were aware of the Christmas Sewing Bee idea were genuinely looking forward to it. So, for those reasons, Charlotte would press on regardless, a firm believer in the old adage, the show must go on. She just didn't know *where* exactly the show would go on quite yet. Or precisely when, for that matter.

Presently, Barnabas the Bear was uncomplaining, sitting patiently on the kitchen table while Charlotte applied the finishing touches to him. With heavy eyelids, Charlotte tied a dickie bow ribbon around his adorable little neck, patting him on top of the head once he was all finished and ready for collection. "How did I nearly forget to make such a handsome bloke as you?" Charlotte offered, though she'd already apologised for her oversight several times, so it likely wasn't necessary to ask forgiveness once more as Barnabas appeared to be the forgiving kind, smashing chap that he was.

Charlotte indulged in a brief moment of satisfaction, immensely chuffed that she'd finished with about an hour to spare before the bear's new owner was expected to arrive. There was, unfortunately, a downside to working on any crafting project against the clock, which included memory bears. And that was the fact that her kitchen presently appeared as if it had been struck by a cyclone, with thread ends, toy stuffing, interfacing, and fabric offcuts strewn in every direction. Indeed, to the uninitiated, it might well have appeared that Paddington Bear himself had walked over and triggered a landmine, as there were bear parts — pieces of fabric flesh and stuffing guts — lying everywhere. But this was a scenario that most experienced crafters would be familiar with, and even prepared for, and Charlotte was no different. With her dustpan and brush within easy reach and a ten-minute power tidy, order was restored to the kitchen just in time to begin preparing Stanley's breakfast.

"Stanley Newman!" Charlotte called up the stairs, hoping to rouse a young person from their sleepy pit. It was her third attempt, with this one being slightly more thunderous than the previous two. Ordinarily, on a Saturday morning, she'd leave him to enjoy the luxury of a long lie-in. But with his dad due to pick him up soon, Stanley still needed to be showered, dressed, weekend bag packed, and fed. "I'm making your favourite for breakfast!" Charlotte shouted, waving one arm through the air, attempting to waft the alluring aroma up the stairs.

Then, shortly thereafter, Charlotte heard the dull thud of two feet landing on the bedroom carpet, with Stanley's sense of smell possibly being more acute than that of his hearing. "Who needs an alarm clock when you're cooking eggy bread," Charlotte mused aloud.

Stanley appeared a few moments later, wrapped up in his dressing gown like a chipolata covered in bacon. "Morning, Mum," he said, trudging into the kitchen, one hand stretched high above his head and the other tasked with removing the sleepy bugs from his eyes. "Ooh," he remarked, clapping eyes on his breakfast, now finished and waiting for him on the table, along with a small metal jug of delicious Lyle's Golden Syrup positioned to the side and ready for use. If he'd needed a firm shove to prise him from his slumber, he certainly didn't need one to polish off his breakfast. A breakfast which was in short order being hoovered down, with the pattern on the plate in danger of being taken right off on account of Stanley licking the plate clean.

"Straight in the shower when you're—" Charlotte started to say, but by the time she'd removed her head from the dishwasher, Stanley's chair was already empty with the sound of splashing water filtering down from the bathroom. And then... "Gordon Bennett!" Charlotte shouted, clutching her chest in response to the bearded figure suddenly pressing its nose against her kitchen window.

"You do know I've got a doorbell?" she asked, upon making her way over and opening the door to a smiling George.

"Sorry, Lotti. It was always fun making you jump, and old habits die hard, I guess," George said by way of an average apology. "So is Stan the Man looking forward to his weekend?" he asked, making his way into the hallway. "We're going bowling this afternoon, pizza tonight, and I've got matinee cinema tickets for that new Marvel whatsit for tomorrow."

Charlotte screwed up her face, sniffing the air. "George," she said, directing her beak towards him. "Don't take this the wrong way, but have you been eating garlic?"

George blew into his cupped hand. "Yeah. Last night," he agreed with a grimace. "And that's after brushing my teeth several times, both last night and this morning. I think it's actually coming out of my pores at this point," he offered with a shrug. "I went for a curry with, ehm..." he started to add, trailing off and looking uncertain if he should continue.

"You can say Vanessa's name, you know," Charlotte happily advised. "I'm not going to collapse in an emotional heap if you do," she told him with a chuckle, along with an *I-do-appreciate-the-sentiment* sort of a smile. "Cuppa?"

George bowed his head a touch. "Sorry. Again, old habits die hard. And yes, I'd love one," he said, following Charlotte into the kitchen. "By the way, I saw Mollie last night when Vanessa and me were walking back to the car," he said by way of conversation.

"Ah. She was on a hot date," Charlotte replied, filling the kettle. "Did she look like she was having fun?"

George ran a hand over his recently shaven bonce, slightly confused. "On a date?" he said. "Sorry, can't say I know anything about that. She was on her own when we saw her. We bumped into her when she was coming out of the kebab shop, and she told us she was on her way to the taxi rank."

Charlotte chuckled again. "Kebab shop? I guess the earlier vegan offering didn't quite do the job," she said to an again confused George. Then, turning her attention to the well-stuffed bin bag in his hand, "Anyway, George, what's with the bag?" she asked. "You know I've long since stopped doing your laundry, don't you? And even if I hadn't, I'm not sure Vanessa would necessarily approve."

"What, this little thing?" George said coyly, playing it down and clearly attempting to build the intrigue. "This is for you," he offered a moment later, making a great show of struggling mightily to lift it onto the kitchen table, for full comedic effect.

Charlotte eyed the bag cautiously.

"Blimey, it's not a bag of snakes," George told her, releasing the yellow plastic drawstring. "Have a look, Lotti."

Charlotte peered inside as instructed. "Its clothes," she said brightly, dipping her hand inside for a rummage. "School uniform, if I'm not mistaken?"

George liberated two teabags from the metal tin marked *TEA*. "Yes, indeed!" he said. "Your ears might have been burning yesterday, in fact, because I was talking about you."

"You were?" Charlotte answered.

George nodded his head, draining the contents of the kettle, now heated up, into two mugs. "Yeah, I was doing some work at this fancy pad in Castletown earlier in the week," he told her. "I happened to mention to the owner about your recycling initiative, and she thought it was a belting idea. So, when I turned up the next day, she had a whole bag full of uniform items waiting for me and the promise of more to come from her mates. I'm no expert, mind, but it all looks to be in top condition, I think, nearly new."

Charlotte broke her attention away from the bag. "You were telling people about ReCyCool?"

"Yeah, of course, Lotti. We're all proud of what you're up to," George answered, applying the finishing touches to their respective cuppas. But when nothing was heard in response, he turned to find Charlotte dabbing her eyes with her sleeve. "Hey, what's up with you?" George asked, uncertain if he should be extending a consoling hand to his ex. But as the sobbing continued, he released his teaspoon, throwing an arm around her.

Charlotte fanned her face with her fingers. "Sorry, George. I've had a few setbacks this week, but this is just what I needed to perk me up."

"You don't really look too perked up, Lotti," George observed. "No offence."

"Trust me. This is me perked up."

Just then, a clean and refreshed Stanley appeared with his weekend rucksack slung over his shoulder. "Daaadd..." he said, shaking his head. "What've you said to her...?"

"It's all right, Stanley, they're good tears, not bad," Charlotte said, answering on George's behalf and jumping to his defence. "Your dad has just given me the motivational kick up the keister I needed," she explained.

"Ah, okay, then," a relieved Stanley responded. "In that case, good job, Dad. Well done, you."

"All in a day's work, kiddo," George replied with a wink, releasing Charlotte as he did so. "So, Lotti, what do you reckon?" he asked. "Now you've got the whole afternoon to yourself, is it some schmaltzy, feel-good film in front of the log burner sort of day?"

"Nope, not today," Charlotte said, wrapping Barnabas up in a snowflake-covered organza bag. "I'm going to jump in the shower, then hand this charming fellow off to his new owner," she told him. "And then, after that, I've an afternoon tea date with three smokin' hot ladies, as it should happen."

"Oh? Can I come?" George joked, jiggling his eyebrows.

"I wouldn't if I were you, Dad," Stanley warned, pulling a face. "Because, just in case no one's told you, you reek of garlic."

With Bride, a sleepy little parish just a short hop from the island's most northerly tip, the Point of Ayre, possessing a modest population of around 400, the quaint, rural idyll was rarely rushed, offering a portal into a more sedate pace of life where traffic jams usually meant two tractors meeting on a country lane. And, as if that wasn't enough of an incentive to visit, it was also home to a charming tearoom, an absolute must for those venturing through the area as Charlotte and her fellow travellers were today.

"I've no idea where you put it all," Joyce remarked, gazing in amazement at Beryl's empty plate. "Have you got a hollow leg?"

Beryl wiped the corner of her mouth with a crisp, white napkin. "The secret is, you have to skip breakfast," she advised. "It's a rookie move to include breakfast first thing in the morning when you know you'll be going out later for afternoon tea."

Bonnie laughed, absorbing this bit of sage-like advice. "I expect that'll be why I only managed two cucumber triangles and a slice of lemon cake?"

"Exactly," Beryl suggested, reaching out towards the tiered cake stand in the centre of the table. "It's all about showing restraint," she added, and yet saying this while selecting *another* vanilla macaron, her third one now, and this coming after everything she'd eaten already.

"Restraint, my eye," Joyce said with a light-hearted cackle. "You're just a bloody gannet!"

"More tea?" an amused Charlotte asked, playing Mum, topping up the dainty china teacups around the table. "Isn't this lovely?" she asked. "Good food, beautiful location, and I suppose the company's not too bad, either."

Charlotte's cheeks often ached whenever she spent any degree of time in Beryl and Joyce's company, and today was no exception. From the moment she'd picked them up to the moment she dropped them off, she'd have a permanent grin on her face. They were like a double act, the two of them. And even though they'd regularly bicker, no offence was ever taken, and before too long they'd have moved onto the next subject, often putting the world to rights in the process. It was an endearing friendship, and their affection for each other was apparent. Indeed, Charlotte could well imagine herself and Mollie being just like the pair of them in years to come, moaning about this, whinging about that, but ultimately, looking out for each other and sharing the good times as well as the bad. And it was a testament to the quality of the old girls' company (one that Charlotte continued to enjoy) that Bonnie, at her tender young age, would willingly give up her Saturday to join them all for afternoon tea.

"So," Charlotte said, once the remaining plates were finally cleared away, placing her opened notepad on the surface of the table. "As I mentioned on the drive here, I need to pick your brains about the Christmas Sewing Bee and harness the collective brilliance around this table."

"Do you mean about the format?" Bonnie asked. "You mentioned that it might be a knockout competition, so how many rounds were you thinking?"

"Hmm, I suppose it depends on how many teams we have entered," Charlotte considered. "My early thinking is that we have three rounds with a timed crafting challenge in each. Then, for example, the judges select ten teams from the first round to advance to the semi-final to battle it out, and then, from there, four teams eventually make it into the grand final? What do you think, too much for one day?"

Joyce and Beryl shook their heads in unison. "It's fine," Beryl suggested. "I've been known to start crafting at dawn and still be going at supper time."

"Agreed," Joyce said, agreeing. "How long for each round? An hour, maybe?"

In her notebook, Charlotte scored a large tick next to the bullet point referencing format. "Yeah, an hour, maybe an hour and a half with a short break between each round?" she said. Then, moving her pen down to the next bullet point on her list, she asked, "And what about our individual team's tactics?"

"About that," Joyce said, looking across to Beryl like they'd already discussed that very point in some considerable detail. "We should wait in the car park for the Knitty Noras to arrive..." she began to explain, receiving a nod of encouragement from Beryl, after which she continued, "And then, when they least expect it, we pounce!"

"Pounce?" Charlotte replied, repeating the word back to her. "Erm, you mean figuratively, right?"

"No, I mean literally. As in, we take out the competition!" Beryl happily declared. "They'd do the same to us given half the chance."

Charlotte offered an uneasy smile, uncertain if the pair of them were being serious. "There will be no pouncing, ladies," she stressed, lest there be any doubt.

"There's a sentence I'll bet you thought you'd never say," Bonnie joked. "Especially concerning a crafting competition."

"With these two, you can never take anything for granted," Charlotte said, pointing her pen to each of them in turn. "Anyway, moving on, I wanted to gauge your thoughts about working collectively on one item? Or, would we prefer to split up, each of us making an item, then submitting the best one to the judges?"

Beryl slowly wiggled her fingers like she was playing the piano. "These stiff fingers might need oiling from time to time, but the brain is still sharp as a tack. So maybe we should work individually and submit the best one?"

"Which is certain to be mine," Joyce said with an assured sniff, although not seriously discounting the others' efforts. "But I agree with Beryl. So let's divide up, each doing our own thing, and between us all we'll come up with a masterpiece."

"Perfect," Charlotte said, scoring another generous tick in her notebook. "That just leaves us with point number three, the festive challenges."

"I was thinking about this last night, actually," Bonnie responded, her face lighting up. "What about making a pair of Christmas pyjamas for round one?"

"Oh, I like that idea," Beryl entered in. "Made from warm, brushed cotton to wear on a cold winter's night."

"Perfect," Charlotte said, taking notes. "And, round two?"

"Christmas-themed decorations?" Bonnie offered, putting forth another idea. "Similar to the ones you've been making at Make It Sew. Stockings, tree decorations, advent calendars, and such?"

"We could make a giant stocking to store all of the presents you're sure to buy me," Joyce told Beryl, receiving a raised eyebrow in response.

"Right. Christmas decorations are on the list," Charlotte confirmed, exaggerating the placement of a full stop with her pen. "And the challenge for the grand final?"

Bonnie raised her hand, running excited eyes around the group, having been the one doing most of the thinking so far, it would appear. "How about..." she said, getting even more animated. "A glitzy night-out theme?"

"Like a party frock?" Beryl asked, gyrating in her seat like she had a sudden itch.

Bonnie took a moment to admire Beryl's peculiar paroxysms which, she assumed, were meant to approximate some form of dancing. Then, she turned to Charlotte again. "Exactly!" she said. "A glitzy, festive, Hollywood-style party frock."

"I like it," Charlotte said, scribbling away. "But that could be a lot of work, so we might want to consider increasing the time slot for the final," she proposed. "And to make it fair to all the competitors, I'll let everyone know well in advance what the challenges are going to be. That way, we don't have an unjust advantage."

"You could always forget to tell some of the other groups," Beryl suggested, with that idea receiving a hearty thumbs-up from Joyce, showing her approval.

"Certain, *select* groups," Joyce added in.

"We're going to play nicely, ladies," Charlotte suggested. "Although I do appreciate your enthusiasm," she added, with a shake of the head and a chuckle. And then, with the running order for the event thus settled, Charlotte closed over her notebook. "Thanks for your thoughts, everyone. Much appreciated."

"Sorry to interrupt," the attentive waitress said, wheeling her dessert trolly in the direction of Charlotte's table. "Our chef has just finished making this chocolate fudge cake," she informed them. "If I can tempt any of you...?" she asked, running her hand invitingly over the trolley like a market stall trader plying their wares.

Charlotte offered a contented sigh. "Thanks," she said. "But I think we're all completely—"

"I'll try a piece," Beryl, the human vacuum cleaner, jumped in, raising her hand so there was absolutely no doubt in which direction the trolley should be heading first.

"Go on, then. One for me also," Joyce entered in. "I can't see Beryl eating on her own."

"In that case, I may as well," Bonnie said, feasting her eyes on the contents of the trolley. "Seeing as how you're heading right this way."

"Well, I don't want to be the one to offend your fine chef," Charlotte begrudgingly added. "Just a sliver, though," she said, using her fingers to illustrate the size of the required sliver.

The women watched on as their respective pieces were cut, looking forward to digging in.

"Oh, sorry about that," Charlotte said to everyone around her, in response to her phone that was currently vibrating on the table. She was about to put her phone in her bag, but the brief preview of the text message intrigued her. "Would you ladies excuse me?" she asked the group, after which she then proceeded to unlock her phone. "It's very rude, I know, but I'll just be a moment."

Charlotte needn't have worried, as the others were too busy salivating over the soon-to-be-served cake than to care one way or the other if Charlotte attended to her phone.

The text was from Mollie, to which Charlotte promptly replied, initiating an exchange between them:

> Mollie: Lotti, guess what I got last night!

> Charlotte: A giant greasy kebab, apparently?

> Mollie: Don't judge me. Vegan portions are tiny!
> But I don't mean that. Guess again.

> Charlotte: On the basis you were on a hot date, do I really want to guess what you got? 😊

> Mollie: Get your mind out of the gutter! Lotti, I've got you a venue for the sewing bee, and you're going to bloody love it!

"What is it?" Bonnie asked, noting Charlotte's incredulous yet delighted expression.

Charlotte lowered her phone for a moment. "I think we've got a location sorted for the Christmas Sewing Bee," she said, scarcely able to believe what she'd just been informed.

"Excellent! Lotti, that's brilliant news," Bonnie answered. "But where?" she asked, leaning forward in her seat, anxious to hear more.

Charlotte offered a shrug, returning her attention to the phone. "I dunno, Bonn. But I'm about to find out...!"

CHAPTER FIFTEEN

Sideways rain battered against the cold window where Larry's cheek rested. The packed bus shuddered into life, moving away from the stop with another punter or two on board, no doubt delighted to be sheltered from the miserable weather. The sudden motion of the bus startled Larry, uncertain if he'd dozed off for a moment. He offered a discreet glance around those sat nearby, concerned that if he had just enjoyed forty winks, then his well-documented snoring would surely have disturbed their morning commute. Fortunately, though, he noticed no scowls being cast in his direction.

Larry peered through his cheek-shaped imprint, using it as a viewing portal past the heavily fogged-up window, hoping to gauge progress and review how much further it would be until the main bus depot in Douglas. And either this particular bus was powered by rockets, or, as he suspected, he had indeed nodded off as progress was more advanced than he'd anticipated.

With the bus soon on its stand, Larry remained seated, allowing those commuters with a busy workday ahead to alight before him. After all, he was in no particular rush, and he figured he'd only get in their way.

"A splendid trip, kind sir," Larry said to the driver a short time later, tipping his dark grey trilby hat when, as the last passenger, he finally made his way to the exit.

"Always welcome," the cheery bus driver offered in return. "And you go easy out there, yeah? It's blowing a hoolie."

"In that case, I should have brought my kite along," Larry joked, chuckling to himself as he zipped up his winter jacket. "Cheerio," he said, waving over his shoulder.

Larry didn't often have cause to visit Douglas, the island's capital and central shopping district, but it was always a pleasure to get caught up in the hustle and bustle, as he often referred to it. Of course, the area had changed beyond recognition since he was a young lad, with modern buildings springing up in every direction or old ones renovated. But even now, years later, if he tried hard enough, he could still picture things as they once were. The happy image of being dragged around every shop by his mum with the promise of a visit to the sweet shop on the way home was still fresh in his mind after all this time.

Other memories brought a nostalgic smile to his face as he wandered leisurely through Strand Street just now, benefiting from the shelter that the row of shops on either side offered from the elements. Memories, for instance, such as his first job as a trainee cobbler in a business long since forgotten by most. Though not forgotten by Larry, of course. In fact, he was often reminded of this first bit of gainful employment whenever he should look down to his slightly misshapen thumbnail, the nailbed having been permanently damaged as a result of whacking his hand with his cobbler's hammer. The shop was now a bookstore, he observed, but for him, it would always remain a salutary lesson to pay attention to the task at hand and not be distracted by the pretty girls walking past the shop window. Especially when using a hammer.

Larry came to a halt, trying to recall the exact location of the jewellers where he'd purchased his wedding rings. But things had indeed changed over the previous fifty-eight years since then, and his memory wasn't as sharp as it once was. It was now a travel agency, or possibly the butcher's shop, but he couldn't be sure which. So he took a mental note to see if any of his friends at the nursing home might know.

Following his brief sentimental journey, Larry reached his destination. "After you," he said, holding the door to the bank open, allowing a shopping bag-laden woman to enter before him.

"You're a gentleman," the woman offered, extending him a warm smile.

Once he'd entered the building himself, Larry removed his hat, placing his gloves inside of it, his chilled fingers tingling in the warm air blowing down from an overhead heater. "Ah," he said, spotting the available cashier directing a cordial wave in his direction.

"Good morning, sir," the smartly dressed young lady greeted him from behind her desk, once Larry had made his way over. "It's a bit parky out there, isn't it," she said, making conversation, though with this delivered more as an observation than a question.

"It's certainly fresh, as they say," Larry remarked, reaching inside his coat for his wallet. "I'd like to make a cash withdrawal if that's possible?"

"Well, you've come to the right place," the girl replied with a cheesy answer of the sort Larry himself might have been proud to deliver had their positions been reversed. "And how much would you like to withdraw today?" she asked, taking possession of Larry's bank card, which he had duly handed over to her.

"Six hundred and forty of your finest pounds, please."

The seated cashier looked up to Larry. "That's a lot of cash to be carrying around, Mr Beasdale. Have you considered doing an online transfer or paying by card?"

Larry immediately shook his head, indicating those options had already been considered and decided against. "Where I'm going doesn't have one of those card-reading thingamajigs, and between you and me, no offence, but I'm not overly trusting of that online banking malarkey."

"Understood," the cashier said, wheeling back in her chair. "I won't be a moment, Mr Beasdale."

Larry helped himself to one of the mints in the glass bowl next to where he'd laid his hat, whistling a happy tune to himself. "Mr Beasdale," another lady said, accompanying the original cashier a moment or two later.

"You're not going to tell me off for eating the schweet?" Larry asked, mouth half-full.

"Not at all," Harriet (according to her name badge) said. "I'm the branch manager, Mr Beasdale," she said by way of introduction. Harriet moved around from her side of the counter to stand next to Larry. "My colleague, Julia, mentioned that you're looking to withdraw a somewhat sizeable sum of money?" she said quietly, and in a tone not designed to offend or embarrass. "If it's not too much trouble, we're required to ask why you'd need that amount of cash."

"I'm buying a new suit," Larry was more than happy to explain. "Made to measure, so it goes over this," he joked, patting his belly. "You have to pay a fair bit of dosh for bespoke, but they do make you look twenty years younger. Well, according to their salesman with all the patter, at least. Oh, and there'll be a bit of money left over, as well, to pick up the Christmas present I'm purchasing for my young friend Stanley, which is also why I'm here in town today."

"A suit, is it?" Harriet asked, making a note on the cash withdrawal slip. "My goodness, I'm sure that was the price of my first car," she recalled, smiling gently. "But you do get what you pay for, don't you, as the saying goes. And if it takes twenty years off you, I might have to pop along and see what they can do for me as well."

"Nonsense, you both look exceptionally smart," Larry said, dialling up his impeccable charm. "Also, I'm not sure if you need to write this down, but the reason for my new suit is that I'm going to be a compère at a sewing event my friend Charlotte is organising. And Stanley, who I'm buying the Christmas present for, is her son."

"I see," Harriet said, sounding perfectly comfortable with what she was being told. "I'm awfully sorry to have asked you,

Mr Beasdale. But, you see, we often get people withdrawing a significant amount of money who are..." she began to explain, though appearing to struggle to choose the right word.

"Old?" Larry said with a chuckle. "You can say it."

"Well, yes, Mr Beasdale. Sadly, the elderly and vulnerable are often targeted by criminals and con artists to withdraw large amounts of cash for them. And it's for that reason we always like to double-check when any relatively substantial sum is involved. I'm sure you understand? So, just to be clear, nobody has pressured you to withdraw cash for them?"

"You're very kind for checking, but I can confirm that this money is most definitely for a tailored outfit," Larry verified. "Although, Charlotte doesn't know I'm investing in a new suit, so it'll be a nice surprise for her on the day," he said, placing a finger against his lips.

"I'm sure you'll look wonderful, Mr Beasdale. My colleague will arrange your cash, but please do take care carrying that amount of money around with you."

With that bit of business soon taken care of, Larry once again stepped outside into the cold, popping his hat back on his bonce. Fortunately, the next stop on his mission was to the toyshop, only a hop and a skip away, located a short walk further up the street. He'd already called ahead to check on availability and had then placed his order over the phone, so it was just the small matter of picking it up and paying for it while he was in town. Prior to this, he'd been quizzing Stanley about potential Christmas gifts over the previous several weeks (though without trying to be too clear about his intentions). But despite his best efforts, he hadn't been able to pin the young fellow down as to any type of firm preference. One minute it was a skateboard, for instance, then a microscope, and then it was something else, and then it was something else again. It was impossible to keep up. So eventually Larry had to concede defeat, changing course and requesting some inspiration from Stanley's mum instead.

And it was for that reason that Larry soon found himself, based on Charlotte's advice, leaving the toyshop with a fine Lego space station tucked safely under his arm, which, though relatively large, thankfully didn't have too much weight to it. Fortunate, then, as he still had a ten minute or so walk to collect his new suit.

Harrow & Sons were a gentleman's tailor operating out of the same premises for over sixty years. And while they were considerably more expensive than, say, the larger chain stores, you were paying for the personal touch, where your garments were skilfully made to measure rather than off the shelf. As Larry walked up Prospect Hill towards their shop, he reflected on how many suits he'd purchased from them over the years. Several, at least. It was Alfie Harrow, Sr, in fact, who'd measured him for his wedding suit all those years ago, and it was a treat to now be dealing with Alfie's grandson, who'd lost none of the original eye for detail and flair for customer service.

Larry knew the purchase of the suit was an extravagance, but he wanted to look his best for Charlotte's event and do her proud. Secretly, he was also looking forward to being on stage again, so to speak, out there under the spotlight with all eyes on him. So yes, the suit was somewhat expensive. But worth every penny in his mind.

The box of Lego under Larry's arm had initially caused no issue, but the further he walked, the more cumbersome it became. Waiting to cross the road, he swopped arms, offering relief even if it was only temporary. Stepping off the pavement, he moved out of the relative shelter provided by the surrounding buildings and was caught by a firm crosswind, the large, flat box acting like a ship's sail, knocking him off-balance so he was teetering about like it was his very first time at sea.

Thankfully unscathed, and now on the other side of the road, Larry took a moment to compose himself, proud of himself for keeping a firm hold on the box. But his joy was short-lived when an even stronger gust soon buffeted him, knocking his hat clear off his head in the process.

"Oh, blast," he said, glancing about for any kind volunteers who might go chasing after it for him. But in typical fashion, there was nobody to be seen, so he hurried after it himself.

Then, like a scene from an Ealing comedy, every time he found himself within reaching distance of his hat, the stiff breeze carried it further away. It was like his hat was attached to the line of a fishing rod controlled by an accomplished practical joker. Finally, right on the verge of giving up his prized hat as a lost cause, it was blown down an alleyway blocked off at the far end, with only one way in and one way out.

"A-ha! Got you now!" Larry declared, quickening his pace past a row of industrial-sized wheelie bins, eager to recover his precious hat before it should find its way into one of the questionable-looking puddles he was currently spying.

"Oi!" a voice called out from behind Larry, echoing loudly as it bounced off the concrete walls.

Startled, Larry turned, greeted by a hooded figure standing at the entrance of the alley, the person's face hidden from view from Larry's position inside the darkened alcove.

Larry instinctively stepped back through what he believed was merely a shallow puddle. But unfortunately, his foot sank into an unseen pothole beneath, twisting the foot back on itself and producing a sickening sound like the snapping of a twig. Larry staggered back, dropping the box of Lego in the process and placing a hand out behind him to brace himself against the imminent fall. But on the way down, as if his injured ankle hadn't been enough in itself, his head caught the rigid green plastic corner of one of the bins, causing an audible thump.

Now on the ground, Larry groaned, placing a hand against his temple, both it and his ankle throbbing in pain. "You put that down!" he said, dazed, and further distressed, even beyond the fact of his injuries, after seeing the hooded figure reach down and pick up the box that he had just dropped in the fall.

"Can you hear me? You give that back!" Larry forcefully insisted, though still very much in a daze. "That's... that's young

Stanley's... Christmas present..." he managed to say, moments before everything faded and he drifted into unconsciousness.

CHAPTER SIXTEEN

C harlotte took a sip of the tea she'd been so kindly provided. It was sweet, just as she'd asked for, but had more milk than she'd perhaps expected. Imperfectly prepared tea was still preferable to no tea at all, however, and grateful as Charlotte was, it's not as if she was about to complain. And she was here at Appledene to receive good news, after all, so there was certainly nothing that could possibly have dampened her mood anyway.

She took another sip, and then gently rested the cup on her knee as she sat patiently, waiting for Sam to come out and join her there in the reception area. As she waited, she stared at the painting on the opposite wall. It was a new one this time, as Sam enjoyed changing them up periodically in order to coincide with the seasons. The current painting featured a striking winter scene, with figures traipsing through the snow. It was mostly greys, but sported hints of colour here and there. It was an older, classic painting, and Charlotte recognised it, although she couldn't recall the title or the artist. She thought of mentioning it to her two art enthusiasts, Beryl and Joyce. But, to be fair to those two, the gentlemen depicted on the canvas were all fully clothed, so Joyce and Beryl likely wouldn't have been any more familiar with it than Charlotte was, this sort of artwork not being entirely in line with the pair's specific interest.

"Bruegel!" said Sam, suddenly appearing beside her.

Charlotte was so startled that she nearly spilt her tea, and, assuming that Sam had just sneezed, she held out her napkin to him, offering it up in case he should need it.

"It's called *The Hunters in the Snow,* by Bruegel the Elder," Sam declared proudly. "It's a nice one, isn't it?"

"Oh! Oh, yes it is," Charlotte answered, retracting her arm, as it was obvious now that Sam didn't need the napkin after all.

"But you didn't come here to talk about art, did you?" Sam replied, all smiles.

"Yes, Mollie said you had some news for me?" Charlotte asked. "Some good news? About a possible venue...?"

"Appledene!" exclaimed Sam.

Charlotte instinctively reached for her napkin once more, but quickly realised, again, that Sam had no need of it.

"Appledene! Right here at Appledene!" Sam told her.

It took her a moment to realise just what Sam was saying. And then, "Oh!" she said. "Oh, my! You're absolutely certain?"

Charlotte received a firm nod in response, which told her all she needed to know. "But why didn't you tell me that over the phone when I called?" she asked, carefully placing her teacup down onto the side table, and then rising to her feet excitedly.

"Well I was going to," Sam gently pointed out. "But then you said you wanted to meet me in person to talk about it, remember? You told me you were heading this way anyway, so..."

"Oh, that's right," Charlotte answered, mildly embarrassed, yet still entirely ecstatic. "Yes, I knew you had good news, but I never imagined—" she started to explain.

"I'm glad you did come along, though," Sam told her, grinning widely. "Because it gave me the opportunity to see your little face when I delivered the news."

"Can I... can I give you a hug?" Charlotte asked, although she didn't even bother to wait for a reply, diving straight in and squeezing Sam for several long seconds, her grip increasing in steady increments.

Eventually she released her hold on him, taking a step back, squirming in her shoes and nearly fit to burst. "Sam, if you hadn't just been on a date with my best friend, I'd give you a huge, sloppy kiss right on the mouth!" she insisted.

"You're very welcome, Lotti," Sam responded, after receiving a rather more respectable quick peck on the cheek, Charlotte doing her very best to restrain herself. "It's the absolute least I can do, considering all you accomplish for not only our care home but all of the others as well."

"I've got a venue for my Isle of Man Christmas Sewing Bee!" Charlotte said, doing a little happy dance, and relaying information that Sam was of course already well aware of.

Sam watched on, enjoying Charlotte's performance. "To be honest, I never even realised you had been struggling to find a place," he said, after she'd had a chance to settle down a bit. "It was only after Mollie happened to mention it that the idea of using Appledene sprung to mind."

"And you're sure the residents won't be inconvenienced?"

"Not at all, Lotti. In fact, I knew you were coming along, so I ran it past them over breakfast just to be sure. Henry and Sid even offered their services as clothing models for the day, which raised a cheer from some of the ladies, who then suggested a swimwear element to your competition?"

"Saucy old devils," Charlotte said with a laugh. "I'll see what I can do," she promised, scribbling an imaginary note to herself.

"Seriously, though, if there's anything we can help you out with, you only need to ask," Sam told her. "And so you know, you can make use of the entire building for the occasion, and there should be ample parking for everyone right on the grounds."

From the moment Mollie broke the wonderful news in her previous text, Charlotte had been on cloud nine. *"Talk to Sam,"* was all Mollie had said when pressed regarding the details, and Charlotte was glad she did!

The lack of an available location for the Christmas Sewing Bee had been playing heavily on Charlotte's mind, so much so that she'd secretly started to doubt the idea's viability and had considered pulling the plug. For that reason, the offer to use Appledene was a complete dream come true. Arguably one of the finest residences on the island, the grand ballroom (which doubled as the dining room), was more than sufficient to accommodate the main sewing event. In addition, Appledene had several other spacious areas that Charlotte could utilise. For instance, the majestic structure boasted a generously equipped library, stocked with leather-bound books stacked high on towering oak stands like something from Harry Potter's school. In this section of the building, Charlotte's vision was selling all of their festive handcrafted goodies, confident the quality merchandise and magnificent backdrop would help to loosen purse strings, all for a very worthy cause. And now that she'd succeeded in securing this venue, Charlotte was finally in a position where she could officially sign teams up and announce to the good folks of the Isle of Man that the Christmas Sewing Bee was coming very soon!

Sam escorted Charlotte through the winding corridors, giving her a whistle-stop tour of the rooms available to her on the day. Of course, she'd been given the grand tour previously, but this time she was looking at things through the lens of an event organiser, permitting her mind to run wild with the available opportunities.

"And you know what else, Sam?" Charlotte said, peering out through the sash windows, admiring the manicured gardens. "We'll hopefully get the sewing crowd coming to support us, but I suspect we'll also welcome a lot of curious visitors, thankful for the opportunity to wander around and soak up the ambience of this building. Or, as I like to do, have a jolly good nosey around."

"Absolutely! And hopefully they'll all be generous when it comes to your collection buckets as well," Sam answered. Sam then drew to a halt outside the kitchen entrance. "Have you thought about refreshments?" he asked, pointing inside the kitchen area. "Because, if you haven't, this will make a superb location. And, if you'd like, Lotti, I'll be happy to man the stand that day with a volunteer or two?"

"I'm sure that Stanley would be delighted to help on the refreshments stand," Charlotte considered fondly. "And yes, that sounds like a fabulous idea. Thank you."

Sam surveyed the spacious kitchen doorframe just before him, rubbing his chin. "You know," he said, thinking aloud. "It wouldn't take much effort to turn the kitchen doorway into a shopfront."

"It wouldn't?"

Sam shook his head. "Not at all. And I've got plenty of wood in the workshop we can utilise to construct a facade here. That way, when people come up to purchase something, it will look like something you'd see at a Bavarian market. And when they do, that's when they're hit by the glorious aroma of my world-famous mince pies!"

"Oh? World-famous, are they?" Charlotte teased, although thoroughly on board with Sam's contagious enthusiasm.

"Well, famous around these parts, at least," Sam replied with a grin. "Now, I noticed you didn't have time to finish your tea earlier," Sam added. "So how about we freshen it up?"

Charlotte smiled politely. "Of course. But let me go through the trouble of making it this time around," she diplomatically suggested, unwilling to criticise the previous person's efforts when they'd been so kind. "You know, Sam..." she went on, pausing to search for the proper words she wished to use. "Sam, you're a genuinely lovely human being," she eventually settled on. And just as she was about to administer another grateful hug, her phone, buzzing in her pocket, distracted her for a moment. "Oh, and *speaking* of wonderful nursing home managers," Charlotte remarked, now looking at her phone's display. "Another one is calling me right now, as it should happen."

Charlotte excused herself, taking a moment to answer the call. "Hello, Emma. Guess where I am?" she said into her phone.

Charlotte waited for a response, but her joyful expression dimmed the moment she started listening to what Emma had to say. "He's what?" Charlotte asked, nervously running her fingers through her hair. "Tell me he's okay?" she added a moment later. Charlotte paced in a circle, allowing Emma to do most of the talking. "I'm on my way, Emma. Thank you for calling."

"Charlotte?" Sam asked.

"It's my friend Larry," Charlotte explained, the anguish in her voice evident. "They think he might have been mugged," she said, scarcely able to believe what she was saying. "I'm going to head to the hospital, so I'll need to leave the tea for another time, Sam, if you don't mind?"

"No, of course. You go."

Charlotte kissed him on the cheek. "I'm sorry to run, Sam. And for what you've done," she said, "I'll never be able to thank you enough."

"You're welcome, Lotti. And I hope your friend is okay."

The drive over to Noble's Hospital passed in something of a stomach-wrenching blur. Charlotte continued to run the conversation she'd had with Emma through her mind. Had she even heard her correctly? Larry mugged? As she said it back to herself, it sounded so absurd. Where on earth would Larry even be to find himself in a position for that to happen?

Charlotte willed the revolving glass doors to get a move on, breaking into a sprint once inside the hospital building.

"Can I help?" a kindly lady volunteered from behind the reception desk, likely noting Charlotte's anxious expression.

"I'm looking for Ward Nine?" Charlotte asked, slowing but not stopping.

"Follow the corridor to your left, then it's up a short flight of stairs once you've reached the end. Would you like me to show you the way?"

"I'm good, but thanks!" Charlotte called out, offering up a grateful wave, heading as instructed and breaking into the sort of running walk you'd do when your final call has just been announced over the airport Tannoy system. She tried to retain a positive frame of mind but couldn't shake the awful reality that she was heading towards terrible news. A fear that wasn't eased when she walked through the doors to Ward 9. There, two police officers were talking to Emma, and even from the doorway, Charlotte could see the concern written all over Emma's face.

Charlotte hovered, not wanting to interrupt, turning her attention to a poster highlighting the symptoms of septicaemia for a moment in order to give herself something to do.

"Charlotte!" Emma said, catching a glimpse of Charlotte from the corner of her eye and waving her over.

"Right. We should be on our way, then," one of the officers said, handing Emma his business card. "We'll be in touch, but don't hesitate to call us if there's anything you need," he added, offering both Emma and Charlotte a comforting smile.

Charlotte studied Emma's face, taking note of her puffy eyes. "Emma, how is he?" Charlotte implored, bracing herself for the worst. "He's not...?"

Emma immediately shook her head. "No," she assured her, taking hold of Charlotte's hand. "The doctor believes he's broken his ankle, and the poor thing has a deep gash on his head as well. They told me he was barely conscious when the ambulance brought him in."

Charlotte struggled to contain her quivering lip. Never had she been so glad to learn that somebody had merely broken an ankle, amongst other injuries. "I couldn't help thinking it was something even more dreadful," she confessed, accepting a hug from Emma while sobbing on her shoulder. "Can I see him?"

"The medical staff are with him at the moment," Emma advised, releasing Charlotte but holding onto her hand. "They don't think there'll be any real, lasting damage, thank goodness."

Charlotte caught her breath for a moment, taking a tissue from her pocket and dabbing at her eyes. "And you said Larry was mugged?" she asked, incredulous. "But who in God's name would do that to such a dear, sweet man?"

"That's what I was just talking to the police about," Mollie answered. "Although it's now looking likely that it wasn't a mugging after all."

"Oh?" said Charlotte, relieved on that count, but confused as to what might have happened if this should be the case.

"The police don't think so, no," Emma explained. "Apparently, a teenaged lad phoned for the ambulance after seeing Larry take a tumble. Then, on arrival, Larry was described by the paramedics as being quite incoherent, suggesting the young lad had attempted to steal from him. As such, the police were called, and the lad was initially placed under arrest. But the boy was devastated."

"So he *didn't* steal from Larry?"

"The police are still investigating, reviewing CCTV and such, but it doesn't seem that way. The lad made a statement saying he'd witnessed Larry struggling to catch up with his hat, which had blown off. Apparently, during the chase for the hat, Larry dropped an envelope. That's when the lad came running over to help, picking up the envelope and following Larry into an alleyway where the hat had landed. That's when he saw Larry twist his ankle, falling over and banging his head on the way down."

"Oh, the poor love," Charlotte said, just wanting to give Larry the biggest cuddle she could.

"I know. So it's starting to look like the young chap saved the day by phoning the ambulance. According to the police, the envelope he handed them had hundreds and hundreds of pounds still inside. So it just goes to show you that there are some kind-hearted, honest people out there."

"Hundreds of pounds? Why on earth would Larry be walking around Douglas with all that cash?" Charlotte wondered aloud.

"Well, that I do know," Emma told her. "The police found a cash withdrawal receipt, so they headed to the bank branch to investigate further. The staff in there knew exactly who the police were enquiring about, and the precise reason he'd wanted that specific amount of money as they'd had a necessary conversation with him about it."

"And what was the reason?" Charlotte asked.

Emma's eyes welled up at the recollection of her earlier discussion with the two police officers. "He told them he was on his way to buy a Christmas present for a smashing young fellow named Stanley," she revealed.

"Oh, bless his soul."

"But that's not all," Emma went on, struggling to contain her emotion. "That only accounted for a smallish portion of the amount, of course. Larry proudly told the cashiers he was going to be a compère at his friend's sewing event, so he was on his way to pick up a specially tailored suit for the big day. From what they said, he had a twinkle in his eye and a huge smile on his face when he told them the new suit was going to be a surprise for his dear friend, Charlotte."

Charlotte looked down to her feet, shaking her head gently. "Oh, Larry," she said, choking on her words. "What a wonderful, wonderful person you really are."

CHAPTER SEVENTEEN

Charlotte often observed that trying to rouse young Stanley from bed wasn't the most straightforward of tasks at the best of times. Throw in the fact that it was a cold, wet Saturday morning this day, and she'd have been forgiven for expecting the first movement from his bedroom to occur not until half past ten or thereabouts. Remarkable, then, that Charlotte had found his bed empty a full few hours before this, a faint Stanley-sized imprint still visible on the bedsheets and his slippers absent. However, after poking her head into the hallway, she knew he couldn't have gone terribly far, hearing a faint *tappety-tap-tap* noise emanating from down below, in the front room of their cosy cottage from the sound of it. She had a fair idea what had woken him at this relatively early hour, but was still surprised nonetheless.

Charlotte ventured downstairs, approaching the living room doorway unheard, which was a minor miracle given the creaky nature of the old staircase she'd just travelled down. But there, hunched over their equally old wooden desk, Charlotte found the apple of her eye staring intently at her laptop screen.

"Morning, mister," she said, approaching to administer the first cuddle of the day. "And what time have you been up since?"

"Dunno," Stanley replied with a shrug, unable or unwilling to break his attention away from the screen, despite having his mum's arms draped around his neck like a scarf. "But I reckon it must have been rather early, because I think I heard the milkman? Either that, or it was a burglar."

"In that case," Charlotte said, releasing her hold on him, "I'll check to see if any milk bottles are waiting in the porch. And, if not, I'll assume we no longer have our family silver in the safe."

"We have a safe...?" Stanley asked, intrigued by this new bit of information, wondering what other sorts of treasures might similarly be ensconced in this steel box his mum spoke of.

Charlotte felt the need to burst his bubble, fearing he'd rip the place apart searching for a safe that didn't exist. "Sadly not," she said. "But we do have your favourite porridge, which is even better, yeah?"

"With a drizzle of Norrie and Esther's honey?" he asked, anxious to sample the delightful golden-liquid offerings of their favourite local beekeepers.

"Yes, with a drizzle of their delectable honey," Charlotte confirmed, opening the curtain to reveal another beautiful day on the Isle of Man. "Ah. And how many are we on now?" she asked, as she set about collecting the batch of empty hot chocolate mugs that had accumulated the previous evening, all with a crusted-on ring inside that would now require a good soaking.

Stanley lifted his head, just for a moment, as he considered the question. Then, he reached for the notepad sitting next to the computer, scribbling some figures and doing a bit of arithmetic, just before slapping down his pen in triumph. "One hundred and twenty-six!" he announced, doing a full 360-degree rotation in the padded office chair.

Ordinarily, Stanley would be subjected to a stern glance for using their furniture as a playground, but not this morning. Charlotte scanned her son's face, waiting to see the glimmer of a smile emerge, indicating he was pulling her leg. But it didn't arrive. Instead, Stanley wore the smug expression of a city trader who'd totally smashed their sales targets and was now headed to the local Porsche dealership to buy a new 911.

"You're kidding, right?" Charlotte asked, though hoping this wasn't the case.

Stanley shook his head in the negative. "Nope," he said, hitting the refresh button on the laptop for good measure. "We had a couple of orders just after the website went live," he told her. "And then, from about ten o'clock on, the orders started to regularly roll in, and they've been coming in ever since. So that's why I got up early, to see just how many came in overnight."

"I don't believe this," Charlotte said, not really believing it, although entirely delighted. "That's absolutely amazing."

"I think I know what's happened," Stanley declared, raising his hand like an accomplished detective about to reveal the solution to a whodunnit. "You know how you often spend the whole day talking yourself out of buying new crafting supplies, trying to convince yourself you don't really need them, even though you desperately want them?"

"Yes, I know that feeling well," Charlotte admitted.

"Well, I suspect it's the same type of thing going on here," Stanley went on, continuing with his somewhat convoluted explanation of the situation. "Because, then, you'll have a glass of wine, tell me life's too short, and then go ahead and buy what you've been talking yourself out of all day anyway, right? So, as I said, I think that's what's happened here."

"You do?

"Yeah. I reckon a bunch of the island's crafters all probably had a glass of wine or two, and after that was when they decided to buy tickets, late at night and into the morning," Stanley replied. "In fact, I was wondering if we shouldn't perhaps give wine to those who haven't yet purchased tickets? You know, to help speed the process along?"

"Stanley, my boy. You'll go far!"

The website that Stanley was so diligently monitoring was one advertising their Manx Christmas Sewing Bee event. It was something Calum had kindly asked one of his team to design. It wasn't overly complicated, really, with just a few pages to navigate showcasing the upcoming event, along with photographs of the marvellous venue, and a section outlining the ReCyCool initiative as well. Importantly, and this was where Stanley had come in, there was also the functionality to purchase tickets online. Calum had explained how he'd need a man he could trust to monitor the online sales and, crucially, ensure that each payment had been successfully processed. Calum had been uncertain as to who this person should be, unsure which one of his top executives he could entrust with this important task. Fortunate, then, that Stanley had stepped up to the plate, offering his services and sparing Calum that tricky decision in the process. All for the princely salary of five pence per ticket sold, which Stanley had been crafty enough to negotiate.

Charlotte finally managed to peel her young entrepreneur away from the computer screen just long enough to enjoy his bowl of porridge.

"You okay, Mum?" Stanley asked, noting his mum hadn't demolished her breakfast like he'd just done.

Charlotte, for her part, sat with one elbow on the table, staring distractedly into the oaty mixture before her. "Hmm? Oh, I'm fine, Stan. More than fine, in fact. I was just running the numbers through in my head," she said. Charlotte then broke her attention away from her porridge, looking across the kitchen table. "Sam said that they've got permission from the fire service to have up to six hundred people on site," she told Stanley. "And at a fiver a ticket, that means we're going to have plenty in the school-uniform-buying budget. And that's not including the competition entry fees."

"Don't forget what those hundreds of people are then going to spend on your festive crafting goodies and cake!" Stanley reminded her, rubbing his little hands together at the prospect. "And on that subject, Mum. I was thinking about my wages for monitoring the website?"

"Oh, I don't know, I'm not sure Calum would be expecting an invoice quite so soon, Stan?"

Stanley smiled, not really sure what an invoice was but liking the sound of it. "If we sell six hundred tickets, Mum. Which we will. Then I'm going to donate my wages to you."

Charlotte lowered her spoon. "My goodness, I didn't think you could melt my heart more than you already do," Charlotte answered. "But you have, Stanley, and that's a lovely gesture."

Stanley pushed his chair back. "I know, Mum," he offered, with a confident wink. "Now, if I'm excused, I need to get back to my sales dashboard. Time is money, you know."

"You do that, Gordon Gekko, and I might look at buying you a pair of braces for Christmas," Charlotte told him, even though, with the quizzical look he was giving her, she knew he had no idea what she was talking about. "Ah. Actually," she said, looking to her watch to check the time. "In fact, you'll need to jump in the shower, as your dad will be here soon, okay?"

"What? But I'm not staying at Dad's this weekend," Stanley was quick to point out. "You've not been on the wine already, have you?" he asked, unable to stifle his giggle.

"No, cheeky chops. Emma and I are going to bring Larry home from the hospital, so your dad's agreed to look after you until I get back."

"What?" Stanley asked, his face dropping in an instant. "But I assumed I'd just be coming to the hospital with you?" he said, sounding wounded.

"Oh, I'm sorry. I suppose I just didn't think you'd be too interested in..." Charlotte began, although before she could even manage to finish her sentence, Stanley was gone. "Stan...?" she said, calling after him.

Charlotte was worried she'd upset him, but he returned only a short moment later.

"Of course I wanted to come, Mum. I've even made Larry a card," he announced, holding it up for inspection.

Charlotte took hold of the card, made from a folded sheet of white A4 paper. There on the front, Stanley had drawn a humorous portrait of Larry in a wheelchair. But this wasn't just any wheelchair, oh no. This was a special edition, no less. "Are these rockets sticking out of the back?" Charlotte asked, running her eyes over his artwork and noticing this peculiar, if delightful, detail.

"Yep!" Stanley was happy to confirm, moving closer with his explaining finger extended. "And because it's rocket-propelled, that's why he's popping a wheelie, see?" he explained. "Because he's just activated them using *that* red button," he explained further, pointing to the big red button.

Then, as the pièce de résistance on his wonderful creation, he'd written the words:

Larry – I hope you get well, Wheelie soon! Xxx

"So can I come?" Stanley asked, with hope-filled eyes.

"You've even drawn him wearing his official Crafternoon apron," Charlotte observed, still admiring her son's amazing handiwork. "Hmm? Oh, yes. Yes, of course you can come," she added, in response to his question. "And I'm very sure Larry is going to absolutely adore his card."

"Sorry!" Emma called out from the driver's seat for what felt like the umpteenth time. "Oh, Larry, I'm so sorry," she said again, only a few seconds later.

"You're not responsible for the Isle of Man's bumpy roads," Larry assured her, sat there in the back of the nursing home's minibus with his leg raised, Charlotte on one side, Stanley on the other.

Despite spending a few days in the hospital, Larry was, as always, in splendid form. Before being discharged, he'd asked his wheelchair pilot, Stanley, to give him a gentle shove in the direction of everyone who'd been so kind to him over the course of his stay. Larry had purchased each and every one of them a little thank you card from the hospital gift shop and wanted to hand it to them personally. And to everybody's immense relief, the medical team confirmed that Larry wouldn't have any lasting damage, with the neat scar on his head healing nicely, and no need for surgery on his broken ankle. The ankle would still need to be in a plaster cast for a month or so, of course, but it was a plaster cast that at least didn't remain unsigned for long, thanks to Stanley.

"Ah!" a delighted Larry said, pulling out the homemade card Stanley had given him and admiring it once more. "I hope you get well, *wheelie* soon," he read aloud, with a snort and a chuckle. "It just works on so many levels," he added, seriously impressed with the creativity of his young friend sitting beside him.

"And you like the rockets?" Stanley asked. "Only my friend Lewis said that his dad is a scientist of some sort. So I reckon, if we ask his dad nicely, he might be able to help us build some *real* rockets?"

Larry pondered that thought for a moment. "Hmm, well it wouldn't hurt to ask, little buddy," he offered, perfectly willing to entertain Stanley's charming proposal.

"There'll be no rocket-propelled wheelchairs in the works, gentlemen," Emma made clear, from her seat up front. "Our insurance premiums are already sky-high as it is," she explained, although certainly not unappreciative of Stanley's whimsical idea.

Soon, Emma manoeuvred the minibus as close to the nursing home's front door as humanly possible without nudging the brickwork. "Here we go, Larry," she said, removing the keys from the ignition. "Home sweet home."

"And that means I get to have another go on the hydraulic ramp!" Larry remarked, always eager to put a positive slant on any situation.

"Can I wheel you inside, Larry?" Stanley asked. "I think I know where I went wrong back at the hospital, so we shouldn't knock anything over this time."

Larry gave the boy a look. "What? That's half the fun, my fine lad. Why have a plaster cast battering ram like this if we can't knock something over from time to time?"

"In that case, Larry, I'll see what I can do," Stanley answered, more than happy to oblige.

Following a controlled descent from the rear of the minibus, Larry took in several lungfuls of fresh, crisp, non-hospital air. "It makes you glad to be alive!" he declared, before cracking his imaginary whip. "Right. Lead on, dear boy. And don't spare the horses."

To be fair to Stanley, he was doing a bang-up job as a wheel-chair pilot. But that didn't stop both Emma and Charlotte anxiously following behind like it was his first time on a bike without stabilisers. "You'll need to give it a bit of gas," Larry suggested, as they approached the slight incline of the wheelchair ramp leading towards the front door.

Stanley buried his chin into his chest, arms outstretched, "Roger that," he said, preparing himself for the final push.

"Or…" Charlotte said, taking hold of one of the handles, "I could just lend a hand?"

The nursing home's automatic doors opened, gliding apart as if to welcome an old friend home once again. A stream of warm air from the overhead heater sent the hair atop Larry's head dancing, much to Stanley's amusement.

"Keep moving, you, or I'll have no hair left," Larry protested, threatening to unleash another crack of his whip. But before he could do precisely that, Larry's eyes were drawn to the left of the reception area, where the corridor ran down towards the dining room. "Oh, my," he said, lowering his whipping arm. "What on earth is all this about?"

Emma placed a hand down on his shoulder. "This is how we welcome our friends home around here," she said, giving his shoulder a gentle squeeze.

Up ahead, the nursing home residents, some standing, some sitting — but all of them smiling — formed a human guard of honour on either side of the corridor. Above them, draped from one wall to the other, was a garland of multicoloured bunting, spelling out the words:

Welcome home Larr xxx

Stanley wheeled his charge several rotations forward, allowing Larry to fully immerse himself in the moment. "What a wonderful, wonderful welcome," Larry commented, smiling broadly at each of his fellow residents.

"Somehow, we've mislaid the Y, I'm afraid," Gladys explained, extending a finger above her head. "We had it yesterday, but, bloody typical, it's vanished. Helen's working on a new one as we speak."

"You can hardly notice," Larry politely suggested, ever the gentleman.

As instructed by Emma, Stanley continued through to the dining room, where the refreshments awaited. "You didn't need to go to all this trouble for silly old me!" Larry exclaimed, feasting his eyes on a table piled high with homemade cakes and sandwiches.

"It's the least we could do," his friend Archie said, poised and ready with a teapot in hand. "And, as you're presently off your feet, I've taken the liberty of assuming to tea urn duties. With your permission, of course?"

"Permission granted, Archie. And we couldn't find a finer man to hold the fort," Larry was pleased to suggest.

Charlotte and Emma took up a position on the periphery, happy to watch Larry enjoying the good wishes of his friends and several slices of cake in the process. He was also dutifully attended to by his loyal chauffeur, Stan, never far from his side and ready to wheel him this way or that at a moment's notice.

Just then, Ken, the receptionist, stuck his head through the dining room doors, running his eyes around the room until they located and settled on Emma. No words were spoken, but Emma appeared to know precisely what Ken's raised thumb was indicating. "Please do excuse me, Lotti," she said, following Ken out of the dining room.

"Mum, I reckon I can get Larry to do a figure of eight," Stanley advised, skipping over to inform Charlotte of this new idea he'd just had. "I'm fairly certain he won't tip over, if only I—"

"Stanley," she lightly admonished him, gently wagging a cautionary finger. "Just you remember he's recovering from a nasty fall, and..." she said, though trailing off as Larry had just appeared, wheeling himself over to where they were presently standing. "Are you okay, Larry? You're not getting overtired, are you?" Charlotte asked, fussing over him. "This isn't all too much for you, is it?"

"I've been lying flat on my back for days, Lotti," a smiling Larry told her. "I'm just glad to finally be up and about. Or as up and about as you can get in this contraption, at least."

Charlotte checked him over once more, and then crouched down a bit. "There was something I wanted to mention to you, Larry," she said, now at the same height as he was.

"If you're going to ask me to dance, Lotti. Now's probably not the best time."

"Well, I expect to be first on your dance card when you're up and running, Larry," Charlotte insisted. "But what I was actually going to talk to you about was the Sewing Bee."

"Oh, right," Larry said, sounding resigned to the situation, like a football manager about to be fired by the chairman.

"The thing is," Charlotte started to say, "I know—"

"But I can still do it," Larry cut across, looking at her with sad eyes, hoping for a stay of execution. "I spent most of my time in the hospital working on my repertoire, Lotti. And I know I'm in this blasted wheelchair, but I've even managed to incorporate a few wheel-based gags because of it. No, I truly had my heart set on this, Lotti, and I won't let you down. I promise. Please let me do it, Lotti, and I swear to you I'll—"

"Larry!" Charlotte said firmly but kindly, sensing he could well go on for some time otherwise. "Larry, dear, I wouldn't dream of firing my host with the most. Not on your nelly. And it was for that reason that I went along to see your tailor."

"You went to see Alfie? Lovely chap. Salt of the earth, that man."

"He sure is," Charlotte was happy to agree. "I explained to him what had happened, and that you're in a plaster cast. Anyway, he's offered to make you an extra pair of trousers, at no additional cost, that'll accommodate your plaster cast. So this way, you can still wear your new suit on the day."

"And I'll be there to wheel you around as well, Larry," Stanley offered. "You just point, and that's the direction we'll go, okay?"

Larry placed the palm of his hand over his chest. "Thank you both," he said, and it was clear from the emotion in his voice that he meant it. "And, Lotti, I really appreciate the..." he began to say, but he never got a chance to finish, as Stanley had just whisked him away, pushing him in the direction of the refreshments table. Which one of them required another dose of refreshing wasn't exactly clear, but Charlotte wasn't overly concerned. It was a party, after all, and eating to excess was to be expected. Besides, Stanley was getting plenty of exercise from wheeling Larry around, Charlotte reasoned.

Returning to the area of the festivities, Emma slipped back into the dining room, a companion following closely behind. "This way," she told him. "I promise they don't bite."

The young lad wearing a black hoody and grey tracksuit bottoms didn't appear too reassured, offering an uneasy smile in return, keeping Emma within range.

"Ladies and gentlemen!" Emma called out. "If I could drag you away from your cake for just a moment?" she asked. "Wow," she added, a moment later, when all eyes turned to her at the first time of asking. "I've usually got to shout at least three times before you lot listen to me," she joked, taking up a position next to Larry. "We're all here today to welcome our lovely friend, neighbour, practical joker and all-around nice guy, Larry, who's back from his short stay in the hospital where he's no doubt been thoroughly fussed over by the pretty nurses."

"It's a hard life," Larry offered. "And you know I'm all about the sacrifice."

"Anyway," Emma continued. "We're all absolutely delighted that you're back home with us, Larry. I can promise you've been dearly missed."

"We've missed you, Larry!" the rest of the group called out in unison, completely unrehearsed.

Emma waved a hand, encouraging the young lad who'd been hovering at the back to come forward. "And we've an exceptional guest here with us today. So, Jordan, if I could ask you to come and join us?"

Jordan smiled awkwardly when all eyes in the room landed upon him. He stepped forward, probably feeling like a meaty, large-bellied warthog venturing into a lion's den.

"This is Jordan," Emma announced to the group by way of formal introduction. "And Jordan..." Emma said, placing her hand on Larry's shoulder. "This is Larry."

Larry smiled politely, but like everyone else in the room, he didn't have a clue as to who their rather nervous-looking young guest was.

"Jordan is the very kind-hearted lad who returned Larry's money," Emma explained to those assembled. Jordan is *also* the one who was there when Larry took his fall, phoning for the ambulance and sitting with Larry until it arrived."

Without being prompted, Stanley started clapping, looking at this Jordan fellow as some sort of hero standing there before him. The applause soon spread through the room, and those that could stand did so, each of them eager to show their gratitude towards this selfless teen.

Jordan, clearly not used to being at the centre of attention, shifted his weight uneasily from one foot to the other. "I'm just pleased to see you're out of the hospital," he said to Larry. "I was on my way home from badminton practice that day when I saw you chasing after your hat and drop your envelope. And that's when I came over to help," he explained.

A look of dismay came over Larry's face as he realised just who this young fellow was, and how gravely he'd misjudged the boy. Larry took hold of Jordan's hand. "Thank you, son. Thank you so much for caring," he said, his shoulders starting to heave. "I'm awfully sorry, Jordan," Larry told him.

"Ehm, what for, exactly?" Jordan asked, flicking worried eyes over to Emma for a moment, concerned he'd upset the old boy.

Larry appeared frustrated with himself and ashamed. "I accused you of stealing from me, didn't I? Oh my goodness, I'm so sorry, truly I am."

"It's fine," Jordan said, making light of the situation. "I saw that you'd just smacked your head on the corner of a wheelie bin, so I didn't take too much offence at what you'd said. How was your hat? It didn't half give you the runaround, from what I could see."

"Good as new," Larry was happy to report. "Charlotte over there very kindly popped it in the wash for me."

"Well, I should probably..." Jordan said, glancing over his shoulder. "I just popped by to say hello."

"Won't you stay?" Larry asked. "We've a lot of cake, and I'd like you to meet some of the gang," he said.

"Ehm, yeah. Go on, then," Jordan said, accepting the plate that was quickly handed to him. "Just for a while."

After a moment or two, Stanley wandered over to Jordan, looking the teenager firmly in the eye.

"Erm... everything okay?" Jordan asked, looking down at the young lad stood about two feet shorter than himself.

Stanley extended his hand. "Thank you," he said, staring up like he'd just met his footballing hero. "Thank you for looking after Larry. He's one in a million and the nicest man you could ever hope to meet."

"Yeah," Jordan said, shaking the hand thrust towards him. "He does seem like he's a cool guy. So what is he, your grandad or something?"

"Not my grandad, no," Stanley said, casting a fond eye in Larry's general direction. "He's my friend, Jordan. One of my very best friends."

CHAPTER EIGHTEEN

Charlotte's modest cottage in the pretty seaside village of Laxey was often full to the brim, with numerous crafting projects typically happening all at once and at various different stages of completion — with some in the planning phase, dozens routinely in progress, several nearing completion, and a few actually finished. (These were what she liked to refer to as her four crafting buckets.) She sometimes imagined a disciplined world in which she'd work on one project, watching it move seamlessly through her production conveyor belt, only jumping onto the next project when the current one was signed off as complete. But, of course, that had never actually happened. Not once. Not even close. Charlotte's issue was that there were just too many tempting patterns to work on and only one measly pair of hands with which to complete them. It was the reason she envied octopus. Oh, what she could accomplish with eight arms and an endless wool supply! Stanley suggested, when Charlotte had mentioned this to him previously, that such a character — a knitting octopus, that is, or rather, *The Knitting Octopus* — might make for an ideal baddie in the next Marvel film. Of course, Charlotte was determined to use her knitting powers for good as opposed to evil, and for now, at least, she'd resigned herself to having to make do with just the two paltry arms. At least until evolution could be coaxed into providing the additional limbs that all devoted crafters both desired and required.

The storage capacity of their cottage was also a factor that occupied Charlotte's thoughts, or more accurately, the lack of it. At present, every square inch of available space had already been requisitioned, turned over to housing a vast array of assorted crafting supplies. It was chaos, but at least it was organised chaos. Ask Charlotte to locate a particular roll of fabric or even a unique coloured thread, for instance, and she could find it for you in seconds. As for Stanley, he didn't mind so much about the clutter. Just so long as the crafting supplies remained outside the boundary line of his bedroom door and thus didn't encroach upon his sacred personal space, then he was perfectly content.

Charlotte occasionally considered the option of a bigger place for the two of them. But the truth, as she well knew, was that if they had any additional space, it'd just get filled quicker than a freshly dug hole in wet sand. And besides, any larger property they potentially moved into would be unlikely to offer up the same charming village location, only minutes from the school and, crucially, the beach.

Charlotte's chronic storage problems were exacerbated at present, even more than usual, owing to the pile of Christmas crafting items stowed in her hallway. With just over a week until the Sewing Bee, she'd been busy as a bee herself, buzzing all over the island, collecting the fabulous festive goodies that the club members had created and kindly donated to raise funds. She'd not compiled a final tally as yet, but there were well over a hundred items by Stanley's reckoning. As such, their cottage was starting to look very much like the staging area for deliveries at Santa's North Pole headquarters.

Fearing she'd soon be unable to open her own front door, her saviour, once again, appeared in the form of Sam. Even though there were still a few days until the event, he was happy enough for her to start ferrying over a few bits and pieces, as required, thereby removing the hoarder-type obstacle course from Charlotte's living space. All she needed to do now was to start the process...

"Right," Charlotte said, speaking out loud to herself as she raised the boot on her trusty little car. "Now, how on earth do you put the rear seats down?" she asked, giving them a little shove, wondering if it might be as simple as that. But it wasn't. "Hmm," she said, pondering if they'd ever actually ever been down during her ownership. So she nudged them again, wondering if, by some miracle, what hadn't worked just a moment ago would for some reason work this time. Only it didn't. "Okay, then," she said, climbing inside through the passenger-side door, hoping an alternative vantage point might help to yield some positive results. Now sitting awkwardly in the vehicle's rear, she ran her hand over the cloth of the backseat, feeling for a lever or hidden mechanism of some kind to release the latch. She knew it wouldn't offer her much more room, but with the seats collapsed, she'd be able to squeeze a few extra bags in, she reckoned, so worth the effort, she thought.

With nothing presenting itself as an obvious solution, Charlotte switched herself to a kneeling position, looking over the seats into the boot compartment. "Come on," she said, stretching and leaning forward so the top of the seat was now digging into her stomach and her posterior was positioned centimetres away from the roof. "Where are you?" she asked, getting frustrated as the blood rushed to her head. "Wait, what's that?" she asked, spotting something glossy in the corner. It wasn't the lever she was looking for, sadly, but she had a moment of elation nonetheless, suspecting it might be the earring she'd lost somewhere around Eastertime. "Eww," she said, as she fumbled for and then successfully retrieved the object she'd spotted. What she'd hoped was her treasured family heirloom turned out to be, in fact, a half-eaten fruit pastille with a bit of fluff sticking to it.

Charlotte righted herself, now sitting back with her head where nature intended.

"Are you waiting for your chauffeur?" came the familiar, cheerful voice of Postman Harry as he walked up the road, nearing Charlotte's cottage. "You do know you can't drive the car from the rear seat, Miss Lotti?" he added, now on a roll, it would seem, as he peered inside the car through the still-opened boot.

"I'm sulking," Charlotte declared, crossing her arms over her chest to emphasise the point. "Twenty minutes, it seems like I've been out here, trying to collapse these flippin' rear seats," she advised. "And so far, all I've managed to do is find a congealed sweet, and I'm reasonably certain I've torn the seat of my trousers in the process. It was either fabric or my hamstring I heard ripping. I'm hoping it was fabric."

Harry lowered his bag, running his eyes around the rear of the vehicle's interior. "What about that?" he said, pointing to a rubber protruding nipple.

"I dunno, what about it?" Charlotte asked, following the line of Harry's extended index finger. "There's one on either side, and I've tried squeezing them, pushing them, twisting them, and I've even tried talking nicely to them, all without too much success."

"Ah, but what about *pulling* it," Harry said, taking a grip of the rubber between his thumb and forefinger. "It's a bit like milking a cow," Harry offered, and following a firm but gentle tug, Charlotte could feel the seatback move as if the mechanism on that side had been freed.

"I think that's it," Charlotte said, sliding over to the other side of the car. "Harry, you're an absolute lifesaver," she said, giving the other rubber nipple its own little squeeze and tug.

"Indeed," Harry said, giving the imaginary medals on his chest a well-deserved polish. "In this game, Lotti, you're not just a postman, you're also a mechanic, plumber, shoulder to cry on, and occasionally a midwife, amongst other things."

"A midwife, eh?" Charlotte replied, climbing out of the car. "Now that's what you call a special delivery."

"It was that," Harry recalled. "Born into this world during the big snowstorm of ninety-one. At first, they were even going to name the baby after me," he said, along with a happy sigh. "That would have been nice, until they changed their mind."

"They didn't like your name?"

"Oh, they did. But it was a baby girl, you see."

"Ah, that's a shame. But what about Harriet, though? That might have worked, yeah?" Charlotte suggested.

Harry offered a shrug. "I suppose," he said. "But it's a bit late now, in any case. She's probably got kids of her own by this point."

"Well, if it's any consolation, how about if I offer my heroic saviour a nice cuppa?" Charlotte asked, walking from the car towards her garden gate.

"Not today, Lotti," Harry said, giving his tum a gentle pat. "I've just had a brew and some cake down the road from old Mrs Bainbridge."

Charlotte feigned shock, her mouth agape. "You're cheating on me with other women?" she said, sounding terribly aggrieved. "Just how many other kitchen tables are you warming your feet under...?" she asked, with a well-timed sob added in for extra effect.

"Ah, but you'll always be my favourite, Miss Lotti," Harry assured her, handing over several envelopes secured together with an elastic band. "But I need to make sure there's enough of me to go around," he said with a wry smile, selfless soul that he was. "Anyway, I'm assuming that lot are heading into the back of your car?" he asked, noting the impressive pile of black bags stacked up next to her front door.

"Yep. That's some of my festive inventory to sell at our Manx Sewing Bee event," Charlotte explained, walking up her garden path.

"Oh, yes. I've already bought our tickets," Harry was pleased to report.

Charlotte's face lit up. "You're coming along?"

"Sure. I'm bringing my old mum and a couple of her pals, Lotti. I'm looking forward to it, I think," Harry said. And then, "Oh, before I forget, I was just talking to Amelia down in the village. She said that if I bumped into you, I should remind you they've got some crafted items for you to pick up. Also, her club is meeting all morning if you should be passing by. So. That's you officially reminded."

"Excellent!" Charlotte said, rubbing her hands in response. "That's more goodies to sell on our charity stall."

"You want me to help you load all that into the car?" Harry graciously offered.

Charlotte shook her head. "No, but thanks. First, I think I'll quickly pop down and see how many bags the Laxey Coffee Morning Crew have for me," she replied. "That way, I'll know how many of *that* lot," she added, pointing to her pile of bags, "I can also squeeze in."

Harry held his arm aloft, offering a hearty wave as he turned to go. "Very good, Lotti. Now I must press on and burn off Mrs Bainbridge's delicious spice cake."

"You're a real Lothario, Harry," Charlotte told him. "A true Casanova of the cake, you could say!"

Harry didn't look back, breaking into a lively skip while whistling a happy tune. "Oh, Charlotte," he said, a moment later, calling out behind him and raising his finger in the air as if he'd just remembered something. "And you were correct."

"I was? About what?"

"You've torn your trousers right across the backside!"

Fortunately, Harry had just been teasing, because as near as Charlotte could tell, the structural integrity of her trouser seams remained intact. And even if she'd managed to overlook a small rip or tear, she was undoubtedly heading to the right place to remedy it anyway.

The Laxey Coffee Morning Crew was awash with talent and an absolutely marvellous place to pop along to if you had a few hours available in your day. And such was the sociable nature of the crafting community (for the most part, at least, and leaving bingo to one side) that Charlotte even found some of her own club members in attendance at times, all of whom were ever eager to satisfy their incessant creative itch. Indeed, it was amusing to note their reactions whenever Charlotte made an appearance. Many among them, particularly the newer members, often squirmed when they spotted Charlotte peering around the door, reacting as if they'd just been caught cheating by their other half. They needn't have worried, though, as like them, Charlotte often frequented other crafting clubs, delighted to find new faces and any excuse for a good natter.

"Uh-oh, competitor warning!" Amelia called out, alerting her membership to Charlotte's current presence, straightening up like a meerkat spotting an inbound predator as she spoke. To this, the assorted crafters filling the Laxey church hall responded immediately, shielding their work like pupils protecting their lessons from the classroom cheat. But it was all delivered with good humour and accompanied by raucous laughter.

"What are we all working on?" Charlotte asked, taking an inquisitive stroll around the populated tables, stopping periodically to admire the array of fabrics being processed.

Gabby, who Charlotte knew from several of the various crafting groups, held up a leg-shaped piece of red-tartan brushed cotton. "Our sewing bee team are putting in a bit of practice against the clock," she was pleased to report.

Charlotte clapped her hands in appreciation. "Very nice. Those pyjama bottoms look good enough to climb into," she offered. "And just who's taking part?" Charlotte asked. "From memory, Laxey Coffee Morning Crew had four teams entered the last time I checked, I think?"

"All of us," Gabby replied, running her hand around her table and then the larger one adjacent.

"And the rest of us have bought tickets to come along and support!" another of the ladies called over. "Go, Team Laxey Coffee Morning Crew!" she added with an impressive whoop.

"I love the enthusiasm, people," Charlotte said, smiling as she continued through the church hall and in the direction of Amelia.

"Our cheering section is thinking of investing in some of those large foam hands," Amelia told Charlotte, once Charlotte had reached her location, though it wasn't clear if Amelia was being entirely serious. "Anyway, nice to see you, Lotti," Amelia offered, giving their esteemed visitor a brief cuddle. "Now, come," she said. "Let's go through to the kitchen and I'll show you what we've all been making for your fundraiser."

"With so many teams competing, I dare say your crew are definitely in with a fighting chance of winning," Charlotte remarked, as Amelia led the way.

Amelia nodded. "We've had so much fun practising, Lotti," she answered. "And the strategy element of the competition is quite genius."

"You mean about the choice of either working individually or together as a team?" Charlotte asked her, pleased to receive the positive feedback.

"Mm-hmm," Amelia replied. "Those who've opted to work as one team are really entering into the spirit of things. For instance, Gabby, who you've just been talking to, has her group working together with the efficiency of a Formula One pit crew, with each of them doing their bit and knowing precisely what's expected of them. Collectively, they could whip a knitted cardigan up in about an hour, I reckon. So, yes, I must confess to enjoying the fresh, invigorating winds of optimism."

Once they'd arrived in the kitchen, Charlotte couldn't help but eye up the pile of plastic bags near where Amelia was standing. Of course she very much hoped they were stuffed with festive crafting fare rather than simply Amelia's recent supermarket shopping, but she didn't want to appear presumptuous. "So… ehm…?" Charlotte said, struggling to contain her excitement.

"Hmm? Oh. Oh, yes. That," Amelia teasingly replied, introducing the bags resting by her feet with a flourish of the hand. "The Laxey crafting elves have been pulling a double shift," Amelia joked. "And Kris Kringle, which would be me, has had their motivational whip on regular deployment," she added, with a sharp flick of the wrist that seemed, curiously, more like the stylings of Indiana Jones rather than Old Saint Nick.

Charlotte joined Amelia, with both now kneeling next to the bags. "You made all of these?" Charlotte asked, as she pulled out some of the contents from the first one. Inside, the plump bag was stuffed with scarves, crocheted baubles, and even a gorgeous table runner that wouldn't look out of place at anyone's fine Christmas dinner. "Amelia, I honestly don't know what to say. This is so impressive."

Amelia smiled a knowing smile. "I know, pretty good, right?" she said. "A lot of our members have school-aged children and grandchildren, so your uniform initiative really resonated with them," she explained. "And for that reason, I didn't need to dispense with the motivational whip quite as often as I thought I would."

Charlotte wiped an imaginary bead of sweat from her forehead. "Phew, that's a relief!"

"Still, I did miss the satisfying sound of the crack," Amelia confessed, pushing herself upright. "Did you bring your car?" she enquired. "I'll help you load this lot if you like."

"I did, and I've reclined the rear seat to make some more room," Charlotte replied, with a little more smug satisfaction than the statement really warranted or deserved. "Do you mind if I just...?" Charlotte asked, hooking a thumb over her shoulder.

Outside the kitchen and back in the main hall, Charlotte cleared her throat weakly. So weakly, in fact, that the only person to look over asked if she perhaps needed a Strepsils lozenge.

"Ladies and gentlemen!" Charlotte said, this time doing a much better job at attracting everyone's attention. "I'm sorry to interrupt you while you're working! But Amelia's just shown me the results of your collective endeavours, and I just wanted to take a moment to offer you my eternal gratitude."

"You're very welcome!" one of the crafters called out.

"We had a blast making them!" said another.

Charlotte looked around the room at those seated, smiling broadly. "I've said this before, and I'll say it again. The crafting community on the Isle of Man are, quite simply, the very best. Thank you. And I do look forward to seeing each and every one of you at the Manx Christmas Sewing Bee next week."

"See you there!" Gabby shouted over. "And you make sure the engraver is ready to carve our name onto the trophy!"

"Hear, hear!" some of the others agreed. "The Laxey Coffee Morning Crew!"

With Amelia's kind assistance, the boot compartment of Charlotte's modest hatchback soon swelled with bags stuffed with community spirit. And once on her way, if she wasn't already feeling Christmassy enough, Chris Rea's seasonal classic playing over the car radio — titled, appropriately enough, "Driving Home for Christmas" — gave Charlotte a warm fuzzy feeling like a generous mug of mulled wine on a cold winter's eve. Singing along to the catchy lines of the chorus, Charlotte drove through the narrow, cottage-lined streets, offering a friendly wave to what felt like every second person or so. Knowing everybody was one of the many delights of living in a charming, close-knit community like Laxey.

Happy in her own little world, Charlotte weaved through the snaking roads leading from the centre of the village and up towards her adorable little cottage. Then, coming through a blind corner, she slammed on the brakes. "Friar Tuck!" she shouted, bringing the car to an abrupt halt mere inches away from the front bumper of the bin waggon menacingly staring her down.

Taking several deep breaths, Charlotte composed herself for a moment, filled with dread at the thought of reversing back down the narrow lane she'd just driven up with her line of sight in the rear-view mirror completely obscured by plastic bags. But when she hadn't moved or given any indication of moving after a minute or two, the lorry driver jumped down from his cab, anxious to find out what was happening and how he might resolve the situation.

"Is that you, Lotti?" the driver asked, shielding the winter sun from his eyes. "Are you okay in there?" he said, giving her passenger-side window a gentle rap with his knuckle.

"Heya, Bryn," Charlotte said to a concerned-looking Binman Bryn, recognising the fine fellow and opening the window to speak.

"You're not hurt?" Bryn asked, leaning over and peering in.

"No, it's not that..." Charlotte started to explain, looking over her shoulder. "I was, erm... well, that is, I was just a bit concerned that..."

"Say no more," said Bryn, the perceptive soul that he was. "How about I back the old girl up and have you on your way?"

"You're sure you don't mind, Bryn?" Charlotte asked, feeling guilty that she was forcing him to reverse a twenty-tonne lorry up a lane.

Bryn shook his head in response. "No, not at all. In fact, it's probably the better option, as I've seen you reversing before," he told her with a chuckle. "Besides, I might have a pair of work trousers for you to have a look at when you can? So, one good turn and all that."

"Drop them by whenever you're passing, Bryn. And thank you."

Charlotte couldn't hide her embarrassment, dawdling along as the stonking great big truck — with about three millimetres clearance on either side — slowly reversed until there was a gap wide enough for her to pass safely by. "Thanks, boys!" she called out, extending a grateful arm through her window, delighted to see clear tarmac up ahead.

With her heart rate returning to normal levels, Charlotte soon found herself parked up in her allocated space in front of her cottage. She turned around in her seat, trying to figure out just how many additional bags she thought she might be able to pack in, in addition to those she'd just collected. "Right, then," she said, clapping her hands together smartly, reasoning it'd be best to just grab a few from the doorstep and see how it went.

Buoyed by Chris Rea's soothingly familiar, classic tune still fresh in her head, Charlotte climbed out, humming along. She then reached for the latch on her garden gate, one eye drawn towards her front door. "Oh no...!" she yelled, pushing open the metallic gate.

Charlotte ran up the garden path in a state of panic, horrified by the absence of the bags she'd left on the outside steps to collect on her return. She unlocked her front door, hoping she'd maybe thrown them into the hall before she'd left, even though she knew she hadn't. "I don't believe this," she said, placing a shaking hand against her forehead. She'd left approximately half of all the bags previously collected on the front steps, and now they were gone. Hundreds of pounds worth of merchandise for their Christmas market, not to mention the hours and hours of work involved, gone. Just like that.

And then the realisation of the situation hit her like a ton of bricks. "Binman Bryn," she said, darting over and looking inside her freshly emptied bin. "Binman Bryn was here," she added, now stating the obvious.

Her heart sank, looking desperately around for someone to provide her with some sort of clue as to what she should do next. Then, with nothing obvious presenting itself, Charlotte ran out onto the pavement on the verge of hyperventilating. "Bryn!" Charlotte screamed, flailing her arms to nobody in particular, as Bryn was of course, by this time, long gone. "Bryn, come back! You've got our Christmas crafts in the back of your lorry!"

CHAPTER NINETEEN

According to the event's dedicated head of marketing, Stanley Newman, ticket sales for the inaugural Isle of Man Christmas Sewing Bee were lively.

And even though it was the day of the big event, he was still up with the lark, eager to man his station at his mum's laptop, hitting the refresh button at regular intervals. By his reckoning, from what they'd sold both online and in-person, they'd shifted in the region of four hundred tickets. Which, at a fiver a pop, was a very welcome contribution to the school uniform initiative's coffers. However, he wasn't despondent they'd not yet sold out. Far from it, in fact, as he knew they were certain to attract some last-minute sales, and it was virtually guaranteed as well that there'd be a good number of walk-ins (those turning up without a ticket, hopeful of buying one at the door).

As far as the number of crafting teams signed up and ready for competitive action, Charlotte was overwhelmed by the response. Secretly, she'd have been thrilled to welcome, say, ten to fifteen, but to have nearly thirty was simply staggering. Not only would it add to the party atmosphere, but, again, their entry fees would be a welcome contribution. It was fortunate, then, that the Appledene nursing home was as spacious as it was, able to accommodate the array of competitors with room to spare. Indeed, Charlotte thanked her lucky stars, grateful she'd managed to secure such a perfect location. She knew it was unlikely that the other venues she'd previously investigated would have had the size and scale to accommodate the stalls, crafting teams, and assembled hordes who'd hopefully be in attendance to support them.

"What do you think, Stan?" Charlotte asked, bouncing into the living room, hands-on-hips, giving him a twirl of the dress she'd created from her most festive of festive-themed fabrics. Then, before Stanley had offered his considered opinion, she jiggled her jazz hands, building up to a big reveal. "Ta-da!" she said, now reaching around to the small of her back, pressing a button on the battery pack she'd concealed there, and lighting herself up like Blackpool Promenade.

"Blinking 'eck, Mum," Stanley said, playfully shielding his eyes. "Everyone will certainly see you coming," he joked.

"Well, at least I won't be alone," Charlotte said, pressing the button once more and activating blink mode.

"You've not made me something?" Stanley replied with a groan, already knowing the answer to his question.

"Stanley, it's not long until Christmas, and your mum is a crafter. So of *course* I've made you something. Not a dress, mind you, but a super cute shirt that I've laid out on your bed. Oh, and remind me to get some more double-A batteries on the way. I'd hate to run out of power during the day. Especially when I've made Calum one, also."

"Yes, that would be a real shame," Stanley suggested with a giggle, pleased that if he was going to be publicly humiliated, at least Calum would be there, flashing away with him.

The doors on the Isle of Man Christmas Sewing Bee weren't scheduled to open until noon, but Calum agreed to pick Charlotte and Stanley up at around eight. The majority of the heavy lifting had been completed in the days running up to the event. However, Charlotte still wanted to be on hand to greet the early arrivals and attend to any last-minute issues, should such need arise.

With the tremendous support from the Appledene staff, in addition to Calum, Mollie, Stanley and others, the scene was looking like something from a Disney Christmas film. When guests first stepped out of their car, they would be greeted by fairy lights in and around the imposing turret and more dangling from tree branches surrounding the building. Sam and the team had even gone to the trouble of piping Christmas music around the car parks just to get those arriving into the proper yuletide spirit. Then, once inside the magnificent building, the already spectacular festive display had grown arms and legs, now appearing much like the American department store Bloomingdale's. It was truly splendid.

And yes, it was a considerable amount of effort to go to for one day. But, as Sam was quick to point out, the Appledene residents would also benefit from enjoying the winter wonderland for the entire month, at least. Although, secretly, he also had to admit that he'd perhaps made a giant rod for his own back, so to speak, as what they'd collectively created was dazzling, and he knew they'd have to come up with something even bigger and grander the following year.

"Uhm, do you think we should switch the lights on our shirts off now, for the drive over?" Calum asked, once the three of them were seated in the car and ready to leave.

"Ah, to save the batteries for later?" Charlotte asked. "Good idea."

"I think he's more worried about pilots seeing the lights and landing their plane on top of the car," Stanley remarked from the back seat.

Calum laughed. "Yes, well, there is that. But I was more concerned about dazzling our fellow road users. Not that I'm not grateful, Lotti, as my shirt is a thing of true beauty."

"Come here," a sceptical Charlotte said, locating the 'off' button for Calum so they could get their journey underway.

Arriving at Appledene shortly after eight, Charlotte was delighted to find plenty of people already milling about. Many she recognised from her crafting clubs and some who'd been involved in the Square If You Care competition. "Blimey," Charlotte said, checking her watch. "If it's this busy now, what's it going to be like come kick-off time?"

"It's going to be a memorable day, I'm quite sure," Calum said, slowing the car to allow a chap carrying a giant stuffed reindeer to cross safely in front.

"And my best boys are happy enough helping out on the Christmas craft shop?" Charlotte enquired, flicking her eyes over to Calum, and then to Stanley.

"Yes, but only when Larry doesn't need me to wheel him around," Stanley reminded her. "Also, I was thinking about calling it the Christmas Emporium, Mum," Stanley offered, having evidently given the matter some thought. "With the quality of the merchandise on sale, I think it's got a classier ring to it."

"This kid's going to go far," Calum suggested, pulling into an available parking space. "And yes," he said, turning to Charlotte, "I'm definitely looking forward to working in the emporium. It'll be loads of fun."

The three of them walked past the magical turret, enjoying the lovely, enchanting music piped through the speakers. Once again, Charlotte's imagination wandered, thoughts of being rescued by her heroic Prince Calum on horseback wearing tight jodhpurs. Charlotte offered a contented sigh as they went inside, giving Calum's hand a little squeeze for saving her once more, even if he was clueless as to what a hero he actually was.

"Here's your office for the day, boys," Charlotte announced, a short time later, introducing both Calum and Stanley to the Christmas Emporium. "And Stan, we've plenty of volunteers, so you'll be fine to come and go whenever Larry needs you."

It was a generously apportioned space, with plenty of room to display their considerable stock on shelving kindly provided by Mollie's farm shop for the day. The rustic blend of aged wood married itself nicely with the vibrant, handcrafted merchandise ready to tempt the inquisitive shopper. Charlotte had skilfully dressed the room with a tastefully decorated tree, an adorable steam train running around the base of it.

"Ah! I thought that was you," said Sam, joining them at the emporium. "And I've already spotted several items here that I surely wouldn't mind purchasing for Christmas presents," he added. "So I suspect today could be costly!"

"Sam, the entire building is like something straight out of a fairytale," Charlotte told him, walking over to administer a hug. "You really have done a remarkable job."

"It does look impressive, doesn't it," Sam confirmed, wide-eyed and happy. "And Mollie's kicking about somewhere, by the way," Sam advised, looking over his shoulder to see if she'd followed him in, though she hadn't. "She's going to help me out on the refreshments stall, if that's okay with you?"

"Only if you two can keep your hands off each other," Charlotte answered, smiling slyly. "Not too much smooching, now. You hear?"

"I can't promise anything," Sam answered with a wink, after which he took an admiring glance around the emporium. "You really do have a lot of stock, don't you?"

"The generosity of the Manx crafters. A wonderful bunch."

"We thought we'd lost half of it," Stanley was quick to point out, offering a sombre shake of the head at the terrifyingly close shave they'd recently experienced.

"Oh, yes. I don't think I've told Mollie about that whole debacle just yet," Charlotte said, puffing out her cheeks and expelling a steady stream of air. She grimaced at the thought, and then proceeded to fill Sam in regarding the worrying situation she'd found herself in with Bryn the Binman, first explaining how they'd met on a particularly tight stretch of a country lane, and then, how after returning home, she'd discovered the big pile of Christmas-craft stuffed bags missing from her doorstep. "And then," Charlotte went on, "I jumped back in my car, catching Bryn the Binman up on their very last stop."

"That's fortunate," Sam said. "And you were able to recover what had been taken?" he surmised, judging by the crammed shelves.

Young Stanley released an amused laugh in response.

Charlotte gave her son a gentle nudge in the ribs. "Well," she told Sam, picking up the story, "I followed the boys back to their base, as agreed, and they very graciously spent the next hour or so sifting through the contents of their bin lorry. By the end of it, the poor chaps were covered in who-knows-what from all the guck that'd come out of the bags. But, sadly, after all of that effort... nothing."

"Nothing? Had they already been crushed or something?" asked Sam, not really too clued up on the inner workings of a bin lorry.

"I wasn't sure at that point," Charlotte said. "All I knew was that they couldn't find them. Dejected, I returned home, filled with dread, and wondering how on earth I was going to break the news to all the people who'd been kind enough to donate that, sadly, much of their hard work had unfortunately been for nought. And that's right when Cynthia, my lovely neighbour, appeared. Apparently, she'd assumed I'd received a large delivery of crafting items left on my doorstep by the postman. So then, with no sign of me about, and rainclouds overhead, the darling had taken them all in for safekeeping."

Sam looked relieved, but then offered a pained expression as something occurred to him. "Wait, so that means you had the Laxey binmen rummaging through the town's refuge for bags that weren't even there in the first place?"

"Yes. But I went straight down to see them and explain the mix-up!" Charlotte related. "I was worried the poor dears would carry on with the search and not stop looking, you see."

"I'll bet you were popular?" Sam suggested.

"Well, let's just say that Binman Bryn and his merry men can now call on me any time they like for any type of clothes alterations or repairs whatsoever, by way of recompense."

"Mum? Can't you just call him The Brynman, like we do at school?" Stanley interjected. "He must like it, I reckon, as he always strikes a pose like Superman whenever we call him it."

Charlotte laughed. "The Brynman...? I like it."

"Well, I'm pleased you got it sorted in the end, Charlotte, and here's hoping for some bumper sales," Sam offered, heading for the door. "Do you want a final inspection of the main hall before the competitors arrive?"

"Lead on, my fine gentleman," Charlotte replied. "Lead on."

In the grand ballroom (which ordinarily doubled as the resident's dining hall), tables were placed on the hardwood floor at regular intervals, with plenty of elbow room between each. Space was the order of the day, as it was Charlotte's hope that the event would be primarily interactive, with the public welcome to walk between the teams, stopping to see what they were working on and have a chat with the competitors. Yes, it was a competition, but ultimately it was a fundraiser and an ideal opportunity to showcase the marvellous crafting hobby to the uninitiated.

On each table, Charlotte had labelled them all with their respective team names, and in the middle, laid out a neat pile of second-hand clothing and previously loved fabric for use during the competition. The inventory each team received was broadly similar with, perhaps, only a variation on the pattern. For that reason, they were all singing from the same hymn sheet, so to speak, with no particular advantage gained from the overall standard of fabric used.

For Charlotte, a considerable challenge had been securing sufficient fabric/clothing to accommodate the ever-increasing number of teams entered. Fortunate, then, that she had a substantial stash from the recycling bins and a passion for frequenting the local charity shops. So much so, in fact, that she was even able to fill a clothes rail with spare stock, should the need arise.

"You don't think I've missed anything, do you?" Charlotte asked, straightening the pile of supplies on the table closest to her, and speaking half to herself and half to those around her. "I went around each table at least several times last night, but I still can't shake the feeling that I must've forgotten to do something, you know?" she asked, turning first to Calum and then to Sam.

Calum smiled his most soothing of smiles. "I'm sure you're fine, Lotti," he assured her. "The place looks wonderful, you've sold loads and loads of tickets, and the competitors are soon to start arriving. Nothing will go wrong!"

"And I'm about to fire up the tea urns, Lotti, so no worries there," Sam was happy to report. "Otherwise, our guests will have nothing to wash down all of those delicious cakes you've dropped off."

Sam left Charlotte to her final, for the final time, *really-final-this-time* last-minute inspection. To Stanley and Calum, all this fuss reminded them of leaving on a family holiday or such, with whatever family member in charge checking to ensure everyone had packed their passports, even though it had just been confirmed not two minutes earlier that all passports had, indeed, been successfully packed away. But Calum and Stanley both knew how important the day was for Charlotte, so if she wanted to double-check anything, well, they were happy to allow her to do precisely that.

After successfully working through the mental tick list in her head, Charlotte finally started to relax, just as the first of the competitors began filtering in.

"Good morning, guys!" Charlotte said, waving her trusty green clipboard at the new arrivals. "Can I just take your team name, and I'll direct you to your workspace for the day?" she offered brightly.

"Yes! Sew It Would Seam!" one particular woman sporting a fetching captain's armband announced, cracking her fingers in a *let's-get-it-on* fashion.

"Right," Charlotte said through her smile, wondering if the clearly wired lady standing before her had indulged in one too many cups of coffee or was just super-excited to get going. "If you'd like to follow me, and we'll get you settled."

Charlotte chatted merrily away over her shoulder, offering some of her finest small talk to put the woman and her team at ease. But with no response received, she was surprised to see, looking behind her, that the team hadn't budged. Instead, the four ladies, all of a certain age, were huddled together in a group. "We've got this!" a voice, possibly that of the team captain, yelled from within the circle of trust. "And what do we do to the competition...?" the voice boomed out, in a scene very much re-sembling the pre-game starting portion of American football.

"WE'RE GOING TO STUFF THEM!" came the collective, as-sured response, the brusque tone of which startled Charlotte.

"Oh-kay, ladies," Charlotte said, introducing the group to their workspace once they'd finished up with their team moti-vational session. "Hopefully, this location will be to your satis-faction," Charlotte offered, really hoping it *was* to their satisfac-tion, as she wasn't prepared for conflict at this early stage and especially without any caffeine onboard. "And if you have any questions before the event, feel free to—"

"Who's judging the event, then?" the team's captain inter-rupted, running her eyes around the room, perhaps hoping to secure some sort of tactical advantage ahead of the other teams' imminent arrival.

"Ah. Let me just check on that for you, ladies," Charlotte said, tapping her clipboard with her pen, and then raising a finger by way of a placeholder to the question.

Charlotte headed over to Calum, who'd just returned from the kitchen, armed with a mug of coffee in each hand.

"Milky with one sugar," Calum announced, dutifully hand-ing over one of the mugs.

With her clipboard tucked under her arm, Charlotte took a dainty yet eager slurp of her coffee, burning her lips in the pro-cess.

"Whoa, cowgirl! That's still very hot!" Calum advised.

Charlotte didn't say anything, staring instead at Calum with a vacant expression, as if she'd just smoked a funny cigarette or something.

"Charlotte?" Calum asked, noting her face had suddenly gone pale. "Charlotte, is everything okay? Have you burned yourself badly?"

Charlotte laughed. Only it wasn't the sort of laugh one might offer in response to a hilarious joke. Not at all. No, instead, this was the sort of reaction you'd offer upon seeing heavy rain-clouds while suddenly realising you've left your umbrella back at home. "I don't believe it," Charlotte said, her eyes flicking up to the gilded ceiling. "Calum, you know when I said before that I thought I'd forgotten something?"

Calum grimaced, uncertain where this was headed, but suspecting Charlotte's explanation wasn't going to reveal anything positive. "Yes?" he prompted. "And... you have?" he replied cautiously.

Charlotte laughed once more. "Oh, yes!" she answered, eyes open wide, like a madwoman. "I've only gone and forgotten to arrange a bloody judge, haven't I?" she said, whispering now, for fear of alerting anybody nearby to this absurd oversight. "How have I managed to entirely forget about a *judge* for today's competition? I mean, *how?*"

CHAPTER TWENTY

The ageing door creaked open, permitting a sliver of light inside the otherwise darkened room. "Hello?" Mollie said softly, easing the door open another few inches. "Anybody home?" she asked tentatively, now stepping inside the janitor's closet. "It's only me," she added, squinting her eyes to compensate for the lack of illumination.

"There's nobody home," responded the dimly-lit figure, down on the floor in the corner, knees pulled into their chest.

"Ah, there you are. Stanley said you'd headed in this direction," Mollie replied, immediately recognising the voice of her friend. "I've been going from room to room looking for you," she explained. "Oh, and be warned, a half-naked Santa Claus is getting dressed in the room next door, so, unlike me, remember to knock if you should go in."

"I'll keep that in mind," Charlotte answered. "So are you now on Santa's naughty list?" she asked, lifting her chin from her knees just a bit.

"I reckon I'll find out on Christmas morning," Mollie offered, moving in close, and then sliding her back down the wall, her bum coming to rest on her heels. "You can't hide away in here all day. You know that, right?" she told Charlotte beside her, saying it softly like she was convincing a child there was no boogie monster and it was safe to come out.

"Oh yes I can," Charlotte replied, and even though she was in relative darkness, it was apparent from her tone that her bottom lip was very likely pressed out.

"Joyce, Beryl, and the other Crafternooners have just turned up," Mollie implored, hoping to coax her friend out from the depths of her hidey-hole. "Your adoring public wants to see you, Lotti."

Charlotte lowered her head back down. "Mollie, they'll string me up when they realise there's nobody to judge the competition. They're competitive crafters, Moll. They take things like this seriously!"

"Beryl and Joyce?" Mollie asked. "I don't think—"

"No, not them. I meant some of the others here," Charlotte clarified.

"Oh, hogwash. They can't be that bad, Lotti."

"But you've not met them, Moll. That mob from Stitch 'n' Bitch, for instance, are a proper nightmare. And as for the Knitty Noras..." Charlotte gravely advised. "Well, they're all here to prove they're the best. And if there's nobody to make that decision, then they'll... they'll, well... they'll rip me a new seam."

"They wouldn't dare," Mollie assured her. "And if any of these crafters *do* kick-off and start trouble, Lotti, then you know I've got your back. Lordy, now there's a sentence I didn't expect to be saying today..."

"Thanks, Moll."

"Seriously, though," Mollie continued, now returning to normal height. "Can't you rummage up a suitable judge from your crafting black book? I mean, there must be somebody qualified to judge, right? What about even doing it yourself?"

Charlotte groaned. "That's the problem, Moll. Everybody I might have asked is already taking part in the competition," she said. "And I did consider doing it myself, but then that bunch of vipers from the Knitty Noras would probably call foul play. Besides, if I volunteered to judge and couldn't participate, then I'd be letting our Crafternoon team down, wouldn't I?"

Mollie didn't have the answers her friend needed. "Come on, Lotti," she said, extending a hand. "We've still got an hour until the start time, yes? Something is certain to turn up. And in the meantime, I'll pop out to the car and fetch my knuckle dusters, yeah? Just in case things go pear-shaped and get a bit unsavoury. Now come on. I need to head next door and apologise for perving on Old Saint Nick."

Eventually, after much cajoling, Charlotte appeared from her darkened cave like a hibernating bear after a long nap. She smiled politely at the dozens of people milling about outside, in the corridor. "It's busier than Piccadilly Circus in here," she remarked to Mollie, taking care not to bump into anybody as they walked along.

"The numbers have exploded in the last fifteen minutes or so," Mollie revealed. "Apparently, the volunteers in the car park are already directing cars to the overflow field."

At this point, Charlotte had precisely zero idea who would judge the competition for her. So, without any other options available to her, she opted to take a wander around the competition hall to see if a suitable candidate might make themselves known. This was fairly unlikely, for the reasons she'd already discussed with Mollie, but in the absence of any other alternative, she'd attempt to remain calm (though with one eye on the nearest exit in case she needed to scarper at a moment's notice). Yes, it wasn't an ideal situation. Far from it, in fact. Still, worse things happen at sea, and all that, Charlotte told herself.

Determined to make the best of it, she knew exactly what might place a smile back on her face, with Calum and Stanley soon standing either side of her as she'd thus requested. "Ready, boys?" Charlotte asked, looking at each of them in turn.

"Ready," came the dual reply. And with that, the three of them activated the button on their battery packs, lighting themselves up like a Catherine wheel on Bonfire Night.

Just then, like an elegant swan on a calm, placid lake, Larry glided silently into view. "Well I'm loving the light show," he remarked approvingly, from the comfort of his wheelchair, leg extended, and coming to a controlled halt.

Charlotte did a double-take, confused for just a moment by the curious lack of either anybody pushing him along or his own hands on the wheels, his wheelchair appearing to move of its own accord. "Larry!" she said, delighted to see him. "A-ha. I see you've gone all modern technology on us," she observed, in reference to his electrically powered steed. "And, if I may say so, Larry, you look absolutely smashing in your new suit."

"It does make me look rather dapper," Larry said, offering no resistance to the compliment. Then, Larry gave his joystick a gentle wiggle, just enough to edge forward a few millimetres. "It's a thing of wonder, isn't it?" he said, about to describe the virtues of his new transport, until he noticed Stanley's dreary expression. "Ah. Well," Larry said, backtracking now. "It's okay, I suppose," he said with a shrug, releasing the joystick. "But it's not the same as the manual version, I reckon, powered by young Stanley."

In response, Stanley's mood lifted, as did his chin. "I was a good pilot, wasn't I, Larry?"

"The best, young Stanley. The best."

Stanley glanced up at his mum, bursting with pride. "And we've been racing, Mum," Stanley admitted, taking a positive spin out of his recent redundancy.

"Have you?" Charlotte asked. "You mean the electric wheelchair?" she said, unsure whether to be impressed or not.

"Yeah!" Stanley gushed. "We were outside on the driveway, racing around a circuit I made from three traffic cones!"

Charlotte shook her head, though offering a modest smile. "Stanley. Larry. The parking monitors will be shouting at the pair of you," she gently chided them.

"Nah," Larry chipped in. "In fact, they were all taking bets on how quickly I could go around."

Charlotte crouched down, admiring the trousers that Alfie Harrow had so kindly provided for Larry. "For a moment, I'd actually forgotten that your leg was in a plaster cast under there," she marvelled.

"I know, right?" Larry answered, stroking the side of his extended leg. "He's made the seam from Velcro, you see? This way, they go comfortably over the cast, while also being fantastically easy to whip straight off."

"Like a male stripper's," Charlotte instantly remarked, though blushing just as quickly.

"Oh? You appear to have some degree of knowledge on the subject," Calum joked, picking up on her squirming.

Charlotte immediately switched gears. "Anyway, Alfie has certainly done wonders on your new suit, Larry," she said. "You look a million dollars, and the workmanship is just marvellous."

"Well, he's certainly not cheap," Larry suggested. "But when you're working with one of the finest tailors on the Isle of Man, you do get what you pay for."

Charlotte didn't answer, and proceeded to stare at Larry so intently that he began to shuffle nervously in his seat. "Erm... everything okay there, Lotti?" he asked, flicking his eyes over to Calum.

Charlotte remained quiet, Larry's words, *the finest tailors on the Isle of Man*, echoing on the inside of her skull, the line bouncing around her currently distracted bonce.

"Charlotte?" Calum asked, sharing Larry's concern. "Are you still with us?"

Charlotte snapped herself back into the present. "Larry, you're a complete and utter genius!" she declared.

"I am?" Larry asked, uncertain as to where this was suddenly coming from. "Why, thank you, I suppose I am," he said, happy enough to accept the kind words despite his present confusion. "May I enquire why, exactly?"

"Because you may have just found me the perfect judge, and saved me from a crafting-led lynch mob in the process!"

A steady trickle of sweat ran down Calum's forehead, making him concerned that if it reached the light display on his shirt it might cause an electrical fire. It wasn't just the large collection of flashing bulbs causing him to overheat. The red velvet Santa hat with faux fur trim was very likely a contributing factor also, plus all the hard work he was putting in as well, of course. Still, he was having a ball, entering into the festive spirit, and wrapping up an order for another satisfied customer.

At the start of the day, Calum was overwhelmed by the sheer volume of stock taking up the shelves in their fine Christmas Emporium. But now, after only twenty minutes, he was concerned they'd have empty shelves before the official start time of the event had even come to pass. Folk, it would appear, were desperate to purchase locally handcrafted items, even more so when said items were being sold to aid such a worthy cause.

And it wasn't just the emporium benefiting from the footfall, either. Nearby, under Mollie and Sam's watch, the refreshments booth was doing a roaring trade, with a steady line of people waiting patiently in the queue. Ordinarily, a queue of any sort would often be met with frustration and the occasional tut-tut. Not here, though. With the splendid decorations, ambient seasonal music, and folks in colourful fancy dress, there wasn't a groan to be heard. Indeed, with the mood entirely jovial, there were only the cheery murmurings of people out enjoying themselves.

Yes, the smiling, happy faces told you that it was indeed the most wonderful time of the year...

"Darn! ... Blast! ... Shoot! ... Fudge...!" Charlotte exclaimed, as she walked from one room to the next, her mobile phone held high above her head. But no matter where she went, the signal strength indicated was woeful. Perhaps it was because of the large number of people in the area, or simply down to Sod's Law (along with its corollary, Finagle's Law), owing to the fact that Charlotte was desperate to make a call. Just then, she recalled a film — was it a Ray Mears documentary, maybe? — where, in a similar situation, a person was seen heading for higher ground where the signal might improve. But then, Charlotte remembered that the lead character might have been suffering from a broken leg. So, perhaps it was a fiction type of film rather than a documentary sort of thing?

Regardless of what it was, Charlotte sprinted up the winding staircase, circling around the towering Christmas tree in the reception area as she did so, leading her towards the upstairs landing. There, to her immense relief, the reception on her mobile jumped up by two glorious bars, sufficient to make a call. Now the only issue that remained was the considerable volume emanating from those arriving through the vast entrance hall below. Why did everybody have to be so merry and chatty!

Charlotte bolted along the corridor adorned with framed portraits of what she assumed to be former occupants of this grand establishment, although she didn't have time to stop to admire them right now. She stepped inside a vacant room, using her hip to close the door behind her and thus block out the noise from below. Then, with a brief prayer, Charlotte pressed the redial button on her mobile phone, willing the call to successfully connect, unlike her previous dozen or so attempts.

"Yes, hello!" she said upon hearing a welcome voice on the other end. "Yes, I was calling to speak with Alfie Harrow, who I'm hoping can save my life!"

Charlotte paced the circular room, outlining the nature of her problem once Alfie came on the line. "You will? That's splendid! Thank you so much!" she said a few moments later, after receiving his response, pumping her fist in the air in victory at this good news. "And you can be here for noon?" she asked, hoping she wasn't asking too much of him. "Oh, Alfie!" she said, resisting the urge to blow kisses down the line. "I truly cannot thank you enough, and I look forward to seeing you very soon!"

With her phone back in her pocket, Charlotte erupted into the sort of dance her son would likely have found embarrassing to watch were he to have the misfortune of witnessing it. But she didn't care. She'd located her judge, and, as a consequence, had now saved herself from a severe tongue-lashing and even possible grievous bodily harm.

"Oh, my," Charlotte said, now taking notice of her immediate surroundings for the first time. She ran a hand over the rough stone wall, moving towards the narrow, rectangular windows overlooking the pretty courtyard below. "I'm in the turret," she remarked, placing a hand over her heart as if she were the star of a musical and a song was ready to burst forth from her lungs at any moment. "How lovely," she said.

But she couldn't stand there all day, this she knew. So she walked over to the door and reached for the handle, a handle... that wasn't there.

"Eh? What's this?" she asked, confused. Then, she spotted the handwritten sign lying there on the floor, nearby. In large letters, it cautioned:

DOOR HANDLE OUT OF ORDER – DO NOT CLOSE DOOR!

In her previous haste, distracted by the urgency of her earlier phone call, Charlotte reckoned she must've missed the prominent warning, knocking the sign off the door as she'd entered.

"Well, I suppose there are far worse places to be locked inside," Charlotte said with a sigh, making light of an otherwise uncomfortable situation.

She reached for her phone again, this time dialling Calum. "Hello?" she said, once connected. "Yes, hello. Is this my Prince Charming?" she asked. "Well, this is your darling damsel in distress, and I'd be very grateful if you could come and rescue me," she told him with a giggle. "No, I've not been drinking. Well, not yet, anyway," she replied to the question just posed. "Where am I?" she said. "Why, I'm in a turret in the highest tower, of course!"

CHAPTER TWENTY-ONE

L arry, egged on by his partner-in-crime, Stanley, hovered a finger over the activation button of his air horn, waiting patiently for the seconds to tick by. And then, at noon precisely, Larry applied firm, consistent pressure to the trigger mechanism, frightening the living daylights out of anyone within earshot and especially those standing closest.

"Ladies and gentlemen! I'm delighted to announce that the Isle of Man's Christmas Sewing Bee is now underway!" Larry declared into his wireless microphone. "Competitors, as a reminder, round one is Christmas pyjamas. You have one and a half hours, and a reminder as well that the judge will consider one entry from each team. Good luck, crafters!"

The judge, Alfie Harrow, was thrown on stage at the mercy of the pack, so to speak, moments after his anticipated arrival time. Initially, he'd received a cool reception from some of the competitors, primarily because many in attendance hadn't previously heard of him. It was only when Larry took it upon himself to detail Alfie's impressive crafting CV that the doubters, including members of the Knitty Noras and Stitch 'n' Bitch, grudgingly accepted his impressive credentials.

The atmosphere in the competition room was a complete contrast to how it had been only a few minutes earlier. Now, rather than noisy chatter and laughter, concentration appeared to be the order of the day as the teams jumped in headfirst, with one big eye on the electronic timer reminding them just how many minutes they had remaining. It was apparent to those watching on, even at this early stage, that some of the teams looked to be seasoned crafters, while others seemed like relative beginners. But whatever stage they were at in their crafting journey, they were all obviously having fun. And for those spectators wandering amongst the tables, with some of them being crafters themselves, the unfolding spectacle made for enjoyable viewing.

Over at one of the Crafternooner tables, Charlotte, Beryl, Joyce, and Bonnie had their heads buried in a sea of fabric, scissors snipping away feverishly. Fortunately, Charlotte's heroic saviour, Calum, had completed his daring rescue, saving his Princess from an uncertain fate. Rather than using a mighty sword to slay her captor, all that had been required was the tip of a screwdriver applied to the latch mechanism inside the door where the door handle used to be. As such, Charlotte had been freed from the tower to join the rest of her team, with plenty of time to spare.

Initially, Charlotte & co's plan of attack, as they had previously discussed, had been to work on individual projects and then submit the group's favoured garment for consideration. However, after several pyjama-making practice sessions in the days leading up to the event, they eventually decided that this wouldn't be practical in the time allotted. For that reason, Bonnie and Joyce were now tasked with creating the pyjama top, and Charlotte and Beryl the pyjama bottoms. But of course this strategy was not without its concerns. As a team, they'd only have one completed garment at the end, for instance, and if it wasn't up to scratch, then quite simply, they'd be out of the competition.

"I see a few of the other teams working on individual projects," Bonnie remarked, running her eyes over and observing the competition, a hint of doubt present in her voice. "We are doing the right thing, aren't we?"

"It's fine," Charlotte replied, furiously cutting out paper pattern pieces. "Keep in mind," she added, looking up for a moment, "that strategy means they've each got to create bottoms and a top in one and a half hours, which is a major undertaking.

And, even if they do manage it, will they have cut any corners to achieve it?"

"I suppose," Bonnie conceded, putting her scissors back to work.

Larry, for his part, was happily weaving in and out of the tables, taking care not to run over any of the paying public in the process. Part of the job description Larry had created for himself involved engaging with some of the competitors, hoping to capture some insight into what competing meant for them, and sharing that with the crowd. He'd always fancied himself something of a roving reporter, and now was the ideal opportunity, he believed.

"Ladies," Larry said into his trusty microphone, turning on the charm as he propelled himself towards the nearest table. "What's your team name, and how are you all getting on?" he asked, holding up the microphone from his seated position. "Ladies?" Larry repeated, waving the device around like a conductor's baton. "If I could just—"

"If you don't get that microphone out of my way, sunshine, I'm going to grab it from you and stick it right up your—"

Fortunately, the astute sound engineer pulled the proverbial plug before the delightful lady could complete her remark. This meant that the audience would never know what she intended to do with Larry's microphone, precisely, although they were certain to have a fair idea.

Unfortunately, for Larry at least, he'd unwittingly wheeled himself over towards the crew from Sew It Would Seam, who, it would seem, were not overly receptive to being disrupted by the self-styled roving reporter. "Oof," a startled Larry said, reversing to a safe distance. "Tough crowd," he commented, giving the sound engineer a nod, indicating he was ready to be reconnected as he made his way onward.

Luckily, the next group Larry deployed his microphone towards appeared somewhat more sympathetic to his advances. This was, in part, because Charlotte had quickly slipped him a little note detailing which of the teams he may wish to consider giving a wide berth and which of the teams might be more approachable.

Larry cleared his throat, buoyed by the warm smile his arrival produced at this next table. "So," he said, into his mic. "It's certainly a hive of activity over here. Tell the audience what's going on?"

A lady wearing an orange jumper that looked very much to be hand-crafted leapt forward. "I like your suit!" she remarked, a twinkle evident in her eye, before returning to the question at hand. "Well, we're a team of crafters from the Laxey Coffee Morning Crew," she said, receiving a whoop of appreciation from the others at the table. "And we're here today to craft, have fun, craft, meet friends, craft, and did I mention craft...?" she joked, cupping her ear for any sort of response from her compatriots and clearly relishing the spotlight.

"And you think you've a chance of winning?" Larry affably enquired.

This generated a polite laugh in reply. "Oh, good heavens no! In fact, we've just realised we've cut out two left legs for our pyjamas," the woman with the orange jumper explained with a sigh. "But of course we're hoping the judge won't notice," she added with a wink, smiling over in the general direction of Alfie Harrow, who was standing nearby and also making the rounds.

"All that matters is that you ladies enjoy yourselves," Larry suggested, retracting his microphone-holding arm and flashing an amiable smile, delighted by his first successful field report.

Taking a short moment to switch his microphone off, Larry looked back up to offer his gratitude to the tangerine-coloured lady. *"Call me,"* she mouthed, splaying out her thumb and pinkie finger to approximate the shape of a phone, followed by a confident wink, causing a startled Larry to fumble for his joystick.

"Ten minutes to go, ladies and gentlemen!" Larry called out. "That's ten minutes to go!" Larry reiterated, lest there be any doubt in anyone's mind.

His announcement was met with panic in some quarters. Namely, from the teams that had absolutely no chance of finishing within the allotted time, thus facing an early bath, so to speak. Others, such as the team with two left legs, for example, knew the dinging of the bell would likely bring their crafting adventure to a premature close. Unless that is, their mismatched creation was somehow still better than the others on display. So this particular group remained hopeful, but that decision, of course, rested firmly on the shoulders of the judge for the day, Alfie Harrow, who'd been pacing throughout the room, taking notes and keeping an expert eye on proceedings.

And one group Alfie appeared especially impressed with was the Crafternoon team of Charlotte, Bonnie, Joyce, and Beryl. The decision to work on one garment, albeit half on the top and half on the bottom, proved inspired. And what Joyce and Beryl may have lacked in nimbleness, they more than made up with raw talent. With a few minutes to spare, the girls were busy applying the final touches, a decorative hem to the sleeves, and snipping off the occasional errant thread. Between them, what they'd created in a relatively short amount of time was nothing short of astounding. Indeed, they'd whipped up a pair of festive pyjamas that wouldn't look out of place on the sales rail of the finest clothes shop in the land.

"That's your time, crafters!" Larry announced, giving his air horn another toot. "Lay down your scissors, please leave your team's selection for judging, and then go and get yourselves a well-deserved cup of tea!"

"I hope you've brought along your hip flask?" Beryl asked of Joyce, stretching her arms high above her head. "I need a little pick-me-up before the next round," she said, confident their efforts would see them progress.

The competitors set down their various implements, after which there was a mass exodus from the main hall. A half-hour break was a welcome relief for the weary crafters, grateful for some time to relax before the next round. The gap in proceedings also provided Alfie Harrow ample time in which to make his final decisions without having competitors' eyes boring into the back of his skull.

At the refreshments concession, Sam, Mollie, and their able crew of volunteers were all hands to the pump, dispensing mugs of tea and plates of cake at a fair old lick.

"Good work, ladies," Joyce said, tipping her silver flask towards Beryl's steaming mug, congratulating their team on a job well done.

"That was so much fun!" Bonnie exclaimed, politely declining Joyce's offer of a snifter, what with her still being underage and all. "And the audience was so lovely, chatting away about what we were working on. Honestly, Lotti, I reckon we're going to be inundated with loads of new members at Crafternoon."

"Here's hoping," Charlotte said, raising her mug to toast that possibility. "Oh, no thank you, my dear," she added in polite response to the offer of something stronger included, placing her hand over her drink. "I think I'll keep a clear head, Joyce. But thanks."

"More for us," Beryl suggested with a happy wink, taking a grateful slug of her fortified brew.

But before they could continue with their team debrief, a bewildered-looking Alfie Harrow edged his way through the assembled crowd towards their location. "Oh. Did you spot my hip flask?" Joyce joked, unscrewing the lid accommodatingly.

"What? No," Alfie replied, offering a polite shake of his head.

With his hair slicked back, and dressed impeccably — as one might expect — in a pinstriped, three-piece suit, Alfie wouldn't have looked out of place standing next to Al Capone in a police line-up. But hearing him speak, it was obvious that he was the gentlest of souls, and in fact right now, Alfie appeared concerned with what he was about to say.

"Ladies," Alfie whispered, just loudly enough to be heard by them. "I wondered if I could take your trousers?"

"Hark at this one," Beryl said, giving Joyce a gentle nudge in the ribs. "One shot of rum between us, and he thinks we're easy meat!"

"But we are, though, aren't we?" Joyce asked, with a shrug and a bawdy cackle.

"I don't mean... that is, what I meant is..." a slightly embarrassed Alfie started to say, cheeks reddening. "Ladies, your pyjama bottoms are not on the table," he explained, opting to just come straight out with it. "And I'm not sure I can judge what isn't there."

Charlotte smiled politely, waiting for a punchline that didn't arrive. "Wait, you're serious...?"

"Yes. Very," Alfie replied, looking down at his watch. "The next round begins in seven minutes. And, at present, there's only half a pair of pyjamas on your workstation."

"I don't understand," Charlotte said, glancing desperately around the group, hopeful for some answers.

"But they were there when we left, I know they were," a confident-sounding Bonnie entered in. "And I know that because I folded them very nicely, placing a little red bow on top."

"Well," Joyce said, casting a suspicious, accusatory eye about the hallway in which they were standing. "The answer's fairly obvious, isn't it?"

"It is?" Charlotte asked, anxious to hear more.

Joyce took a sip of her tea, shaking her head gravely before responding. "Yes. Someone must have nicked them," she said, unconcerned by the rising volume of her voice. "Someone's trying to sabotage our chances of winning."

"Foul play?" Charlotte asked, narrowing one eye and sounding somewhat sceptical. "You really think so?"

"*Exactly* so," Joyce proclaimed. "There's *foul play* at the Isle of Man Christmas Sewing Bee!"

CHAPTER TWENTY-TWO

Around this time, Alfie Harrow might have wished he'd never answered Charlotte's call earlier in the day. First, the poor chap thought he'd agreed to judge a charitable crafting competition, and now he found himself embroiled in controversy, theft, and intrigue.

Following the first round of judging, over half of the competing teams were eliminated, including all but one of the groups from the Crafternoon Sewcial Club. However, as it should happen, one of those teams *not* making an early exit was Charlotte's particular team of Crafternooners, despite the bottom half of their pyjamas having mysteriously gone missing. To the relief of Charlotte and her teammates, Alfie was kind enough to offer them something of a lifeline. During the competition, he'd been circling the room, admiring the workmanship on display. Among the garments he was particularly impressed with was that produced by the Crafternoon team. And while the pyjamas had disappeared before the 'official' judging at the conclusion of that round, Alfie was gracious enough to feel that he'd seen enough to mark them through to the next phase of the competition.

As a consequence, when Alfie announced which teams had progressed to the second round, there was some degree of uproar from certain, less charitable factions, with some declaring that rules had been broken and going so far as to demand a recount, even though no counting (or recounting) would be possible on account of there not being any type of election having taken place to begin with.

It was left to Larry, as chief announcer, to explain that there weren't, in actual fact, any official rules to break. Other than a general running order of the day's event, Charlotte hadn't even considered hard and fast rules of engagement to be a major consideration, never imagining such a thing to be necessary.

And so, despite some grumblings, fourteen teams in the Isle of Man Christmas Sewing Bee had progressed onto round two. During the break, the staff had removed the tables vacated by the eliminated teams, laying out those remaining in two equal rows, ready to compete in the festive decorations segment of the competition.

"Look at those miscreants," Joyce said, elbows resting on the table, scowling her sternest scowl across the hall.

Beryl nodded in agreement, glaring in solidarity. "Em, which team, exactly?" she asked, unsure where she should be directing her ire, offering a long stare at no one in particular.

Judging by how she was presently darting her eyes between several tables in quick succession, it was apparent that Joyce wasn't entirely sure about the finer details. All she knew for certain was that somebody was very clearly guilty. She just didn't quite know who that particular guilty party was.

Charlotte, arranging some items on the workspace before her, glanced up momentarily. "Ladies. Don't forget we've only got one hour for this challenge," she advised, calling in her distracted troops in hopes of readying them for the coming battle.

For this challenge, instead of working collectively, they'd decided upon the individual approach, with each member creating their own festive fancy this time around. That way, they'd hopefully have four completed items by the time the clock ticked to zero. By their own admission, Beryl and Joyce's mantra was slow and steady wins the race. This meant that, with the race limited to an hour, there would be little opportunity for half of the group to spend precious time perfecting their Miss Marple impressions by observing or investigating the perpetrators of the apparent sabotage.

With round two of the Sewing Bee soon underway, trade at the concession stands faltered, at least for a while, allowing the teams of volunteers to pop their heads out for a nosey and see what was going on.

"Don't they all look so serious!" Mollie remarked to Sam and Calum, both of them standing on either side of her. "Lotti's nibbling her lower lip, which means she must really be concentrating."

"Either that or she's worried about Larry's driving skills," Stanley jokingly offered, joining the group while watching his friend in the plaster cast travel unceremoniously through the hall, forcing those standing in his path to move for fear of being run over.

"Larry's a bit like the old Austin Metro I had back when I first passed my driving test," Calum suggested. "It had a blockage in the fuel line, so it either dawdled at five miles an hour, or it erupted to maximum speed, without warning. Not ideal when you're trying to park at the supermarket."

"You know, Calum, I think you may have hit the nail on the head," Sam replied. "Larry's throttle control does appear to be rather erratic," he observed, just as Larry proved this very point by careering into an impressive yucca plant that was hardly inconspicuous standing at over six feet tall.

Young Stanley laughed along as two bystanders righted the stricken plant while scooping up handfuls of dirt that had escaped onto the wooden floorboards. "Maybe he thinks he's a jousting knight?" a cheeky Stan suggested. "You know, using his extended leg like a lance?"

"Stanley, go and slow him down, will you, before Sir Lance-a-Lot ploughs somebody down and spends a 'knight' in the cells?" said a concerned Mollie, while managing to splendidly incorporate two puns at once.

They say a watched pot never boils, but where crafting against the clock was concerned, the minutes for all concerned seemed to slide by faster than a river crashing over a waterfall, and soon...

"Ten minutes to go, ladies and gents! That's ten minutes to go!" Larry announced, with Stanley providing him a steady escort, staying close by his side and keeping a watchful eye on the throttle.

"Oh, bother," Beryl said, dropping the partially stuffed reindeer she'd been working on and throwing her hands above her head for a moment in frustration. Unfortunately, Joyce wasn't faring much better, with the collapsed, yet-to-be-stuffed snowman she'd been working on presently resembling a puddle rather than a cute tree decoration.

"Don't worry about it," Charlotte said with a warm smile, hoping to put the two at ease. "We're here to spend some quality time together and have fun!"

Neither Beryl nor Joyce had mentioned it up to this point, but Charlotte could now see the pair were struggling. Joyce, in particular, suffered from arthritis in her left hand, and Beryl's back was giving her gyp from sitting hunched over for so long. Of course, Charlotte was there to offer assistance, which she absolutely did, but the progress of her own project suffered, and any hope of finishing in time was now looking unlikely as a result. Because of this, the hopes of the Crafternooner crew thus fell on Bonnie's tender shoulders, and, for one so young, she was really demonstrating a flair for the hobby.

"Bonnie, I can't believe what you've managed to produce in less than an hour," Charlotte marvelled, looking up to check on Bonnie's progress. "It's so wonderful!"

"Aww, thanks, Lotti. I've been practising this one so much, I've got the pattern consigned to memory," Bonnie confessed. "There. Done!" she said, holding up her masterpiece, a traditional velvet green elf boot stocking decorated with jingle bells and finished off with a luxurious red inner lining.

It was indeed a thing of beauty, and such a lovely vision, in fact, that it drew admiring glances in Bonnie's direction from some of those competitors nearby. Which was a compliment in itself, considering the esteemed crafting circles in which Bonnie currently found herself.

Not long after, Larry tapped his index finger on his trusty microphone, sounding like a woodpecker on a new tree. "That's your lot, ladies and gentlemen! If you'd like to lower your scissors, and please leave your team's selection in the middle of your workstation."

"I think we can agree that we'll leave Bonnie's Christmas stocking for judging?" Charlotte proposed, receiving a firm bob of the head from both Joyce and Beryl. "Come on, ladies," Charlotte said, enjoying a well-earned stretch, "I think we all deserve a nice cuppa, and the next round's on me."

Charlotte took a slight detour along the way, popping her head in to see Calum and the other elves toiling away in the festive emporium. "Wow, that's amazing!" she said, stretching up for a kiss from Calum, which Calum, being no fool, was only too happy to administer.

"What is?" Calum asked. "Oh, you mean my special shirt?" he joked. "Ah. My girlfriend made it for me."

"Well, your girlfriend must be *exceptionally* talented, then," Charlotte suggested, running her hand down the length of his arm, impressed that his lights remained illuminated. "No, but what's amazing," she said, running her eyes over the empty shelves, "is how much you've all sold. You have sold it? I mean, you've not been burgled?"

Calum unzipped the cash belt secured around his waist for inspection. "Check it out," he said, flicking his thumb over a crisp pile of banknotes. "We could have sold some of those crocheted tree decorations ten times over, Lotti. Honestly, it's been manic, but so much fun. And, from what Mollie was saying, they've been just as frantic over at their post, if not more so."

"I can't thank you enough. This is absolutely—" Charlotte started to say, before a tap on her shoulder interrupted her.

"Can we have a quick word?" Joyce said, Beryl beside her, and both of their expressions earnest.

"Yes, of course," Charlotte answered. "But if it's about that cup of tea? That's where I'm off to next, I promise, ladies." But Charlotte suspected that wasn't what this was about, actually, and had an inkling as to where in fact this conversation might be heading.

Once outside the emporium, and away from prying ears, Beryl took up the reins, first looking to her mate Joyce, and then to Charlotte. "Charlotte," she started tentatively, "I know there are no guarantees we're going to make it through to the final, but..."

"If we don't make it through to the final with Bonnie's masterpiece, then it's a bloody travesty," Joyce commented, cutting in. "Sorry," she then said. "Please continue."

"You'll get no arguments on that front," Beryl answered, in complete agreement. "But Lotti," she continued, pulling the conversation back on track. "Lotti, the thing is, both Joyce and I are not as young as we once were."

"Or sober," Joyce insisted, though it didn't sound like she was being entirely serious.

"Speak for yourself," Beryl said, but throwing in a well-timed *"hic"* for comedic effect just the same. "Anyway, we didn't quite know how to tell you this, Lotti. But I... well, that is we... think we need to bow out of the competition. Assuming our team hasn't already been eliminated, of course."

"My hand's seized up," Joyce explained. "And Beryl's walking around like the bloody Hunchback of Notre Dame. No offence, Beryl."

"None taken," said Beryl.

"So if we continue, we're afraid we're going to be more of a hindrance than a help. We hope you're not too disappointed?"

"Disappointed?" Charlotte scoffed. "Yes, of course I'm disappointed. But only because two of my dearest friends are in discomfort. Now, let's say we go and fetch you both a nice, comfortable seat on which to enjoy your cuppa?"

"And some ice?" Joyce asked.

"Consider it done," Charlotte said. "But is the ice for the contents of that hip flask, or for your painful wrist? Just so I know."

"Get enough for both," Joyce answered. "Just to be on the safe side."

CHAPTER TWENTY-THREE

Four tables positioned about one metre apart from the corners formed a broad rectangle shape in the middle of the marvellous ballroom. With the grand final scheduled to get underway in a few short minutes, hopeful competitors and enthusiastic spectators filtered back into the main hall, daring to dream.

During the break, each of the second-round creations had been laid out for the spectators to get an up-close and personal view. And what was utterly apparent was the quality of work-manship and obvious talent on hand.

Then, to build tension ahead of the grand final, the four winning creations from the previous round were laid out separately, concealed from view by a Santa-patterned fabric covering, ready for the big reveal.

"Well, here we are!" Larry announced over the PA system. "After what I'm sure you'll agree has been a magnificent day with the backdrop of this festive wonderland, we're down to the fabulous final four!" Larry paused for applause, and the packed room did not disappoint. "And let's not forget," he continued. "Today is not just about witnessing the island's finest crafters in action, but also raising funds for a truly wonderful and worthwhile cause. Your generous support will go some way to ensuring the island's schoolchildren have the uniforms they need and coats to keep them warm."

Larry's second pause for applause didn't disappoint any more than the first, and he was immensely enjoying this MC gig judging by the cheesy grin on his chops. "Right," he said, edging himself closer to the display table, resulting in the crowd shuffling forward for an improved view. "And now to reveal the finalists!" he announced, extending his hand towards the protective Santa-themed shroud... but not quite reaching it. "Erm, just a moment. That is... any minute now..." he joked, playing off as if this delay were deliberate, even though it was not. But try as he might, he just couldn't get close enough, unable to navigate his chair into the proper position.

"I've got this," Stanley declared, never far from his friend's side. But whereas Larry's intention had been to tease the fabric away, slowly unveiling the finalists' creations, Stanley gripped a handful of the cloth, quickly ripping it free in one go like a magician clearing a dinner table. As a result, those teams lucky enough to progress became immediately aware of the fact, able to see their work plainly revealed.

"Yes!" yelled Bonnie, jumping up and down like a pogo stick. "We did it!" she said, turning first to Charlotte, and then to Joyce and Beryl, giving them each a warm hug.

Joining the Crafternooners in the grand final were Stitch 'n' Bitch, the Knitty Noras, and a jubilant team from Amelia's Laxey Coffee Morning Crew, all basking in the appreciative glow of the assembled audience.

One notable absence in this quartet, however, was the feverishly passionate team from Sew It Would Seam. Indeed, so fervently enthusiastic were the team that Larry and Alfie Harrow deliberately maintained a safe distance, unsure what sort of reaction the group might offer for not making the final cut. But as dedicated crafters themselves, the Sew It Would Seam group couldn't deny the quality of workmanship that had made it through to the final round, so had little choice but to accept the judge's decision without too much complaint. Besides, they had more significant issues on their plate at present, as Joyce and Beryl, it would appear, had decided they were now the prime suspects in their ongoing sabotage enquiry. So team Sew It Would Seam probably felt it best to watch their step if Beryl and Joyce's aggressive posturing was anything to go by.

"Ladies," Larry said into the microphone (a microphone that would likely need to be surgically removed from his hand, such was his fondness for it by this point in time). "And I say ladies without fear of being berated, as the last of our male contingent graciously bowed out in the previous round. But there's always next year, lads. Anyway, to business. The grand final of the Manx Christmas Sewing Bee. And with the theme of this final round being… Hollywood glitz."

Larry invited each of the four teams to take up a position at the finalists' tables. Bonnie paused for a moment, hesitating before heading over. It didn't feel right to her to go over there without Beryl and Joyce by her side. In response, Joyce, from her seat, instinctively reached up and took her hand, gently stroking it.

"It just won't be the same without the two of you," Bonnie told them both, her expression heavy.

"We're not going to be too far away," Joyce reassured her.

"And you know what would make us really happy?" Beryl asked, a devilish twinkle in her eye.

"What's that?" Bonnie asked.

Beryl wiggled her finger, beckoning Bonnie nearer.

"Yes…?" said Bonnie, leaning in close so that Beryl could speak directly into her ear.

"Get out there and knock their bloody socks off!" Beryl joyfully advised. "Show them what the Crafternooners are capable of, yeah?"

"You've got it," Bonnie said, and then, with a tear in her eye, Bonnie stood, noticing not only her friends in the audience but her dad, who'd been there to support her throughout the day. Then, like a boxer heading into the ring, she took up a position next to Charlotte, ready for the bell to sound so they could both come out, arms swinging, so to speak.

"Are we settled on Audrey?" Charlotte asked, carefully laying out her crafting paraphernalia like a brain surgeon preparing for a long, delicate operation.

"Oh, yes. Absolutely, Lotti," Bonnie replied, in ready agreement. "Does anything say Hollywood glitz more than Audrey Hepburn in Breakfast at Tiffany's?"

"I don't think it does, Bonn. I really don't."

Due to a pre-existing appointment for a wedding suit fitting, Alfie Harrow temporarily excused himself. But with the final round being allocated an hour and a half, he promised it was plenty of time to get to his shop and back in time for the final judgement. Plus, as he pointed out to Charlotte, his decision would then be based entirely on viewing the finished garment, with no chance of him being swayed during the creation phase.

Over by the overflow clothes rail for the competitors, Larry parked himself up, accompanied by his able wingman, Stan. "I don't know if the battery on this microphone or the battery on this wheelchair is going to run out first," Larry remarked, tapping the wheelchair power display as if this would make any difference.

"Maybe we shouldn't have raced you for so long?" Stanley suggested.

"Yeah, but it was some flippin' good fun, though, wasn't it?" Larry offered.

"It was," Stanley agreed. "The best."

Stanley rested a hand up against the metal clothes rail, casually leaning against it as if he were about to do some shopping. He ran his eyes over the assortment of garments hanging there, many of which he recognised from being previously stored at his house for weeks on end. "Here, what's this?" Stanley said, looking first to Larry, and then crouching down to a crudely folded pile lying there on the floor below the rack of clothing. "Is that not...?" he asked, peeling away various articles until he'd reached the one he was looking for that was peeking out from underneath the others.

"Ah. That's my fault," Larry confessed, glancing over each shoulder as if he'd committed a heinous crime. "After the first round of the competition, I was a little heavy-handed with the throttle," he explained. "As a result, I dinted the wheelchair and took out a few tables in the process. Some materials dropped onto the floor, so I gathered them up and set them there."

Stanley stood to attention, holding in his hands the one particular item he'd singled out from the rest, an article of brushed cotton adorned with a cheery festive pattern.

"You don't need to hang them up at this point, Stan, I don't think," Larry said. "I'm not sure the competitors have even used this clothes rail judging by the amount still on it."

"Erm... does this not look slightly familiar?" Stanley asked, unable to contain his nervous smile, allowing the item in his hands to unwind, falling towards the floor like a Venetian blind opening.

Larry ran his tongue over his lower lip, staring intently, offering perhaps a flicker of recognition, or perhaps not. It was difficult for Stanley to tell. Then, several seconds later, Stanley could see the precise moment the penny dropped through Larry's skull, rattling around his rib cage for a while, before tickling the soles of his feet.

Larry darted his eyes about, frantically searching his brain for any alternative explanations that might present themselves, though without success, for by this point he already knew exactly what young Stanley held in his hands. "Are they...?" Larry started to say, before taking a moment to clear his throat. "Are they the Crafternooners' pyjama bottoms?" he asked.

"I think they might well be, yes," Stanley answered, raising an eyebrow in acknowledgement.

"I just scooped up the items that'd fallen off the tables," Larry explained, like he was in a court of law facing serious jail time. "I had a quick look through them, and from what I could see, I thought they were just offcuts and such. That's why I placed them over here."

Stanley didn't know to fold things neatly, so he rolled up the pyjama bottoms, like a sleeping bag after a night camping in the great outdoors.

"I won't say anything if you don't," Larry offered with a wink, more through hope than expectation, and fluttering his bushy eyebrows for good measure. "I mean, your mum's team did still end up qualifying for the next round, after all, so there's no real harm done, right?"

"I suppose," Stanley said, gently returning the offending article back underneath the rest of the pile, where he'd found it. "Although..."

"Although?" Larry asked.

"There might be a bigger issue," Stanley suggested.

"Such as?" Larry said, quickly making sure the switch on his microphone was in the off position.

"Such as Joyce and Beryl still think it was sabotage, or espionage, or some kind of other thing like that," Stanley advised. "They're convinced they know who's responsible and are intent on revenge."

Larry didn't appear overly concerned by this information. "Joyce is ninety-something, and Beryl's not too far behind," he said. "They can't get up to *that* much mischief, can they?"

"Water bombs," Stanley said with a gulp, remembering an earlier interaction he had with the ladies.

"Water bombs?"

"Yes, they asked me for my packet of water bombs."

Larry shot him a glance. "What on earth are you doing with a packet of water bombs at a crafting competition?"

"Larry, I'm ten years old," Stanley answered, an explanation which seemed more than sufficient in his eyes.

"Bloody hell. This could start an island-wide crafting war, the likes of which have never been seen before," Larry dramatically declared. "If we want to avoid a skirmish, there's only one solution."

"You're going to tell everybody the truth?" Stanley asked him, innocently enough.

"Good heavens, no!" Larry answered. "No, lad. You need to get the water bombs back from those two loons Beryl and Joyce!"

CHAPTER TWENTY-FOUR

I might need to borrow this once we're finished," Bonnie remarked, feasting her appreciative eyes over their very own little black dress, so synonymous with the iconic film from which they'd taken their inspiration. "It's funny how something so sombre, colour-wise, could appear so chic."

"You'd look amazing in this, Bonn," Charlotte replied, with a needle clenched between her teeth and a line of thread running down her chin. "All you'd need to find is a handsome boyfriend to buy you some pearls to wear with it."

"And take me somewhere elegant to wear it, as well," Bonnie added in.

Neither Bonnie nor Charlotte had been paying too much attention to their immediate surroundings or what was going on around them. Other than a brief interruption when Larry appeared with a few questions from the audience, they'd had their eyes glued to what they'd been working on. If they'd examined the other tables, like the spectators were, they'd have seen a 1920's Gatsby-inspired flapper dress, a strapless fuchsia number, and finally a sleeveless V-neck red cocktail dress with a daring split up both sides that Jessica Rabbit would probably die for. And in keeping faithful to the popular TV programme — *The Great British Sewing Bee* — upon which their own event was based, four willing models (friends of Bonnie, as it should happen) would be on hand to walk the four finished garments up the catwalk. Both Beryl and Joyce didn't take too much offence when their own offer of modelling services had been politely rebuffed, with Charlotte noting that, while she was appreciative, all vacant positions had already been filled for the day. But of course, with Beryl's dodgy back and Joyce's pesky arthritis, the old girls probably hadn't been serious anyway.

The day so far had been thoroughly enjoyable for all involved, but challenging for the competitors, requiring every ounce of their concentration. And even Charlotte joked that she might need an extended period to recharge her crafting batteries after the competition's conclusion. However, those closest to her doubted her sincerity on that matter, never knowing her to be without a crochet hook within arm's length and a ball of wool by her feet for any real length of time.

With the electronic timer almost on the ten-minute mark, several sets of eyes fell upon Larry, the roving reporter and erstwhile announcer, expecting him to leap into action as he'd done before. But rather than pressing the microphone to his lips in anticipation, unleashing his dulcet tones to signal the final stages of the competition as per usual, Larry was sitting uncharacteristically motionless, staring vacantly off into the distance.

Mollie, standing nearby in her jam-splattered apron from the refreshments stand, headed his way just to make sure that he'd not been taken unwell.

"I'm just checking in, Larry," Mollie said, crouching down beside his wheelchair. "Everything okay, dear? Do you need anything?"

"What?" Larry replied, slightly startled. "Oh. Thanks. No, I'm fine and dandy," he insisted, issuing forth a double thumbs-up to reinforce this statement despite the fact that he didn't sound very convinced of it himself.

"Well, it's just that..." Mollie said, deliberately tapping her watch, and then flicking her eyes suggestively over to the electronic timer which now read closer to nine minutes than ten.

"Oh, crap," Larry replied, holding up an apologetic hand for those that may have been watching and waiting. "The thing is, Mollie," he whispered, from out of the corner of his mouth, lips unmoving, like a ventriloquist. "The thing is, there's no sign of

Alfie Harrow, and I'm starting to get worried," he said, smiling, and still giving a little cupped-hand wave to any onlookers, as if everything was just fine and there was absolutely no cause for alarm. "You see, without him to announce the winner, people will look to me for answers, and what am I going to say? After all, I'm just the witty and talented announcer, aren't I?"

"You'd think of something, Larry, brilliant as you are," Mollie assured him, trying her best to bolster his ego. "But I wouldn't be overly concerned, yeah? I'm sure Alfie is on his way back. If it helps set your mind at ease, though, I could get his mobile number from Lotti and give him a call?"

Larry's face lit up in response to Mollie's kind offer. "If you wouldn't mind?" he said, breathing a sigh of relief.

"Consider it done, Larry. Now, your public awaits," Mollie told him, thankful that Larry's unusual demeanour a few moments ago had simply been down to worry over an overdue judge as opposed to, say, a funny turn, medically speaking.

"That's eight and a half minutes, ladies!" a chirpy, reinvigorated Larry announced into his microphone. "Eight and half minutes, if you please!"

Despite the fact that there were upwards of four hundred spectators in attendance, you could hear a pin drop (as was quite literally the case on more than one occasion, the result of one nervous crafter with a somewhat shaky hand). And aside from a few final instructions shared between team members, not a word was heard in the hushed hall. It was a nail-biting climax to a fabulous day, and right now, the main enemy for the finalists was the ticking clock. After their valiant efforts, it would have been devastating if all their hard work were to come undone by not being able to finish the current project by the deadline.

For Bonnie and Charlotte, the last few moments of the competition were spent casting fatigued eyes over their dress, hoping to catch and sort out any last-minute issues or imperfections. Fortunately, as far as they could tell, there weren't any. Now finished, satisfied, and reasonably happy, they lifted their heads from the workstation the moment Larry sounded his air horn bringing the day's final challenge to a close. And first to hurry over and congratulate them on a job well done were Beryl and Joyce, thrilled that their early retirement from the team hadn't dulled the group's chances of victory.

Larry trained one cautious eye on Beryl and Joyce, concerned to see them so animated, as the threat of crafting warfare was ever-present in his mind. But it was a struggle to maintain his surveillance, as he soon became inundated by a steady stream of well-wishers issuing forth.

"Do excuse me," Larry said, navigating through the sea of legs around him. "Coming through, yes, yes, lovely day. So good to see you," he went on, but progress was slow, like wheeling himself through sand. Undaunted, Larry pressed on, sharing pleasantries along the way, his hands clammy.

He'd really dropped a clanger with the whole pyjama bottoms faux pas, and, concerned that matters might soon get entirely out of hand, he decided that honesty might possibly be the best policy after all. Gradually, bodies sufficiently parted, presenting Larry an avenue through the crowd. He teased his joystick forward, head down, eyes fixed on his two targets.

"Are you playing hard to get?" the woman in the tangerine jumper from earlier cooed, suddenly placing herself directly in Larry's path. A brave move considering Larry's rather questionable braking skills.

"Do excuse me," Larry said, looking around the orange-hued obstacle. "I just need to..."

"I didn't give you my phone number earlier," said the obstacle, scribbling a series of digits on a scrap of paper in her hand, periodically flicking her eyes in Larry's direction as she did so and batting her eyelashes seductively. "There," she said, once finished, carefully folding the paper, leaning forward, and then sliding it in behind the handkerchief in Larry's breast pocket. "My name is Valentina," Larry's special new friend whispered softly, through pouted lips.

Larry started out again, aiming his wheelchair to the left, attempting to go around the woman, but this manoeuvre was immediately countered, his path once again blocked. "You're a cheeky one," declared Valentina, wagging a finger like he was a naughty little boy.

But Larry wasn't really listening. Instead, he'd caught a brief glimpse of a cackling Beryl, sharing a joke with Charlotte and Bonnie. But that in itself didn't concern him. Rather, it was the plump, generously-filled waterbomb displayed on the palm of her hand that did.

"No, it's all been a mistake!" Larry called out, ignoring poor Valentina's advances. He successfully navigated around her, flailing his free hand to shoo any stragglers out of the way as he advanced. "Beryl!" he shouted, approaching at maximum speed. "Stand down, Beryl, it's all my fault!" he declared, mere moments before careering into a leg of the table they were all gathered around, scaring the bejeezus out of everyone nearby.

"Would you sort out that bloody throttle control of yours?" Joyce scolded him, clutching her chest and then checking herself over for injury.

"You don't need to do this, Beryl! The missing pyjamas were all my fault!" Larry confessed, raising, and then slowly lowering his hand, hoping Beryl would do the same. "Please. Drop the weapon, Beryl..."

"Oh, relax, silly," Beryl said, softening her grip. "Stanley's already told us exactly what you've done."

"And just in time, too, as we'd been right about to launch these bad boys," Joyce entered in, relieving herself of her own weapon and handing it over to Beryl. "Ah, well," she said with a sigh.

Beryl stood with both waterbombs in either hand. She stared down at them, giving them a gentle jiggle, offering a wistful smile. "Ah, that takes me back to my youth," she declared, giving them another jiggle.

"It's never too late to go under the knife," Joyce suggested to her friend. "I'm not sure how much it would cost, but you did receive that nice little tax rebate," Joyce reminded her. "Hmm, maybe it's something I'd also consider?"

Larry didn't want to dwell too much on any potential plastic enhancements that may or may not happen, just relieved the imminent crisis had been averted and the matter put to rest.

"Well, thank heavens for that," Larry mumbled to himself, carefully looking over his shoulder before reversing as all good motorists should. Unfortunately, however, and unbeknownst to Larry, his extended leg supported the corner of the table he'd hurtled into, and the moment he removed it, the table collapsed towards him. Fortunately, it was a lightweight folding table, so no physical damage was inflicted. Still...

"Don't move an inch!" Charlotte shouted, lurching forward, and then making a dive at the black fabric gathered by Larry's rear wheel.

"Oh no," Bonnie said, quickly dropping down onto one knee to render assistance as well.

But it was already too late. During the table collapse, Bonnie and Charlotte's little black dress had been pitched to the floor, landing in a crumpled heap, where it promptly got caught up in the maelstrom of Larry's revolving wheels, with Larry unable to stop in time despite Charlotte's warning.

Larry looked down in horror. "I'll... I'll just move forward a bit...?" he suggested, and then did precisely that. But sadly, all his corrective manoeuvre served to do was eat more fabric.

With the assistance of Sam and Calum, Larry was soon transplanted from his steel chariot to a comfy armchair procured from over at the reception area. Then, with the wheelchair tipped on its side, Charlotte utilised her trusty, well-used crochet hook to recover the portion of the dress caught up in the wheel. With this accomplished, Charlotte tentatively rose, the dress still scrunched in a heap in her hand as she stood.

"Well?" Bonnie asked, watching on through a small opening in the fingers held up to her face.

Charlotte slowly opened the folds of fabric, barely able to look, afraid of what she might discover. Those who'd formed a circle around them held their collective breath, none more so than Larry, who was chewing on his knuckle.

Charlotte shook her head, and then, in resigned defeat, held the dress out in front to reveal the damage. The noticeable smear of oil across the front may have been salvageable, but the tear on the backside area was beyond repair. She could see the concern written all over Larry's face, and, as did Bonnie, tried her best to mask her disappointment. "Houston, we might have a problem," Charlotte said jokingly, with a laugh, so as not to contribute further to Larry's obvious distress.

"This probably isn't the best time," Mollie said, making her way through the crowd of concerned onlookers. "Scrap that. I can see this isn't the best time. But Alfie Harrow's on his way. Apparently, the car park was so full that he was struggling to find a space."

Larry placed his head in his hands. "Oh, no," he said, digging his fingernails into his scalp. "What have I done? I've ruined everything. I'm a clumsy old fool who's ruined everything."

Charlotte took his hands, gently easing them away so she could see his face. "Ruined everything? Larry, you've done no such thing," she insisted. "Do you hear me? No such thing."

"But... your dress? The competition...?"

Charlotte laughed. But it wasn't a sarcastic sort of laugh at all, despite the circumstances. Rather, it was the sort of laugh you'd offer when recalling a fond or happy memory. "Larry," Charlotte told him, wiping away a tear that'd rolled down his cheek. "Larry, when I look back on today, I'll remember being surrounded by my delightful, if slightly bonkers friends. I'll think of you tearing around this magnificent hall, looking like a million dollars in your wheelchair. And, okay, yes, I *may* think about our pretty dress having a chunk ripped out from the arse. But I'll probably chuckle when I do, all right? I promise."

"Don't forget the waterbomb warfare that almost very nearly occurred," Bonnie entered in. "And the talk of plastic you-know-whats," she said with a laugh.

Charlotte grinned at either image forming in her mind. "Can you imagine if Stanley hadn't spilt the beans, and *those* two..." she said, looking over to Joyce and Beryl. "If those two had staged their surprise attack? Oh, my days."

"So, you're honestly not annoyed at me?" Larry asked of both Bonnie and Charlotte.

"Nah," Bonnie said, waving away his concerns. "Although I have to admit, I was hoping to wear that dress at some point."

"There's plenty of material left, kiddo," Charlotte remarked. "We can always make another one, yeah?"

"Can we? That would be grand," Bonnie answered, pleased at the thought of this.

"Yes, indeed. And I know just who can help us with it," Charlotte said, giving Larry a friendly stare.

"I'll help any way I can, ladies," Larry happily promised, before looking over to Stanley. "Come here, Stan, will you?"

Stanley held his hands in the air like he was about to surrender. "I had to tell them about the pyjama bottoms," he said, setting out his stall ahead of his arrival and worried he'd thrown his pal under the bus. "It was the only way to end the war, as I could see that battle lines were being drawn."

But Larry appeared unbothered, having taken absolutely no offence. "You did the right thing, lad, don't worry," he said. "In fact, I'd just been on the way over to come clean about it myself, only you beat me to it," he revealed. "No, we're fine. What I actually wanted, though, was to perhaps ask a little favour?"

Stanley nodded. "Of course. Anything."

"It's the electric wheelchair," Larry explained, looking over to the collapsed table, and then back again. "I don't think I'll ever master that beast. So I'm thinking of handing back the keys, so to speak, before I cause any more damage."

"Understood," said Stanley, offering a smart salute. "And what is it you need from me?" he asked, still saluting.

"Well, if I reverted to the manual version, I wondered if you'd help wheel me about again?"

Stanley pushed out his lower lip, thrilled to step up. "Larry, it'd be my pleasure," he said, giving his pal one last salute for good measure. "One thing, though, before we switch back to the old model?"

"Oh? What's that?" Larry replied, perfectly open to any sort of suggestion Stanley might have in mind.

"Can we go outside and try to beat your lap record before you do?" Stanley enquired.

"No, you cannot!" Charlotte interjected, gently but firmly nipping this little notion right in the bud before any possible shenanigans were able to commence. "Larry's got one plaster cast already, and he certainly doesn't need another."

"Here, Lotti," Beryl said, attracting Charlotte's attention, as there seemed to be something important on her mind.

"Yes, Beryl?" Charlotte asked, happy enough for a distraction of any sort, away from matters of wheelchair racing. "What is it, dear?"

"Whaddya reckon?" asked Beryl, the two waterbombs still held in her hands, and now cradled in front of her chest. "Just enough, or could I go up a couple of cup sizes?"

CHAPTER TWENTY-FIVE

For someone so utterly captivated by everything Christmas, Charlotte Newman was nevertheless delighted when the month of January arrived and thoughts turned to packing up the tree and returning it to the loft for another year.

It's not as if she hadn't enjoyed herself over the festive period. Quite the opposite, in fact. And therein lay the problem: her expanding waistline. As a very active member of the island's vibrant crafting scene, Charlotte's social calendar had been in danger of exploding in the run-up to Christmas. It was, of course, a most pleasing problem to have had, and each event she attended was thoroughly gratifying. The issue was that crafters, generally speaking, like cake. Lots of cake. Both making and eating. And especially eating. And even though you're regularly attending several social clubs each day, it would be considered terribly rude to refuse what had been so lovingly prepared and so graciously offered, especially during the season of goodwill.

There was even one notable week in which Charlotte had attended three Christmas lunches, consuming a large turkey meal with all the trimmings at each one.

As such, the welcome arrival of January would hopefully prevent Charlotte from being such a gannet. And, once again, reinstalling the Couch-to-5K app on her phone showed a willingness to shift some of her recently acquired poundage. Still, if she was ever feeling a little down in the dumps about the struggle, all she had to do was cast her mind back to the Christmas Sewing Bee to raise an immediate smile.

Sadly, there had been no fairytale ending for her team of Crafternooners on that day, but that was all right. Ultimately, Alfie Harrow, who'd so generously given up his time, could only judge what was presented before him, of course. Unfortunately, unlike the missing pyjama bottoms, Alfie had never actually laid eyes on their finished black dress, so he was only able to consider the mangled effort they eventually ended up with. But there were absolutely no complaints from Charlotte and the others, who were delighted enough to see one of Amelia's Laxey Coffee Morning Crew teams crowned as the inaugural Isle of Man Christmas Sewing Bee champions.

For a while, at least, there had been some talk about making Larry wear the mutilated black dress along with an Audrey Hepburn wig so they could enjoy a group photo opportunity — the ideal opportunity for a souvenir of a wonderful day and a reminder for Larry to go easy on the throttle. But, to Larry's immense relief, it was decided he simply didn't have the cheekbones for it, and the idea had eventually fallen by the wayside (and was one that Larry didn't appear particularly keen to remind them of).

Aside from copious amounts of entertaining, Charlotte had also been busy juggling work-related activities, namely the ongoing rollout of the Make It Sew programme, her nursing home crafting sessions. In addition to these duties, there was also the consideration of the school uniform initiative she'd introduced, which required urgent attention if, as Charlotte and her band of merry helpers had been working towards, it was to be properly implemented in time for the start of the new school term in January — the time when some of the island's children needed it the most. It was a herculean effort by all involved, but one they were delighted to see come to fruition and in good time.

The Christmas Sewing Bee and the surrounding publicity it had attracted, as was hoped, had been a real game-changer for the ReCyCool campaign. Since the event, Shoprite reported a steady stream of uniform donations island-wide in their recycling bins. So much so, the staff were delighted to report that they'd already welcomed many families in store, grateful for assistance at a time of year when the purse strings were already stretched.

And there was the cash the Manx Sewing Bee had generated as well. Virtually all of the Christmas stock had been sold, and nary a crumb remained on the cake stands when the Sewing Bee had concluded. If you took into account the money thrown into the collection buckets, there was a substantial pot available to supplement the uniform donations when needed.

For Charlotte, it had been a humbling experience to both be involved in and witness. To see ordinary, everyday folk so selflessly offering up their time, money, energy, and resources for such a noble cause was just one of the many reasons she adored this little island in the middle of the Irish Sea and loved living where she did.

And presently, today, there was the possibility of raising the ReCyCool profile further after Charlotte accepted the offer of an interview and photo opportunity with the local press. And with her unofficial PR adviser, Mollie, en route to pick her up, all she needed to do now was find her favourite lipstick, which was somehow evading her, last seen in the darkest recesses of her handbag...

"You look nice," Mollie remarked as Charlotte climbed inside her car. "And is that a new dress?"

"Thanks, Moll. Yeah, this is the new dress Calum bought me for Christmas. I thought it would be perfect for having my picture taken in."

"Impressive. The boy's got exceptional taste. But what I'm guessing you mean is that you dragged him around the shops and pointed to the one you liked?"

"Pretty much," Charlotte was happy to confirm. "And thanks for coming along with me today," she added, giving Mollie's thigh a gentle pat as they headed on their way. "I always get a little excitable whenever I've been interviewed in the past."

"I remember. What was it you started singing on the radio that one time?" Mollie asked.

"Bohemian Rhapsody," Charlotte answered, lowering her head in shame. "You know I'm bloody useless with any awkward silence. He let me go on for an entire chorus before he finally cut to a commercial break."

"So, you want me to make sure you don't waffle on and say something stupid, or otherwise make a spectacle of yourself?"

"Yes. That would be most appreciated."

The suggested and agreed-upon rendezvous point was just in front of the green recycling bin outside Shoprite's flagship store in Douglas, the island's capital. And even though it would likely only result in a small article in the local paper, Charlotte couldn't help but feel a smidge nervous as they parked up. And her nerves were not allayed when, after ten minutes, there was still no sign of Patrick, the journalist...

"Do you think he's stood us up?" Charlotte asked, flapping her arms like a bird, hoping to restore blood flow to her chilled extremities and regretting that she hadn't worn a coat.

"I'm sure he'll be here soon," Mollie said, casually leaning up against the recycling bin. "Relax."

"Oh, wait, this could be him," Charlotte said, perking up as she spotted a chap bustling in their direction. Her hopes were raised further when he stopped directly in front of them.

"Patrick?" Charlotte said, about to extend her greeting hand.

"Erm, no," the middle-aged fellow replied, likely wondering why two women were resting up against a recycling bin. "It's Simon. Nice to meet you?" he said politely.

"My mistake," Charlotte said with a chuckle. "I could have sworn I'd read the name Patrick on your email. Anyway, where do you want us?"

"Want us?" the man asked with a nervous smile.

Charlotte placed a hand on her hip, pouting her lips. "How's this, Simon?" she joked, looking Simon up and down. "For the camera, I mean."

"Camera?" he said, again repeating Charlotte's words back to her.

Mollie felt obliged to step in at this point. "You're not Patrick, the journalist and photographer, are you?" she surmised.

Simon shook his head, holding up the plastic bag that'd been tucked under his arm. "No, I'm just Simon. Simon, who's hoping to put this bag in the recycling bin. Simon, whose wife is sitting in the car, probably thinking I'm chatting up two attractive women by a recycling bin and wondering why one of them is posing for me seductively?"

"Attractive?" Charlotte said, delighted, and forgetting for a moment all about the issue of mistaken identity. "It's a new dress, and I thought..." she started to explain, but then thought better of it and remembered the reason they'd gathered there. Charlotte reached for the metal access drawer of the recycling bin, gently swinging it open to accept Simon's generous donation. "Never mind. There you go, Simon. Much appreciated, and it's all for a wonderful cause."

"I should probably go," Simon said, placing his bag into the opening.

"We're waiting for a journalist and photographer," Mollie explained, just to clarify the situation.

"I see," replied Simon, looking at the two of them, the large green bin behind them, and then back to the ladies once more. "Well, it's a lovely location you've chosen. And, ehm... I'm sure there'll be a photographer along at any moment?" he said, appearing to choose his words very carefully, probably feeling it unwise to upset the two women before him who were quite obviously barmy as a box of frogs.

"Well at least he thinks we're attractive," Charlotte said a moment later, waving as Simon's car drove past and flashing him a beaming smile.

"Simon's going to have a fun journey home," Mollie observed with a chuckle, clocking the sour expression on his wife's face.

A further ten minutes elapsed, and with the imminent onset of hypothermia becoming a very real danger, Charlotte glanced down to her watch. "I wonder if we've turned up to the wrong Shoprite store," she mused aloud. "Perhaps we should just go?"

But that decision quickly became unnecessary, as just then...

"Charlotte? Charlotte Newman?" a somewhat breathless chap with a well-manicured ginger goatee enquired, as he bounded towards them.

"Ah. You must be Patrick," Charlotte responded, spotting the Nikon camera bag slung over the fellow's shoulder. "Did you get lost?" she asked, though not in an *I-am-furious-with-you* sort of way. Curiously, he appeared to have come from the direction of the store's entrance, as if perhaps he'd just performed a bit of last-minute shopping.

"No, no! Sorry about that!" Patrick replied, shaking his head, and appearing genuinely regretful. "No, just a few things I had to check on," he explained. "Well, I suppose we should get on with your interview, shouldn't we?" he offered, correctly sensing that none of them were getting any younger as they stood there. "Shall we, then?" he said, extending a hand, as if there were someplace else they were supposed to be standing.

Charlotte looked around, uncertain as to where they were meant to be going. She had thought, after all, that they were precisely where they ought to be.

"Oh. Did I not say in the email? I thought I said in the email," Patrick answered, and looking over to Mollie for some reason. "I thought we'd first get a few snaps instore," he told Charlotte. "That way, we can have the school uniforms hanging up in the back of the shot, showing the public what it's all about, yes?"

"Ah, I see. All right, then," Charlotte said, turning towards the store, happy enough for this unexpected change of plan as the interior of the store was almost certain to be warmer than the area outside. "Lead on," she told him. "We're in your hands."

The last time Charlotte was in this location, she'd been doing a recce on the donated uniform stock levels with Calum and Stanley. And it had been slim pickings, to say the least. Indeed, with the racks all but empty, one could easily have assumed that particular section of the store had just been looted. But things had hopefully progressed since then. And Charlotte's contact in the store had actually sounded optimistic when they'd last spoken over the phone, leaving Charlotte with a distinctly positive impression.

Once inside, Charlotte couldn't help but notice Mollie was acting a wee bit peculiar. She'd run up ahead and was talking to Patrick through the corner of her mouth. For a moment, Charlotte wondered if the poor fellow was perhaps getting a tongue lashing for keeping them both waiting outside. Charlotte picked up her pace, catching up with them and drawing alongside. "Everything okay?" she asked, hoping to defuse any potential unpleasant situation.

"Oh, yes," Mollie said as they passed by the pet food section. "We're absolutely *marvellous*," she answered. And she said this so enthusiastically, in fact, that it came across as a bit Scooby-Doo villain, only missing the enthusiastic "Mwaha-ha-ha!" at the end to punctuate the sentence.

Then, coming around a corner, the three of them came to a halt. There in front, two staff members in Shoprite uniforms had wheeled a whopping great trolley into their path, packed high with empty cardboard boxes. It was so large, covering the entire width of the aisle, that it was preventing Charlotte and the others from continuing on, along with obscuring their view ahead as well.

Mollie stepped forward, as if she knew just what was going on, raising her hand and offering the two staff members a spirited wave. In response, they trundled the unwieldy trolley forward, moving slowly like a freight train leaving the station.

"Mollie?" Charlotte said, tilting her head quizzically. "What's going on?"

The trolley disappeared up the cleaning products aisle, revealing the previously obscured section of the store, and more importantly, dozens of people standing around the ReCyCool display just ahead.

"SURPRISE!" a collective cheer called out, nearly knocking Charlotte flat on her arse. Charlotte couldn't take it all in, looking instead to Mollie for answers.

"Go on," Mollie said, giving her friend a gentle nudge. "This is for you, Lotti. It's all for you."

Charlotte pressed her fingers to her mouth, with her cheeks turning a lovely shade of scarlet. She wasn't sure what exactly was going on, but amongst the crowd of people were a handful of familiar faces, including Calum, Larry, Joyce, Beryl, Bonnie, and Sam, along with a solid contingent of those who'd made the Manx Sewing Bee possible.

"What are you all doing here?" Charlotte asked the group. "Can somebody tell me what's going on?"

A smartly dressed chap Charlotte didn't know extended a hand in her direction. From his bearing, he looked like he could have been a lawyer, was Charlotte's initial thought.

"Charlotte, my name is Alex Adler," the fellow said, waiting for a glimmer of recognition that didn't immediately arrive.

"As in Alex Adler, Minister for Education...?" Charlotte said after a moment, realisation finally dawning.

Alex nodded. "The very same," he answered. "We spoke over the phone several weeks back?" he added, refreshing her memory in case that was needed.

"Yes, I remember it well!" Charlotte insisted, despite not recognising his voice at first.

Alex spoke up so that the others in attendance could hear their conversation. "Charlotte contacted my department a little while ago with a daring vision. And that vision was that every family who needed such support should have access to school uniforms. To say I was impressed would be an understatement. And to see what you've achieved, Charlotte, in so short a time, is nothing short of staggering."

"Well, I couldn't have done it without any of these fine folks," Charlotte answered, running her hand in the direction of her assembled friends, determined to give credit where credit was due. "They've been absolutely brilliant," she said fondly.

After allowing Charlotte time to blow kisses to them all, Alex continued. "Your friend Mollie here contacted my department, inviting me along today," he said. "And I'm pleased that she did, because it allows me the honour of delivering some news which you may enjoy, face to face."

"I *knew* you were up to something, Mollie," Charlotte said, smiling like a fool and anxious to hear more of what Minister Adler had to say.

"Charlotte," Alex went on, "I've just recently received approval from the government which offers you matched fundraising for your ReCyCool initiative."

It took Charlotte a moment or two to properly digest this little snippet of information. "Wait, are you saying that for every pound we raise, the government will match it...?" she asked him, gobsmacked.

"Yes," Alex was delighted to confirm. "Not only that, but we can also offer it for every pound you've *already* raised."

Charlotte was unusually lost for words, taking it all in for a moment or two. "That's... that's spectacular news," she said, once she'd composed herself, for the most part. "I mean, that's utterly fantastic!"

"How about a nice group picture at this time?" Patrick gently suggested, herding everyone in, encouraging them all to stand closer together.

Charlotte moved towards Joyce, Beryl, and the others. "You managed to keep all this from me?" she said, gently admonishing them. "Of course it's wonderful to see you all here," she said, doling out a quick round of hugs.

"Minister," Patrick suggested, lining up the shot. "Would you mind getting in the centre of the shot, next to Charlotte?"

"Get yourself tucked in here," Joyce said, taking a slight step to her left.

"Plenty of room for a handsome young thing like you," Beryl chimed in, taking a similar step to her right, with both she and Joyce allowing ample room so that Charlotte and Minister Alex could stand together in the middle, as instructed.

"Oh, what about Larry?" Charlotte said to no one in particular, concerned about Larry's ability to wheel himself over and into the shot, as she wanted to make sure he was included.

"Don't you worry about me," Larry responded, gliding effortlessly into view. "I've got my trusty assistant to lend a hand."

Charlotte looked over, doing a double-take. "Stanley?" she said, shocked at the presence of her son, who she had dropped off at school earlier. "Stanley, what on earth are you doing here?"

"We've one more little surprise," Mollie confessed. "Stanley, would you be so kind?"

"On my way," Stanley replied, leaping into action and running off momentarily.

A minute or so later, Stanley was at the head of a column of uniformed schoolchildren, who'd apparently been waiting in the wings, all of them filing in now, in a single row, like they were attending a school assembly.

"Just over here," Patrick cheerfully instructed, directing the new arrivals to an area right in front of Charlotte. There, they fell down onto their bottoms, smiling in advance of their photograph being taken.

"Oh, how interesting. They're not all from Stanley's school?" Charlotte observed, noting the different uniforms on display.

"Yes, we've got thirty-two primary schools in all on the island," Minister Adler explained to her. "I wanted to do something to give you a visual representation of the admirable work that you and the others are involved in. So for that reason, we invited a representative from each of those primary schools, including your son Stanley, of course. I did think about extending the invite to the secondary schools, but Patrick suggested it might be a bit of a squeeze getting us all in the picture."

"We'll just need to snuggle up a little closer," Beryl suggested with a cackle, linking the minister's arm.

"Okay!" Patrick called out, loud enough to be heard over the lively chatter from the assembled group. Not an easy task with over thirty children sitting in front of him. But upon closer inspection, it became obvious that it wasn't the children making the lion's share of the noise. Rather, it was the grown-ups, carrying on loudly behind them. "Ladies and gentlemen!" Patrick barked, getting everyone's attention from his elevated position halfway up a stepladder. "Three… two… one… ReCyCool!" he shouted, finger hovered above his camera's shutter button.

"ReCyCool!" shouted the kids, as well as each of the adults, likely causing the in-store shoppers to wonder what all the fuss was about.

"Perfect," Patrick confirmed, looking back up from his view-finder. "That's going to be an absolutely cracking picture!"

Later that same day, Charlotte cuddled up on her sofa between the two men in her life, Calum and Stanley, a nice glass of red within easy reach and the log burner roaring.

"Lotti, did I tell you how proud I am?" Calum asked.

"Several times, but a girl never tires of hearing such things. So do continue," Charlotte answered.

"I'm proud of you as well, Mum," Stanley added, dipping into the box of chocolates resting against his knee. "Wait, was that the pizza man?" Stanley said, jumping up like the family dog who'd just heard the postman. "Ah, false alarm," he said, return-ing a short moment later, deflated, while consoling himself and his pangs of hunger with another chocolate or two.

"I've done something impulsive," Calum confessed, turning the volume down on the telly so he could speak to them both. "I hope you don't mind?"

"Well, that depends what it is, I suppose?" Charlotte replied.

"Yes, it depends what it is," Stanley quickly agreed, though in truth he liked all surprises.

"Well…" Calum said, sucking in a lungful of air through his teeth while pausing for dramatic effect. "Well, I've booked us a little holiday," he disclosed.

"A holiday!" Stanley shouted in delight, all concerns about his rumbling tum immediately forgotten. "To where?"

"Center Parcs," Calum revealed, unsure if his surprise would get the positive reaction he'd hoped for. "I remember your mum telling me how much she'd like to take you there."

"Are you joking?" Stanley said, leaping onto the sofa, bouncing up and down like a jackhammer.

Calum laughed, shielding his wine glass with his hand. "No, I'm not joking," he was only too happy to report.

"Can I... can I bring my bicycle?" Stanley asked, so excited he was struggling for air.

Calum looked over to Charlotte, receiving only an impassive stare in response. "You fancy a little trip away?" he asked, a little worried, hoping he'd not overstepped the mark.

Charlotte shrugged indifferently, and then rose to her feet, as if she were about to wander off. But then...

"We're going to Center Parcs!" she yelled, scooping Stanley up and pulling him straight off the sofa. "We're going to Center Parcs!" she yelled again, jumping around in circles with Stanley like the two of them were performing a rain dance.

"I guess I'll take that as a yes, then," Calum responded with a chuckle, placing his glass down on the table. "Here's the thing, though. I've booked one of those massive lodges," he said, as if this was in some way a problem. "You know, the ones with a hot tub and BBQ area? Only..."

"Only?" Stanley said, worried where the 'only' was leading.

"Only it's probably too big for us alone," Calum advised. "So I might have invited Mollie and Sam along."

"You're being serious?" Charlotte asked, setting Stanley and herself off on another jubilant rotation around the living-room rug. "They're coming with us?"

Calum nodded. "Yep!" he was pleased to report.

"Oh, I cannot wait!" Stanley said, punching the air in delight.

Calum raised his index finger like there was something else he needed to tell them. Something important. "You know when I said I'd booked a massive lodge?" he said, darting his eyes between the two of them.

"Yeah...?" Charlotte asked cautiously. "What are you up to?"

Calum was struggling to contain his cheesy grin. "Well," he said. "The problem with a *massive* lodge is that there are plenty of rooms to fill, aren't there?"

"Go on," Charlotte said, liking the direction this was going.

"So we may just have a few extra people joining us if we can sort out all the arrangements," Calum informed the pair.

Stanley looked up to his mum, and then back over to Calum. "Do you mean Larry and the others?" he asked, daring to believe.

Calum nodded. "Larry, Bonnie, Joyce, and Beryl, so far. But it's an awfully big lodge, so plenty of room for even more people if they should want to come."

"This is too good to be true," Charlotte said, reaching for her wine glass and shaking her head in happy disbelief.

"You're certain you don't mind?" Calum asked, though suspecting he already knew the answer judging by the happy faces staring back at him.

"Do I *mind*?" Charlotte said, taking a huge mouthful of wine to enjoy, before continuing, "No, of course I don't mind! I can't bloody wait!"

"The Crafternooners are going on holiday!" Stan called out, jumping up and down once more. "And I'm pretty sure I've just seen the pizza man's car pull up outside as well! Blimey, this is the best day ever!"

The End for now (But they're coming back)

The Crafternooner gang will all be back soon! You can pre-order *The Crafternoon Sewcial Club 3* at:

www.authorjcwilliams.com/the-crafternoon-sewcial-club-3

For a complete list of the author's other books and to subscribe to his newsletter, please visit:

www.authorjcwilliams.com

You can also find all of his books on Amazon globally in Kindle, Paperback, and Audiobook formats.

Finally, if you'd like to learn more about the Isle of Man's real-life Crafternooners who inspired this book, please visit:

www.makeitsewiom.com

Printed in Great Britain
by Amazon